The Rack

A. E. Ellis

The Restored Edition

Restoration by

Alan Wall

Zephyr Books
Ashgrove Publishing
London

Introduction to *The Rack*

•

On reading this remarkable book on its first publication Graham Greene declared it a great work. He always had a sure critical sense, and he was undoubtedly right in this instance. Penguin confirmed its status when they issued it as one of their Modern Classics. *The Rack* is the greatest novel of medical confinement in the English language. To find its equivalent we would have to travel abroad. The subject is life inside a sanatorium in the years after the Second World War. Most of the inmates are victims of pulmonary tuberculosis. And yet the book cannot be confined in such a strait-jacket: it uses its medical subject to explore the ultimate significance of living, which means that it is much preoccupied with the subject of dying, too. Its themes appear universal. Nevertheless, we cannot for long evade the question of T.B. The novel's hero, Paul Davenant, endures its ravages, and so inevitably do we, as the compelling narrative situates us inside his life and mind.

Until Robert Koch demonstrated the nature and *modus vivendi* of the tubercle bacillus in 1882, tuberculosis – or consumption, as it was so often called – could be interpreted any way you chose. In that respect, it was a diagnostician's delight. Its causes? Bad air, poor sanitation, inadequate diet, genetic inheritance. And then, of course, there were the psychologists. Then as now their name was legion. Tuberculosis was the physical expression of a pathological withdrawal from life. The wasting-away of the body was not a primary expression of any medical aetiology: it was an emblem for the withering away of the spirit. This mode of thought long outlasted Koch and his precise aetiology. We find it in Kafka's letters and diaries. There he mused to himself that the disease which was killing him wasn't the real cause of his momentous problems, only their outward expression, their physical displacement into flesh. Four decades after Koch had shown *mycobacterium tuberculosis* to be the causative agent, Kafka could conceive his own terminal condition as a kind of lethal metaphor; a transference from soul to body of transcendent, life-denying forces. Like the benighted officer in his own story 'In the Penal Colony', the patient would seem to employ the machinery of pain in order to prove himself guilty of ultimate bad faith.

In fact, tubercle bacilli are ejected in minuscule droplets from the infected lungs of a sufferer. The uninfected then inhale, and rapidly become infected in their turn. Even if the droplets do not find a home first time around, they are tiny enough to be sustained in the air for a long period. So the area of infection then becomes any shared airspace. A living-room, for example; or a bedroom. Dust offers an alternative home, for many months at a time. And the same dust when disturbed swirls up into the air, and may then be inhaled. The bacilli travel into the lungs of the inhaler, and settle down, sometimes for good.

Over the years, we have been given vivid enough accounts of the effects of this terrible affliction, some fictional and some historical. First John Keats nursed his brother Tom, as he died from its ravages, then one day he saw the blood on his own bedsheets. He promptly announced: 'I know the colour of that blood; it is arterial blood; – I cannot be deceived in that colour; that drop of blood is my death-warrant – I must die.' And of course he did die, not long after. His unillusioned self-diagnosis was based on the sound medical knowledge he had acquired; he recognised the symptoms that announced the onset of consumption. Keats knew what he was talking about from his own earlier medical studies. And in any case, Tom had already made the journey before him.

And then we have Ralph Touchett in Henry James's *The Portrait of a Lady*. In a curious way, he represents all the clichés that gathered around the condition. His vivid moral awareness, his imaginative intensity, his seeming detachment from material values; all these represent the intellectual complement to the devastation of the physique which the condition enforces. Like Mimì in Puccini's *La Bohème*, Ralph is often bed-ridden, but he is not institutionalised, any more than were the Brontës. But it does start to seem, in all these cases, that the shorter the physical existence, the more exalted is the concomitant intelligence. And frequently enough, the beauty, too. The Pre-Raphaelites' phthisic women often looked like embodiments of the consumptive mode. Lizzie Siddal appeared tubercular, whatever the actual nature of her mystery life-long illness, laced as it was with laudanum and daily grief. It was part of the consumptive myth that the devastations of the disease could bestow irresistible sexual attraction. It could even, as in the case of Doc Holliday, imbue a man with preternatural gifts as a ruthless and accurate killer. A consumptive, apparently, was a good man to have as a companion at the O.K. Corral.

Everything changes, though, the moment we enter the sanatorium, an institution and a word that appears only after Keats is dead. The purpose of such institutions high in the mountains, like the one Paul Davenant travels to here, was to be translated to better air, pure mountain air, far away from the smoke and fever of the city where, as Keats put it – with his brother Tom in mind – youth grows pale, and spectre-thin, and dies. Now up in the high atmosphere of a Caspar David Friedrich painting, all that fever and fret should be left behind. And the tubercle bacilli might now have their work cut out for them. There is only one problem, however, and that 'problem' is the core of this book, for the consumptive is inevitably incarcerated with fellow-sufferers, and subjected to the attentions of the doctors who are the gods of these human eyries. Both medicine and psychology became concentrated, compressed into a place and a space, and there can be no escaping either except by reaching that final terminus which never seems too far away in any case.

What ensues in these pages is what we might call a classic drama of confinement, whose progress, in all its complications, is the subject of *The Rack*. Like Thomas Mann's *The Magic Mountain*, which preceded it by a more than three decades, *The Rack* explores the inter-relationships of a group of highly strung and sorely afflicted human beings, all of them at a time in their lives when they should theoretically be full of vigour. Instead they are full of *mycobacterium tuberculosis*. And don't they all know it. The high mountains might have become their remedial domicile, but the tubercle continues to make a domicile of them, and what a persistent and troublesome tenant it proves to be. The commentators upon their condition, the self-proclaimed warriors against it, are the doctors, who are a daily presence in every patient's life. They are an integral part of the drama presented here.

A. E. Ellis (aka Derek Lindsay, whose pseudonym it was) had himself spent a lengthy spell in a European sanatorium. This book could not have been written without that personal experience. In *Illness as Metaphor*, Susan Sontag wrote brilliantly of how easily we turn medical conditions into states of mind, expressions of philosophic acclamation or denial. Consumption, she points out, was the prime subject for this kind of manoeuvre for many years. But we very soon realise that there is nothing metaphorical about *Les Alpes*, the sanatorium up near Brisset in this book. Instead, we sense on every page of the novel the reality of the gruelling experience underlying it. Unlike Mann, who gathered his data regarding the sanatorium from an illness of his wife's, Lindsay himself underwent the experiences so brilliantly and graphically conveyed here. It might be possible to fictionalise what goes on in *The Rack*, but no one could have simply made it up; not without all the first-hand experience which renders it so credible. You could never ask for more evidence of first-hand experience than we are given in this novel. Where Mann is relatively uninterested in the actual medical details of the procedures being pursued up in the mountains, preferring long philosophical discussions, the writer Ellis spares us nothing. We know with every page that this is an account, as vivid as any could possibly be, of actual experience transmuted into fiction.

Koch had provided an explanation and an aetiology. But what about a cure? The pneumothorax which recurs throughout these pages consisted of deliberately collapsing the affected lung so that treatment could be applied. The process was lengthy and all-too-frequently exhausting. It was also frequently unsuccessful. The word was already out that the age of the wonder drug was at last arriving. Streptomycin appeared to be the great new hope, and certain characters in this book plead to be given it. Some of them do receive it (and sometimes find out that they are resistant to it in any case), but the medical staff remain committed to the practice of the pneumothorax, and we are given indisputably graphic evidence of what it was like to undergo this operation in a post-war sanatorium. The writing is so fastidiously detailed that the reader feels as though he or she has undergone the experience for themselves – well, almost. We can always turn the page, of course; Ellis (or Derek Lindsay) couldn't.

Medical practice lags behind medical discovery, often by a matter of decades. Joseph Priestley, great scientist that he was, still believed that there was something called phlogiston, an essence of heat and fire. The discoveries of chemistry in the first half of the nineteenth century showed that there was in fact no such substance, and yet for a hundred years afterwards, medical journals and medical experts discussed varieties of 'phlogistic' inflammation in regard to muscles. Ellis's desperate patients also hear joyful whispers of new antibiotics that might soon be used, in place of the knife, to sort out their physiques and physiologies, but the old processes of the sanatorium grind on all the while. The effect of this grinding on their psyches is a large part of the subject of this book. Its central character, Paul Davenant, is in effect a mobile intelligence unit, travelling through the ravages of sanatorium life at the time. An 'Oxford undergraduate and sometime captain in an infantry regiment', he is highly intelligent, deeply troubled, and vastly manipulated by the medical machinery to which he is unrelentingly subjected. He continually disappears into this machinery, the way Chaplin disappears into the machine he is supposed to be tending, in his film *Modern Times*.

The details of this life are portrayed with such particularising brilliance that it is impossible not to notice that we are in the presence of great writing. This is indeed the work which so impressed Greene, and it achieves a finesse of horrified observation which would surely have struck Flaubert as exemplary. Here, for example, is Paul describing the sanatorium food:

> Even within the enforced limitations of the *régime*, the food was trumpery. The soup was the lachrymal secretion of empty heads and empty larders; the *pasta*, in its centimetre of cloudy exudation, looked like a dish of etiolated, disintegrating octopus; the permitted daily ration of fruit was composed solely of grapes of the size and rigidity of small marbles, testicular pellets taut with a surfeit of seeds set in a glutinous and bitter fluid.

You have to look long and hard at food to see it as vividly as that, and you have to be a writer of remarkable command to convey the matter so succinctly. In the drama of confinement that constitutes life in a sanatorium, assuming you are a mobile intelligence unit with the exquisitely functioning senses of Paul Davenant, you have time to scrutinise all this data fastidiously. The obsessions are: first the medical treatment, then the food, then the environmental conditions, and finally the doctors whose regulations rule your existence. Here is a description of the flies that beset the institution at certain times of the year:

> Dusty, slothful flies like miniature hedgehogs, the oviparous philoprogenitive, all-season nurslings of the primitive central-heating installation, were emerging from their places of concealment, dipping stridently across the room to Paul's bedside lamp and, like their forebears eighteen months earlier, transforming the glass bowl into an illuminated, transparent hive. Eviction was complicated and purposeless – the swarm would return as to a carcass.

Paul observes the insects with the same dispassionate coldness as he is observed in his turn by the medical authorities. Such detailed observation, such imagistic precision, amounts to a form of reverse erotics. The object of the gaze, the subject of obsession, produces loathing instead of love. But the same unswerving fascination remains. Such words reconstitute a world.

Like military conscription, life in the sanatorium throws together all sorts, however socially separate they might have been on the outside. De la Marelle, the aristocrat, finds himself rubbing shoulders with people whom he would normally expect to be employed as his servants. In fact, he tends to talk to them as though they still are his servants; even when he is proposing marriage to one of them. The one element he knows he cannot command, however exalted his genealogy, is the reign of the tubercle within his lungs. These swarms might be the riff-raff of a physiological Third Estate, but they have stormed his barricades, all the same, and are taking control of his palace.

And yet, one should be careful not to give the wrong impression. This is not merely an account of passive suffering. Paul's emotional life represents a kind of heroic endeavour. And his passions run high, particularly when they are engaged with the one person in his life who seems capable of beckoning him out of his life of illness and confinement. This part of the narrative cannot be summarised; one must simply read the novel. The appearance of Michèle Duchesne could have been the one cliché in a work remarkably free of them: what is called in the trade 'the love interest'. But it does not turn out that way at all. She is as vividly real, and as potently believable, as the diseases that predominate around her. What follows in the narrative could hardly be called predictable.

We are presented with a rich array of characters here, starting with Monsieur Halfont, the director of the sanatorium called *Les Alpes*. He is suave and mendacious by turns. Then there are the various doctors, including Vernet and Bruneau, who are sometimes cheerfully brutal, sometimes incompetently affable. They often breeze through their surgical procedures as though they were taxidermists stuffing animals rather than surgeons invading the bodies of sentient human beings. A character called Desmond Beale seems to have strolled out of the pages of an Evelyn Waugh satire of the 1930s. He is in effect a living gargoyle, splendidly portrayed in all his inebriate ghastliness. And yet, like so many of the characters in Waugh, he is not in fact mere caricature; he comes alive on the page. There is even a character called Emile, the sanatorium's mysterious odd-job man, who sometimes makes off in the night with the dead, like a sepulchral assistant to Burke and Hare.

Here we should point out that the restored version of the book before you contains a great deal that has never been seen in any of the previously published editions. More than 25,000 words have here been rescued from the original manuscript. When James Michie edited *The Rack* for Heinemann in 1958, he cut an enormous amount of the author's manuscript. It seems that he wanted to emphasize the aspect of existential parable which the work undoubtedly exhibits. Read in such a manner, the novel can be seen as an account of the dark quest, combatting shadowy forces, just as much as certain famous narratives by Camus or Sartre. If the editors of the time saw it as such an existentialist novel, in one sense they might have been right. But it seems now that they were over-programmatic in excluding so much of the human warmth and engagement which the original manuscript contained. If this occasionally meanders, then so does life. The text presented here now displays far more of Derek Lindsay's darkly comedic talent as a writer. Ellis writes in that great, savage tradition of British humour, a tradition which includes Ben Jonson, Dickens and Evelyn Waugh.

In Thomas Mann, the sanatorium provides each medical inmate with a podium from which to expound his philosophy, metaphysics and politics. This can sometimes feel like the real subject of *The Magic Mountain*. In *The Rack*, the physical devastations never leave anyone alone long enough to permit such uninterrupted disquisitions. We are frequently treated to the ultimate nightmare of German Expressionist cinema: incarceration in an institution run by those who exert complete control over your life, and have precious little care for your distress, however eloquently it might be expressed. Like Keats, gazing forensically upon his body's own announcement of mortality, Paul Davenant learns how to read the signs of his life, both inside and outside the sanatorium. As we watch his moral progress on this journey, we can only marvel at the achievement of this extraordinary book.

Alan Wall
University of Chester
2016

Jacqueline

PART ONE

CHAPTER ONE

•

The small town of Uhle in the Haute Savoie lies on the route of the Paris–St. Gervais express. It is neither a watering place nor a centre of industry; nevertheless no train halts there for less than several minutes. Indeed so disproportionate is the size of the station to that of the town which it serves that passengers travelling this way for the first time often spend anxious moments as they seek assurance that the train has not brought them ahead of schedule to their destination.

Nor is their uncertainty diminished by the sight of the passengers who descend at Uhle, for they are in appearance as cosmopolitan as any who may be encountered on the platforms of European termini. Voices in most European and many Asiatic languages can be heard demanding *renseignements* of all kinds; individual passengers attach themselves rapidly to small national groups, presenting infinite variations of physique and colour. Imperturbable porters, cigarette stubs adhering to their lower lips and cases strapped to their backs, thread their way through the files of passengers and baggage-littered *quais*; small electric trolleys, transformed into quivering skyscrapers by their loads of crates, trunks and hampers, hoot neurasthenically as they speed up and down the platforms.

For Uhle, while not a centre of industry, is nevertheless the gateway to an industry, an industry which attracts its clients from all parts of the world. It is located several thousand feet above sea level on the site of a small village which formerly was frequented only by peasants and their herds. This village, which still retains its original name of Brisset, has, during a period of some fifty years, developed so considerably that what originally was a compact settlement of châlets and stables now straggles in all directions about the place of its original foundation.

For those who live up in the mountains, as well as those who have only gone to stay there for a certain period, Uhle has a symbolic importance. It is, as it were, a kind of free city situated upon the common border of two neighbouring countries, the citizens of each of which are permitted to associate on equal terms. For cross-currents of the world converge at Uhle, and there divide into two such disparate streams that the contrast between each is more significant than that between members of different nationalities and races.

The territory, the borderline of Uhle, must be crossed to gain access to the mountains. Those engaging upon a temporary *séjour* at a high altitude will traverse and re-traverse its brief confines each time a fit of disenchantment drives them to make an excursion into the outer world. And those who cannot descend for some time (and who, perhaps, may descend no more) will, from their balconies on a clear and star-filled night, see the lights of Uhle flickering far below them.

Whatever the reason (and despite its commonplace main street and insignificant shops), Uhle rarely fails to make a distinct impression upon those who pass through it for the first time. Its atmosphere, even on the sleepiest midsummer afternoon, has a tenseness which gives an extra-dimensional relief to the façades of its buildings, and sharpens the silence of its squares. But it is not in midsummer that we shall see it first.

Towards the middle of November, some time after the end of the Second World War, the small electric train which connects Uhle with the mountains had picked up its passengers from the station and was slowly returning along the streets before mounting the steep track which leads to Brisset. Periodically they come down from the mountains for business reasons or '*pour se changer les idées*'; they will go to one of the towns in easy reach in order to visit a theatre or a restaurant or perhaps go on a shopping expedition, for choice is limited at Brisset and prices are for the most part higher than elsewhere.

Then in groups of two or three, or perhaps singly, were the devotees – their excursion of a few days to the bottom of the mountain now ended, they were returning in silence to continue their *cure*. There were also the new arrivals, replete with boxes, cases, *articles de sport*, and usually accompanied by relatives or friends. Hailing each other cheerfully, and mostly sitting together, were the residents and merchants of Brisset.

At one end of the coach was a party of six young Englishmen whose ages varied between twenty-two and twenty-seven. They were attempting to peer through the frosty windows at the brightly-lit, snow-lined street through which the train was passing. Each a member of a British university, and each having served in one of the armed services, they were the protégés of the I.S.O. or International Students' Organisation, a society affiliated to the majority of European universities which devoted its funds to the welfare of its members. They were in France as a consequence of the initiation of a new project by the directors of the I.S.O. whereby treatment in the mountains was to be provided for a period of several months to a limited number of students from a dozen different nations.

The members of the British party, amongst whom an easy friendship was already forming, had met for the first time on the previous day when they had assembled at a London station. There they had been received by a courier of the I.S.O. who had been appointed to conduct the party to the mountains.

Only one of their number appeared noticeably unwell, an impression arising more from his colour and bearing than from his physique. Tall, heavily built and wearing an army officer's greatcoat from which all insignia had been removed, he was finding it difficult to remain upright in his wooden seat: his fair hair had fallen over his brow, whilst his head rested against the freezing interior of the window. A sudden jolt of the train and his head fell forward, and a student sitting beside him grasped his shoulder, and asked:

'Paul, are you all right?'

And Paul Davenant, an Oxford undergraduate and sometime captain in an infantry regiment, shook himself, raised his head, opened his eyes and smiled at his interlocutor. At that moment the I. S. O. courier, Mr. James, walked up the centre of the coach.

'We'll be climbing soon,' he said cheerfully. 'The train turns round, then goes up in the other direction. It's really snowing outside.'

He rubbed energetically at the inside of the window with his handkerchief, oblivious of the fact that the obstruction to the view was caused by the heavy layer of frost which had formed outside. Then the train came to a halt, a few more passengers climbed in, the guard cried: '*En voiture!*' and, as Mr. James had predicted, it set off in reverse. But, changing to another line, it left the region of Uhle and started to ascend the mountain. 'Well, here we go, lads,' said Mr. James, and as no one replied he leant over and, slapping a young man on the shoulder, cried out: 'How are you doing, Cambridge?'

Mr. James, belly, bosom and buttocks in uncompromising relief under his tight uniform, was a card, a clown, a little light entertainment provided by the I.S.O. Without a word of French, and never before having travelled on the continent, he had been escorted by the party rather than the reverse. Before the boat had left Dover he had leant over the side of the rail to stare at the water, and his thick spectacles had fallen from his nose into the sea. During the subsequent train journey, he had managed twice to mislay his hand baggage, once to lose his own ticket, once the tickets of the whole party.

But these slight *contretemps* in no way reduced his spirits; it was all one long picnic to Mr. James. When not searching desperately through vast pockets for an elusive and essential document, he joked, jested and bantered. Members of the party he addressed either by the name of their university or the region of the country from which they came.

Between Paul Davenant of Oxford and the student whom Mr. James had recently addressed as 'Cambridge', and whose name was John Cotterell, he had attempted to promote a healthy sense of rivalry, awarding or deducting marks according to some system of his own which led him from time to time to cry out: 'That's one to you, Oxford,' or 'Keep it up, Cambridge – you're only a length behind!' To other members of the party he allocated 'blues' or 'half-blues' for the performance of any act of communal value. Sometimes he would stare disdainfully at the party as a whole, and cry: 'Crikey, what a bunch! One Oxford, one Cambridge, one Taffy, two Scotties and a Yorky. Fancy me having to take a load like that across Europe,' and then he would whistle low and long between his teeth.

The coach was now mounting steeply; its interior – all but hermetically sealed by sliding steel doors – was warm and humid. The chatter of the passengers subsided; they sat rigidly, their bodies braced against the angle of ascent, their feet in pools of water formed by the melting of the snow brought in upon their boots. In the dim, yellow lighting they appeared to grow out of the benches, and their outlines, so indistinctly revealed, merged one into another. Outside was all black but for a certain luminosity caused by the reflection of the lights of the train upon the banks of snow heaped on each side of the track.

Paul Davenant, without consciously directing his gaze, found himself staring drowsily at a French woman seated opposite. She was dressed in a carefully pressed costume and was wearing a hat which sought a marriage between the practical and the frivolous; the lapels of her jacket were smartly turned, and the white blouse showing beneath had been cut in severe yet feminine lines. Everything from the nylons which covered her determined and sexless legs to the lacquered bunch of artificial violets pinned above her left breast, proclaimed the painstaking and scrupulous lack of taste of the French middle classes.

She started, all of a sudden, to speak to her neighbour, a plump, pink-faced *gendarme* in his fifties who was smoking a cheroot and reading a newspaper. The conversation rapidly became animated, and although she did not raise her voice, its pitch was already high and penetrating. And at the same time that she spoke she looked in every direction save that of the *gendarme* and it was as though she were addressing her remarks to the whole coach. '*Alors je lui ai dit: "Que voulez-vous que ça me fasse?"*' she repeated tonelessly, and as her neighbour started to laugh, she added: '*Ah non, dites, mais je ne rigole pas, vous savez.*'

The train came to a sudden halt, and a few passengers descended. Mr. James once more rubbed frantically at the window with his handkerchief as he tried to see the name of the mountain station; then he grasped the shoulder of a workman seated beside him and stammered: '*Voulez dire... la station ici... je veux...*' when to a shout of '*En route!*' from the guard the train continued on its way. Mr. James, shading his eyes with his hands, pressed his nose against the window and was rewarded with nothing more than his own ill-defined reflection peering back.

The woman resumed her conversation with the *gendarme*, adjusting the volume of her voice to the buzz of the train, the two in conjunction forming a toneless and unpleasantly persistent duet. Then the female voice, capable of a greater virtuosity, broke free, soared, and became completely audible again: '*Alors je lui ai dit, "Vous savez très bien que vous ne devez pas faire de ski avec votre pneumo, c'est pas sérieux, ça."*' She had been looking at Paul, and had appeared to be addressing her remarks directly to him, when suddenly, her mouth wide open in the act of articulation, she turned back to her neighbour and met with a great *bouffé* of smoke which he had just puffed from between his teeth. Momentary spluttering succeeded by a series of coughs, as sharp, distinct and compelling as her voice; pats on the back and cries of '*Pardon, Madame,*' from the *gendarme* and a choking '*Je vous en prie, Monsieur,*' from the lady. A temporary *accroc*; the mechanism swiftly adjusted itself and the human counterpoint to the buzz of the train recommenced unimpaired.

'What does *"pneumo"* mean?' Paul whispered to John Cotterell; it was the key word to an otherwise incomprehensible sentence. 'It's a medical term. It means – oh, never mind. We'll be hearing it all too frequently soon enough.' John Cotterell dug his hands deep into the pockets of his trenchcoat and, in an effort to restore his circulation, drummed with his feet upon the floor of the coach.

'I reckon we should get there any minute,' said Mr. James, now rubbing the glass on his watch with his handkerchief. Then the windows of the coach became suddenly bright, and despite the frost it was possible to make out the shape of a large and brightly lit building. 'We're here, we're here!' cried Mr. James, as the train came to a stop. 'No, you are not 'ere,' was shouted in English by a guard who had just come through to the coach. 'It is a stop. I will say when you are 'ere. It is the next stop.'

Through the open doors it was possible to catch a glimpse of great banks of snow, and the outline of square, modern buildings. The place could be no more than a halt, for nothing indicating the existence of a station was visible. Half a dozen *réligieuses*, members of a nursing order, apple-cheeked, their veils grotesquely lined with snow, climbed up into the coach. The guard passed a number of parcels and a mailbag through an open window. Then came the cry of '*En route!*' The steel doors slammed, and the train set off once more up the slope.

As the track became steeper the noise of the train became more insistent. Then suddenly the passengers started to bestir themselves; hats were adjusted, journals were folded and stored in pockets. The corpulent *gendarme* got up from his seat and re-fastened the belt and lower buttons of his tunic. Mr. James, oblivious of the implications of these signs, opened a small paper packet and took out a hard-boiled egg, which he began to shell. Paul Davenant turned his head, laid his cheek against the freezing window and closed his eyes; to lose consciousness for a second was to lose it, during that second, for eternity.

'*Brisset Village*,' a guard shouted, as the train came to a halt, and he jumped out from the coach on to the platform. Immediately there was great activity. Two porters who had climbed up into the coach started to hand down baggage from the racks which ran along its whole length; a family made its way along the centre of the coach, each member holding a pair of skis horizontally above his head. The *gendarme*'s neighbour dropped her bag on the floor, and the *gendarme*, bending down to pick it up, lost his own peaked cap, which fell from his head on to a heap of melting, dirty snow. Mr. James stuffed what remained of the hard-boiled egg into his mouth and was temporarily robbed of speech. The students formed up in a line behind the other passengers who were filing slowly out of the coach.

The first impact of mountain air on a November evening. One breathes deeply and the interior of one's chest becomes suddenly, deliciously, frozen. One breathes out and the air crackles in one's nostrils. The condensation of the breath of the guard, as he helped passengers down the steep steps of the coach, escaped from his mouth like ectoplasm.

The small station was well lit; the snow cleared from the track had formed into great mounds at the extremities of the platform. Uniformed concierges, the names of the sanatoria to which they were attached printed in gold upon their caps, were alert for new arrivals, whilst porters, not occupied elsewhere, started to remove the baggage, which filled the whole of a large trailer attached to the rear of the second coach. From outside the station came the sound of horses and sleigh bells.

Mr. James marshalled his little squad, now fluttering and coaxing like a hen, now rapping out orders like a sergeant-major, now making a cautious appraisal of the unfamiliar location like the leader of a Resistance group newly parachuted into hostile territory.

A concierge with the name *Les Alpes* upon his cap sighted the party through the throng of passengers on the platform, and walked briskly towards it. 'You are the British students?' he inquired first in French and then in English. His query answered, he explained that the sanatorium for which they were bound was some two hundred metres from the station, and that they should now follow him. The baggage, assuming it had been properly labelled, would be sorted out and brought up separately by sledge.

With Mr. James in the lead, the students followed the concierge out of the station. Snow fell lightly as they mounted a slight incline in the direction of a building indistinguishable in appearance from the type of large hotel constructed on the sides of French lakes in the early part of the century.

Standing at the entrance, protected from the snow by an awning, stood a tall and portly man wearing a tight, double-breasted black suit; one arm was folded behind his back, the other extended stiffly before him in a gesture of welcome. He shook hands with Mr. James, and then, majestically opening the doors, invited the students to enter.

They found themselves in a lofty, oak-panelled entrance hall, furnished with a number of armchairs and settees upholstered in dark brown leather. A concierge's counter cut off one corner. The whole was illuminated, rather dimly, by a series of pendant lustres, suspended both from the ceiling and from bronze-figured brackets on the wall.

The black-suited gentleman first shook hands formally with each of the students, then conducted them to some chairs and bade them sit down. He regarded the party thoughtfully for a moment, glancing swiftly from face to face with slightly furtive eyes which bulged incongruously out of deep recesses set above the inflated contours of his cheeks. His nose was heavy but pointed, the lips were thin, the mouth impersonal and uncommitted.

A tentative assessment completed, he took a typewritten list from his pocket. 'The roll-call,' he said in English, but with a strong accent; 'it is for each one to answer in his turn.' When the names had all been called, he clasped his hands behind his back, and, staring at the floor, declared: 'It is all correct, quite O.K. Now I introduce myself to you. I am Monsieur Halfont, the director, or, as you would say in England, the manager of this sanatorium. It is my wish that you made a good journey and you are welcome here.' He looked up suddenly and suspiciously, searching the faces before him. 'No,' he said, as though someone had contradicted him, 'I mean it sincerely that you are welcome.'

The preliminaries concluded, he touched briefly on certain details concerning the organisation of the sanatorium. Besides the students who were under the auspices of the I.S.O., there were a certain number of private patients. Four of the seven floors were reserved for private patients: the remaining three would be devoted exclusively to students. The only difference between private patients and students was that the latter would be accommodated two to a room; this would constitute no hardship since the rooms were quite spacious.

M. Halfont then asked the students if they would decide immediately with whom they wished to share, in order that the bedrooms might be allocated. Paul Davenant and John Cotterell agreed to share; so did the two Scotsmen, John MacAllister and Angus Gray; which left the remaining room to the Welsh student, William Davis, and David Bean who came from Yorkshire.

'Good,' said M. Halfont. 'Now I will have you led to your rooms, for in half an hour your meal will be ready. After your meal you will go to bed, for you will necessarily be fatigued. Tomorrow you will see our medical director and his assistants, and they will tell you what you must do. Whenever you have difficulties or require something you will come to me and I will aid you. And now I wish you a good stay and a prompt recovery.'

A series of embarrassed 'Thank yous' from the students, a request from Mr. James as to where he was to pass the night, and then a *chasseur* was detailed to conduct the party to the appropriate rooms. Those of the students adjoined each other and, like all the rooms in the sanatorium, were connected by inter-communicating doors. They appeared comfortable, and were agreeably furnished with built-in cupboards, a large marble-topped commode and twin beds in veneered mahogany. Illumination was provided by a light-fitting set into the ceiling, and uncurtained, double french windows led out on to a wide balcony.

During the intervening half-hour there was time for a wash, a settlement of the choice of beds, and a quick glance at the dispositions of rooms, corridors and landings.

The meal was served in a small annexe leading off the main dining-hall, which remained in darkness; Mr. James sat at the head of the table, *en père de famille*, whilst the students sat in rows of three on either side of him. They were quiet and over-elaborately polite; they took pains to refill each other's tumblers, and to pass each other bread.

During the course of the journey, which had lasted a day and a half, certain characteristics had become discernible, indicating to some extent the personalities of each member of the party. But each student had laboured under a certain reserve. In consequence, his character was no more than adumbrated; it resembled the outline of a drawing to which many details had yet to be added.

John Cotterell had already exhibited a natural inclination to cheerful leadership; he had a good command of French and he had managed all the small formalities of the journey, the checking of tickets and passports, the passage of luggage and the location of the reserved second-class compartments. He had pushed Mr. James into the train when the latter, believing that he had lost his ticket, was in danger of being left on the platform at Calais; he had propelled him along corridors of moving coaches, impelled him both in and out of station buffets at various halts along the way, and finally delivered him upon this summit of a French Alp. How Mr. James would get back by himself was a matter for some speculation.

William Davis, the Welsh student, had appeared good-humoured and taciturn – very content to leave the management both of the journey and of Mr. James to John Cotterell. A tall, well-built, fair-haired young man, with shrewd eyes and a healthy complexion, he looked like what in fact he had been – an outstanding athlete at his university.

David Bean, who was studying medicine, and who was to share a room with William Davis, had revealed himself during the journey as the member of the party least given to compromise. His lean face was intelligent and bitter; despite the fact that he was obviously at pains to appear amiable, he had at times made little effort to conceal reactions of impatience and irritation. On several occasions when the trend of a conversation had displeased him he had taken a paper textbook from his pocket and begun pointedly to study it.

The two Scotsmen, John MacAllister and Angus Gray, were strongly contrasting types. The former was tall and very thin; he spoke with a soft Edinburgh accent and was gentle in manner. Glasgow-born Angus Gray was stocky and dark; he had thick eyebrows, a heavy moustache and a prominent, bony nose. He was humorously cantankerous; during the journey he had busied himself with a series of calculations regarding the exchange rates between France and England and had become rapidly competent in assessing any sum of money in the currency of the other country. Visitors to foreign countries were notoriously open to exploitation by the natives, but he commented grimly that here the French had met their match. Both he and John MacAllister were also medical students.

The remaining student was Paul Davenant. At twenty-seven he was the oldest member of the party, as in appearance he was undoubtedly the illest. During the journey his discomfort had been all-too-apparent; he had been continually embarrassed by his incapacity to do much for himself. (John Cotterell, with whom he was to share a room, had assisted him good-naturedly throughout the journey.) He had often appeared unconscious of his surroundings. When his companions laughed (which they did frequently), he laughed with them, though it was apparent that he had little idea what it was they were laughing at.

Now at table he appeared preoccupied and detached. Each time that he became conscious of his drooping posture, he sought to remedy it by an elaborate straightening of his back, but before the meal was over he was supporting the whole weight of the upper part of his body on his elbows, which he rested on the table.

Mr. James, safely arrived at his destination, felt liberated from any remaining inhibitions; overflowing with good-humour, he chattered ceaselessly and senselessly. The meal provided both the occasion and the audience for a series of anecdotes about his life. It soon appeared that there was no capacity in which he had not, at some time or other, been employed, no situation which he had failed to render both ridiculous and humiliating. He was consciously a dupe, a stooge; his loud and self-indulgent laughter prefaced the *dénouement* of each shameful recitation.

When the meal was over, the party moved towards the door. Paul Davenant was wearing an old battle-dress. Mr. James, wearing his own curious uniform, now ran forward, pulled the door open, at the same time pronouncing in a simpering, mincing voice: 'Three pips to two: you go first, *mon capitaine.*' And bending from the hips and arching his back, he raised his hand in a trembling salute.

When Paul Davenant and John Cotterell entered their room they found that their trunks and cases had arrived. On the marble-topped commode were two glass containers shaped like immense wine-glasses, but supported on short, thick stems, and by their side two blue-tinted glass jars with screw-on lids. One set was labelled with the name 'Davenant', the other bore the name 'Cotterell'. Two white enamel mugs with lids, each containing an inch of strong disinfectant, completed this initial issue of equipment.

'I am a beginner,' confessed Paul. 'What precisely are all these things for?'

'You have never been in a sanatorium before?' asked John Cotterell.

'No. You have, I believe.'

'Yes. I spent six months in a sanatorium before coming here.'

Paul looked with surprise at his companion, thinking: 'He looks well, but he must have been very ill to start with.'

'Are you negative or positive?' John Cotterell asked suddenly.

'I've no idea. What should I be?'

'It's better, far better, to be negative.'

'And these containers. What are they for?'

'The jars are for a specimen of sputum, the glasses are for urine. The mug you had better keep by the side of your bed.'

'I see. Thank you.'

In silence they unpacked certain necessities from their cases, and whilst Paul was undressing he was seized by a fit of coughing. He hesitated for a moment, then guiltily, surreptitiously, grasped the white enamel mug, removed the lid, and released the sputum which had been raised by the cough. Through the corner of his eyes he watched John Cotterell, who appeared not to have noticed. 'Perhaps John, having been in a sanatorium, is used to that sort of thing,' he thought to himself. He replaced the mug on top of the commode, and then, remembering John Cotterell's advice, took it up again and placed it on the *table de nuit* by the side of his bed.

He wanted to lie down. As he looked at his cases and at the accumulation of hair-brushes, tablets of soap, bottles of hair-lotion and shaving tackle spread out on his bed and on the floor, he felt that he would never manage to impose upon them any semblance of order: all his efforts seemed to manage no more than the transposition of one heap of articles from a chair to a table, and then back again. But although he was exhausted, something in his nature made him delay the moment when, by entering his bed for the first time in a sanatorium, he would commit himself to it.

Suddenly an impulse was translated into action; he stopped what he was doing and, throwing his greatcoat about his shoulders, unfastened the double windows and went out on to the balcony. It had stopped snowing now and there was no wind. But the floor of the balcony was deep in snow which had drifted high into the corners, obliterating all but the head-rests of two wooden *chaises longues*. Even the rail of the balcony and the ornamental metalwork beneath were lined with narrow fringes of snow several centimetres deep.

Under a full and yellow moon, the mountains stood in brilliant relief, their rugged surfaces smoothed to a glazed consistency by the crevice-filling snow. Below the mountains lay the vast Vallée de la Plaine, spread out as though for immolation, its chaste, wedding-cake surface broken only by the black, winding channel of the River Arve. At the further edges of the valley flickered an infinity of lights, which in their tiny groups appeared like tributary stars fallen in clusters from the golden stream of nebulæ that, at seemingly no greater lateral distance, filled great areas of the sky.

A well-executed backdrop which, in the lives of so many of the dwellers on that narrow ridge set high above the Arve valley, had assumed the proportions and status of a permanent set. Its essence was implicit in the prickly, frozen and odourless air which, with each breath Paul took, flooded the antennæ-like structure of his bronchi and whipped into the deepest recesses of his damaged lungs.

He could not move from where he was standing, nor avert his gaze. Deep and primitive principles of association and recognition were forming a complex series of reactions in his subconscious mind; he felt as much a part of what lay before him as the whole mountain range of its foundations, and the river of the course which it had marked out for itself along the snow-covered expanses of the valley of the Arve.

CHAPTER TWO

•

Several hours later Paul was awoken by the morning light. An instant of panic, a shudder, instinctive as the movement with which a dog shakes itself free of water after a swim, and then the painful down-gearing which checks the course of the undisciplined waking mind.

John Cotterell was still sleeping; his face was turned away from Paul, his one visible ear looked like an oyster. Paul glanced at his watch – it was just after seven.

He looked about the room, impersonal, traumatically bright in the sun: the wash-stand, the white-painted doors of the built-in cupboard, the smell of disinfectant from the polish on the linoleum. His eyes lingered on the only familiar objects – the anguished paraphernalia of baggage, shabby fibre and battered leather, mute but lucid witnesses to the state of his fortunes. Soon they would all be emptied and stored away; pledges to be redeemed not by money but by time.

By the side of Paul's bed lay a thermometer case, and, opening it, he examined its contents. It was a continental thermometer, a flat glass tube marked in centigrade, its scale rising from 35° to 42°; normal was indicated by a red line at 37°.

Footsteps in the passage; guiltily, clumsy in his haste, Paul replaced the thermometer. Then the double doors were thrown apart. As John Cotterell opened his eyes, a young nurse entered, propelled more by the force of her energy than by the locomotive power of her legs. She announced herself in English, rapidly and without ceremony. She was *Sœur* Jeanne; she was in charge of this, the second, floor. Then, having demanded of each his name, she made two impatient ticks with a ball-point pen on a typewritten list.

'Now,' she said. 'Now...' There followed a concise and practised résumé of the first day's routine. Patients, unless instructed to the contrary, took their own temperatures twice daily – once on waking, once at six o'clock in the evening – and immediately recorded the results on their temperature charts. Breakfast was served in the *salle à manger* at eight o'clock prompt. ('You get there late and you have no breakfast. Next time you get there at the right time.') After breakfast, patients undressed and got back into bed. Later in the day medical examinations would take place, when all questions would be answered. Was that all quite clear? *Sœur* Jeanne closed the windows and left the room as briskly as she had entered it.

John Cotterell put his thermometer in his mouth, and Paul self-consciously followed his example; it was some ten years since he had taken his temperature. He wondered vaguely whether the instrument would now take its revenge for so protracted a period of neglect. At the end of exactly two minutes he jerked it from his mouth; to his astonishment the mercury had barely reached the red line. 'Why, it's sub-normal, it's only 36.9,' he cried; he then noticed that John Cotterell still retained his thermometer in his mouth. 'I keep it in for ten minutes,' explained the latter indistinctly, opening his lips, but keeping his teeth clenched upon the glass tube.

With great satisfaction Paul marked his temperature chart with a dot fully one division below the red line. Perhaps he was really not so ill after all; perhaps after two or three months of rest he would be able to return to England. In his imagination he already saw himself packing his cases, reserving his tickets, saying goodbye to the doctors… John Cotterell removed the thermometer from his mouth. 'Exactly 36.3°,' he announced.

Paul was amazed. 'But that must be terribly sub-normal,' he objected.

'Not for a morning temperature. It goes up as the day wears on.'

'But why do you keep it in your mouth for ten minutes?'

'For T.B. ten minutes is the minimum. Two minutes gives only a very approximate result.'

Further discussion was prevented by the opening of the door, which admitted Mr. James, his uniform well brushed, his buttons gleaming. 'What, Oxford and Cambridge still in bed! Come on out of it, it's time for breakfast. If you're not ready in a quarter of an hour, I'm going in with the other boys, so get a move on.'

When at last John and Paul arrived in the dining room, the British party was already seated. It was an enormous room, perhaps one-hundred-and-fifty feet in length, and one whole side comprised a single window overlooking the Arve valley. Vast imitation marble columns and pilasters sprouted from the variegated mosaic of the floor, terminating in a splay of plaster cartouches at their incidence with a vaulted, whitewashed ceiling. The three walls were respectively painted shades of pale yellow, chocolate and red. The room had been divided into two sections: the first was filled with a number of separate tables which were all unoccupied (these were reserved for the private patients who breakfasted in bed), and the second contained three long trestle tables, at the end of one of which the students were seated. John and Paul exchanged nods with their former travelling companions, and Mr. James, drawing up his sleeve, stared ostentatiously at his chromium wristwatch.

'You're late, but if you can manage to find an empty place you can sit in it,' he said with high sarcasm.

They sat down at the table. In the centre of a paper tablecloth was a basket filled with thick slices of nearly black bread, whilst on each plate were three shavings of butter twisted into *coquilles*, and a spoonful of jam. The coffee was thin and sweetened.

'I've got something to tell you all, a little bit of information that I managed to pick up last night,' said Mr. James. His voice dropped mysteriously and then stopped altogether as a *garçon* approached the table with another basket of bread.

'What is it?' asked John MacAllister with interest.

'Keep your mouth shut, Scottie,' hissed Mr. James as he watched out of the corner of his eye until the *garçon* was beyond earshot. 'Couldn't you wait till he'd gone?' he demanded chidingly. He gave the offending MacAllister a look of displeasure, then, leaning forward in his chair, he whispered: 'If you want to know, I've found out that there are other students expected here – *foreign* students!' Mr. James sat back, the better to watch the effect of his pronouncement.

'For God's sake!' cried Angus Gray. 'We knew that before we'd set foot out of England!' John Cotterell, who had been drinking his coffee during Mr. James's impartment, swallowed wrongly and started to splutter. Mr. James looked at him austerely. 'When my son grows up, I won't send *him* to Cambridge!'

'Did you think you were telling us something we didn't know?' insisted Angus Gray, rapping on the table with a teaspoon, his thick eyebrows twitching.

'Never you mind. You can now treat it as official,' said Mr. James loftily.

'But it was official all the time,' roared Angus Gray.

'Now don't shout. You're not in Glasgow.'

'When you say *foreign* students, where do you imply they come from?' demanded John Cotterell, who had regained his breath.

'What do you mean, where do I imply they come from? From abroad, of course.'

'And where do you come from?'

'Oh, shut up, Cambridge, you're getting on my nerves.'

'Don't you realise that here it's *you* who's the foreigner?'

Mr. James was at last thoroughly piqued. 'Me a foreigner! Are you cracked?' And pulling his elusive passport out of his pocket, he thrust it under John Cotterell's nose. 'British passport,' he pronounced distinctly and witheringly, syllable by syllable, as though addressing a retarded child. 'I suppose they teach you to read at Cambridge?'

John Cotterell signalled to a waiter, and indicating Mr James, demanded, '*Ce monsieur-là, c'est un étranger ou pas?*'

The waiter glanced towards Mr. James. '*Oh oui, il est Anglais, n'est-ce pas? Evidemment c'est un étranger.*'

'I'm sorry, this waiter says you're a foreigner,' said John apologetically.

'For Christ's sake!' said Mr James.

'And the French are foreigners!'

'For Christ's sake! Of course they are!'

'Language!' murmured David Bean.

'Language yourself! You lot would make a bloody saint blaspheme.'

'Alas, we have,' said John MacAllister.

'Yes, of course. St. James, Knight of the I.S.O.,' commented John Cotterell.

'A bloody saint! St. James of St. James's Bloody Park!' commented William Davis.

'St. James of St. James's Palace!' cried John MacAllister.

'St. James of England!' shouted John Cotterell, getting to his feet. 'One hundred per cent, home-produced, home-killed, British saint. Holy giblets, tripes and offal on sale at your registered butcher.' He leant over and snatched the handkerchief out of Mr. James's breast pocket. 'One pure and inviolate nose-rag guaranteed to have been worn by St. James on the day of his martyrdom – certified cure-all to those who touch it and have the true faith. Protects against King's Evil, the sweating sickness, divers humours, all distempers and the common cold. Relics, sacred relics,' he cried.

Everyone was laughing and attempting to touch the handkerchief which John Cotterell was flicking backwards and forwards above the table. Mr. James, with an unusually adroit movement, shot out his hand and retrieved it.

'All right, all right, you lot, you can laugh – now that I've got you here.' And before this remark could provoke fresh merriment, he added: 'Anyhow, you won't have the chance to laugh at me much longer. I'm off back this afternoon.'

The idea of Mr. James leaving, and of his leaving alone, brought the true nature of the situation into sudden relief. Up to this moment it had been obscured by the prominence of many incidental details – the journey, the new associations, the strangeness of the surroundings; it had been very much as though one were still in the services, and had been posted to a new and rather eccentric unit. When Mr. James left, this tenuous sense of security would automatically leave with him; it was a sobering thought.

And before the students dispersed to return to their rooms, William Davis said that he for one would miss Mr. James, and as everyone else immediately expressed agreement with this view, Mr. James became mollified. 'I'd be the last,' he said, 'to resent a joke at my expense, and by and large I don't mind admitting that I'll be sorry to go. You've been a hell of a bloody handful all the way, but I've had worse lads to deal with in the past, and I expect I'll have worse again in the future.'

Once back in his room, Paul undressed, put on his pyjamas and climbed into bed. During the meal his breathing had caused him uneasiness, and he had not spoken for fear of precipitating an attack of coughing. As soon as he lay down the attack came, and it lasted several minutes. The colour mounted in his cheeks and his eyes watered, but when it was all over, and his bronchial tubes were cleared, he felt impregnated by that sense of permanent alleviation (so false, and so often the experience of consumptives), attendant upon the temporary resumption of unrestricted breathing.

'I suppose,' he said at last to John Cotterell, 'you were also pretty-ill to start with.'

'Not really. I had the good luck to get diagnosed very early.'

'But you told me last night that you had already spent six months in a sanatorium.'

John Cotterell laughed. 'Six months with this illness is not a very long time.'

'It isn't! Then how long do you think that I will be here?'

'I'm afraid that it's very difficult to say.'

'But how long could it be?' insisted Paul.

'There isn't really a time limit. It all depends on what happens.'

'I see.' Paul was silent a moment. Then: 'Well, I suppose there is one compensation. I mean that in the last six months you must have got through a great deal of work.'

'In actual fact, not awfully much. Of course I intended to do a lot at the outset, but somehow one tends to drift. If you want to work you've really got to set yourself a minimum each day, and get it done however you are feeling.'

'That's what I shall do,' said Paul decisively.

And he gave the impression of being about to start that very moment, so much so that John laughed again. 'You can take a holiday today, I think. Besides, there will be a number of interruptions; there's sure to be a medical examination, and then probably X-rays. Tell me, is there very much wrong with you?'

'I don't know,' replied Paul guardedly. 'I hope not. But then I know nothing at all about... about T.B.'

'How did you find out that you were ill?'

'It was like this...' said Paul. And there followed a story which adhered to an all-too-familiar pattern. After leaving the army he had suffered from a fatigue which at last had forced him to restrict his activities at the university. Insofar as he had sought any explanation, he had believed it to be partly due to leading a sedentary life, partly due to the fact that the Oxford climate was so notoriously relaxing, though damp.

At the end of a year he had started to feel physically ill, and he had paid a visit to a G.P., who, after a medical examination, had pronounced him completely fit. 'Tired? Well of course, and who isn't? Perhaps with a Conservative Government, and a little red meat...' A second doctor, consulted some months later, gave him a tonic, and a third, at an interval of a few more months, prescribed a course of Benzedrine. A fourth doctor, after examining him cursorily, regarded him through half-closed eyes and spoke darkly of psychosomatic disorders and of the almost universal need for analysis. Here Paul had left the matter until, nearly a year later, bordering upon a state of complete collapse, he had once more felt impelled to seek medical advice. He was about to describe the outcome of his final consultation when there came a crash at the door, and in burst all the remaining members of the British party.

'Quiet please, gentlemen,' said John Cotterell, raising one hand. 'The Captain is just summarising the diagnostic capacities of Oxfordshire G.P.s. Up to the time of going to press four of them have pronounced him physically fit, though one has prescribed a change of Government, the second a tonic, the third a course of Benzedrine and the fourth psychoanalysis. New readers now start here – on you go, Paul.'

Paul looked in confusion at his friends, who had seated themselves either on his or on John Cotterell's bed, and who, by their silence, invited him to continue with his story. 'But there's really nothing more to tell,' he said.

'Get on with it, man, and don't blather,' said Angus Gray. John MacAllister added that he did not wish to miss an opportunity of studying the methods of those prodigies of science who practised south of Hadrian's Wall.

'What did finally happen?' demanded William Davis.

'Oh, something utterly ridiculous. I couldn't – '

'Get on, man, we can't wait all day,' said Angus Gray testily.

So Paul repeated briefly and haltingly the events which he had just recounted to John Cotterell.

'And what about the last doctor?' demanded John MacAllister.

So Paul described how one day, feeling altogether too ill to work, he had left the library and had taken a disconsolate walk in the Oxford streets. Passing a house with a brass plate bearing the name 'Dr. Thompson', he had given in to a sudden impulse and had knocked at the door. He had been shown straight into Dr. Thompson's consulting-room.

Once seated, and having introduced himself, Paul had recounted his story. He had described the progressive intensification of what had started merely as a malaise: he had dwelt in detail on each symptom. Then he had summarised briefly the findings of the doctors he had so far consulted. Dr. Thompson had listened with attention, only interrupting to pose a pertinent question or to request a more exact definition of some particular aspect of the narrative.

When Paul had finished, the doctor pressed the tips of his fingers together, sat back in his chair, and, closing his eyes announced that in order that everything should be quite clear in his mind, he wished to make a summary of all the principal points. For the next five minutes he expounded to Paul the latter's story; it was surprisingly accurate, the doctor making an occasional error in respect of date, or the exact sequence of events, but in nothing else.

'And this has been going on for more than two years?'

'Yes.'

'And not only do you feel no better, but you feel progressively worse.'

'Yes. Very much worse.'

'Well, my friend, it is my considered opinion that there is certainly something the matter with you.'

A silence.

'Then what should I do? What do you advise?'

'Heaven knows... You have already consulted four doctors... But I suppose you really must consult a fifth.'

'A fifth!'

'Yes.'

'But – Well, I mean – ' A pause. 'But you're a doctor...'

'Yes – of economics. Now, if there is anything you want to ask me about my own subject, just fire away...'

At this point Paul's listeners broke into such a roar of laughter that *Sœur* Jeanne, who had been passing in the corridor, came running into the room.

'*Mon Dieu, les Anglais!*' she cried indignantly. 'What are you all doing here? Do you not know that it is the morning *cure* and that you should all be in bed? If Dr. Vernet comes along and finds you, you will not laugh then, that I promise you.' And ferociously she bustled the still-laughing students back into their rooms.

CHAPTER THREE

•

'And how did you find out in the end what was wrong?' asked John Cotterell, when the students had all left the room.

'Oh, the usual way, I suppose. One morning while I was still in bed I started to cough, and when I put my hand in front of my mouth, it got stained with blood. Then I found I couldn't stop coughing and suddenly blood started to stream out.'

'Was it very much?'

'It must have been. Everything seemed to get covered in it.'

John Cotterell stretched himself lazily; the Alpine sun had transmuted the fawn-coloured wallpaper into sheets of gold. The only sound came from the *choukas*, gull-like birds in Jesuitical black, ridiculous and ungainly in their walk, superb in their flight. Squawking angrily and disconsolately, they wheeled about the balconies of *Les Alpes*, or, grouped together in great clouds (which resembled the myriad of germ cells revealed by a microscope in a drop of contaminated water), soared in a communal flight about a distant mountain.

The snow which had formed on the balcony soon melted; the summits of the mountains, clustered together as thickly as sand-dunes, shone with an electric radiance. It seemed foolish to lie in bed when outside it was so warm. Accordingly, John and Paul got up and transferred a few blankets on to the wooden *chaises longues*, and, covering their bodies with their bed-clothes, lay back with the rays of the sun streaming full upon them.

Lying thus in the sun one is liberated from doubts and from misgivings; it is not that problems and difficulties are resolved, it is that they are banished. The sun's radiation penetrates the mind as well as the body, anæsthetising thought, suppressing progressively all disharmony of spirit until the dulled but ecstatic brain vibrates with a continual shimmer of pleasure.

The young men were not to experience their sense of well being for very long. '*Nom de pipe!*' cried a voice, and *Sœur* Jeanne, her face taut with horror and indignation, came running on to the balcony. '*Oh, mon Dieu, que vous êtes fous!* Who told you you could lie out there?'

She grasped the corners of the blankets on each *chaise longue* and dragged them back into the room. 'Listen,' she said, as both John and Paul followed her, 'for you the sun is death. For the rest of your lives you will never be able to support the full sunlight. You do not understand what it means to be ill, you carry on just like children. Why, in one hour the sun can open lesions on the lung which have already healed, and in no time you can start a fresh evolution. One day Dr. Vernet may allow you out on the balcony with the sun-blind lowered, and' – turning towards Paul – 'for you at least, *mon cher*, that will not happen for a long time.'

The rebuke, justified and unanswerable, was offered and accepted; at the same time it served as an initiation into the status which illness imposes on the individual. John and Paul looked embarrassed and apologetic; *Sœur* Jeanne, feeling perhaps that she had been over-harsh, modified her severity and explained that she was not angry on her own account but purely for the good of her new charges, who in future must co-operate, and not be '*de mauvais garçons*'.

She then explained that she had come to fetch Paul, who was to have an X-ray and a medical examination. She helped him on with his shabby grey dressing-gown and then hurried him down the passage to the lift, a garish and rickety bird-cage which groaned and trembled its way between the floors.

The *Service Médical* was on the fourth floor – to enter it one had to pass through a white door with a glazed glass panel. One then found oneself in a narrow corridor, smelling strongly of ether. Lining each side were doors on various of which were painted: '*Salle d'Attente*', '*Rayons*', '*Médecin Chef*', '*Bureau*', '*Département de Larynchologie*', and most ominously, '*Salle d'Interventions*'.

'You wait here while I tell them that you have come,' said *Sœur* Jeanne, and she knocked at the door of the bureau, entered and closed it behind her. Paul experienced an excess of nervous excitement which drained the strength from his legs; he leant against the wall to stop himself from swaying. He felt as though he were swinging a great wheel into motion, which, once turning, would carry him with it. His instinct was to run, to quit, whilst still able, this hygienic, aseptic world on top of the mountains.

There was the opening of a door behind him. The emergence of a white-coated figure. The glimpse of a face without colour surmounted by a thick tuft of ginger hair; the whole expanse of hair dramatically substituted for the face as the figure hinged at the centre in a bow. Then the hand, candle-white, produced like an unexpected gift and extended towards Paul. A gesture in lieu of a verbal summons; another bow; and Paul passed through the doorway.

'I am Dr. Bruneau, deputy *Médecin Chef.* I speak no English. Do you speak French?'

'Very badly,' replied Paul.

'Good. You will soon learn – necessity is the best tutor. Sit down.'

Very lean, with swift, pouncing movements, a disproportionately large head and hard, green eyes, Dr. Bruneau looked like a starveling ginger cat dressed up in a white jacket, a figure from a children's post-card of the turn of the century: a firm jaw and a loose mouth, high cheekbones tightly covered by transparent flesh, ginger eyebrows pointed at the corners like the ends of a sergeant-major's moustache, wiry, rippling hair as unmanageable as a handful of uncoiled springs.

Sitting down at a desk, he motioned to Paul to draw his chair nearer, then, taking a file-cover from a pile which lay beside him, he opened it and started to write inside. Once he stopped and searched for some papers from a drawer; as he read he grunted and nodded, occasionally directing a glance of curiosity towards Paul. At last he put down his pen.

'*Alors, cher Monsieur,* we will begin our acquaintance by learning a few particulars about you. Your parents are both living?'

'Dead.'

'*Ah, voilà!*' he said with the satisfaction of a man who has just located the missing piece in a jigsaw puzzle, and he was about to inscribe this in Paul's dossier, when the latter corrected him.

Sensing a misunderstanding, Paul added quickly: 'They died in a car accident when I was two years old. I was brought up by my uncle.'

'A car accident! *Tiens!* Then they were not ill?'

'No. They were perfectly healthy.'

'Then which members of your family had tuberculosis?'

'None. I am the first.'

'That, *Monsieur,*' said Dr. Bruneau, waving his pen at Paul, 'you do not know. Many are ill and never know it. I have a theory... However...

He now posed a number of questions about Paul's occupation and background, repeating the answers as he wrote them. He spoke with a curious distinctness, and in such a way as to leave no doubt as to the intended punctuation, a consequence, probably, of many conversations with invalids whose knowledge of French was rudimentary.

'*Monsieur*,' he demanded suddenly, and almost as if with the object of catching Paul off his guard, 'have you ever spat blood?' Paul nodded. 'How many times?' 'Only once.' (It was now the question and answer of the confessional.) 'It was much?' 'Yes.' 'Ah. It is all written down here,' said Dr. Bruneau, looking at a sheet of typewritten paper from which earlier he had been copying.

He then inquired about the nature of past symptoms and the events which had led to diagnosis, until with confusion and fatigue Paul's French became incomprehensible. Either because he now had sufficient information, or because he realised that he could extract no more, Dr. Bruneau closed the file, and then subjected Paul to a thorough physical examination.

'*Eh bien*, now I will screen your chest.' He led Paul through an intercommunicating door to the adjoining room; its ceiling was vaulted, there were no windows, the air was heavy and the only illumination was provided by a dim, blue-tinted electric bulb. Machines of complex construction towered obscurely beyond what was discernible of their façades. It was as though the workshop of Dr. Coppelius had been resurrected in the catacombs.

Dr. Bruneau seated himself on a music-stool in the middle of the floor, and, lowering his head, clasped his hands over his eyes. Paul, who had no idea that Dr. Bruneau was merely accustoming his eyes to the darkness before attempting to distinguish the ill-defined shadows which would be projected on to the screen of the X-ray machine, stood motionless and perplexed; he felt like a visitor who, having come to inspect the interior of a cathedral, has found a service actually in progress, and was unable to make up his mind whether he would cause more disturbance by remaining or attempting to leave.

'Now take off your jacket and step into this cabinet,' said Dr. Bruneau, pointing with one hand, whilst keeping the other over his eyes. Paul dropped his jacket on to a chair and climbed cautiously into a wooden structure shaped like an up-ended coffin. He heard the sound of the music-stool being dragged across the floor. Then Dr.

Bruneau's voice, slightly muffled but very close, ordered him to stand forward with his chest against the screen. Paul shivered as his flesh came into contact with the cold glass. 'Now your hands on your hips and elbows forward'; a panel opened in the front of the machine, and Dr. Bruneau's hand was inserted to guide Paul's inexperienced movements. The resultant tactile sensation was one of great intimacy, as though two people buried alive by an explosion had found each other at last.

A click as Dr. Bruneau pressed a switch with his foot; the dim light was extinguished, and Paul heard for the first time the characteristic buzzing of the X-ray apparatus, a sound as insistent and directionless as if a bee had been imprisoned in the orifice of each ear.

'Lean backwards. Lean forwards. Turn half about,' ordered Dr. Bruneau. 'Now back again. Halt! Breathe in. Breathe out. Stay like that.' The buzzing stopped. 'Don't move. I will now fetch Dr. Vernet.' The opening, closing, opening, closing of a door, and then the *Médecin Chef* of *Les Alpes* was also peering at Paul Davenant's shadowy interior. The two doctors conferred in whispers; Paul sought desperately to catch a significant word, but without success. The blue light was turned on, and he was told to leave the cabinet.

'*Je vous présente le Docteur Vernet*,' said Dr. Bruneau, and Paul bowed slightly to a white-coated figure. '*Enchanté, Monsieur*,' said Dr. Vernet, shaking Paul's hand. 'Come now into my bureau. After having viewed the interior of a patient, I like always to see his exterior – if only for the purpose of co-ordination.' Dr. Vernet's English was mannered but fluent, and, although he spoke with a marked accent, it was unidentifiable.

'*Mais je n'ai pas encore fait la radiographie*,' objected Dr. Bruneau.

'*Bien. Faites-la vite. J'ai tous le temps, comme toujours*,' said Dr. Vernet mildly.

When the X-ray had been taken, Dr. Vernet led Paul into his bureau, and both men regarded each other in the light. Dr. Vernet was a little above middle height, and in his late forties. His body was thick, he had a short neck and firm, round features, His eyes were alert and highly intelligent. On the apex of his left cheek was a small mole which compelled attention whenever the angle of his face brought it into view. His smile was so broad that it caused his cheeks to bulge and the thin line of his lips to extend to twice its normal length.

Suddenly, and with no change of expression, he seized Paul's hand, as though with the object of shaking it a second time; instead he turned it over and examined the fingernails, even running the tip of his own finger very delicately over their surface. '*Mais vous voyez…*' he murmured to Dr. Bruneau.

'And now I auscult you,' he said. And as he sounded Paul's chest, he repeated: 'Breathe deeply. Cough. Say *trente-trois*.' When the stethoscope moved fairly rapidly, Paul felt relieved; when it lingered in any particular area, he was filled with apprehension.

When Dr. Vernet had covered the whole terrain, he directed Dr. Bruneau to take a stethoscope and to follow his own from one point to another, and each time Paul felt the pressure of the two instruments, he breathed deeply, coughed and said *trente-trois*.

'*Bien. Allez chercher Florent*,' said Dr. Vernet at last. Dr. Bruneau left the room to return shortly with a young doctor of most timid aspect. 'Come, Florent,' said Dr. Vernet, giving Paul the smile of a confederate. 'Come and give us your opinion of the condition of *Monsieur* Davenant.' And, still smiling, he seated himself on the corner of his desk whilst Dr. Florent ran his stethoscope over Paul's chest, telling him at the same time to breathe deeply, to cough and to say *trente-trois*.

Paul stared at the opposite wall; he felt dehumanised and exhausted. The pitch of his voice was unrecognisable as, every few seconds, he cried out: '*Trente-trois*.'

'A little quicker, Florent; *Monsieur* Davenant is getting tired, I think,' said Dr. Vernet, and as Dr. Florent started to stammer a diagnosis, he cried: '*Halte! Ça suffit*.' Then, turning towards Paul and still smiling, he announced: '*Monsieur*, you have many cavities and lesions at the base of your left lung, and infiltrations at the apex. On the upper lobe of your right lung there are a number of minor infiltrations. I will have to reflect upon your case before I decide what treatment to attempt. In any case you will return to bed and remain there, for you are too ill to be up.'

The consultation was over and the doctors were about to withdraw. 'Excuse me,' said Paul hurriedly; he felt lonely and abashed in his sickness and his semi-nudity. 'Excuse me, but I should be grateful for even the roughest indication of how long you think I shall have to stay here?'

Dr. Bruneau glanced over his shoulder: 'You should know, *Monsieur*, that this is not the sort of place to which you come for three weeks.'

'Yes, yes, of course, I understand that. All I ask is the very least idea.'

'*Monsieur*, we are doctors – not prophets,' replied Dr. Bruneau, as he hastened after his colleagues.

When Paul returned to his room he found it empty, for everyone was at lunch. He was glad that he would miss the meal, glad that he was alone, glad that in quietness he could climb back into bed. But as soon as he lay down he had a bad attack of coughing, and then for several minutes could not clear his throat. At last, completely exhausted, he lay back and shut his eyes.

He fell instantly into that sort of half-sleep in which thoughts and memories, heightened by the partially hallucinatory perception engendered by a tubercular fever, become synthesised in a specious impression of reality. 'Excuse me,' he had once said, somewhere, for some reason; occasions, possible, half-remembered, drifted across his memory. 'Excuse me' to people he had inadvertently jostled, 'Excuse me' as a preamble to uncongenial explanation, 'Excuse me' to the blockers of doorways and passages through which he had wanted to pass... 'Excuse me,' he had said to Dr. Vernet, in an anguished attempt to gain some knowledge of the implications of his condition. 'Excuse me. Excuse me...'

Doorways and passages... He reviewed and re-saw them, familiar, forgotten structures, each with its grey associations. Doorways were quickly passed, passages stretched as far as the imagination: the narrow, unilluminated passage of a block of flats in which he had once lived, the wooden passage of an army 'spider' leading to a disinfectant-drenched wash-house, the bare, discoloured passage of School House...

The associations fell into alignment. School House, the fagging duty bungled, the prefect who seemed twice his size, the eternity in the passage, then 'I'll see you later'. 'Excuse me,' Paul had said, knowing already the answer, but impelled by panic to imprudence, 'excuse me, but what are you going to do to me?'

He woke with his face covered with sweat, and, as he wiped it away, he saw that the pillow was soaked. More sweat returned to his forehead, and his pyjama jacket stuck to his back. He looked incredulously at his watch; only five minutes had passed since he had last consulted it. He took a brush and comb from the *table de nuit*, but as he started to brush his moist hair they fell from between his fingers. Before he could attempt to retrieve them, he heard the sound of footsteps and the voices of the British students; the door opened and they all came in.

'What are you doing in bed? Why weren't you at lunch?' demanded Angus Gray, who was the first into the room. Paul explained that he had had his medical examination, and had been told to return to bed.

'Have you had your lunch?' asked John Cotterell.

'Yes,' lied Paul.

'You're looking very flushed,' commented John MacAllister. 'How did you get on? With your examination, I mean.'

Paul, who was now sitting up in bed, shrugged his shoulders. 'God knows. I don't.'

'What do you mean, you don't know? What did they say to you?'

'That I was ill.'

'Brilliant diagnosis! Nothing contagious, I hope?'

'Oh no! Merely what French novelists call "*un peu faible de poitrine*".'

'"A wee bit chesty," as they say up our way,' said Angus Gray.

'Certainly no more than that.'

'I should hope not. I wouldn't stay here a minute if I thought otherwise,' said William Davis.

'Nor would I,' said Paul, amidst laughter.

'You're all taking it very lightly,' commented David Bean. He sat down on a chair and raised his feet on to Paul's bed.

Everyone looked at him in surprise.

'Well, how do you think we should take it?' demanded John MacAllister.

'A little more realistically.' David Bean turned to Paul. 'Yesterday you were shooting your mouth off about one of the great advantages of T.B. being that it was painless. I wondered at the time whether you had ever seen anyone dying of T.B. Have you?'

Paul shook his head.

'Well, then, I advise you to reserve your judgement.'

'I didn't make a judgement. I merely said that if I must have a disease, I preferred it to be painless.'

'Who wouldn't?'

'Precisely.'

'Which is just the reason for not choosing T.B.'

For a moment there was silence. Then Paul said very deliberately: 'Well, David, if you're in a lot of pain I must confess you're disguising the fact very courageously.'

'You think so. Maybe.'

'In fact you give the impression of being in as little pain as I am.'

'As little pain…' cried David Bean. His face turned scarlet, and his whole body began to tremble. 'What in God's name do you know about pain, you who are only beginning? Do you think there is no pain in rotting in your bed for years until one day you drown in your own blood? Do you think that there's no pain in knowing you're a pariah? Do you think there's no pain in having to apologise for your sickly presence everywhere you go, in being shunned by your friends because they think you a plague-carrier, in being afraid to kiss a girl in case she finds out that you've got T.B.? Do you think that there's no pain in being confined to your own knife, fork, spoon and plate when you're eating in the house of your own parents? Do you think – ' he paused to take breath.

'Well done! Bean's potted guide to T.B. Of course you'll be speaking from years of personal experience,' said John MacAllister sarcastically.

'Yes, I am. My brother died of T.B. a year ago. I nursed him in the last months and caught it from him.'

'I see. I'm sorry.'

Paul said very quietly: 'That's pretty bad luck, David. But it doesn't mean that we're all going to die. I can tell you that I, for one, intend to get completely cured.'

David Bean was not placated, and he replied in a measured and remorseless tone: 'The first thing, Davenant, that you can get out of your head is the idea of being completely cured. Nobody who gets touched by the tubercle can ever get completely cured. The best thing that you can hope for is to obtain some compromise with the bug which will enable you to live with it on fairly amicable terms.'

'What absolute nonsense!' cried John MacAllister. 'With collapse therapy it is possible to cure it definitively.'

David Bean's eyes narrowed contemptuously: 'I refer you to your textbooks,' he said. 'In my second year of medicine I assimilated one principle concerning T.B., and I have seen its vindication ever since. It is this: T.B. is a general disease with local symptoms which may appear anywhere in the body. By various methods you may clear up the local symptoms; the disease itself you will never touch.'

'You're out of date, man,' said Angus Gray, also a medical student. 'Our surgeons have long ago unmasked that fiction. The danger from T.B. is in the symptoms, not in the disease, and when the symptoms are overcome the disease itself often has a mysterious way of packing up of its own accord. I've seen people die as a result of pulmonary cavitation, but never from a general disease exhibiting no local symptoms!'

'Splendid! How very encouraging for the surgeons. But I seem to have come across a surprisingly large number of cases where local symptoms have been suppressed by some form of collapse therapy, only to break out in another part of the lung or somewhere else in the body.'

'I don't know what you mean by collapse therapy, but it's common knowledge that enough people got over T.B. long before any sort of treatment existed,' interjected Paul.

'They probably didn't have T.B. Every wasting disease was once called consumption,' said David Bean.

'André Gide had T.B., and seriously enough to be considered a hopeless case. Nevertheless without going near a sanatorium he managed to clear it up some fifty years ago. And then again, Somerset Maugham doesn't seem to be getting on too badly,' replied Paul.

'A pity that Keats, Lawrence, Katherine Mansfield and a few others couldn't have found out the secret,' was David Bean's acid reply.

'And a pity, as you've decided to decline and drown in your own blood, that you couldn't have done it at home instead of coming out here,' said William Davis, who up to now had taken no part in the argument.

'But I haven't decided to,' replied David Bean coldly, 'and I am effecting just that compromise with the bug about which I was speaking. The fact that I am managing very nicely was confirmed by Vernet when he examined me this morning. In any case I've never had any more than a faint shadow at the apex of my right lung, and it has now gone completely. But I've no illusions about the permanency of my recovery, despite the fact that Vernet insists that I am quite well, and has allowed me up for all meals and out for walks. It is my intention to consolidate my improvement, and that will not be by running about the mountains. I shall spend as much time as I can in bed, and the next ten years of my life (if I have the good luck to avoid complications and relapses) I shall pass very quietly indeed.'

'What a revolting prospect! I should prefer to be dead,' said John MacAllister.

'Which is just the alternative available to you – choose as you wish. In any case, I have chosen. I – ' David Bean broke off as the door opened and in came *Sœur* Jeanne.

'Two o'clock,' she cried, 'It is the *cure de silence.* For two hours you must all get right into bed, and you may not talk or read or do anything. Now get along and don't make a noise. *Bonne cure, tout le monde!*'

As the young men got up to leave, they ceremoniously wished each other '*bonne cure*', and laughed heartily having done so. But '*bonne cure*' was a joke which, subjected to repetition by all new patients, tended to stale with the passage of time.

The late afternoon saw the departure of Mr. James. He came into the room shared by John Cotterell and Paul Davenant at the end of the *cure de silence*, and found, as he had anticipated, that the other students were also assembled there. His mood was both truculent and sentimental. First of all there was a bun for everybody. He opened a paper bag, which he handed round from student to student, delivering at the same time cautions and admonitions. ('Go easy lads, one each,' and a flood of indignant banter when John Cotterell pulled out a bun to which another was attached.)

While everyone was eating, he related a curious incident which had occurred when he had been taking leave of M. Halfont. Not having sufficient French money, but wishing to give M. Halfont a tip, he had pressed a packet of cigarettes and half a crown into his hand, explaining that he could undoubtedly change the latter coin at the bank. M. Halfont had examined the cigarette packet and the half crown, and had then handed them back to Mr. James, saying: 'Thank you for showing me. They are most interesting.' Mr. James, touched by M. Halfont's unworldliness, had explained that they were a tip, at which M. Halfont, despite the fact that he seemed to understand English, had turned and walked down the passage. Mr. James had followed him, trying to explain in French, but it was useless. 'Which,' as Mr. James pointed out, 'just goes to show that their English is not always as good as they like to make out.'

Then Mr. James had had an interview with Dr. Vernet, and a fact of great significance had emerged from it, which under no circumstances should he ever reveal to the students. But... The door opened and *Sœur* Jeanne entered, and Mr. James seized a magazine lying on a bed, opened it at random, and started ostentatiously to read aloud. When she had left again, Mr. James signalled to everyone to gather about him.

'More news about foreign students?' asked John MacAllister.

'Shut your mouth, Scottie,' said Mr. James tartly.

'Dr. Vernet also refused his tip?' suggested John Cotterell.

'For crying out loud!'

'Well, what is it that you mustn't tell us?'

'You don't bloody well deserve to know.'

'Well, tell us all the same,' pleaded John Cotterell.

'I shall do so – for the sake of the others,' said Mr. James with great dignity.

And he explained that he told Dr. Vernet that, although his responsibility had ended with the safe delivery of the British party to Brisset, he could not deny that he felt the keenest interest in their future. 'What, frankly, and in complete confidence,' he had asked Dr. Vernet, 'is their chance of ever getting out of here alive?' and Dr. Vernet had replied, after only a moment's reflection, that in his opinion all the members of the British party were curable!

'And I make this great breach of confidence purely for your peace of mind. If Dr. Vernet had made even one exception I would never have so much as breathed a word of it.' Then he commented that that afternoon he had provided not only mental nourishment, but also physical nourishment, for everybody had received and eaten a bun. Now it was his intention to provide a little spiritual nourishment. He did not know the religious views or denominations of any member of the party, and he wasn't interested. For himself he couldn't claim to be a great religious authority, and he didn't mind admitting that he was very far from being a saint. But he had learned one thing, and he was going to pass it on for what it was worth – the power of prayer.

And he related an experience which had befallen him during the war. One evening there had been an air raid and he had heard the sound of a falling bomb, and he had known by a sort of second sight that it was coming straight for the house in which he was living. He had fallen on his knees and prayed as never before. There had been a terrible detonation, he had thought that he would be buried alive, but no… The bomb had fallen on the house next door. 'There,' said Mr. James, 'was the power of prayer.'

'Was the house next door occupied?' asked William Davis.

'A family of seven, not counting the lodgers, and all blown to smithereens,' said Mr. James impressively.

'And was your house badly damaged?'

'Not touched but for a couple of windows out at the back.'

And before the effect of his story could diminish he took from his pocket a packet of faded, paper-covered prayer books, and handed one to each student. They were headed in heavy type: *A Soldier's Shortened Version of the Book of Common Prayer for Use in the Field*, and underneath appeared the date: 'August 1914'. 'A job lot – I picked them up at a ha'penny each on a stall in the Portobello Road,' explained Mr. James.

Time was getting short. It was not easy, he admitted, for him to leave them just as their period of trial was about to begin, and when in many ways they would most have need of him. But he believed that they would emerge chins up and banners flying; they would show the French that the British knew how to take it in peace-time as well as in war. One day they would all meet again, for preference and for old times' sake outside the Foreign Departures platform at Victoria Station, and he would stand them all a dinner at any Soho restaurant they might care to name. Till then it was 'watch and pray'; they would be in his thoughts.

Except for Paul, they all escorted Mr. James to the entrance hall, where last hand-shakes were cut short by the arrival of the concierge who was to conduct him to the station. Then the students returned to their rooms for the evening *cure* which lasted from half-past five till seven o'clock. When the *cure* was over, they found the passages full of baggage; this indicated the simultaneous arrival of the French, Polish and Hungarian parties. Tomorrow, *Sœur* Jeanne told them, the parties from Italy, Czechoslovakia and Greece were expected, whilst the last party – from Finland – was due at the end of the week.

Throughout the evening and night it snowed heavily.

CHAPTER FOUR

•

Paul Davenant was preoccupied by a number of thoughts before he at last fell asleep. He did not, however, pass any time in reflection upon the fate of the little blue jar which bore his name in capitals on the label, and in which he had expectorated early that morning. Indeed, had it been possible for him never to have heard of the matter again, it is probable that he would have forgotten it completely.

But this act of expectoration was – though Paul could not have known it – of infinite significance. New rules of conduct, new standards of behaviour, new systems of rewards and punishments, new concepts of virtue and vice, of character and its lack, of wisdom and its absence, would be formulated according to the result of the analysis of the matter hygienically sealed within the small blue container.

If the sputum contains no trace of the dreaded *Bacille de Koch*, B.K. – this will be inscribed on the chart of the patient concerned; if the microscope reveals the presence of the bacillus, the marking on the chart will be B.K.+.

Thus in this new and shadowy world is established the measure by which each member of the community must pass; the aristocracy and the commonality are divided respectively into the negative and the positive. Analyses are carried out monthly, when all charts are collected to be inscribed in red with the individual result.

Mutations take place from time to time, and members of each society change place. Some bettering themselves, some losing caste. Those who are irrevocably positive know little more each month than the confirmation of their dejection (though who among them does not, each month, hope secretly that he has emerged from his category?); the real arpeggios of nervous excitement on the gamut of dread are known only to the negative; a + suddenly replacing a series of –s, will mean the postponing of the cherished date of departure, and perhaps a relapse into the dreadful gulf from which a patient, at the expense probably of months or years of treatment, had thought to have extricated himself.

Though Paul was unconcerned about the fate of the little blue bottle, he nevertheless showed a marked interest in the flat glass tube which twice each day he was required to hold between his lips: it provided the only verifiable evidence of his condition from one day to the next. The previous evening at six o'clock precisely he had retained his thermometer in his mouth for the regulation period of ten minutes, at the end of which time the mercury had risen several divisions above the red line which indicates normal; a rapid calculation had shown this to be under 100° Fahrenheit, and with confused memories of boyhood temperatures he felt that it could have been considerably worse.

On waking the following morning he had instinctively stretched out his hand for his thermometer case; probably as a consequence of a whole day's rest, his temperature would be lower than it had been twenty-four hours previously. At the end of five minutes (he was too impatient to wait the whole ten) he saw that it was actually two divisions higher. Irrationally he felt that this was a confirmation of his worst fears, and he speculated gloomily upon his condition and its implications. Dr. Vernet had spoken about treatment. But what other treatment was there, he wondered uneasily, apart from prolonged rest in bed? Stray words and phrases of his comrades had provided hints so horrible that at the time he assumed that they must have been joking. But now he searched his memory for every detail, attempting hopelessly to distinguish the truth from the total mass of fanciful exaggeration.

An hour later a waiter brought in his breakfast on a tray. John Cotterell, who had been sleeping until this moment, got up and dressed hastily and went to share the communal breakfast in the *salle à manger*.

Whilst John Cotterell was still away, Paul decided to get up and wash. His image in the mirror above the basin arrested his attention; familiar but impersonal, he could not wholly associate it with his own person. With the detachment of a lecturer identifying a condition to medical students, he said to himself: 'This is the face of a man who is chronically ill.' The traditional details – the pallor of the cheeks merging into burning apices, the encircled eyes, themselves moistly bright, the drops of sweat where his hair-line joined with his forehead – for the first time since the diagnosis of his illness he recognised and acknowledged what he saw. With difficulty he withdrew his attention from the details in order to study the whole; he saw then a face mask-like in its lack of mobility, a coloured plate from a medical book on toxicology, the sort that one opens at hazard and instantly regrets.

As he began his toilet he was seized by so violent an attack of coughing that he was forced by breathlessness to sit on the end of John Cotterell's bed. His throat was blocked and in order to free it he gulped and expelled air, producing a primitive and hollow croaking, the cry of the very disease within him, a sound which Paul had never heard before and which he could not believe proceeded from himself. His efforts provoked a fresh series of coughs which seemed to have their beginning in the extremities of his toes and which dragged a raucous and eerie progress up the length of his whole body. Then suddenly the sputum lodging in his throat was expelled, and he spat it into the *crachoir* at the side of his bed. Instantly his breathing returned to normal, his throat felt splendidly clear, and the silence in the room seemed by contrast even more astonishing than the dreadful noises which he had been producing a few minutes earlier. He dried his eyes, which had been secreting, and continued with his wash; the spasm over, it seemed unthinkable that it should ever start again.

But during the course of the morning it happened only too frequently that Paul's arm serpented from his bed to grasp the white enamel *crachoir*. And he noted with melancholy interest that, since he had taken to his bed, the disease was declaring itself with far greater intensity than formerly.

The only visitor during the morning was Emile, the concierge. Twice a day he delivered letters to the patients in the sanatorium, and this morning he had nearly half a dozen for John Cotterell. Paul Davenant anticipated no letters, and was not surprised when Emile turned to him and said in concierge's English, 'Nothing for you this morning.'

This Emile was a small, solid man in his middle-fifties. He had silvery hair and a red face; protruding blue eyes sheltered under tufted eyebrows; his white, cropped moustache showed yellow at the extremities. He was a prominent character both in the sanatorium and in the village of Brisset; his laugh, unmirthful and insinuating, was well known and, in certain quarters, not a little feared. Several times during the day he would descend to the station, either to collect letters or to meet passengers, and on the way he would call at a little *bistro* where a *fine* always awaited him, which he would swallow in a single gulp. Progressively through the day his eyes would become moister, his gestures more expansive, and his laugh lose any inhibiting restraint.

He received only a nominal salary, the greater part of his income being derived from the *commissions* which he made each day for the private patients; bills were rendered monthly and he charged a flat rate of 10% on each. In addition he received a substantial discount from the shopkeepers. What he did with the money that he earned – apart from what he expended on alcohol – no one knew; there were concierges who had bought shops, *estaminets*, cinemas and even clinics out of their savings. He had been employed at *Les Alpes* for more than thirty years.

Just before lunch the British students assembled in Paul's room in order that they might all go together to the *salle à manger*. The last of them had received his medical examination, and the results for the party as a whole were good. No one, apart from Paul, was sufficiently ill to be confined to bed. With this reassurance all attention could now be directed to the new arrivals, and to speculation about the future.

Greetings had already been exchanged with the French contingent. It was thought that greetings had been exchanged with the Hungarians. But the Hungarians (or were they Czechoslovaks?), had only spoken German, of which language not one of the British party had even a superficial knowledge. In consequence the Brisset Esperanto had been employed, a sort of basic French mixed freely with the words of any other language known to the speaker, which depended for direction and edge more upon intonation than eloquence.

And it was wondered if the only difficulties would be linguistic. In common with the members of the British party, all the other students had served in the armed forces of their respective countries, and these countries had been divided fairly evenly between the two opposing sides during the war. And some countries previously Fascist had now Communist governments; to which (if to either) side would the students coming from such countries incline? And would previous loyalties lead to discord in the community?

Paul only gave part of his attention to what his friends were saying. All morning he had speculated upon the nature of T.B. treatment. He knew that John Cotterell could have answered most of his questions, but he feared that the latter's account would be over-circumspect. It seemed to him that John MacAllister would probably be the person least likely either to exaggerate or to spare him.

So, because he felt that he could bear the uncertainty no longer, he had decided during the morning that when John MacAllister came in with the others before lunch, he would ask him directly for the information which he sought. But now that all the students were assembled, he shrank from carrying out his intention; a number of times he was on the point of speaking, but he hesitated and then the opportunity was lost. He wanted to say: 'Look, I know that I am desperately ill. I am a moral coward. I think that I am not frightened by the prospect of death, but I am frightened by prospect of treatment, and I am still more terrified that my terror should become apparent. But most of all I fear the scope of my imagination. Tell me what I must expect, tell me the worst that can happen to me, and then certainty, however bad, must bring relief.'

But how, how could he ask? Somehow the discussion amongst the students had reached the point where John Cotterell appeared to be providing a demonstration of how a Hungarian ballet master whose second language was German would instruct a French class to dance czardas, whilst Angus Gray and William Davis (as his pupils) scampered across the floor and jumped over the beds. Then some French students hearing the noise opened the door, and, without hesitation, they too joined in the dancing. John Cotterell jumped on to a chair and started to sing in an improvised Hungarian; everyone either pranced about wildly or clapped his hands to the rhythm. The uproar came to an end with a furious knocking on the floor of the room above. And then, because it was now lunch-time, the students, breathless with their exertions and with laughter, filed out of the door and left Paul to his introspection.

But in a sanatorium there is one topic of conversation to which everyone, sooner or later, always returns. William Davis had appointed himself treasurer for the British party, and he had purchased a packet of cakes, which he shared out at the end of the *cure de silence*. While everyone was eating, John MacAllister made a passing reference to the X-ray apparatus in use in *Les Alpes*, and David Bean, swallowing quickly, seized the opportunity to express his views. Long before X-ray apparatus had ever been thought of, he observed, there had been doctors who, with a simple wooden stethoscope, had been capable of making a far more accurate diagnosis than a modern specialist with all his streamlined equipment. Perhaps in the future doctors would do better to rely a little more on the evidence of their ears than of their eyes. If anyone were interested in his opinion, he believed that it would have been no loss to medicine if X-ray machines had never been invented, and one day he intended to write a thesis on the mistakes in diagnosis arising from their use. The majority of operations for appendicitis, he insisted, were quite unnecessary, being based on the erroneous interpretations of X-ray plates. And in T.B. it was notorious that every doctor interpreted the shadows in X-rays as he wished, and he could quote cases where X-ray plates, and even tomograms (a series of X-rays in depth), had shown nothing to indicate the existence of disease, though subsequently a P.M. had revealed extensive damage.

Angus Gray congratulated David Bean on so lucid an exposition of his views, but suggested that they did not go quite far enough. Discard all X-ray apparatus, of course, but on what grounds retain the stethoscope? Had there not been doctors capable of recognising consumption long before stethoscopes had been invented? And then again what doctor of real integrity would ever care to make a diagnosis of a patient's condition before having attended his post-mortem?

As everyone laughed, David Bean said sarcastically: 'Oh, we all know that the information provided by any little gadget or magic box is worth its weight in gold to the modern practitioner so long as it saves him the trouble of thinking. I must say, Angus, that I envy your future patients.'

'And quite frankly I envy yours – for the tonic effect your personality will have on them,' replied Angus Gray.

'And talking about tonic effects, gentlemen, I think that we might do well to remember from time to time that Paul here is still awaiting a decision about treatment,' added John MacAllister.

Everyone was astonished, everyone had quite forgotten.

'You mean to say that you still don't know what they're going to do to you?' said Angus Gray.

'No.'

'Give them time. He only had his medical yesterday,' said William Davis.

'It's true. But it seems as if we've been here weeks already.'

'What do you think they'll do to me?' asked Paul, trying to make the question sound quite casual, though he addressed it pointedly at John MacAllister.

'I can't say – it will depend on all sorts of things. Are both your lungs affected or only the one?'

'Both; but I gather that there's not much wrong with my right lung.'

'Well, it's always possible that they'll try to give you a pneumo on your left lung, and then if it's not too badly damaged the right could clear up by itself. But don't take that as official, they may do something quite different. Besides, it's not really possible to express any opinion without much more knowledge of your case.'

'I wish you'd explain to me what a pneumothorax really is; I haven't the first idea about it or any other form of treatment.'

So, briefly, John MacAllister explained the nature and the function of the pneumothorax. The basis of all treatment for T.B. was rest, which gave the affected tissues a chance to heal. The pneumothorax, which artificially reduced the function of either (and if necessary both) lungs, brought the principle of rest directly to bear on the affected part.

It was accomplished in this way. Air was pumped between the exterior of the lung and the interior of the chest wall, which had the effect of compressing the lung to a fraction of its original size. Although it continued to breathe, its activity was greatly restricted, and healing could start to take place. Unfortunately the process was not always straightforward, for sometimes adhesions existed between the lung and the interior of the chest wall. Often, however, it was possible to sever these adhesions by the performance of an operation called a thoroscopy.

Because the air so introduced between the chest wall and the lung (into what was called the pleural cavity) was absorbed during a certain period of time into the bloodstream, it was necessary to maintain the pneumothorax by reintroducing fresh supplies of air at regular intervals, which varied normally between one and three weeks. Both refills of air and the initial induction were made in the same manner: a hollow needle was passed between the ribs, and the air was pumped directly into the pleural cavity. This was effected with a minimum of trouble, and did not take more than a few minutes.

Was it necessary to remain in bed all the time that one had a pneumothorax? John MacAllister shook his head; complete bed-rest was only required during the initial stages, after which it was possible to lead a semi-normal life. To the question of how long it was necessary to maintain the pneumothorax, John replied that it depended on the individual case, and that the time varied usually between two and six years.

'Well,' said Paul, 'it appears to me to be a good solution. I think I shall ask for one.'

'You are splendidly naïve about all this,' commented David Bean. 'It will be more a question of what Vernet decides for you than what you want. Besides, John has given the impression that a pneumothorax always works, whereas in point of fact it quite often can't even be induced. Then again it occurs not infrequently that there are adhesions, and if these can't be cut, then the pneumothorax has to be abandoned.'

'I see,' said Paul. 'Does that mean that no further treatment can be carried out?'

David Bean laughed. 'Something in the tone of your voice tells me that you wouldn't be wholly disappointed if I told you that that was the case. No, there are still quite a few specialities. The enthusiastic fish, for example, can always be filleted.'

'Filleted?'

'Have his ribs out. An intricate and engaging little process performed without the benefit of a general anæsthetic.'

'Without a general anæsthetic?' exclaimed Paul, now thoroughly startled.

'David's putting it ridiculously,' said John MacAllister. 'The operation is performed under a very powerful local anæsthetic. The object in removing the ribs is to obtain a permanent collapse of the ill part of the lung.'

'A method which might be compared to cracking a walnut with a steamroller,' commented David Bean.

'But the operation must be appalling,' said Paul.

'It's not a picnic. Actually one doesn't feel the removal of the ribs; the worst part comes later when the effect of the anæsthetic has worn off,' said John MacAllister.

'And of course there's no question of feeling the ribs coming out,' added Angus Gray quickly.

'One may not feel them coming out, but one certainly hears them,' said David Bean. 'I've been present at a number of thoracoplasties and

I've never found the sound particularly stimulating, quite apart from how it must strike the person who is actually undergoing the operation. I certainly would not propose myself as a candidate.'

'Obviously nobody volunteers for one,' said John MacAllister, 'but at least it can usually be looked upon as a permanent job, and you don't run the same danger of fluid which so often wrecks a pneumothorax.'

'What do you mean by "danger of fluid?".' asked Paul, his voice sounding strained.

'Well, it can happen that a pneumothorax provokes an irritation of the pleura, which then results in an effusion. Sometimes it clears up by itself, but if not it can always be aspirated.'

'And as the aspiration often re-irritates the pleura, you then get a fresh secretion, which in due course is followed by another aspiration. It can, in time, become quite tedious,' said David Bean.

'Well, I think that I won't perhaps ask for a pneumothorax after all,' said Paul.

There was some laughter, in which Paul joined.

'David's putting the wind up you,' said John MacAllister. 'You needn't think that complications are inevitable or even likely – a tremendous number of people have had a pneumothorax with very satisfactory results. There's no reason in the world why you should be unlucky, if it proves possible to induce one. And if it doesn't work, there's always the second line of defence.'

'And when the thoracoplasty turns out not to work, what's the third line of defence?' asked David Bean.

'Stop blethering, man,' cried Angus Gray. 'You might have the decency to keep all your pessimistic drivel to yourself. I've heard of people like you amongst the patients, but for a medical student to speak as you do is a damned disgrace.'

'The damned disgrace is to pay lip service to a whole system of treatment which doesn't repay its existence by its results,' replied David Bean, slightly raising his voice. 'I would advocate any method, however radical, if I could see that it served its purpose. But how many times have we all seen examples of treatment producing clinically satisfactory results, and then the whole thing breaking down for some inexplicable reason at a later stage? Why does no one start to reflect that there is something infinitely mysterious and subtle about tuberculosis? Why, for example, should we, from our comfortable middle-class homes, well-nourished, well-developed, fall victims to a deficiency disease? And why, if we have got it, should we expect to overcome it by suppressing its symptoms? Would we try to cure a skin eruption by rubbing on some quack ointment advertised in the popular press?'

'It's probably all a lot less mysterious and subtle than you're trying to make out,' said John MacAllister. 'If you've had a primary infection when you were a child, you've been able to build up a resistance against it. But if for some reason you haven't, down you go the first time you come into contact with a big dose.'

'You're over-simplifying. I don't believe that a person in a state of mental and physical equilibrium could catch the bug even if he hadn't had a primary infection.'

'No, and probably one wouldn't have caught it before the Fall of Man. What's the use of speaking of mental and physical equilibrium in the abstract? The question is, Man having undoubtedly fallen, what methods have you to substitute for the treatment which you find so unsatisfactory?'

'I haven't said that I have anything to substitute, but, because a specific is lacking, I don't believe in resorting to witchcraft. If Man has fallen, then the thing is to try and get him up again. Once one can re-establish mental and physical equilibrium in a patient, I am positive that the disease will disappear of its own accord. There are various fairly obvious methods of going about this, depending on the case. Congenial surroundings, good food and plenty of rest will help. Then what? Analysis? The priests? The almoners? I don't know. The patient is disequilibrated and the reason must be found; each is an individual case and must be treated individually. The doctor who does not acknowledge this is criminally negligent, and will never succeed in producing permanent results.'

'You're talking absolute nonsense,' said John MacAllister. 'I've seen the most appalling cases completely cleared up by treatment.'

'I don't doubt it. But I'll tell you with every confidence that the cases, however appalling, of which you speak, would have got equally well if no treatment whatever had been administered. Either the body produces its own resistance against the disease, or it collapses. Yesterday someone was citing Gide and Somerset Maugham as examples of people who recovered from tuberculosis. Does it occur to you that both had something in common? They both of them got better without any form of treatment whatever? Now, if they'd fallen ill today, what would have happened? Pneumothoraxes, ribs out, God knows what. And all the resistance which they needed to combat their disease would probably have been employed in trying to combat the effects of the treatment. Gide would have done well with a double pneumothorax, with probably a double purulent pleurisy to follow.' David Bean turned towards Paul: 'It's no use being depressed through hearing the facts, and it's far worse learning the truth afterwards, when the miracle which you were expecting doesn't happen. You may be lucky and you may come out of this all right – I hope you do. But at least you ought to know a few of the issues which are involved.'

The discussion was interrupted by the entry of *Sœur* Jeanne, who was carrying a number of prints in her hand.

'These are the copies of your X-rays,' she said, distributing one to each of the students. But the copy which was due to Paul she put inside a folder affixed to his temperature chart.

'What is mine like?' he asked.

'*Ce n'est pas très joli, mon pauvre garçon.* Do not look at it.'

The other students were occupied in examining the copies of their own X-rays, when there was a knock at the door, and the young Dr. Florent peered into the room, a look of embarrassment on his face.

'*Monsieur Cotterell, pouvez-vous venir un moment? J'ai quelque chose à vous dire.*' Dr. Florent had no English.

John went out into the passage, and returned a few minutes later. 'It's the result of the sputum analysis,' he said briefly. 'We're all negative, except for Paul, and…' he broke off, realising too late that he would have done better not to have hesitated.

'Well?' asked Paul.

'Well, I'm afraid I've got to move, that's all. As far as I'm concerned, I wouldn't do so, but Florent says that it's an order; I'm sorry, Paul. Florent says that there's a Pole who's been ill a long time, and he's going to have him put in here with you.'

And as the day was already advanced, and as John had been told that he must move before the evening, he started on the removal of those of his possessions which two days previously he had stored in cupboards and drawers.

CHAPTER FIVE

•

Kubahskoi was a Polish student in his middle twenties. He spoke English with many curious turns of phrase, and expressed considerable pleasure at the prospect of sharing a room with Paul. His manner was courteous and refined; his references to himself were modest. Above middle height, he had a solid physique and a sensitive, slightly melancholy face. His forehead was high, his eyes unmistakably Slavonic and rather secretive; he had a heavy, drooping moustache. When dressed he looked like a German student from the pages of a nineteenth-century illustrated novel.

He installed himself with a rapidity which implied considerable experience, and indeed, during the five years that he had been ill, he had been an inmate of many sanatoria. He had fallen ill during the Occupation, whilst studying law at Warsaw University. A pneumothorax had been induced (which had been maintained ever since), but he had remained obstinately positive; apart from this he looked and felt relatively well, and he was not confined to bed.

Like many Slavs, he possessed an exceptional faculty for languages; he spoke four fluently and two others with proficiency. English he had started to study only a few months previously, and by speaking it with Paul he made rapid progress. He was equable in temperament and very studious; there were times, however, when he would be overcome by the wretchedness of his situation, and then for hours he would lie back with his head on the pillow, motionless and silent. Paul, seeing him thus, was always reminded of the pencil sketch made of Nietzsche on his deathbed – the great brow, the heavy moustache, the staring, unseeing eyes.

Once each morning one or other of the assistant doctors would pass on a routine visit, usually demanding no more than: '*Tout va bien?*' Deliberately, Paul posed no questions. 'Perhaps they are deciding to give me no treatment now that they see the improvement I am making through bed-rest alone,' he thought. Some days, indeed, it seemed to him that he was coughing less and that he felt better, though if he sought corroboration from the mirror above the wash-basin, he was rapidly disillusioned; at times he would be so irritated by the sight of the deep flush on each of his cheeks that he would slap at them violently with his hand, punishing their redness by turning them scarlet. For the rest, the graph of his temperature chart plotted an eccentric and irregular course, recoiling on some evenings, only to bound more precipitously the next.

The British students continued to visit Paul, though less frequently than at first. But John Cotterell, with whom Paul shared a number of common interests, came once or twice each day, often passing a whole evening with him when Kubahskoi was playing bridge in the room of one of his fellow-countrymen.

From the various details which emerged during the conversation, Paul became familiar with the uncomplex background of John Cotterell's life.

He was the son of the headmaster of a small private school, at which he had received his education and from which he had gained a scholarship to a public school, Another scholarship had taken him for a brief period to the university, which he had left to join the navy; he left the navy with the rank of lieutenant-commander. One year after returning to the university he had fallen ill.

Happily, his illness had not evolved beyond its earliest phase; an initial pleurisy had long since cleared and his lungs were free of infection. He felt no misgivings, therefore, about the future. After taking his degree at Cambridge he intended to devote his life to teaching, for which he believed he had a vocation. He was engaged to a girl whom he had met during his naval service, and of whom he kept several photos conspicuously displayed by the side of his bed.

Sometimes John questioned Paul about his own background. Paul always replied that there was nothing which merited relating. No, he admitted, he did not live with his parents; he had been an orphan since the age of two. Apart from the fact that he was an orphan, everything had been ordinary, everything conventional. When John attempted to commiserate with him on the grounds that he had no parents, Paul silenced him instantly; not having known his parents, he had not missed them. In truth, he said, he would not have wished his life to have been otherwise. No, he had not been deprived of family life; he had been brought up by an uncle, his father's brother, and in the company of a number of young cousins. No, he had not been a good scholar at school, nor indeed had he been a scholar of any sort or description. This was not modesty, he insisted with some asperity; it was only too true that he had been well below average, that indeed his development had been retarded.

'And your war service?' inquired John Cotterell.

'As uneventful and undistinguished as the rest of my life,' said Paul with finality.

'A man without history; *ergo* you must be a very happy man,' said John Cotterell.

'Why not?' replied Paul, dismissing the matter. If Paul were little disposed to discuss his past it was because he was still less disposed to think of it. That past, as he had declared, did not merit discussion. Nevertheless he never thought of it without disenchantment. And yet, as he would have freely acknowledged, by most standards it had been enviable: the usual middle-class pattern – day-school, boarding-school, public school.

In his early years, subsequent to the loss of his parents, his state bordered on idiocy; in isolation his conduct was inoffensive, but the least constraint or any human contact provoked ungovernable and interminable fits of weeping. Left alone he had a limitless capacity for doing nothing.

Paul's uncle, a benevolent and moderately wealthy man, had been appalled by the condition of his ward, and had sought, without practical issue, the advice of a number of doctors. Fearing at last the effect of Paul's continued presence on his own children, he had put him out to board with a retired doctor who thus became his tutor and virtually his guardian.

He made a gradual but unspectacular improvement. When he reached the age of fourteen it was decided to send him to a public school, into which he would have not gained admission but for the fact that it was second-rate, and – specialising in the production of extroverted young toughs (mostly the sons of wealthy manufacturers from the Midlands) – did not exact even minimal educational standards. He was bitterly unhappy, the butt of every boy, the despair of every master.

His only consolation lay in his twice-daily attendance, with the rest of the school, in the chapel; the building represented at first a refuge, and later a place hallowed for a limitless series of prayers and supplications. He turned to religion with the special fervour of the mental defective, addressing prayers to his creator at all times of the day, and falling asleep over his devotions at night. In trouble with his fellows or form-master, his lips were often observed to be moving, a fact which intensified the anger of those who were forced to associate with him. It appeared as though he were engaging in some curious form of mockery (an idea completely at variance with the agonised expression on his face); he was praying desperately to gentle Jesus, meek and mild, to turn away the wrath of the tyrant. He was beaten regularly, and beyond all else he dreaded the humiliation of these occasions; he sought to avoid them with endless prayer and the performance of innumerable penances. His housemaster regarded him with incredulity; he had never been required to deal with so wretched, so miserable a boy.

Two years later, when it had become too evident that his state was deteriorating, his uncle removed him from the school and returned him to the care of his guardian.

Nothing more than good behaviour now being required of him, he was left entirely to his own devices. After an initial period during which he remained in a state of nervous apprehension – either a reflex from his time spent in school or a fear, despite assurances to the contrary, of being sent back there – he began slowly to re-adjust himself to his simple environment. Setting himself at last to work, he consolidated and then augmented the little knowledge which he had assimilated before going to school. In the years which followed, natural tastes developed; progressively he extended the scope of his reading. The change which was taking place was too subtle to be smoked-out by the doctor; he considered his charge's preoccupation with books as yet another inauspicious symptom of the original disorder.

Paul's twentieth birthday occurred soon after the outbreak of war. Obviously unsuitable for military service, it was intended that the details of his case history should be submitted to the appropriate authorities as soon as he received his call-up papers. But Paul, who believed that for some years he had possessed complete insight into his condition, entered upon a course which he had secretly meditated ever since the war; disclosing nothing of his earlier disorders, he volunteered for service in a regiment of Artillery.

He might as well have attempted to dispossess himself of his shadow as of his past; for a year he managed to struggle against the breakdown which had stalked him from the day of his attestation – it declared itself definitively at the end of the first leave he was granted after receiving his commission. He spent seven days alone, and in a state of the most intense introspection, in a small provincial hotel.

In an army mental home he experienced a temporary recapitulation of his earlier symptoms. The great difference, however, between his present and his original condition was that he maintained his capacity for ordered thought; the symptoms disappeared but were replaced by an all-enveloping despair.

The religious faith which had sustained him in his youth he had lost; having nothing to substitute for it he now became obsessed by the apparent futility of everything. How could he manage to re-commit himself to the perpetual and joyless struggle for self-adaptation which was all his existence, when life was without meaning, without significance? 'If only I were dead,' he repeated endlessly to himself and to the psychiatrist in whose charge he had been placed.

He dreaded the prospect of returning to the army. At the same time he was convinced that if he received his discharge, he would – through consciousness of his failure – deteriorate progressively until he had reverted to the state of his childhood. It was this last which at all costs must be avoided.

Several months after his admission to the hospital he was summoned before a medical board – it had been decided in advance that he should receive his discharge from the army. He contrived, however, to simulate a perfect air of normality and composure. It was a trick at which he was gaining great proficiency, and he pleaded so earnestly to be allowed to rejoin his unit, that the president of the board – despite the opposition of his colleagues – insisted on reconsidering the case. The outcome was that Paul was allowed to return to the army, though all his eloquence could not prevent the imposition of two conditions; his medical category was permanently to be reduced, restricting him to service with a static unit, and at the same time he was to be retained only in a temporary capacity, the extension of which would always be subject to satisfactory reports on his progress and behaviour from his future commanding officer.

Posted to an anti-aircraft battery, he carried out his duties efficiently and zealously; he was promoted after some months to adjutant. His conflicts were unresolved, his mental condition was little improved, but to all appearances he was well-adjusted. The price for the suppression of his true state was a form of nervous fatigue which, transferring itself imperceptibly from a mental to a physical plane, was the forerunner of future disorders.

By this time, Paul had completely lost touch with his uncle, who in any case he had not seen for several years. The aged doctor, his guardian, long since submerged in senility, had been killed in one of the last air raids of the war.

Paul's immediate problem – and at the same time the problem of a great number of other young ex-servicemen – was solved in the most fortunate way possible: the institution of army grants for study at a university. Paul presented himself at an Oxford college and was accepted. It was in his second year that he was found to be in an advanced state of consumption.

At the beginning of a stay in a sanatorium, most patients exhibit one of two clearly defined reactions. The representatives of the first group sit in their beds in a state of sullen fury because no notice is apparently taken of them by the medical staff, and their reiterated question to anyone who will listen is invariably: 'Well, why don't they get on with it?' Those of the second group prefer to evade attention, and when occasion brings them into contact with their medical advisers, seek to avoid discussion of their symptoms or condition. Paul, after initial resistance, could now be said to belong to the latter.

And as the days passed at *Les Alpes* and nothing happened, he gained a certain wary confidence. In particular he looked forward to the weekends, for he felt that at such times he must surely be immune from uncongenial summonses to the *Service Médical* and the initiation of treatment. In the same way he awaited impatiently the approach of Christmas, which he hoped would promote a state of interregnum in the sanatorium until the New Year.

Encouraged by the example of Kubahskoi's exceptional application, Paul also started to work. In the evenings (like the weekends, temporary periods of immunity), if no one visited him, he read.

Then one day the smiling Dr. Vernet came to Paul's room and announced: '*Monsieur*, after Christmas your holiday will be over. We shall then start to torture you.'

'What do you intend to do to me?'

'That, *Monsieur*, depends on the result of certain tests which we shall make. As your famous politicians say: "Wait and see."'

And, smiling still more broadly, Dr. Vernet left the room.

CHAPTER SIX

•

By the end of the first week in December all the students had assembled; they numbered just less than a hundred and filled three of the seven floors of *Les Alpes.* Only a small proportion were confined to their rooms, for a clause governing their selection had required that the condition of the majority should not have evolved beyond the earliest stages of the illness. A considerable number, like John Cotterell, were actually convalescent. For the most part they tended to remain in their national groups, strolling together in the corridors, eating together, and congregating in the evening in the rooms of those who were confined to bed. On the days of mass screenings and consultations the *Service Médical* resembled the clearing-house of an international port; individual accents were lost in the general uproar and only gestures and colouring remained to indicate the nationality of otherwise anonymous, half-nude bodies.

Everybody was well installed; everybody was pleased to be in the Haute Savoie at so treacherous a period of the year; those who were allowed out delighted in the crisp air and the sunlit snow. But by the end of the first week, various private and unexpressed impressions attained quite suddenly the status of a communal conviction, and as such became the subject of general discussion – the food was rotten. The nearly black bread served for breakfast was often stale and sometimes sour; there was no general allocation of milk and all beverages were pre-sweetened with saccharin; the two main meals were insufficient and prepared from inferior ingredients; tea could only be distinguished from breakfast by the fact that there was even less butter and no jam, and the thin coffee was replaced by what John Cotterell termed 'tea-type tea'.

Dissatisfaction at last became vocal. M. Halfont and Dr. Vernet received the complaints sympathetically, and explained that the organisation of the kitchen – the staff of which had recently been considerably augmented owing to the sudden increase in the numbers at the sanatorium – was temporarily imperfect. But it was only a question of remaining patient for a little longer, after which it was hoped that a *cuisine* agreeable to everybody would be available.

The approach of Christmas became evident through the initiation of extensive preparations at *Les Alpes*. Private patients took their meals at different times from the students, but it had been decreed that at the special dinner to be served on Christmas Eve everyone would eat together. All the separate tables were to be placed end-to-end in a gigantic horseshoe; private patients, nurses and staff would be seated at one half, the students at the other. Then it was announced that the dinner was to be followed by a fancy-dress ball, and everyone who was going to attend was requested to busy himself or herself with the preparation of a costume. Private patients telephoned a local costumier; the students set to work with needle and cotton, ransacked the attics and store-rooms of the sanatorium for old curtains and worn-out, discarded linen.

A great Christmas tree was erected in the *salle à manger*, and stars, crescents and lanterns decorated the lofty ceiling. Individual rooms reflected the taste and temperament (and often the state of health) of their occupants. In some the walls disappeared under a mass of improvised decorations; in others the owners had arranged elaborately dressed trees or *crèches*; in most was greater or lesser evidence of festivity. But here and there was a room which – like an extinct star still fixed within its radiant galaxy – lacked even the addition of a single candle or Christmas card to mitigate the austerity of its habitual appearance.

Angus Gray and William Davis went out together one afternoon and came back with branches of holly, which they divided among the rooms of their compatriots. John MacAllister and David Bean modelled in silhouette from cardboard and coloured paper a disconcerting variety of surgical instruments. John Cotterell was wholly occupied with the design and execution of his costume.

The snow fell in such quantities that the roads of the village were impassable each morning until after the passage of the snow-plough.

Two days before Christmas there arrived for each student a gaily wrapped packet from the headquarters of the I.S.O. It contained a bar of chocolate, a tablet of soap, a tube of toothpaste and a pictorial calendar of Switzerland. So human and unexpected a gesture was greatly appreciated. Deliveries of mail were non-stop. Emile, combining seasonal exertion with seasonal indulgence, staggered at all hours up and down the passages, muttering and recriminating, eyeing his clients both defiantly and ingratiatingly, and distributing parcels like curses.

Paul was able to watch all these preparations quite dispassionately; he had been informed some days previously that he could not be permitted to attend the Christmas meal.

As the hour approached, his door opened every few minutes and someone entered either to exhibit his costume or to demand advice or assistance in respect of an adjustment. Feeling like an aged seamstress behind the wings of a provincial music-hall, he sat up in bed and acquitted himself as well as he was able, sewing and pinning, altering and fitting.

The costume varied from the ingenious to the indelicate. Kubahskoi made a passable mandarin, John MacAllister an impressive *chef de gare*. (He had engaged the co-operation of the stationmaster of Bris-set.) Angus Gray had gallantly sacrificed his great moustaches to the accomplishment of a change of sex. David Bean had covered his face with burnt cork and had suspended brass curtain rings from his ears. On his head was a turban made from an old towel. Besides this he had draped himself in a sheet; secured a doormat to his back, and, from a plaited string belt about his waist had slung a carving knife. With unerring taste and technique he had affiliated himself to the D.P.s of every improvised fancy-dress ball, that roving, ubiquitous band of gipsies cum sheiks cum pirates cum hunters cum dustmen.

John Cotterell, all but crushed at last by the accumulated weight of his own ingenuity, tore up all his intricate designs, and, to the scandal of the sanatorium, wore nothing more than a set of *Sœur* Jeanne's underwear and a top hat.

By dinner-time the rooms and corridors on Paul's floor had become deserted and silent. It was the moment which secretly and with impatience he had been awaiting.

Ever since Dr. Vernet's announcement in respect of treatment to come, Paul had decided that, when alone on Christmas Eve, he would engage in a systematic appraisal of his situation, after which he would re-orientate himself to it. How would he accomplish this? He had no very exact idea. But each time that he suffered a sudden moment of anguish in thinking of what lay ahead, he had managed to calm himself by saying: 'I need not trouble myself with this now. I will settle it all on Christmas Eve.'

At last, it had required little effort to refer all his doubts and dread to this single evening of resolution. 'After all,' he had told himself, 'I am free. If I stay here and accept treatment, it is of my own volition. If I decide that I don't wish it, I have only to explain to Dr. Vernet, and then pack my bags. The worst I have to fear is death, which, after all, is always inevitable. On the other hand if I stay and agree to undergo whatever treatment is proposed, I can regard it dispassionately, almost in the light of an experiment which I myself am making. All that matters is that it should be *I* who consciously make the choice; on Christmas Eve, when completely alone, I shall weigh up all the alternatives and decide.'

And now the evening had arrived, and, instead of carrying out his intentions, he lay basking in the voluptuousness of the silence and the sensation of being alone. 'Oh,' he thought, 'I have time, I have the whole evening before me.' On a sudden impulse of curiosity he got out of bed and wandered about the room, considering its changed aspect from various unfamiliar angles. For a few minutes he stood in the doorway, figuring to himself how it must appear when – he and Kubahskoi both in their beds – Dr. Vernet entered on one of his rounds.

His feet dragged about in a pile of paper wrappings, lengths of paper streamers and clippings of material. Suddenly irritated by the general disorder, he started to sweep the floor, using at first the edge of one of his slippers, then a carton and a newspaper. He closed the cupboard doors, aligned scrupulously the drawers of the commode, tidied the beds and the bedside tables, rearranged the bottles on the glass shelf above the wash-basin. Then he glanced through Kubahskoi's books, all of which were in languages which he did not understand.

As he climbed back into bed he reflected that it would be a pity not to take advantage of the rare silence by reading until the arrival of his supper tray. 'For even when I have finished eating,' he told himself, 'there will still be some hours before me in which to make my decision.'

It was symptomatic of the way in which he was tending to substitute unlimited procrastination for an objective assessment of his situation. Thus the fauna of a volcanic island which is being reclaimed by the ocean, repair to progressively higher levels, ignoring the fact that unless they can develop gills or wings, they must perish at the last.

By nine o'clock his meal had not arrived; he realised with indifference, even with a certain satisfaction, that, in the course of all the extra activity in the kitchens, he had been forgotten. He remembered that in the pocket of his greatcoat there was a packet of biscuits which he had purchased during the journey but which he had not opened. He fetched it, ate those in the top layer which were broken, and then resumed his reading.

Some time later he heard the sound of singing from the direction of the *salle à manger*; it swelled then fell completely away. There was no wind and through the window he could see the snow falling as lightly and silently as within a Victorian glass globe.

In this preternatural silence Paul found that his attention was being compelled hypnotically by the rhythm of the sentences he was reading, whilst he was not assimilating their meaning. Then the print seemed to project three-dimensionally from the page, and to slide across it. It was all a trick of his position and of the lighting; to break the spell he heaped up the pillows behind him and sat up with the book resting on his lap.

Then the noise made in turning over the pages disconcerted him, so he eased them up at the corner, raised them lightly and silently compressed their surface with his free hand. Another hour passed and there was still no sound to indicate that the dinner was over and that the diners were returning.

He took a handful of biscuits from the packet on the *table de nuit*, but the subsequent noise of crunching was so startling that he replaced the remainder by the side of his bed. His reading was once more becoming compulsive, and the silence of the sanatorium, earlier so welcome, began to oppress him. He felt suddenly that he wasn't alone in the room and twice looked up sharply in the direction of the door.

At last he closed his book, but lay for a long time without changing his position. The tendency of everything to slide… he clutched involuntarily at consciousness and shuddered with the jolt as the dissolving room reintegrated. 'It is true,' he thought, 'one does *fall* asleep. I was, literally, *falling*…'

A faint sound caused him to turn to the window. A face was pressed against the glass, eyes were watching him. His body grew rigid as the window started to swing apart.

Into the room, walking, tottering, came the slight figure of a young woman. She was dressed in a sleeveless nightdress, her matted hair was thinly veiled with snow, her bare feet were thickened with contusions. She knocked over a small table, staggered and nearly fell. Then, steadying herself by holding on to the wash-stand, she fixed Paul with her eyes and raised a warning finger to her lips.

Like the shackled protagonist of a nightmare, Paul watched as, supporting herself against the wall, she edged her way along it. As she approached, he threw aside the blankets. Then her knees sagged; falling forward, she collapsed across the end of his bed.

The sound of voices in the corridor. She started to shudder, tried desperately to speak, but when she opened her mouth, she could do no more than swallow and exhale great gulps of air. Then, with a gesture of impatience, she thrust her hand into the bosom of her nightdress and pulled out an envelope. The sound which she succeeded in forcing at last from her throat came in the form of an uncontrolled, inarticulate cry. Terror in her eyes, and a restraining hand clamped too late to her lips as she grasped the significance of her error. Silence. The clatter of approaching footsteps. Then the sound of rapid footsteps in the corridor; exchanging a glance of mutual horror with Paul, she flung him the envelope and backed unsteadily towards the window.

The door was thrown open and in ran the doctors Vernet and Bruneau, unbuttoned white coats flying, flapping over carnival costumes. The young woman crouched back against the wall; the doctors closed in on each side of her. She darted suddenly forward, falling to her knees as each grabbed a separate arm. Between them they dragged her to the door. '*Assassins! Assassins!*' she screamed, throwing herself backwards, her head barely clearing the floor, her hair sweeping it. As Dr. Vernet pulled open the door, her face banged against the handle. She screamed and started to struggle violently. Once in the passage she gave another scream but this time it was cut short. Silence.

Paul lay staring at the trail of wet footprints which led from the window, the only perceptible evidence remaining of his recent visitation. Already they were drying. Then suddenly he remembered the envelope. Where was it? With shaking hands he pulled aside the duvet, then the top blanket; it fell out of a fold on to the floor. The writing was indecipherable, the stamp torn and stained.

The door had swung shut; it reopened briskly to admit Dr. Vernet.

Now carrying his white coat over his arm, he was dressed as a rather stocky harlequin.

'A little accident, *Monsieur*,' he explained, smiling broadly. 'Normally I treat patients' visitors with more respect.' Then noticing the letter in Paul's hand, and saying, '*Ah, vous permettez*,' he plucked it away. '*Tiens!*' he commented, 'another letter to her husband – that would have caused unnecessary grief and misunderstanding. She is mad of course, tubercular meningitis, the last phase is approaching. And she thinks' – he laughed pleasantly – 'she thinks that we are trying to kill her. As if nature needed any assistance from us. But what is irritating is that she will try to write to her husband that we are murdering her, and she now suspects, moreover with complete justification, that we are intercepting her letters. Thus the reason for her visit to you – she was looking more for a postman than a lover. She must have clambered along the side of the balconies, really a remarkable achievement in her condition. She would have been moved from this floor with the other private patients when the students arrived, but I didn't insist, for I knew that she hasn't long. And of course normally she is not left alone, but Christmas Eve...' and he shrugged his shoulders.

Dr. Bruneau walked into the room. '*Maintenant tout va bien*,' he said to Dr. Vernet. In one hand he was carrying a hypodermic syringe with a long needle attached, in the other a false nose. He went straight over to a mirror, slipped off his white jacket and rearranged his costume. He was dressed as a Renaissance jester.

'Have you ever reflected on the recalcitrance of the human organism, *Monsieur* Davenant?' asked Dr. Vernet mildly as he watched his colleague adjusting his gartered hose. 'It seems often to be possessed of a will which delights in opposing itself to our own. And whilst in many instances it may be too stubborn to get well, it can at the same time be too stubborn to die. But I fear, nevertheless, that the night air will not have helped the condition of our patient; her temperature was 41° at six o'clock.' Then, looking at his watch: 'Nearly midnight, we must get back to our festivities. A pity you cannot be there, but in another year, perhaps...' He tapped Dr. Bruneau's shoulder with a wand and cried: '*Hop-là, Bouffon, tu viens?*' Dr. Bruneau leapt in the air in mock surprise.

A scream came from down the passage. '*Merde!*' cried Dr. Vernet, and both men raced from the room. Paul jumped from his bed. A second scream came from the direction of the balconies. Stopping only to throw his greatcoat about his shoulders, he ran out through the still-open windows. Leaning over the balcony rail he saw, four floors below, the body of his visitor, her night-dress about her waist, one arm stretched above her head, the other crumpled beneath her. Also leaning over the balcony of a room a little farther up were the doctors Vernet and Bruneau. A nursing sister was explaining hysterically what had happened: she had only turned an instant to refill her syringe with morphia, when her patient, who had appeared unconscious, had slipped out from her bed and rushed to the window. Dr. Vernet silenced her peremptorily and the three figures re-entered the room.

'*Taisez-vous, idiote, et ne me faites pas vos excuses banales,*' said Dr. Vernet and his voice was full of menace.

Paul looked down at the body; broken and disjointed, its stillness betokened no serenity.

It had stopped snowing and the night was now brilliant. The sky hung like a gold lace shawl above the infinite winter landscape; the vast Arve valley, seeming to radiate its own luminosity, shone with the quiet distinctness of an illuminated shop window in a midnight town. The village clocks began to chime and were joined an instant later by the bells of the churches. From a nearby Catholic church came the faint sound of the singing of midnight mass.

Down below, three figures emerged with torches from the entrance of *Les Alpes*; Paul distinguished Dr. Vernet and Dr. Bruneau, the latter still carrying his false nose in his hand. The third, a short, broad-shouldered man, was revealed by his staggering gait as Emile, the concierge. In a little posse they advanced towards the corpse, their steps hampered by the depth of the drifted snow. Dr. Vernet arrived first, seized for a moment the girl's wrist, then let it fall back to the ground. He muttered an order to Emile, and returned with Dr. Bruneau to the porch of the building. Emile bent down, grasped the corpse about its waist, and started to drag it across the snow, its heels marking two parallel lines. Then, in answer to an impatient cry from Dr. Vernet, he stopped, leant over and heaved it on to his shoulder. A false step, the snow reached up to his knees, and he nearly fell; swearing, he righted himself, then, trying to catch hold of a waving foot, the heel of which was banging against his back, he turned in a series of frustrated circles like a senile dog pursuing its tail. '*Dépêchez-vous*,' came angrily from the porch. Emile secured the ankle, and stumbled to where the two doctors were waiting for him.

Paul remained staring down at where the body had been lying; its outline could barely be distinguished, for the snow which marked it had been trampled flat. Then as the cold began to penetrate his great-coat, he turned away.

When, some hours later, Kubahskoi returned to his room, Paul was lying in bed with his eyes closed and the light extinguished. Kubahskoi, believing Paul to be sleeping, undressed quickly and quietly in the dark.

At last Paul did sleep, and it was to dream that he was wandering about *Les Alpes*, which had become as empty as an abandoned shell; the rooms and corridors were thick with weeds, and the walls were lined with creepers. He entered his own room, which was derelict; the unmade beds and furniture were covered with undergrowth and foliage. Under some compulsion he crossed to the wash-basin and turned on the light above the mirror. Reflected in the glass, staring back at him, was a skull.

He woke as the sun was colouring the summits of the mountains in shades of rose and crimson, and he discerned in his nostrils the acrid smell of his own mortality.

And as he started to cough and to expectorate, which he always did on first waking, he wondered in great wretchedness of spirit to what end the dreary formality of treatment was soon to be initiated, when his course was so clearly set for death.

The concept of death circumscribed all his thoughts. He remembered how once he had watched a group of young children playing in a tomb-strewn churchyard during a long afternoon in midsummer, running between the irregular headstones and over the grave-mounds as unaware of what lay beneath as mice frisking about the lids of coffins in the funeral parlour of an undertaker. Under the short summer dresses and the daisy chains, locked tightly within the confines of each skull was death, death which would feed and blossom on the tender soil of their flesh, absorbing first beauty, then health, then existence itself. And they would return to their playground at the last, but to lie beneath its surface, and other children would play above their heads, whilst even the last remnant of life, the little flesh still adhering to their bones, would be eaten away.

And it seemed to Paul that youth was bred by age simply so that, at the end, its eyes might be closed and the shame of its nakedness be hidden in the ground. And he reflected how the last descendants of man will lie unburied, and their flesh will be hacked by carrion from their bodies in full sight of a hostile sky; and those who have already managed to escape to the grave will rejoice in their obscurity.

Over the mountains the sun was rising, transforming all that it illuminated, metamorphosing the mute wastes of white into glazed expanses of red and gold. Before the monstrous light, shadows were dispelled, shrinking, turning in upon themselves, retreating down the sides of the great slopes, uncovering in their flight the surfaces of immense forests and glaciers, drifting, falling away like the wisps of dreams in the brain of a waking giant, as they dissolved in the onrush of the self-renewing sun.

And Paul, who asked for no more than the shadow, buried his head beneath his pillows to avoid the sight of the heartless illumination of the world. And he felt, like a blow upon his back, the utter indifference of nature for man, and the indifference was more bitter than hostility, for hostility is personal and related to its object.

His sickness was of life, and he knew within him that that sickness had preceded the sickness of his body, rendering propitious the terrain of his lungs for the hosts of tubercles which they now pastured. And drenching his mind with the force of a cloud-burst came the realisation that in rejecting life he had of necessity chosen death, and that from death, when it is self-willed, there is no escape.

Throughout the following day he appeared absorbed in thought, and he spoke to no one of the events of the previous evening. And when it was again night, and the students assembled in the passages to sing the carols of each nation, he lay with his head on his pillow and his eyes shut, oblivious of the sound they were making from without.

He was dominated by the idea that it would be better if he killed himself now, voluntarily, before the machine of hygiene swabbed him out of life with antiseptic and hypodermic. A violent death, proudly chosen, at least expressed the protest which the other in its muteness lacked; and as a swimmer rubs water on his back and shoulders to condition himself to full immersion, so Paul envisaged and rehearsed mentally that moment when, poised upon the rail of his balcony, he would precipitate himself into space. And he thought of how little pain would be involved in gaining so great a good, and he twisted with exasperation in his bed at the thought that he did not leap up that very instant to throw himself in the wake of his visitor of Christmas Eve.

CHAPTER SEVEN

•

One evening, soon after the beginning of the New Year, Paul was informed that the following morning he must eat no breakfast. It was the approach of another weekend; he had believed himself safe for still a few more days. 'At last,' he thought, 'at last it begins ...'

He did not sleep until after midnight, and the next morning felt so ill and weak and coughed for so long that he was convinced that his disease had undergone a new evolution, and begged Angus Gray to examine his chest. Angus complied in order to calm him, and announced that he could discern no change in his condition.

In the middle of the morning the telephone sounded in the passage, and *Sœur* Jeanne told Paul to put on his dressing-gown quickly and follow her to the *Service Médical*. Dr. Vernet was waiting for him, dressed in a white jacket which was so starched that it crackled when he moved. Through the half-open door of the *Dept. de Larynchologie*, Paul glimpsed *Sœur* Miriam, the head nurse, who was engaged in selecting instruments from a steriliser.

'*Monsieur*,' said Dr. Vernet, 'I have summoned you with the purpose of making a test. It will not be painful, but disagreeable. Upon its result will depend what we shall do to you.'

Another door opened and out came Dr. Bruneau and Dr. Florent. '*Bonjour*,' Paul murmured, but either they did not hear or else they considered his greeting to be inappropriate.

Dr. Vernet motioned him into the *Dept. de Larynchologie*. He entered; it was a small room, almost a cubicle. Three of the four walls were lined with glass-fronted shelves, all containing graded rows of instruments. *Sœur* Miriam had ranged a selection of them upon a chromium trolley.

It was this which held Paul's attention. What could be the special and combined function of these giant, blunt-ended, scissor-like instruments, these squat, opaque bottles, these basins and swabs? *Sœur* Miriam opened the lid of another steriliser, revealing a slender coil of rubber tubing submerged in liquid; she prodded it with a pair of pincers, and raised one end; it had all the air of a fair-booth atrocity, a long-defunct, serpentine abortion preserved in alcohol for the edification of amateur teratologists.

Dr. Vernet pointed to a stool at the side of the instrument trolley, and Paul seated himself. Dr. Bruneau and Dr. Florent closed with difficulty the door and stood wedged against it; Dr. Vernet adjusted a chromium reflector on his forehead; *Sœur* Miriam fastened a cloth about Paul's neck, then stood beside him holding a kidney-bowl.

Dr. Vernet sat down opposite Paul, and directed him to open his legs. In the space between Paul's thighs he inserted his own knees, at the same time drawing his chair closer. Dr. Bruneau touched a switch by the door which extinguished all the lights except one; this, shining on to Dr. Vernet's reflector, enabled him to re-direct its beam in whichever direction he turned his head.

A preliminary examination of Paul's larynx, facilitated by a thin wooden spatula, which, pressed on to the base of his tongue, precipitated retching and a flow of hot tears down his cheeks. '*Bien*,' said Dr. Vernet.

He selected an instrument, slim as a bridge pencil and nine inches long, affixed a piece of cotton-wool to its end, dipped it in a bottle of liquid anæsthetic, and, telling Paul to keep his mouth wide open, inserted it down his throat. It touched Paul's uvula, and he retched violently. Dr. Vernet waited impassively for the end of the attack, the cotton-wool recharged with anæsthetic, the instrument poised for the next insertion.

Paul swallowed the ill-tasting fluid which had trickled down his throat; instinct had dictated that he should exaggerate the subsequent coughing and spluttering in the childish hope that this might bring the whole operation to a premature conclusion. Implicit in Dr. Vernet's manner was recognition and acknowledgement of this manœuvre, coupled with the tacit assurance that it would not succeed.

As Paul opened his mouth again, it was seized and held in this position by Dr. Bruneau, whilst Dr. Florent, threading an arm between the shoulders of Dr. Vernet and *Sœur* Miriam, grasped the tip of Paul's tongue between two strips of cotton wool. The instrument was once more inserted with a similar result; vomiting and coughing, he wrenched his jaw free; *Sœur* Miriam placed the kidney-bowl under his mouth to catch the falling saliva.

A third, a fourth, a fifth insertion; in the intervals of spasms Dr. Vernet watched for a suitable opening, and when it came whipped the instrument in and out of Paul's throat with the speed of a chameleon's tongue. Paul gulped, retched, swallowed quantities of anæsthetic, which every few minutes he vomited back into the kidney bowl. Slowly his throat was losing all sensation; it felt as though its interior were metal-plated.

Then, in order that Dr. Florent might gain some practical experience, Dr. Vernet told him to continue in his stead. An exchange of seats. Dr. Vernet gazed laconically at his young assistant as the latter nervously affixed a reflector to his forehead. In his anxiety to cause Paul as little discomfort as possible, Dr. Florent inserted and withdrew the instrument before it had wholly performed its function. Dr. Vernet watched, advised and criticised; at last, losing his patience, he seized Paul's jaw, inspected his throat, and then flicked on the lights. The air was stifling. Dr. Florent's face had become as red as Paul's own.

A respite? Half-time? 'If only this were all, it would not have been too bad,' thought Paul. Then he noticed that *Sœur* Miriam was uncoiling from the interior of the steriliser the length of rubber tubing.

'Which is your better nostril, *Monsieur*?' demanded Dr. Vernet. Taking the tube from *Sœur* Miriam and holding it between a pair of forceps, he inserted one end up the nostril which Paul had indicated, thence propelling it down into his throat. '*Vous voyez, ça descend très bien,*' he remarked in an aside to his colleagues.

He continued until some two feet of its length had appeared; then he injected down the free end of the tube the contents of a large syringe. 'For several days, *Monsieur*, you will have the disagreeable experience of coughing up oil and iodine,' he commented.

There was a loud knocking at the door and a female voice cried: 'Dr. Vernet, you are wanted on the telephone.'

'I can't come. I'm very busy.'

'It's long-distance. They say it's very urgent. *Il faut qu'on vous parle.*'

With an exclamation of annoyance Dr. Vernet peeled the reflector from his forehead. Dr. Bruneau and Dr. Florent flattened themselves against the wall in order that their chief might pass through the door.

Taking a piece of adhesive tape, Dr. Florent secured the end of the tube which protruded from Paul's nose to his cheek. Dr. Bruneau and

Sœur Miriam started to discuss an American comedian whom they had seen in a film recently at Brisset. 'One must admit he's got something,' conceded Dr. Bruneau.

'Got something! He's an absolute scream!' insisted *Sœur* Miriam, bent double with laughter at the evocative power of the name.

Paul wanted to ask what was to happen next; he wished to make his voice sound casual, even jocular, to pronounce some such banality as: 'Well, what's the next item on the programme?' But owing to the carefully controlled breathing necessitated by the presence of the tube in his throat, his attempt at speech caused him to choke.

Dr. Bruneau tapped him impersonally on the back.

'We could fix him now,' he remarked. Then, bending close to Paul's ear, as though the latter were deaf as well as mute, and employing the wheedling tone with which one might address a temperamental and difficult child, he demanded: '*Monsieur*, would you like to give Dr. Vernet a nice surprise?'

Paul nodded his head.

'Well, come along, then.'

They led him from the *Dept. de Larynchologie* to the *Salle d'Interventions*, *Sœur* Miriam aided him up a little flight of stairs on to the operating table. As he stretched himself out on it, Dr. Vernet bustled into the room. 'I'm leaving for Paris in three-quarters of an hour,' he cried. Then to Paul: 'You understand, we must move quickly; in three-quarters of an hour I must go.' *Go now, go now,* thought Paul.

Dr. Florent and Dr. Bruneau leant forward at the same time and clamped Paul to the surface of the table; Dr. Vernet seized hold of a handle at its side and started to turn it. Paul suddenly found himself with his feet in the air and his head nearly touching the ground.

He felt he was falling, desperately contracted his muscles, gripped at the side of the table with his hands. Then the table swung level again. He raised his head in bewilderment. 'Lie still,' shouted Dr. Vernet. The table tipped once more and his head banged against the top; an instant later and it was level. Then up and down regularly, rhythmically. Paul closed his eyes, the juxtaposition of wall and ceiling was making him dizzy. The essential was to concentrate on breathing, to try to time each breath for when the table was either level or on end. He attempted to count the number of times that the table tipped, but became confused to the point of having no clear idea from one moment to another in which position he found himself.

'*Allez! Passons-le en scopie*.'

Paul was pulled from the table. He staggered, and was supported by Dr. Bruneau and Dr. Florent. They took him out of the *Salle d'Interventions* down the narrow corridor of the *Service Médical* and through the door marked '*Rayons*'. Dr. Vernet was already seated in front of the X-ray machine.

As soon as the image of the interior of Paul's chest was projected on to the screen, Dr. Vernet called out to Dr. Florent, who grasped the end of the tube protruding from Paul's nose and pulled at it. '*Cinq centimètres, Docteur*,' he cried. '*Encore deux*,' called back Dr. Vernet above the humming of the machine. Dr. Florent pulled again at the tube. '*Halte! C'est trop*.' The tube was stuffed back slightly.

A new piece of adhesive tape secured the end of the tube to his cheek, the contents of another syringe of oil and iodine were discharged down it. He was led back to the operating table, tipped several more times, and then returned to the *Salle de Scopie*. Dr. Bruneau now controlled the level of the tube, whilst Dr. Vernet watched intently its shadowy ascent or descent on the X-ray screen.

Back again on the table, Paul felt incapable of bracing himself against the incline as it tipped. Dr. Florent, who had insufficient hold on Paul's feet, lost it completely, and, his weight being too much for Dr. Bruneau, Paul would have crashed from the end of the table had not Dr. Vernet, with the grip of a stoker, seized the top of his tightly corded pyjama trousers. '*Idiot!*' he shouted at Florent, '*Espèce d'imbécile!*'

The position of the tube had again to be adjusted; Dr. Vernet gave impatient directions from the front of the X-ray screen. Every time the tube moved, Paul felt that he was choking; saliva trickled down the corners of his mouth and dropped on to his chest. Coming out of the X-ray cabinet he fell forwards and was caught by Dr. Bruneau, and had to be carried back into the *Salle d'Interventions*. Both assistant doctors and *Sœur* Miriam secured him face downwards to the table top as Dr. Vernet turned the rotary handle. As the table tipped he felt himself losing consciousness, his mouth fell open as his head reached the floor, and blood-flecked, frothy saliva mixed with oil and iodine gushed across his face to the ground.

Success. The screen of the X-ray machine now revealed that whatever might have been the purpose of the manipulation had at last been obtained. The three doctors gathered about it and conversed in whispers. X-ray plates of both the front and side of Paul's chest were taken, then lights were turned on and doors were opened.

Dr. Vernet pulled off his white jacket, threw it across a chair, and without a word to anyone hurried from the room. 'He looks as if he's in a hurry,' observed Dr. Bruneau with a laugh. Dr. Florent extracted the tube from Paul's nose and helped him to a *chaise longue*. He found that he still had to breathe through his mouth, and his heartbeats came so loudly that it was possible to count them without recourse to his pulse.

An hour later he was led back to his room, but it was evening before his breathing reverted to normal and he was able to answer any of the questions put to him by his compatriots. He paid no attention as the medical students in the party discussed and argued about the nature of the test which had just been carried out; he now felt as uninterested in the test itself as he believed himself indifferent as to its result.

CHAPTER EIGHT

•

Apathy, if complete, is not devoid of compensations. In the days which followed the test Paul neither worked nor read; for hours he lay without talking and without movement, always on the border of sleep, often crossing it. He had not sufficient interest even to speculate on the result of the test, still less to seek exact information about it from any of the visiting doctors. And if Dr. Vernet had come to tell him that it had been decided to saw him in half that very evening, he would have received the news with neither surprise nor consternation.

But when nothing happened, and no information of any sort was volunteered, and the length and dreariness of the days had driven him once more back to his books, the reversion to his earlier routine prompted a relapse into the state of malaise which had accompanied it.

To his dismay he found himself half listening for the ringing of the telephone in the passage; nor, when once it had rung, could he continue his reading until the sound of *Sœur* Jeanne's footsteps disappearing down the passage indicated that it represented no new summons to the *Service Médical.* If, after answering the telephone, *Sœur* Jeanne should direct her steps towards his room, his heart would beat more quickly and his apprehension mount until she had safely passed the door.

One morning *Sœur* Jeanne entered with the miniature X-ray prints which had been made at the conclusion of the test, and which she now placed in the folder of Paul's temperature chart. Paul continued with his reading, ostensibly taking not the slightest notice of what she was doing; but the moment she had left the room he seized his chart and extracted the prints. At a glance he recognised as his own the heavy skeletal outline, the solid osseous casing, the deep thorax with its wide inter-costal spaces. But the bronchi, rendered opaque by their content of iodine and oil, sprouted like gigantic tentacular growths. What fresh horror now lay revealed?

Cursing his lack of knowledge of anatomy, he scrutinised each detail of the little prints, seeking by the intensity of his examination to penetrate their mystery. At last, rationally accepting his inability to make any valid interpretation, he replaced the prints in the folder of his chart.

But a few minutes later they were again in his hands, and he was holding them up to the light, comparing them with the original X-ray taken on his entry to *Les Alpes*, seeking to explain to himself the implication of each secretive and subtle shadow. Oh why, he wondered with exasperation, had he not studied medicine? How could he have been so blind as to devote his time to a subject so utterly without application to his condition?

He took care not to show the prints to any of his friends, and if Kubahskoi happened to be present at a moment when he felt impelled to re-examine them, he concealed his activities behind the folds of his duvet.

But by the next day they already seemed more remote, and a few days after that it was as though they related to a much earlier condition, and he could look at them and say to himself: 'Heavens, I must have been in a poor state when these were taken.' Then familiarity effaced the last traces of novelty, and he left them undisturbed and unconsulted in the folder to which they had first been consigned.

Besides, there were other current distractions; at the moment everyone's attention was focused on what later became known as 'the first food incident'.

It had been discovered that two separate *cuisines* were served in the sanatorium, one for the private patients and the other for the students. This of itself would not have provoked complaint if the latter diet had been adequate and of reasonable quality. But despite the assurance of M. Halfont and Dr. Vernet it had not improved; indeed there were signs that it was deteriorating.

And now, just when criticism of the food had become general, there was served a supper consisting of a single debatable and grisly sausage, a few lettuce leaves which, tired some days previously, were now in the last stages of exhaustion, and – unprovoked libel on an undistinguished city – a helping of *pommes Lyonnaises* (beneath the fat-smeared surfaces of which it could be clearly seen that they were rotten.)

There was a murmur of indignation in the *salle à manger* as each student made this discovery and commented on it to his neighbour; then abruptly there was silence. To a burst of applause John Cotterell got to his feet and, taking hold of one of the platters of offending potatoes, marched with it across the dining-hall towards the exit. Instantly a representative of each of the other nationalities also seized a platter and joined up behind him in single file.

John Cotterell led the way down the corridor to M. Halfont's bureau, but, seeing through the glass panels that it was empty, he changed direction and made for the kitchens. There, one after the other, he and his party slammed down the dishes of potatoes before an angry and demonstrative chef.

Then a spontaneous meeting of all the students took place in one of the public rooms. Speeches were made in French, German and English, each speaker affirming that the time had now come for a corporate organisation and corporate action. A representative committee should be elected to make direct representations to Dr. Vernet or even, if necessary, to the headquarters of the I.S.O.

And, the moment being propitious, each national group selected a member to serve on this committee, after which the committee, voting among themselves, appointed a president and a vice-president. To this first office was elected Grominoff, a French student of Russian origin who had fought with the Resistance Movement and been imprisoned in a German concentration camp. The vice-presidency fell to John Cotterell.

Paul had his own food problems. For over ten years he had eaten neither fish nor meat. (Initially he had been unable to reconcile himself to the slaughterhouse. Later – when it had seemed to him that every principle was arbitrary – flesh-eating as such had become repugnant.)

In the army his diet had frequently been hopelessly deficient; it seemed that it would not be any better in a French sanatorium. Fresh vegetables were rarely served; a diffident request for a vegetarian diet had resulted in the substitution of a piece of cheese (always of the same indeterminate brand) for meat. For some weeks now he had received a twice-daily serving of cheese, potatoes and gravy.

But the nature of his diet was no more than an irritant. Far more significant and destructive was the trend of his mental processes. When he woke in the morning, racked by coughing and the restriction of his breathing, he would think: 'Let anything happen to change this.' But as his physical state grew easier as the day progressed, he became obsessed by the prospect of treatment and by the fear that he would reveal his fear in the face of pain. Then this mood would be succeeded by another: there would be periods of stoicism, periods of indifference, periods of contempt for himself, for the doctors and for the entire medical machine. Often, the cycle completed, he would fall into a feverish and hypnotic slumber, and when he once more became conscious, his first horrified reaction would again be: 'Let anything happen to change this.'

And still he based all his days on the hope of indefinite procrastination, measuring them out, anticipating the danger periods when it was most likely that he would be summoned to the *Service Médical*, counting the hours until the evening, when he esteemed himself to be safe. And when the evening arrived, he would wonder dismally why he had awaited it with such impatience, for – the sense of immediacy momentarily suspended – it allowed him to reinforce his natural apprehension over the following day with all the potentiality of his destructive imagination.

The weekends loomed before him like the shores of friendly islands. This period of respite had always the same prelude.

Each Saturday morning the three doctors made a tour of every room in the sanatorium. It had about it the precision of a military inspection. The floor sister would throw open the door and announce: '*Le Médecin Chef.*' Dr. Vernet would then march in, followed by Dr. Bruneau and Dr. Florent.

The temperature chart of each patient was laid in readiness at the bottom of his bed; Dr. Vernet would seize it, assess it, toss it back. A question, a few rapid and indistinguishable remarks between Dr. Vernet and Dr. Bruneau, and then, with a curt '*Bonjour, Monsieur*,' the *défilé* would march out, and its progress could be assessed by the sound of the opening and closing of doors as it continued rapidly from room to room along the passage.

It was just such a Saturday morning. The routine visit was safely over; Paul, congratulating himself at the prospect of another respite, was settling down to a book which all morning had lain unopened by his side. Then the telephone rang, he caught the phrase, '*Oui, tout de suite*,' and after that the sound of rapid footsteps coming down the passage. He glanced incredulously at his watch. Half-past twelve on Saturday morning! He felt the moral indignation with which a civilian, after the sounding of the 'All clear', hears the unmistakable drone of enemy engines approaching.

The footsteps stopped, his doors were thrown open, and in came *Sœur* Jeanne, crying: '*Service Médical, vite, vite!*'

She chided him for his slowness as he tried to pull on a pair of heavy socks, bustled him into his ancient and shabby dressing-gown, and preceded him from the room. Down the passage, dressing-gown billowing, cords dragging along the floor, as he tried to keep pace with her. Then frustration at the lift shaft. *Sœur* Jeanne pressed the button, rattled the outer handle, but the lift would not come; like a gilded pantomime coach wedged in the mechanism which should have raised it to the stage, it lay two floors below, golden light streaming tantalisingly from its fretted roof. '*Ascenseur! Ascenseur!*' cried *Sœur* Jeanne, shaking the lift-shaft door. There was the sound of gates being slammed; with a mechanical groan the garish box tumbled upwards, shuddered momentarily and menacingly at the floor where *Sœur* Jeanne and Paul were standing, then soared up to the roof. '*Nom de Dieu,* we walk,' cried *Sœur* Jeanne, motioning Paul to the staircase.

In the narrow passage of the *Service Médical* the three doctors were awaiting Paul's arrival. Dr. Vernet directed him through the door marked '*Rayons*', and ordered him to remove his dressing-gown and pyjama jacket. He then screened him, at the same time making comments in a low voice to his assistants, who were grouped about the X-ray cabinet. Then, turning off the controls and illuminating the dark-tinted bulb, he told Paul to climb out of the cabinet. In a very even tone of voice, he said: '*Monsieur*, I am going to try to create a pneumothorax. If this can be done there will be no more danger.'

Dr. Bruneau opened an inter-communicating door, and Paul passed into a small room furnished with a *chaise longue*, a table and a few wooden chairs. *Sœur* Miriam was standing in the corner, holding Paul's temperature chart; she did not look up as he entered.

'You will take off your dressing-gown and your pyjama jacket and you will extend yourself, *Monsieur* Davenant,' said Dr. Vernet. In his studied and precise English even the mistakes sounded authoritative.

Paul removed his dressing-gown and laid it over the back of a chair, then started to unbutton his pyjama jacket. Under this, as an added protection against the cold, he was wearing a thin vest; he pulled it over his head, feeling self-conscious about the tufts of hair beneath his armpits and on his chest. Then, untying the cord of his pyjama trousers, he readjusted it, pulled it tight and retied the knot. *Sœur* Miriam laid an elongated and narrow bolster across the top of the *chaise longue*.

'We are waiting, *Monsieur*,' said Dr. Bruneau.

Paul stepped out of his slippers, climbed on to the *chaise longue* and, reclining at full length, laid his head on the narrow bolster. Dr. Vernet smiled momentarily, and, pulling the bolster from under Paul's head, placed it under his shoulder-blades. Then he instructed him to turn over on his right side, and to raise his left hand in such a way as to bare the whole of his left side. Dr. Bruneau readjusted the bolster in order that Paul's ribs should be elevated into greater prominence, whilst Dr. Vernet extended a forefinger in the area of the fourth and fifth rib and began to feel for an inter-costal space.

Dr. Florent raised on to the table a curious apparatus fronted by two glass containers, graduated along the surface and each showing equal levels of liquid: a length of tubing protruded from each side: one terminated in a rubber bulb. At the same time *Sœur* Miriam offered Dr. Vernet a lidless metal box. Dr. Vernet's hand hovered above it as he scrutinised the contents – it was as though he were seeking to distinguish one brand of cigarette from another. Then, the choice made, his fingertips descended, he abstracted a very slim metal tube about four inches long, and by pulling at one end revealed it to be a miniature cannula-and-trochar – a hollow needle containing a removable solid needle.

Dr. Bruneau took a match-stick, about the end of which was a twist of cotton-wool, dipped it in iodine and coated an area three inches square just below Paul's armpit. Dr. Vernet smeared his own forefinger with iodine, and sought again the space which he had located a minute earlier.

Then he suspended the double needle above it. 'You will feel two distinct stabs. The first will be as the needle penetrates the surface of the skin, the second as it reaches your pleura.' He eased the needle through the epidermis and it sank rapidly, was momentarily obstructed by the surface of the pleura, then pierced it and sank deeper still. Paul lay rigid, not daring to breathe lest the needle penetrate his lung. Suddenly Dr. Vernet extracted the needle. Coating his finger with more iodine, he again felt for the spaces between Paul's ribs. 'Good, we try once more,' he said at last, re-plunging the needle into Paul at a spot slightly above the place where it had first entered. It sank swiftly; Paul gasped as it passed through his pleura. Then Dr. Vernet pulled out the trochar or inner needle, leaving the cannula embedded between his ribs. To the end of the cannula he affixed one of the rubber tubes from the apparatus at his side, and then took the rubber bulb attached to the other and started to squeeze. The levels of liquid in the glass containers trembled; air began to be pumped between Paul's chest wall and the surface of his damaged lung.

'Breathe!' commanded Dr. Vernet. Hesitantly Paul took a breath. 'Again, much more deeply.' Fearing that his lung must be punctured, he nevertheless complied. The levels of the liquids fluctuated.

'Good. Four hundred c.c. of air. Pressures: minus five; minus four,' called out Dr. Vernet. Repeating this information, *Sœur* Miriam wrote it in red on Paul's temperature chart. Then Dr. Vernet disconnected the rubber tube, replaced the trochar in the cannula and pulled the reassembled needle from between Paul's ribs. A small bead of blood formed over the mark of the puncture; *Sœur* Miriam dabbed it with an iodine-soaked swab.

With bent and contracted shoulders, Paul shuffled his way back into the X-ray cabinet. Dr. Vernet flicked on the controls. '*Pas mal*,' he cried in an agreeably surprised tone of voice. *Sœur* Jeanne helped Paul out of the cabinet and Dr. Bruneau and Dr. Florent stood to one side as Dr. Vernet strode out of the room. Then the two assistants followed, but Dr. Florent, who was, as usual, last, turned round before leaving and whispered encouragingly to Paul: '*La guérison commence*.'

Back in bed, Paul lay stunned with relief and a sense of anti-climax. Was it just for this that he had passed weeks in a state of dismayed anticipation? Liberated from the tyranny of his imagination, he grasped the extent to which he had been its dupe. 'Never again,' he said to himself, 'never again will I let it subjugate me in such a shameful way.'

The discomfort which he felt in his chest was very welcome; it reassured him that something had really happened. *Sœur* Jeanne came to see him every few minutes, Kubahskoi was infinitely solicitous and attentive. Within the next three hours each of the doctors had called on him. Towards the end of the afternoon, announcing 'Some visitors for you,' *Sœur* Jeanne admitted the whole of the British colony.

They were all smiling mysteriously, self-consciously. One after another each took hold of Paul's temperature chart and scrutinised it as though it were a concert programme.

'Four hundred cubic centimetres of air,' they commented in hushed voices. And David Bean, who was all astonished satisfaction, drew everyone's attention to what he termed the negative pressures. 'For,' said he, 'the existence of negative pressures shows clearly that there must be few, if any, adhesions, an almost unbelievable stroke of luck for anyone whose lung is in as bad a condition as Paul's.'

'David, it almost sounds as if you were on my side,' murmured Paul.

Encouraged by the general air of approbation, David Bean continued. He had not, he claimed, expected that the induction of a pneumothorax would prove possible, and he had thought that even if Dr. Vernet succeeded in finding a space into which some air could be introduced, the existence of multiple adhesions would restrict the induction to a minimal and inefficacious amount. But four hundred c.c.s, and with negative pressures! 'Which just goes to show…' commented William Davis.

At nine o'clock Paul took his temperature, and as he did not feel feverish, he was surprised to see that it had risen to 37.7°. An hour later Kubahskoi extinguished the light, but Paul lay on his side looking out through the window at the moonlit mountains; he felt too excited to sleep. Running ceaselessly through his brain was the phrase: '*La guérison commence.*'

'*La guérison commence…*' It was as though a veil had been lifted and he could see clearly for the first time. His carefully argued pessimism, his consistent attitude of negation, where were they now that recovery was imminent?

Projects, hopes and resolutions jostled in his brain. He became overwhelmingly aware of the value, the almost religious significance, of the illness which had brought him so low, but from which, phoenix-like, he would arise renewed. The world of prospective recovery was bathed in golden light; how could he, who had been so ill, and who in the depths had learned that life was precious, ever again be subject to accidie or despair? His affirmation had all the irrational conviction which hitherto had characterised his pessimism.

As the hours passed, and the clocks in the village sounded midnight, one, then two o'clock, and sleep receded before him like the horizon before a swimmer, his thoughts became progressively less coherent. He was not always certain of his location or circumstances, and could only substitute fresh fantasies of time and place for those which his intelligence managed to reject. Sometimes a sudden access of pain in his chest would restore him to momentary lucidity, and he would reflect with dismay on what his state must be the following day as a consequence of so troubled a night.

He fell into a heavy sleep just before the dawn and awoke covered with sweat on the arrival of the *garçon* with the breakfast tray. Instinctively he took his temperature; it registered a little less than on the previous evening. Kubahskoi advised him to try and eat some breakfast, but he felt disinclined to take more than the coffee. Then, getting out of bed, he stripped completely before the hand-basin and washed himself all over.

Sœur Jeanne came to inquire about his morning temperature, and she returned about half an hour later with Dr. Vernet, whose manner was formal and uncommunicative. From time to time one or other of the British students would come to ask how he was feeling; the taciturn William Davis confined himself to inserting his hand round the door, two fingers extended in an emphatic V-sign.

He read for most of the morning, sustained in his tiredness by the reflection that it should conduce later to a good night's sleep; and the next day he would feel completely well, for had not everyone assured him that the induction of a pneumothorax provoked no reaction?

In the afternoon his head began to ache and he stopped reading. He closed his eyes against the bright mountain light which streamed unchecked through the high, uncurtained windows, but his eyelids, like tinted filters, merely converted his vision into a uniform expanse of dazzling scarlet. Rolling up a handkerchief into a bandage, he placed it over his eyes, and lay motionless on his back for the remainder of the afternoon. By six o'clock his temperature had risen to 38°.

Throughout the day he had been sweating, but when he got up to wash, he found that he had difficulty in standing at the wash-basin. 'Heavens,' he thought, 'I shall be glad when it's tomorrow and I feel better.'

Sœur Jeanne gave him a sleeping pill for the night. The next morning he awoke feeling slightly drugged, but completely well. He placed his thermometer under his tongue and confidently awaited the result – without a doubt it would be normal. But it showed – he stared incredulously at the glass tube, sitting up with his back to the light to make sure – yes, it showed 38°. Then he smiled as he suddenly understood what had happened; he was looking at the temperature recorded the previous evening, he had obviously forgotten to shake down his thermometer after taking it. Now shaking it down with great care, he placed it for a second time under his tongue. Five minutes later the mercury had risen to 38°.

When he got out of bed to wash, he felt unsteady and very sick. His breakfast arrived and he left it untasted; his head started once more to ache; his body burned. An intensive resumption of his headache precluded the possibility of reading, at the same time his body felt too overheated and painful for him to lie very still. In the afternoon the light forced him to re-bandage his eyes, and Kubahskoi placed a basin of water at his side in order that he might soak a succession of handkerchiefs and apply them to his forehead in the form of cold compresses.

Each of the doctors visited him during the day; of each he demanded: 'Is this usual?' and 'How long will this last?' Each replied in a way characteristic of his temperament.

Said Dr. Vernet: 'Everything depends. Your temperature will surely come down…' Said Dr. Bruneau: 'If I could foresee the future I would select the winning ticket in the *Loterie Nationale*.' Said Dr. Florent: 'Everything is going very well. In no time at all you'll feel quite yourself again.'

His headache became less acute towards the evening, but his temperature reached 39°. John Cotterell and William Davis filled a basin with water and helped him to wash in bed. That night his sleeping pills had no effect; he coughed continually and violently; his body felt so tender that there was no position in which he could lie for more than a few minutes at a time. Kubahskoi's night was inevitably only a little less disturbed than his own.

The next morning the need for evacuation drove him to stagger from his bed to the lavatory which lay at the bottom of the corridor. But when he got there he found that it was in use; the shape of the seated occupant was plainly visible through the glazed glass panels in the door. In despair he seized the handle and rattled it; then with a slight moan he turned back down the passage.

Suddenly feeling that he could get no farther, he made for the wall and, supporting himself against it, stood with one hand clasped over his eyes. At that moment William Davis came into the passage and, seeing that Paul was on the point of falling, grasped his arm and guided him to his room. Back in bed, Paul closed his eyes; across the interior of his eyelids shapes and colours were gliding like sparks above a wood bonfire.

The door opened and in came John Cotterell; William Davis beckoned him into a corner of the room, and they whispered together. Then William Davis went out, and returned a few minutes later with the only wheelchair belonging to the sanatorium. John Cotterell and Kubahskoi helped Paul into it, and William Davis propelled him down the passage. *Sœur* Jeanne, engaged in sorting and rearranging the contents of her medical cupboard, gaped at him as he passed. The mind which is emancipated from all shame in respect of the body's sexual rôle, often remains inhibitedly sensitive in connection with its other functions. As other students walked up and down the passage, glancing at him with curiosity, Paul, despite his condition, stared at the ground and wished that William Davis had not stationed him so obviously outside the door of the lavatory.

When, a little later, William Davis wheeled Paul back to his room, John Cotterell and Kubahskoi had just finished making his bed. They helped him out of his dressing-gown; William Davis filled a bowl with hot water, and as Paul only fumbled with soap and flannel, the former took them both and washed him rapidly and efficiently.

Towards the middle of the morning Dr. Vernet called, in company with his assistants. Paul pulled away the rolled-up handkerchief from his eyes; his face was tense with pain.

'You feel no better?'

'I can't lie still. Wherever my body touches the mattress it feels as if it were on fire.'

'All fires extinguish themselves at the last.'

'But often only when everything's been burnt.'

Dr. Vernet shrugged his shoulders: 'Tomorrow I will screen you,' he said.

Paul's lunch came and was returned untouched; repellent even to a fit man, it was beyond the capacities of one who was sick. John Cotterell, who was in the room when it arrived, went to see Dr. Vernet to ask whether Paul could be given a special diet. Dr. Vernet agreed and told him to order from *Sœur* Jeanne anything he thought that Paul might eat. John Cotterell then went to find *Sœur* Jeanne and asked her to order a light and simple meal to be served to Paul that evening.

During the afternoon Paul's condition deteriorated; his eyes felt as if they had been scalded, his body as if it had been skinned. Forced by exhaustion to lie in the same position until he could bear it no longer, he would then twist himself from one side of the bed to the other. At six o'clock his temperature had reached 39.7°.

The supper tray arrived an hour later. John Cotterell, who intended to force Paul to take a little nourishment, was waiting for it. But when he lifted the lid of the *réchaud*, he saw that it contained a blackened meat-ball and greasy potatoes. Angrily he went to the kitchen, where he was told that, although a special order had been received, it could only be executed if signed by Dr. Vernet. John then went in search of Dr. Vernet, but it was late, and he was nowhere to be found.

A heavy dose of sodium amitol. Paul fell asleep, but woke again before midnight and coughed uninterruptedly until the dawn. In the morning his temperature stood at 39°; it was apparent that his physical reserves were at an end. William Davis gave him the most perfunctory of washes, Kubahskoi and John MacAllister arranged his bed without his leaving it.

John Cotterell obtained the menu sheet, duly signed by Dr. Vernet, and waited in Paul's room for the arrival of the lunch. It came; it was the same as that being served to the rest of the students. Trembling with rage, barely able to speak, John Cotterell went to find M. Halfont. M. Halfont was in his bureau; he inquired sympathetically about Paul's condition, he expressed deep regret about the menu: '*Vous voyez, Monsieur* Cotterell, one must always do everything oneself. This evening I engage myself to speak to the chef for *Monsieur* Davenant's *régime*.'

In the afternoon the students carried Paul bodily to the wheelchair, and William Davis pushed him to the *Service Médical*. Dr. Vernet gave him a quick screening and then directed that he should return immediately to his room. Back in bed he fell into a state of semi-coma.

Dr. Vernet came to visit him in the evening and confirmed by the gravity of his expression that the moment of crisis had been reached. Asked whether there was anything which might ease his condition, Paul said that if only a duvet could be placed between his body and the mattress it would give him relief. Dr. Vernet agreed, but when, afterwards, John Cotterell asked *Sœur* Jeanne to procure a duvet, she said that it was not possible – the sanatorium was full and every duvet was in use.

Paul's temperature now stood at 41° and he seemed to boil in the secretion of his pores. His evening meal arrived – the ingredients were unchanged. Without hesitation John Cotterell went to Dr. Vernet's private apartment. 'There is no error – this is deliberate,' he cried furiously. Dr. Vernet telephoned to the kitchens and to M. Halfont. There was no reply from either.

'Tomorrow,' said Dr. Vernet, laying a calming hand on John Cotterell's shoulder, 'tomorrow I shall send Dr. Florent to *Monsieur* Davenant; in future he will be personally responsible for the order.'

When John Cotterell returned to Paul's room, he found that the other students had assembled there. Paul was semi-delirious; he was talking as much to himself as to those about him. Frequently he renewed his request for a duvet. For a few minutes he would lie quite still, then in a sort of spasm he would arch his back, or raise his body on his hands in a desperate attempt to obtain relief from the pressure of the mattress. Repeatedly he renewed his request for a duvet.

John MacAllister had also tried to obtain a duvet. 'His condition is desperate,' he had insisted to *Sœur* Jeanne, but she had turned on him sharply: 'Now you make me angry with all this talk of duvets. You are as mad as he is if you think a duvet would do any good.'

John Cotterell remained in Paul's room after all the other students had left. He asked whether there was anyone with whom Paul wished to get into touch. Paul shook his head, his eyes tightly closed.

'I am sorry to provide such a spectacle,' Paul said.

'It will go.'

'It must. It must.'

'Could you drink an egg beaten up in milk?'

'No. No, thank you.'

'Or just milk alone?'

'No. John…'

'Yes?'

'I've got something to tell you.'

'What?'

'Promise you won't tell anyone.'

'I promise.'

'Are you sure no one's listening?'

'Of course no one's listening.'

'Well, it's this.' Paul raised himself slightly on his pillow. 'I've just learned in strict confidence that we're all curable.' He gave a sort of laugh. Then he retched and turned over on his side. John Cotterell watched him helplessly. He lay back gasping – his laughter had caused him to choke.

The door opened. In came John MacAllister. He was carrying a duvet from his own bed.

'Come on,' he said grimly. With John Cotterell's aid he inserted it under Paul's body.

Paul stretched himself. The feather-filled duvet moulded itself to the shape of his body; by allowing an equal distribution of his weight it relieved those parts of his limbs which, hitherto supporting him, had become most painful through contact with the mattress. Experimentally he turned on his side; the anticipated reflex of pain did not come. He closed his eyes, stretched himself again. By lying very still it was almost as if … it was almost as if one might… John MacAllister and John Cotterell left the room; Paul had fallen asleep.

The next morning *Sœur* Jeanne noticed that a duvet was missing from John MacAllister's bed. She admonished him angrily, and he – which was rare for him – lost his temper. Then the *gouvernante* of the sanatorium produced from somewhere an ancient duvet, which was substituted for the one on which Paul had passed his night.

Paul's temperature was lower than it had been for several days. Dr. Florent, who had come to take his order for lunch and dinner, could hardly believe it. '*Mais c'est épatant*,' he kept on repeating.

Although his body was much easier, his headache developed during the morning with no less intensity than on the previous day. At half-past twelve his luncheon tray arrived: the *réchaud* contained a sausage and some oily potatoes. John Cotterell led Dr. Florent to Paul's bedside.

'But I don't understand,' declared Dr. Florent.

'I think that I understand,' said John Cotterell. 'Anyhow I'm going to telephone the British Consul. Paul must be taken away.'

'But why?' demanded Dr. Florent, turning red.

'Because he's eaten nothing for a week and if he doesn't eat soon he will die.'

Dr. Florent pleaded with John Cotterell to take no action before the evening; he would speak to Dr. Vernet, he would speak to M. Halfont, he would speak to the chef. If necessary he would go into the kitchen, take off his jacket and cook the meal himself...

And that evening there was a change; the floor-waiter brought a tray on which was a jug of milk, a plate of noodles and a dish of apple *purée*.

Paul again slept for most of the night and the next day Dr. Vernet took advantage of his more rested condition to screen him and to make another injection of air between his lung and his chest wall. This provoked no reaction.

And with each succeeding day the improvement was maintained, and at last even the headaches – the most redoubtable of his symptoms – diminished. He remained very weak but in no discomfort. Dr. Florent called each morning to arrange his menu for the day; John Cotterell and William Davis continued to look after him with the devotion which each had shown from the outset of his fever.

CHAPTER NINE

•

Each day Paul continued to receive what M. Halfont proudly called '*Le Régime*'; it approached the standard, probably, of the diet served in the sick bay of a penal colony. Free interpretation of his requests led to the serving of almost identical meals: a plateful of unflavoured spaghetti or macaroni, *pomme purée* and a jug of watery milk. 'A man ill enough to require a *régime* is too ill to gourmandise,' explained the *chef de cuisine* when John Cotterell inquired why Paul never received the poached egg on toast which he regularly ordered. But M. Halfont, who never liked to miss an occasion for making an exhibition of '*bonne volonté*', would rush out of his bureau whenever he caught a glimpse of John Cotterell, and, beaming, demand: '*Monsieur* Davenant receives always his *régime*?' or '*Monsieur* Davenant retakes always his forces with the special *nourriture*?'

Nevertheless, Paul's temperature dropped consistently until, two weeks after the critical phase of his fever, it was little higher than during the period preceding the induction of his pneumothorax. Then suddenly it soared: headaches, pain, *crises de toux*: Paul was convinced that he was entering upon what would prove to be the final relapse. Three days later his temperature had again settled, and his symptoms had disappeared.

'Ah,' said Dr. Vernet, studying the new peak on his chart, 'it is classical, quite classical. You are a medical student, *Monsieur* Davenant? No. It is a pity. You see your temperature curve makes the outline of an inverted frog. First *you* think it goes down, but *I* know it goes up. Then *you* think it goes more up, but *I* know it goes down. Science, I think, is very interesting.'

One morning the telephone sounded in the passage; even when he was expecting no fresh summons to the *Service Médical*, Paul heard it with misgiving. Then footsteps growing ominously louder. The door opened and in came William Davis, propelling the wheelchair. 'Come on, get togged up,' he said abruptly. Behind William Davis was *Sœur* Jeanne, pushing and scolding: why was time being wasted? Paul was fit enough to walk – he would only need the chair to bring him back!

Dr. Vernet was waiting for Paul at the entrance of the *Service Médical*. 'You are now well enough for a new torture, one that I think you will not like at all,' he announced very affably. And ceremoniously he bowed the chair into the *Salle d'Interventions*.

Instinctively Paul scrutinised the preparations made for his reception. In the middle of the room was an operating table on which were ranged a series of hypodermic syringes. On the other side was a glass-topped table.

Dr. Vernet rolled up his sleeves and started to scrub his hands; Dr. Florent helped Paul off with his dressing-gown and pyjama jacket and then aided him on to the table. Dr. Bruneau filled a syringe with distilled water and aimed a thin jet at a passing fly. *Sœur* Miriam was engaged in examining and opening a number of small bottles of local anæsthetic.

Then Dr. Vernet selected a hypodermic, affixed to it a long needle, and seated himself at the side of Paul's chest. He smiled down at him, holding the syringe poised above him like a dart. 'Shall we use anæsthetic for *Monsieur* Davenant or, since he is a captain of the British Army, perhaps he would prefer it without?' he said playfully to Dr. Bruneau.

'*Qu'est que vous dites? Je comprends* "British Army".' replied Dr. Bruneau.

Dr. Vernet laughed delightedly. 'You see,' he said to Paul, 'he does not understand to perfection the language of Shakespeare.' It seemed that this common language provided a new bond between them.

'What are you going to do?' asked Paul.

Dr. Vernet, shaking with laughter, looked from face to face, the corners of his mouth reaching back to his ears.

'But he is insatiable. When he is not suffering, it is just so much time wasted.'

Sœur Miriam could contain herself no longer; her laugh swept out with the force of a cataract.

'Good,' said Dr. Vernet, speaking with the precision of one determined to control himself, whatever the cost. 'I am going to make a *ponction sternale*. It is very interesting. You are not a medical student? No, I remember. A pity – perhaps one day you will become one. How do you say "ponction sternale" in English? Sternal puncture, perhaps?

Is that right? It makes sense?' He turned to Dr. Bruneau. '*Voyons, mon cher Bruneau, l'anglais est très facile – tous les mots sont les mêmes qu'en français.*'

'*Ponction sternale*, sternal punction,' repeated Dr. Bruneau. 'Punction' *veut dire "ponction"; oui, c'est facile, ça.*'

'*Et maintenant, Florent, dites:* "Sternal puncture,"' ordered Dr. Vernet.

'Sternal puncture,' repeated Florent awkwardly.

'*Voilà! Nous sommes tous des polyglots! Maintenant travaillons!*'

Dr. Vernet pressed the tip of a finger about Paul's sternum, indicated by an intensification of the pressure that he had located a suitable position, then swabbed the whole region with iodine. He inserted the needle a little way below the surface of Paul's flesh, at the same time depressing the plunger of the anæsthetic syringe. A click; the needle had made contact with his rib. Dr. Florent leaned over to get a better view, at the same time laying a hand on top of the glass table.

'*Mais flute, alors!*' cried *Sœur* Miriam as she noticed Dr. Florent's hand; Dr. Florent, realising his error, withdrew it quickly, but not before it had been noted by his chief. 'Florent, *vous m'empoisonnez l'existence*,' said Dr. Vernet wearily. The table top had been rendered sterile, and was now sterile no longer. Dr. Florent rapidly set himself to rubbing its surface with ether.

'Now I shall endeavour to make a little hole in your rib,' announced Dr. Vernet. He inserted another and thicker needle into the track of the first. Then needle followed needle with great rapidity, boring and enlarging. Both assistant doctors and *Sœur* Miriam watched with an admiration which even communicated itself to Paul (whose fascinated gaze only left the region of the hole in order to glance quickly at the next instrument to be inserted into it). And the whole time Dr. Vernet sustained a commentary for the benefit of his assistants, with occasional asides to Paul. 'This will not hurt,' he would say, inserting another needle into the aperture, or dryly and with candour: '*Attention!* This will hurt.' He raised a lancet, and Paul objected: 'I won't have that in.' '*Ach, ach,*' replied Dr. Vernet. 'No, you can put it down. I won't have it.' 'You have always murders in England because your policemen don't carry revolvers,' said Dr. Vernet, plunging the lancet into the hole. With its progressive enlargement came the accompanying sound of the splintering of bone.

At last Dr. Vernet lowered a thick needle into the aperture, and it remained upright. To the free end he affixed a hypodermic syringe. 'Now I draw out your marrow blood. It will hurt.' As blood gushed up into the transparent cylinder Paul's chest twisted forward despite the fact that both assistant doctors had been securing his shoulders to the table.

Dr. Vernet then released all the blood from the syringe on to the newly-sterilised glass table, and Dr. Florent rubbed specimens of the blood on to slides. *Sœur* Miriam fastened a dressing over the wound. Paul made a movement to descend from the table.

'*Halte!* We have not finished,' cried Dr. Vernet.

'*Quoi maintenant*?' demanded Dr. Bruneau.

'Hospitality. I like *Monsieur* Davenant. I like his Oxford accent and his schoolroom French. He has been our victim – he will now be our guest. *Sœur* Miriam – the cognac.'

Sœur Miriam went over to the cupboard and brought out a bottle and three glasses; Dr. Vernet filled them generously. He handed one to *Sœur* Miriam, one to Paul, and took one himself. 'Once we had six glasses, but now three are broken and we are forced to live *à la bohème*,' he explained. 'Happily Florent does not drink, while Bruneau has evolved his own special and charming method.' And he handed the bottle to Dr. Bruneau.

And Dr. Bruneau, seeing that Paul was watching him, smiled slyly, smoothed back with one hand the copper quills which sweat had caused to adhere to his corpse-like forehead, and seizing the bottle made as if to raise it to his lips. 'Excuse. Not for gentlemens,' he said in English. Then with a dexterity which argued practice he lowered a hypodermic syringe into the bottle, raised the plunger with his thumb, and discharged a cylinder of cognac down his throat.

Back in his bed Paul wondered whether the rest of his life was going to comprise a succession of refills of air and *ponctions sternales*. The very sight of a needle now emasculated him. '*Ce n'est pas mal ici*,' said Dr. Vernet, pointing reassuringly at Paul's sternum during the course of a medical round a few days later. Paul made no reply, his expression a mixture of gloom and doubt.

Whenever he was depressed, he had the faculty, sooner or later, of relating his depression to life itself. He did not want to live, he had never wanted to live. Why, therefore, had he gone to such trouble, and endured such wretchedness in order to attain an end he so little desired?

Nevertheless the outcome of the treatment was becoming daily more apparent. He coughed less; the volcano at the apex of each cheek was extinct; his eyes no longer resembled the rear lights of Tube trains disappearing down tunnels.

The tedium of the days became oppressive, then their tenor was broken, in consequence of which they immediately attained the stature of a golden age. For to Paul's disgust he was again summoned to the *Service Médical* and another *ponction sternale* was performed. *Ah*, he thought, *if only I could be left in peace. I ask nothing more of life than that.*

He decided at the first opportunity to ask Dr. Vernet for a statement as to his condition. 'Ah no, *Monsieur*, you are too indulgent,' Dr. Vernet replied, arching his eyebrows, 'I know too well that you have no interest in the matter and that you are only asking out of courtesy and in order to encourage me.' He would have left the room if Paul had not detained him. Well, if M. Davenport really wanted the truth… Dr. Vernet hesitated, looked embarrassed. Paul appeared now to be '*hors de danger*'; his pneumothorax was working well; his analyses were almost negative. And if – the worst blow possible – the next analysis should prove to be completely negative, he would have to think in terms of leaving his mountain retreat during the next few months. He would then be free to wreck what would be his considerable expectation of life in whichever way his ingenuity might dictate.

'But my other lung?' inquired Paul.

'A little shop-soiled, but certainly serviceable,' replied Dr. Vernet.

With this reassurance, Paul started to impose a pattern on his days. He worked a few hours in the morning; in the afternoons he extended his limited knowledge of French. In the evening, wrapped in his battered dressing-gown and an additional blanket, he was allowed to lie on a bed in the room of one of his friends. And before long, as he got better and his right to a daily *régime* was revoked, he found himself sharing the general excitement and indignation of the rest of the student population.

The position was undeniably one of stalemate.

There had been regular committee meetings of what John Cotterell called 'the little Balkan States'. A direct representation had been made to Dr. Vernet; it had had no effect. At last, after considerable deliberation, the committee had addressed a letter to the headquarters of the I.S.O. In consequence a representative had been sent to *Les Alpes* to talk to the students and to investigate their complaints.

The representative had confirmed that the situation was unsatisfactory; he would make known his findings to the directors of the I.S.O., and he was confident that in a matter of days there would be a considerable improvement in the diet. Two weeks went by and there was none.

A weekly allowance of four hundred francs was made by the I.S.O. to each student. Such incidental expenses as haircuts, toilet requisites and writing paper accounted for a large part of this sum; the rest was of necessity devoted to supplementing the diet.

John Cotterell had inaugurated a milk round, buying milk in bulk from the local dairy and supplying it to any patient at a fifth of the price charged in the sanatorium. Then the Italians applied themselves to the preparation of simple meals; they purchased spaghetti and cooked it in saucepans normally reserved for the boiling-out of hypodermic syringes. The practice spread. Bedroom cupboards rapidly became repositories for crockery abstracted piece by piece from the trays of bed patients.

Supplies of food arrived by post; students whose families were in good circumstances received minor items of cooking equipment. Each group endeavoured to reproduce its national specialities. On Sunday afternoons the sanatorium did not provide tea. Angus Gray's foresight had been fully vindicated – he had brought with him a primus stove. Each Sunday the stove was set up on the marble-topped commode in Paul's room. Slices of black bread were purloined from the *salle à manger*, tins were opened, sandwiches, two inches thick and containing baked beans, sardines or pilchards in tomato sauce, were handed round, tea was brewed until it obtained the consistency of gelatine. Paul loved lying back on his pillow on these wintry afternoons, watching the jolly, surging, extrovert flames of the primus, illicit Sunday visitors, freebooters from the British main who openly mocked the alien austerity of their surroundings.

Fresh farm butter from England, salami from Italy, smoked hams from Poland: a judicious system of exchange was instituted and the arrival of the parcel post transformed the end of the corridor into a market square. Suddenly it was necessary to call a halt – excessive customs duties forced each student to request that the contents of the parcels he received be restricted to minimal essentials. The Poles took the greatest exception to the attentions of the *Douane*; their regular consignment of sausages was subject not merely to duty but frequently to exploratory incisions made in a zealous search for small contraband.

Gradually the students settled down to a routine which – treatment apart – resembled that of an international summer school. Rambles and excursions for those who could go out; lectures, gramophone concerts, language classes for those who could not. There was no shortage of organisers – in number they frequently exceeded the members of the audience. Private lessons in languages were often exchanged. Paul received help in his French studies from Kubahskoi and in return he gave his room-mate regular tuition in English.

'Look,' said Kubahskoi one day, and he passed Paul the old copy of *The Tatler* which he had been reading. Oxford during Eights Week. Photos of tea-parties on the river, groups at dances, self-conscious young men in dinner jackets eating cold collations. 'Explain, please,' demanded Kubahskoi – his appetite for details of Oxford life was omnivorous.

Paul glanced idly at the photos. Then suddenly he laughed. A face had caught his attention and he designated it with a thumb.

'You recognise someone?'

'Yes,' said Paul. He laughed again.

'Show me, please.'

Paul passed *The Tatler* back to Kubahskoi, indicating with his forefinger a young man seated with a number of others about a dinner table.

'What is his name?'

'Desmond Beale.'

'He has been drinking very well, I think.'

'Almost certainly.'

'You know him?'

'Better than anyone.'

'Tell me about him please.'

Paul lay back on his pillow and half-closed his eyes. The task was not simple. How best could he evoke for Kubahskoi one of the least likely representatives of post-war Oxford?

'Desmond Beale,' said Paul, laying back on his pillow. The days were long – one could take one's time.

'Desmond Beale,' repeated Kubahskoi thoughtfully; as was his habit he started to make notes in a little exercise book headed: 'English Conversations'.

'Desmond Beale *was*, I mean *is*, an ex-fighter pilot who returned to St. John's College after the war.' Then he stopped. Words were simply inadequate.

'Go on,' said Kubahskoi.

'It was like this…' said Paul.

Lacking the stimulus of danger, Desmond Beale, back in Oxford, sought other distractions. He drank immoderately and spent recklessly; in the midst of bottle parties, broken engagements and mounting debts, whole terms would pass without his opening a single textbook.

Impatience with life, with all that was ordered and pedestrian, drove him to embrace any supposition with a tenacity that was in proportion to its ridiculousness. The violence of his enthusiasm, the precipitate nature of his moods, the spontaneity of his reactions, combined to provide the necessary volition to translate it into action.

A passing conviction would obscure all faculty of judgment. In this way a theory formulated for the sake of paradox over morning coffee would by lunch-time have attained the status of an established truth. If Desmond Beale claimed idly that sleep was a matter of habit, a neurosis, that tiredness was no more than a sublimated form of hunger and could be countered by eating, then he would talk of nothing else until it had been put to the test. The filling of his room with provisions, the three days and nights of vigil, the subsequent eighteen hours, fully dressed, covered with crumbs, stretched out fast asleep on his armchair, all this followed as inevitable routine.

His lodgings varied with his fortunes. He had lived in a disused stable ('The Studio'), in a tent erected in a coal cellar, in a rowing-boat (covered at night with a tarpaulin) which, at the sight of his creditors, he would discreetly row into the middle of the Isis.

He had given a celebrated party on board a leaky barge (on which he happened to be living at the time). Periodically through the evening the deck had sunk level with the water; a warning cry and the guests had manned the pumps and baled out the hold. Reduced vigilance – the outcome of love-making and general intoxication – and at two o'clock in the morning the barge had slipped silently beneath the surface of the water.

Kubahskoi listened with amused incredulity – this was not at all the foreigner's conception of Oxford. Occasionally he interrupted Paul's narrative to pose questions both sociological and linguistic. It was often his practice on these occasions to write a *résumé* for Paul's correction.

Thus the days passed monotonously but tranquilly; there were no more *ponctions sternales*, the refills were spaced to weekly intervals. Paul gradually ceased to lie half-listening for the sound of the telephone. He was not yet allowed out on the balcony but he often stood at the window, looking across the great chain of mountains. Despite the approaching spring, all the high ground was as thickly covered with snow as on the day that he had arrived, but the valley showed green and the sunlight limned in dazzling reflection the winding course of the Arve.

CHAPTER TEN

•

A small incident which was to lead to one of greater significance occurred one evening when rissoles were served for dinner. When opened, they gave off so great a stench that not only was eating them out of the question, it was not even possible to keep them in the room until such time that the trays could be removed by a waiter. Quite spontaneously a dozen were collected, wrapped individually in tissue paper, and despatched to M. Halfont with a label bearing the legend 'Analyse, S.V.P.'

M. Halfont was aggrieved – the incident implied disrespect, the students were not *sérieux*. They must be dealt with. Accordingly an announcement was placed on the notice board summoning the representative committee of the students to M. Halfont's bureau, where he would address them upon the topic of food.

And when they were all assembled, M. Halfont, wearing an immaculate double-breasted blazer which swelled over his immense stomach like a maternity gown, swept into his bureau and, deliberately not asking anyone to be seated, pulled a chair away from his desk, sat down adroitly, crossed one sausage-like thigh upon the other, polished the finger-nails of one paw upon his sleeve, scrutinised them, then glanced up at the faces of the students. '*Eh bien, messieurs...*' he said very coldly.

It was an ill-chosen phrase and it evoked a multi-lingual response. M. Halfont got up from his chair with great dignity and raised a hand for silence. Then, referring to the incident of the rissoles, he commented that the affair was unworthy, that he was accustomed to dealing with '*des gens sérieux*', and that such behaviour reflected little credit upon the students as a whole. There had been a number of representations (he preferred to call them misrepresentations) to the authorities of the I.S.O. about the nature of the *cuisine*; all this was unwarranted and had to stop. There was nothing wrong with the food, and he and his family ate, and would think of eating, nothing else. But people who were ill were notoriously difficult to please, and it was universally acknowledged that of all invalids none was more exacting than the sufferer from tuberculosis. Now the time had come for the students, who presumably could be considered intelligent and reasonable people (a note of irony was discernible), to employ a little psychology in order to gain some measure of insight into their condition. Let them start with this premise: the food was good. And not only was it good, it was prepared by a first-class chef.

But here, let us face it, it could not be denied that a difficulty arose – the preparation of the food was in the French manner, and therefore might seem less palatable to certain individuals than if it had been cooked in the style of the country of their origin. But what could be done? The problem defied solution. If the cooking, for example, were in the Hungarian tradition, then all the Hungarians would be very satisfied, but everyone else would complain: there would be the same reaction if he adopted the English, French or Czechoslovakian *cuisines*.

At this juncture Grominoff, the President of the Students' Committee, interposed that complaints were concerned not with the preparation of the food in any national manner, but solely with its quality and quantity.

M. Halfont drew himself up proudly. '*Monsieur*,' said he, 'I am a man of honour, and for the quality of the food I myself will answer. You have my personal assurance that no better food exists anywhere. As for the quantity, well…' and he drew in his stomach sharply, 'we do not cater for *gourmands*. But it is sufficient and very healthy.'

To a complaint about the black bread which was served for breakfast, M. Halfont replied that it was specially ordered on account of its high vitamin content, such vitamins being essential to the preservation of health and protection against minor ailments. It might be less delicate than other breads which undoubtedly made greater appeal to effeminate palates, but one was not here to titillate one's gastronomical fancies, merely to get well. His family had grown accustomed to eating black bread for breakfast and would now refuse anything else.

The morning coffee was sweetened with saccharin? Next complaint, please, *that* issue was frivolous. No, it was regretted that it was essential that the coffee be sweetened before it reached the table – the provision of sugar-bowls containing lumps of sugar would involve far too much labour. 'What labour would it involve?' inquired John Cotterell. 'Why, having to count out the lumps,' replied Mr. Halfont.

'The question of butter,' said Grominoff, but M. Halfont interrupted him with a raised hand. Butter was one subject about which he was willing to hear no complaint. Two hundred grammes of the finest, freshest butter were served each week to every student. And where in the world, except perhaps in the fleshpots of America, in the fabulous establishments maintained by the leaders of commerce and the cinematograph industry, would one find anyone so privileged as to consume two hundred grammes of butter every week? Two hundred grammes!

M. Halfont looked about him in triumph; who would be so brazen as to claim that two hundred grammes of butter was insufficient? M. Cotterell had something to say? Well? So. M. Cotterell wished to suggest that the allocation of three *coquilles de beurre* for breakfast and another two for tea could not possibly weigh two hundred grammes over a week? Good. It was very simple. If M. Cotterell chose not to accept his word, let him save up his butter for a week and then weigh it.

'Is it not a fact that, despite all you say, the *cuisine* for the private patients is very much superior to our own?' demanded the representative of the Czechoslovak students.

'Yes,' replied M. Halfont candidly. 'Nevertheless your *cuisine* is comparable to that served in some of the best houses in France. It is what I could call "*la Haute Cuisine Bourgeoisie*".'

'And what would you call the *cuisine* of the private patients?'

'That,' said M. Halfont, rolling his eyes, 'is incontestably "la *Haute Cuisine Classique Française*".'

'Where we shall catch out the rascal is over the butter,' said John Cotterell, addressing the members of the committee when the meeting with M. Halfont had reached an end. He proposed that M. Halfont should be taken at his word and that one week's supply of butter should be weighed. To save time, it was agreed that the following morning thirty-five students should each bring one *coquille de beurre* to the room of President Grominoff; this would represent the issue of butter to one student for a week. It would be carefully weighed and subsequent action would depend on the result.

There was no difficulty in finding thirty-five volunteers. A balance was borrowed from the laboratory, and immediately after breakfast the next day Grominoff's room filled rapidly. When all the butter had been collected, it was weighed amidst complete silence. Grominoff waited until both sides of the balance were still, then, in his very precise voice, he announced: 'Exactly forty-five grammes.'

A great cry of mingled triumph and indignation. Then spontaneously, and without a clearly formulated intention, John Cotterell seized the balance and holding it above his head marched to the door, the donors of the butter falling into line behind him. The procession passed down the corridor, and, as news of the result of the weighing spread from room to room, doors opened all along the landings until, with the exception of those too ill to leave their beds, the whole of the student population was marching behind John Cotterell.

To the sound of a great clattering of boots the procession mounted the stone staircase which led to the corridor where M. Halfont's bureau was situated. Semi-moribund private patients peered timorously round half-open doors in order to see what was accounting for the uproar. Dr. Bruneau was sighted for a moment as with a white and ghastly grin he watched the proceedings from behind the lift-shaft; then he disappeared, apparently well-pleased to leave so purely an administrative matter in the hands of M. Halfont.

With rhythmic step the demonstrators marched down the corridor to M. Halfont's glass-panelled bureau, where two frightened clerks were just in the act of climbing through the window on to a narrow ornamental balcony. 'Where is *Monsieur* Halfont?' cried John Cotterell as he threw open the doors. 'We don't know,' said one and 'He's out' cried the other. As this information reached the students wedged outside the bureau, there arose a great cry of 'Hal-font, Hal-font,' and one section of the students detached itself from the main body and, marching up and down the passage, shouted with hypnotic insistency the two syllables of the name of the *directeur* of *Les Alpes*, whilst the remainder stamped their feet in unison to the cry of '*Beur-re, beur-re*'. The uproar increased in intensity, reaching the ears of private patients on other floors, who left their rooms and began to assemble at vantage points on the stairs from where they could discreetly survey the gratuitous spectacle. Emile the concierge, an expression of gravity ill-masking the satisfaction which he felt in contemplating a situation so pregnant with unpleasant possibilities for everyone but himself, was describing for the benefit of new arrivals the events which had led up to the demonstration.

Then Grominoff called for silence. He mounted a chair and began to address the students. As he was speaking, a face was observed to be peeping through one of the glass panels of the bureau. Undoubtedly attracted by the silence, M. Halfont had entered his office through a side door; too late he realised his error. Everyone cried aloud his discovery. John Cotterell, brandishing the scales, raced towards the bureau, a swarm of students behind him.

M. Halfont ran forward and tried to turn the key in the lock, but he was too late, and the door shot open and was all but pulled from its hinges as student after student forced his way into the bureau.

'*Canaille!*' hissed M. Halfont, backing behind the counter and towards the window. '*Beur-re, beur-re, deux cent grammes de beurre, beur-re,*' chanted the students. '*Disposez instantanément ou je vous foutrai dehors,*' cried M. Halfont, his cheeks becoming glaucous. A great laugh greeted this challenge, and the crush in the doorway grew more solid, more menacing.

M. Halfont had now his back to the window; he could retreat no farther. Pressure from the crowd without forced those at the front more deeply into the bureau. '*Vous faites encore un pas et je vous –* ' M. Halfont broke off; someone had seized one of the pats of butter and had hurled it at his face. A protest from Grominoff; a pause. '*Salauds!*' cried M. Halfont. Losing control, he aimed a blow at the student nearest to him. A dozen hands sought a *coquille de beurre* and the air became charged with yellow pellets. Direct hits on M. Halfont's forehead, nose and chin. Dramatically the window opened behind him and two pairs of arms pulled him out backwards on to the narrow balcony. The window was slammed down again; behind it, gasping and panting, with rolling eye and drooping jaw, M. Halfont looked like an expiring globe-fish in an aquarium.

A very powerful Czech shouted out for everyone to follow him and to pelt M. Halfont with snow from outside the building, but Grominoff called the demonstrators to order and warned them that they had already gone too far. 'Any more force will weaken our position,' he said, and there was assent from the more moderate elements. He ordered everyone to return quietly to his room for the cure, whilst a committee meeting would take place in the evening to decide on the best action for the future.

And at the meeting it was decided that an exhaustive report should be prepared about the food. As soon as the report was completed, it would be submitted to the authorities of the I.S.O., whilst copies would be circulated to Dr. Vernet and the management of *Les Alpes*.

The next morning all the students were summoned by Dr. Vernet to a meeting in the entrance hall. He spoke quietly but angrily. There were never again to be such demonstrations as had occurred the previous day, no matter what grievance, supposed or actual, the students might have. The sanatorium had been gravely disorganised, patients who were seriously ill had been inexcusably disturbed and harassed. M. Halfont had been insulted and ill-used – he would have been justified in summoning the police, for the action of the students was criminal.

If ever such an event should occur again, then not merely the ringleaders but all concerned in the demonstration would be expelled from the sanatorium, irrespective of their condition. The students might make what they considered legitimate representations in a lawful and orderly manner, but hooliganism was not looked upon with a favourable eye in France. 'And now,' said he, terminating his discourse, 'return to your rooms, and try in future to behave like worthy representatives of your individual countries.'

The speech had a sobering effect upon the students, and Grominoff in particular was bitter about the turn the demonstration had taken. He claimed that until then the behaviour of the students had been irreproachable, and that this one lapse had given the advantage to the authorities. But he also believed that the decision not to act against the instigators of the demonstration was prompted no less by prudence than by benevolence, and that the management of the sanatorium was not particularly eager to promote a course of action which might lead to an extensive inquiry. In accordance with this belief he decided to concentrate all his efforts on the composition of the food report, and he appointed a sub-committee of the medical students who would be responsible for it, and worked with them over each detail.

The students who were not directly concerned with the production of the food report had no very constructive outlet for their energy. Certainly a considerable number studied for a part of the day, and, besides this, looked after their sick nationals, shopped and catered for them. But they were high-spirited, and their enforced idleness often led to juvenile behaviour. They bombarded each other with snowballs in the streets, they ran and slid along the highly polished floors of the sanatorium corridors, they dressed up as doctors, as postmen, as *gendarmes*. A very fat student borrowed a nurse's uniform and, raising the skirt high above his plump thighs, paraded up and down the passages for the delectation of his fellows.

One day Paul jumped back, on leaving his room, to avoid being knocked over by a tea trolley harnessed to four Finnish students who were racing down the corridor. Precariously seated on a chair on top of the trolley, rocking from side to side, hallooing, cheering on his team and cracking an improvised whip above their heads, was John Cotterell.

Returning one day from the *Service Médical* after a refill of air, Paul found that his half of the room had been assembled at the end of the passage. His bed, carefully made and invitingly turned down, stood against the far window; next to it on the *table de nuit* were Paul's water-carafe and thermometer case; slippers at the bottom of the bed, temperature chart – covered with the traditional peaks of a hospital cartoon – laid across the pillow; and on a chair – more functional in appearance than any structure of Le Corbusier – had been placed a Gargantuan urine bottle. Laughter up and down the corridor; students poured from their rooms, pointing, gesturing, bent double. Dr. Florent, appearing on one of his rounds, was conducted to the foot of the bed, had the temperature chart put into his hands. Then a chair was fetched for Paul, and half a dozen students with hammers and spanners cheerfully set themselves to dismantling the frame of the bed whilst others carried back to the room the mattress and furniture.

The larger the group, the more precipitously the mental age of the students diminished. Now that Paul was better he was required to attend the communal consultations and communal refills. Some twenty students, pressed together and stripped to the waist, would assemble in the small X-ray room, which was sealed against external light and without ventilation. The air would rapidly become heavy with the stench of sweat and nudity. Despite the cramped space there were always two who mimed a boxing match, others who tickled the bare ribs of their neighbours. The noise was without precedent as the students shouted to each other in a dozen different languages.

They would grow quiet and a way would be cleared when Dr. Vernet entered, followed by his assistants and *Sœur* Miriam. Then the lights would be extinguished, and, forming up in file, they would pass, one after the other, through the cabinet of the X-ray machine. The skeletons projected on to the phosphorescent screen varied considerably in size; there was one student whose physical development was so retarded that the X-ray revealed what appeared as no more than the frame of a monkey.

At the instigation of Dr. Vernet the skeletons would turn first to one side, then to the other, then turn about. This curious *danse macabre* first fascinated, then oppressed. Paul at last would shut his eyes, endure the hateful and intimate contact of the flesh of those before and behind, allow himself to be propelled indifferently in the pushing, bustling queue. Those who had left the cabinet crowded behind Dr. Vernet's back, studying the images on the screen, attempting, for the later edification of their comrades, to overhear his whispered comments.

Dr. Vernet was not always in attendance at these mass screenings; sometimes there would only be Dr. Bruneau and Dr. Florent, and occasionally Dr. Florent by himself. Then the jokes, the *belles farces*, would commence. Amidst suppressed, anticipatory laughter a student would enter the X-ray machine with a fork or a pair of scissors or a watch suspended across his chest, and everyone would wait for the confused and horrified gasp that Dr. Florent invariably emitted the moment he distinguished the object apparently encased deep within a lobe of the student's lung.

Dr. Bruneau had had a bad day: Dr. Vernet was operating at Lausanne, Dr. Florent was in bed with a temperature. In the morning there had been a tedious series of aspirations preceded by a rapid and obligatory visit to the rooms of the *grands malades* and the *grands opérés*. During the afternoon and at irregular intervals there had been half a dozen new arrivals, each one posing frivolous questions; at five o'clock Dr. Bruneau had tried to lie down for an hour prior to starting on the consultations for Paul's landing, when an invalid who was setting out for the station (having just been discreetly discharged home as incurable) had had a violent hæmorrhage and died on the very threshold of the sanatorium.

Then the mass screening. Dr. Bruneau's eyes were red with staring at the fluorescent screen. His throat felt suspiciously dry. Was it the beginning of *la grippe*? Now the individual consultations, and again the same questions. 'When will I be well?' 'When can I think of starting work?' 'When will I be fit enough for my operation?' How could he or anyone else answer them?

What was there that was particularly offensive in Paul's manner as he came into the consulting-room? His step was lighter, his bearing more confident than usual. Implicit in his appearance was the consciousness of returning health. Dr. Bruneau looked at him sourly; twice while ausculting him he was forced to stop owing to an attack of coughing. Then, with eyes watering, he took hold of Paul's dossier.

'*Eh bien, Monsieur*, you have now a pneumothorax.'

Paul nodded his head.

'And you are pleased with yourself?' He silenced Paul's reply by quickly resuming: 'But why do I ask, when it is all too evident? And of course you have some questions?'

'Well, yes. I – '

'You want to know when you can return to England. Will I please give you a date so that you can book your ticket. Then when I have answered that question, you will ask me when you can again start work at the university.'

'As a matter of – '

'What a wonderful thing is science,' interrupted Dr. Bruneau. 'You came here a few weeks ago a dying man, and now, *grâce à un pneumothorax*, the clouds have rolled away, you contemplate returning to your work, perhaps for all I know you are secretly thinking of marriage, of becoming *père de famille*.'

'Is such a thing impossible?'

'*Ecoutez, mon cher Monsieur*. In this life nothing is impossible. Please sit down.'

He indicated a chair to Paul, at the same time sitting down at his desk. Then, leaning forward, he placed his elbows one foot apart on the inlaid leather surface of the desk, bent his hands at right angles to their wrists, brought the tips of his middle fingers together, and lowered his chin to the point where they met.

'*Monsieur*, you have a pneumothorax and you believe yourself to be cured. And yet…' and he turned a page in Paul's dossier, 'and yet what do I see here? If this entry is not incorrect, you are not even negative, that is to say that the *bacilles de Koch* are still present in your sputum. And why are you not negative? Experience has taught me that a patient becomes negative very shortly after the induction of a pneumothorax (assuming that there are no complications in the way of adhesions) unless of course his case becomes similar to that of your unfortunate room companion…'

'Dr. Vernet told me that he believed that I would be negative next month.'

'He did indeed – I was there when he said it. Nevertheless even if you should be negative next month it is not the end of the story. Your lung was very ill, is very ill, it can reserve a number of unpleasant surprises for you. Many patients far less ill than you have had pneumothoraxes which have led them quite a merry dance. And then there are cases where a pneumothorax works quite well but for one reason or another it has to be abandoned. It would be a little premature for you to believe yourself cured when in actual fact you are still navigating a dangerous channel.'

So it seemed there could still be unpleasant surprises…

'I didn't know…' said Paul.

Dr. Bruneau laughed. 'You didn't know. Well, the lacuna is now supplied.'

Both men looked at each other. The blue-grey light of an oblong, glass-fronted case affixed to the wall and used for the display of full-sized X-ray plates illuminated the side of Dr. Bruneau's face, discolouring it, modelling the curve of his nostrils and the contours of his jaw, which was so compounded of weakness and of strength. In the last hour he had ceaselessly run his fingers through his hair, twisting it, pulling it, erecting a series of irregular, rippled horns.

'What are you trying to tell me?' asked Paul in a low voice.

'Nothing.' Dr. Bruneau cleared his throat. With clarity and finality he repeated: 'Nothing.'

'It has all been useless?'

'Who knows? God perhaps – certainly neither Dr. Vernet nor myself.'

'The future?'

'It is always the past – recapitulated.'

'There are differences. We change.'

'Only externally.'

There was a long silence. '*Monsieur*,' said Dr. Bruneau at last, 'I too have had a pneumothorax – ten years ago. It was maintained four years; since it was abandoned I have had three – ' and he raised three white fingers – 'three pleurisies. After each I was forced to pass six months in bed. When I was first taken ill I was gaining a reputation as a surgeon. Look at me now. Since my last pleurisy three years ago I have not dared to leave the mountains, and here I am still an assistant doctor in *Les Alpes*, and never likely to be anything more.'

'I see,' said Paul.

'You think I enjoy my life?'

'No.'

'*Allez*. If I tell you these things it is because I was once like you. I also thought that because I had a pneumothorax, I was cured.' And, getting up from his desk, he signified that the consultation was at an end by replacing Paul's dossier in a large filing cabinet.

CHAPTER ELEVEN

•

During the days which succeeded the incident, M. Halfont maintained so injured and, withal, so dignified an aspect that he could not bring himself to acknowledge a salutation from a student other than by raising a little farther the already elevated arcs of his eyebrows. The ringleaders he ignored completely. His nude scalp shone with self-righteous polishing – possibly he had rubbed into it a little of the butter which had landed there a few days previously.

The food report at last reached completion. Besides a detailed analysis and abstract of the menus there was also an account of the various unsuccessful attempts made by the students' committee to obtain an improvement in the diet. It was submitted to Dr. Vernet, who agreed to forward it to the headquarters of the I.S.O.

The food continued bad, but, pending the outcome of the report, there was no further action to be taken; like a clock which has broken down with its spring fully wound, all activity was suspended but the tension remained. Routine assumed the double function of goad and halter, forcing and curbing movement. Everybody became suddenly conscious of, and oppressed by, the succession of little disciplines enforced, the diurnal sequence of *cures de silence, heures de repos, promenades gradées.* A feeling of mass irritation swept the students' corridors with the edgy persistency of a mistral.

The formality of medical rounds; the humiliating perspective from which the horizontal view the vertical. As the quarters on an antique clock are sometimes marked by the emergence of one grotesque, the hours by a little procession, so weekdays brought to each room a single doctor, Saturdays the three together.

It was this weekly synthesis or compound of medicals which was the most dispiriting.

'*Attention! Le Médecin Chef!*' the *sœur de l'étage* would shout, throwing open the doors of one bedroom after another. First Dr. Vernet would stride across the room with the jerky step of a marionette whose feet never quite touch the ground. Jerky but without speed, sickly, cynical, discouraged and detached, Dr. Bruneau would follow. Dr. Florent, wedged in a flurry of sisters, would rarely manage to cross the threshold.

Temperature charts were laid in readiness across the bottom of each bed. Whilst Dr. Vernet assessed keenly the implications of the interlaced graphs of temperature, weight and pulse, Dr. Bruneau would loll apathetically against the wall, stare out of the window, or, if a book or magazine lay to hand, would seize it so purposefully as to suggest that its perusal constituted the sole reason for his visit.

It was the weekday visits, however, which revealed that Dr. Bruneau's disinterest in temperature charts was merely feigned; left to himself, he was at his esoteric best. Seizing a temperature chart, he would fold back its flap, apply it at right angles to his cheek, and gaze, whistling and muttering, along the extended range of little peaks. Only those in his special confidence were informed that by this unique method he was able to obtain an invaluable *racourci* whereby he could distinguish subtle trends and arid tendencies of temperature unsuspected by his colleagues.

Dr. Florent, too young in the art of healing to embark upon such a display of virtuosity, would merely rise like a ballerina *sur les pointes*, more than content with such trends and tendencies of temperature as he was able to distinguish from his tentative standpoint between the double doors.

On one occasion a malicious patient, instead of marking his temperature in a series of little peaks below the red line (which was its true position, for his temperature was subfebrile) inscribed it in the same relative position above the red line, thus giving the impression of a nightly temperature of 38° or over 100° Fahrenheit. Each day the graph was either foreshortened by Dr. Bruneau or focused from afar by Dr. Florent; every Saturday it was scrutinised and assessed by Dr. Vernet; none remarked what had happened until the patient, tiring at last of so restricted and private a jest, dropped the temperature curve to within its actual limits.

It was a Saturday morning visit which brought two contrasting items of news to Paul and Kubahskoi. As Dr. Vernet had predicted, Paul's latest analysis proved to be negative. He was to be allowed up for his midday and evening meals; in a week he could take his first walk outside.

Kubahskoi was still smiling his pleasure and congratulations when Dr. Vernet turned towards him. A few days previously Kubahskoi had had a routine X-ray.

'You have the result, *docteur?*'

'*Oui, mon cher. Ce n'est pas très bien.*'

'*Pas très bien,*' repeated Kubahskoi. He was still smiling, but his features had become as rigid as those of a china Buddha. Dr. Vernet touched his shoulder sympathetically.

'The X-ray has revealed why, after five years with a pneumothorax, you still remain positive. It is because your second lung is infected.' He paused; medical tidings in tuberculosis, like ground glass, are often painful to digest. Then the monody became formalised: the implications of the newly discovered lesions; the dangers of procrastination; the necessity for a few more months of patience. Briefly, in a word, it was essential that a second pneumothorax should be induced.

And then the crystallised cherry tossed into the middle of the bitter citrus fruit: 'If the second pneumothorax can be effected without complications, there is no reason why you should not completely regain your health.'

It was the beginning of the era of the wonder drugs. For months the newspapers had been full of reports. Kubahskoi – clutching at a straw – asked whether instead of a pneumothorax he might be given a course of streptomycin. Dr. Vernet shook his head. '*Non, mon vieux,* for you it would do no good. You must have a second pneumothorax. I will create it in a few days.'

The day before the induction, Kubahskoi neither ate nor spoke to any of his friends. Throughout the whole of the afternoon he sat on the balcony, his chin resting on the rail and stared fixedly across the mountains until the sun had set and the forests were lost in shadow.

And there were no complications; Dr. Vernet described it as the perfect pneumothorax. An analysis was made a fortnight after the induction – the result was positive; two weeks later there was a second analysis and the initial result was confirmed. When Dr. Vernet was making his Saturday round, Kubahskoi pointed dejectedly to the two red crosses on his temperature chart. '*Mon vieux,*' said Dr. Vernet, 'it is, alas, well known that with a second pneumothorax one never becomes negative before a period of six months.'

* * *

When he compared his situation with Kubahskoi's, Paul became increasingly conscious of his own good fortune. But it was only when he was able to get up and make the acquaintance of other students who were in bed that he could assess the depth of the abyss from which he had escaped. And the symbol of his escape was now inscribed in red on his temperature chart: B.K. How easily – merely at the cost of several critical days – he had achieved it.

Now he met young men and women who had been ill for several years, who had undergone appalling operations, who had witnessed the passing of their youth from a bed in a hospital ward, and whose case-histories, biographies and autobiographies were summed up, concisely, synonymously, on any one of the multifarious leaves of their temperature chart by the sinister, the Damoclean, marking: B.K.+.

Some of these students had been imprisoned in concentration camps; the conditions in which they had lived had induced T.B. of the bone or of the lung, sometimes both. One form of imprisonment had been exchanged for another; where they had been confined to cells, they were now confined to beds, where they had lain in fetters, they now lay in plaster casts. And where they had previously existed in daily dread of summary death, it was now only the method, not the threat, which had altered.

Their families were sometimes displayed; more often they had long since been annihilated. The regions where once they had lived were now either uninhabitable (politically or racially) or absorbed into the zones of other powers. They had no past and no future, and the present had little to commend it.

An Alsatian giant, forced into the German Army, who – having lost both legs on the Russian Front – jerked up and down the corridors like a vertiginous robot, was waiting until he was sufficiently fit to undergo the removal of seven ribs in order that his lung might be collapsed. He said: 'I go on living in the same way that the middle-aged go on copulating – not because it's a pleasure, but because it's a habit.'

Paul knew himself well: he had neither the courage nor the stoicism of his fellow patients, and the thought of physical pain demoralised him. A line from Milton ran often through his mind: 'Square my trial to my proportion'd strength'. He could have borne no more than he had suffered, and his suffering, as each day he realised more fully, had been as nothing.

It was the first occasion that he had left the sanatorium since he had entered it five months previously. Wrapped in his old army greatcoat and wearing his stoutest shoes – for despite the fact that it was nearly April the roads were thick with snow – he walked down the slope which led from *Les Alpes* to the station, and recalled the freezing December evening of his arrival. At that time the weight of his greatcoat had left him breathless and he had even contemplated quietly abandoning it in the snow. Having reached the bottom of the slope, he started to mount a slight incline – the relative lightness of his step was the most tangible evidence of his recovery.

Crossing a small bridge over the railway he heard a train ascending the steep track. A curious, disconcerting, utterly distinctive sound – how was it that he had forgotten it? He stopped, closed his eyes, attempted to break down the concert of sounds into its component parts: the noise of the diesel, the groaning of the couplings between the coaches, the click of the ratchets biting into the slotted track. Then he resumed his walk. Perhaps when, in a few weeks, he left for England, he would again forget it, though, like certain stilled voices once familiar, its echo would persist in some recess of his brain, ever available – in appropriate circumstances – to establish instantaneous prodigies of recognition.

The sun was shining brilliantly. It glazed the surface of the great mounds of snow which lined the edge of the pavements, and through which, at intervals, gaps had been cut to provide access to the road. The traffic was composed mainly of horse-drawn sledges bearing provisions and merchandise; the few cars to be seen had chains wound about their wheels.

Brisset was divided into an upper and lower village, the two connected by a steep *escalier*, a quarter of a mile long. Descent by foot was arduous, ascent – for all but the very fit – impossible. The *escalier* could be avoided by use of the *crémaillère*, but its timetable precluded the making of a two-way journey during the periods between the *cures*. Most of the patients, therefore, confined themselves strictly to the village in the area of which their sanatorium was situated. For one patient to encounter another a few hundred yards above or below his particular territory would provoke astonished greetings, and the demand: '*Mais qu'est-ce que vous faites en ces pareges*?'

Paul was astounded at the way each turn in the road provided fresh vistas of sanatoria. They varied from large modern buildings to châlets on the wooden façades of which were painted: '*Sanatorium-Pension. Bons Soins. Tout Confort. Cuisine Soignée. Prix Très Modérées*'. They were everywhere, on all levels, clustered as tightly and haphazardly as booths at a fair-ground.

The narrow main street of the upper village had been constructed along a natural ridge in the mountain. One side was lined with low, modern shops, the other dropped away as sheerly as the edge of a precipice. Paul hurried across the road, anticipating an extended view; but there was only the outer belt of Brisset, its *faubourgs, environs, départements*, a density of sanatoria covering all that was visible of the lower slopes.

Farther down the street he came upon a series of step gardens, levelled with snow, their parterres showing like December graves in a paupers' cemetery. Low trees skirted the periphery of the gardens, their lopped-off branches forming the skulls of white carnival heads brought to a state of dripping decomposition by the sun's rays.

On a fine day it was here that many patients came for their *promenades*. They were of all ages, though the young predominated, and their dress and deportment suggested a variety of backgrounds. Brave youth of Brisset, bravely attired, *jeunesse aussi dorée que possible*! Young girls in ski-clothes, eyes a little too bright, cheeks a little too flushed, figures a little too slim... Young men, firm, vigorous, golden-skinned, the pears or peaches of a dishonest fruit vendor, resplendent without and rotten within.

Paul went into one of the crowded cafés and sat down alone at a table. The languages! What was being spoken all around him? His untrained, insensitive ear could not distinguish Hungarian from Czechoslovakian, Turkish from Arabic. But there were key words – keys not to the origins of the speaker, but to his condition. '*Pneumothorax*', '*pleuroscopie*', '*thoracoplastie*' – all rolled with equal facility about Oriental and Western tongues. It seemed that everyone was discussing his own condition or that of his neighbour! Paul pushed aside the cup of coffee which he had just ordered, paid an inflated price and left the restaurant.

Every Wednesday the billiard-room of the sanatorium was turned into a cinema. Admission: three hundred francs for private patients, who sat in armchairs; one hundred-francs for students, waiters and kitchen staff, who sat on benches.

Who and what were the private patients? They lived on their own floors, gave parties in their rooms, ate their meals at different times from the students, and in the evenings congregated in their own *Salon des Privés.* Occasionally they would be seen chatting in twos and threes at the foot of the main staircase, or in little groups advancing self-consciously but aloofly through noisy ranks of students to the *salle à manger.* Sometimes, hands in the pockets of their dressing-gowns, they wandered aimlessly up and down the corridors; sometimes they strolled into the music-room, where one would strum on a piano and another would tap a lethargic accompaniment on the drum. It was only at the cinema that they could be encountered in a body.

The films chosen for projection had generally been made some years previously and for the most part were American with French and German sub-titles. There being only one projector, there were a number of intervals of some minutes whilst the reels were changed. Owing to the maladroitness of the projectionist the reels would sometimes overrun, always with the same curious consequences. The picture and soundtrack, in the middle of a gesture, a word, would suddenly change to a crowd of half-naked studio Indians executing a war dance. Then the camera would focus on a small group of dancers, then on one, a girl. Waving a tomahawk and wearing only buckskin trousers which did not reach to her navel, she would shimmy, retreat and bend backwards over a great drum. Her breasts would grow taut, her pectoral muscles tensing, and then, as the audience stamped and cheered and the projectionist woke up, the mysterious and tantalising film would end in a shriek from the soundtrack, and the screen would reflect nothing more than the glare of the projector lamp.

Between reels, the screen illuminated, the hall in partial darkness, certain of the private patients would seek to distract themselves from the boredom. Leaning forward in their armchairs, they would pull the hair of friends seated in the front row, hit them on the head with screwed-up cellulose wrappings of the sweets they were sucking. The essence of their jests lay in anonymity; the hair pulled, the pellet thrown, and they would instantly regain their place and appear fixed in contemplation of the screen on which other, more creative members of the audience were throwing the images of bats and rabbits. Discovery, laughter, retaliation, more laughter, more projectiles, catharsis.

The quality of the sound was poor: in an American or English film an English-speaking member of the audience could often only interpret the dialogue by following the French or German subtitles. As the private patients were composed of even more disparate nationalities than the students, and as, more often than not, they were confined to one language, their own (which frequently corresponded neither with the language of the film nor its subtitles), they would talk throughout the film to their fellow nationals either endeavouring to interpret the action or, if it had ceased to hold their interest, discussing their state of health, their symptoms, their treatment, or the nature of the operations with which they were threatened.

It was in this way that Paul became acquainted with a new cult-cry: '*Liquide.*'

'What is "liquide"?' he whispered to Kubahskoi, whilst the reels were being changed. For answer, Kubahskoi took a bunch of miniature X-rays from his pocket, and, selecting one, passed it to him. One side of the chest was clear; on the other a level, opaque mass reached as high as the fifth rib. 'Pleural fluid,' he explained. It had been the consequence of a visit to Geneva, where he had passed a few hours in a night-club and had subsequently caught a cold. He had been fortunate. After a month of aspirations the fluid had stopped and it had been possible to maintain his pneumothorax. Usually fluid caused adhesions between the lung and the chest wall, and then there was nothing for it...

'Ribs out?'

'Ribs out!'

Immediate panic resolutions to avoid catching cold. Woollen waistcoats, extra underclothes from England, always a coat when out walking. During the rest of the film Paul could not prevent himself from experiencing in anticipation what was now surely inevitable. The slight indiscretion, the change in the weather, the chill, the next X-ray, Dr.

Vernet sympathetically patting him on the shoulder, the cracking sound as rib after rib was torn from his side…

At the end of the film he encountered M. Halfont in the passage. This gentleman greeted him affectionately, took his arm, and strolled with him towards the lift shaft.

'Ah, *Monsieur*,' said he, 'it gives us all great pride and pleasure that you have now so good a *mien* – at the time of your bad days we were very frightened for you. Each day I asked your news of Dr. Vernet. You have pulled yourself well out of it – the *liquide* can play you some dirty turns…'

'*Liquide*! I had *liquide*?'

'Oh yes – up to here!' And very gravely M. Halfont stubbed his thumb into Paul's chest. And whilst Paul stared at him in amazement M. Halfont took his hand, shook it loosely, then scuttled down the stairs flanking the lift shaft, his arms and legs working like those of a toy miller swarming down a pole.

And M. Halfont's information was quite correct. At the next consultation Dr. Vernet confirmed that one of the facets of Paul's critical state after the induction of the pneumothorax had been a serious pleural effusion. And the great danger had been the formation of adhesions which would have necessitated abandoning the pneumothorax. But by exceptional good luck the fluid had been absorbed, and had caused no complications.

'And so,' said Dr. Vernet, 'you are our triumph – a most successful case. We took a risk, *bien entendu*, but, as you will agree, it has been vindicated. There is a quotation, *Monsieur*, that you will recall for me from Hamlet – a play to which I was much addicted at the university. It was that bad diseases need big remedies.'

'Diseases desperate grown…' quoted Paul, and Dr. Vernet listened intently and bade him to repeat it three times. Then Dr. Bruneau walked into the bureau, and Paul was ordered to recite it once again, and very slowly, whilst Dr. Vernet translated it word by word for his colleague.

'You see Voltaire was quite wrong about Shakespeare,' cried Dr. Vernet. 'This phrase I will have engraved in stone above the door of *Les Alpes*, and inset into the walls of our operating theatres!'

'*Il y un proverbe français qui dit que le remède est souvent pire que le mal…*' replied Dr. Bruneau.

Dr. Vernet laughed. 'I will engrave that as well so that my patients can consider both sides of the question.' He turned to Paul. 'I am lucky to have a metaphysical assistant who secures me from the wild excesses of my natural optimism!' Then somewhat tartly to Dr. Bruneau: '*On peut aussi bien dire que souvent le mal est pire que le remède...*'

'*Ça dépend le mal, et ça dépend le remède...*'

'*Evidemment!*' Dr. Vernet's mood had changed. 'And whilst philosophers theorise on what depends on what, men of science are getting on with their work – which is what we shall do now. And remark well – when philosophers fall ill they come to doctors to get cured. But I have not yet found anyone whose state required him to have recourse to a philosopher.'

Dr. Bruneau bowed assent. Dr. Vernet resumed his official manner, and initialled Paul's temperature chart to signify that the consultation was over. 'You will see,' he said, 'that I have changed your *horaire*. You are now to go for walks in the morning as well as in the afternoon. After the evening *cure* you will stay up until ten o'clock.'

In the way that all advance contains elements of regression, that all celebration is not without a seasoning of regret, so Paul was both delighted and defeated by his new *horaire*. He had formed the habit of studying all morning; now it was required that he should get up and dress at eleven o'clock. And being basically undisciplined and only capable of real application when there was no alternative to it, his concentration wandered, he continually looked at his watch, and the now very attenuated morning managed both to drag unbearably and, for all practical purposes, to pass in a flash.

Then, sickened by his capacity for repining, no matter what his circumstances, he made a conscious rejection of the new conflict which was threatening to drain all satisfaction from the first part of the morning, all enjoyment from the second. 'After all,' he told himself, 'I might very well be dead.' What did it matter if he lost a few more weeks or months of study? The important, the primary, thing was to convalesce.

Usually he took his morning walks alone, exploring the roads and pathways about *Les Alpes*, sometimes looking in the bright shop windows, noting each item of their highly priced contents as admiringly and impersonally as a visitor gazing into showcases in a museum. One morning, encountering Angus Gray and David Bean out together, he joined them for some distance. Then, at a place where the road forked, Angus Gray left them, for he had some purchases to make in the village. Paul and David continued together.

'You know,' said David Bean, smiling, 'you have completely upset my calculations and theories.'

'How is that?' asked Paul.

'Well, it's like this. Probably you didn't know, but I spent a year in a sanatorium in England before coming out here. There was not much wrong with me, just a few infiltrations on one lung, but they were obstinate and took a long time to clear. Now, in the sanatorium there was a nursing sister who had been there for over twenty years, and she had developed an extraordinary faculty, known to the doctors but not to the patients. I learned of it because as a medical student I was allowed to take part in some of the ward rounds, and when they were over I heard her observations to the doctors. She had the gift of being able to predict with unbelievable accuracy the outcome of any case, irrespective of diagnosis or prognosis. What was even more astounding was that she would make her prediction without any foreknowledge of the patient's condition or his case history; in fact, her findings were based on no more than a casual glance at the patient during a ward round. Often her opinions would appear utterly without foundation, and in the early days the doctors would laugh when she pronounced a light case with an excellent prognosis as hopeless. But events invariably showed her to be right. In the same way, she might see a patient who was clinically in a very bad way, and if she said of him, 'He'll pull through,' then he did. At last the staff came to accept her powers as miraculous and left it at that.

'I was able to see her faculty at work. Whenever I questioned her about what it was she looked for, she told me that in fact she looked for nothing at all. All her judgements were based upon an immediate sensory impression, in which she allowed her reason to play no part, and she insisted that she possessed no faculty which another person could not easily develop.

'From then on I began to make independent judgements on new patients, after which I would compare my own findings with hers, and to my astonishment I found that, except in cases where I had let my reason interfere with my first intuitive impressions, they always corresponded. So gradually I learned to rely on my intuition, and at last I reached the point when she and I were in complete agreement about all the new cases that we saw.'

The two young men had now passed above the village and were branching off on a narrow mountain path which led circuitously back to *Les Alpes*. The sun had become obscured by clouds and an icy wind cut into their faces. Paul buttoned his khaki greatcoat up to his neck.

'What bearing has all this on me?' he asked.

'It must be fairly obvious, and since you have proved me wrong there is no reason why I should not tell you, though I would never have done this before. When I first saw you on Victoria Station, I had the immediate impression that you would never return to England – you and one other of our party. Then, when we arrived at *Les Alpes*, I received every corroboration from your X-ray plate – though I must emphasise that, even without this, my opinion would have been in no way affected. And now it seems that I am wrong.'

He became silent, and they continued along the path for several minutes without exchanging a word. An unexpected gap in the side of the mountain brought into view a great forest of deciduous trees, the peaks of which protruded grotesquely through a uniform covering of glazed and brittle snow. Clouds like breakers rolled up the valley, whilst below and slightly preceding them, a gigantic shadow flowed along its whole expanse: in no time the basin of the valley was completely obscured by a swirling sea of clouds, the extremities of which no sooner lapped the edges of the mountains than they swelled and started to rise.

'Who was the other you thought would not survive?'

'I obviously can't tell you. Besides, I've probably made another howler there. And anyway it's only because I've been proved so utterly wrong in your case that I'm mentioning the matter at all. A few days ago I saw your latest X-ray, and whilst of course the lung is still in a very bad state, there is no reason why one day it should not be completely healed.' He laughed self-deprecatingly. 'I won't deny I feel a bit piqued to see my theory tossed overboard, but I'm glad for you at any rate.'

'Thank you, That is generous!' said Paul. He reflected for a few minutes. Then he said: 'In a sense, I, too, made the same mistake. But if it's of any interest, I will tell you that my own powers of intuition led me astray.'

'Ah! In what way?'

'I also thought at the outset that my case was hopeless.'

'And you think that you were mistaken?'

Paul raised his eyebrows: 'I don't understand you.'

'I mean, wherein do you think your error lay?'

'It lay,' said Paul, and he spoke a little acidly, 'it lay in confounding my pessimism with what I took to be my powers of intuition. Premonitions which relate to oneself are probably symptoms of a sickly temperament; when they relate to others, it seems to me that they are more likely symptoms of something worse.'

'You explain your own error,' said David Bean, laughing, 'but I don't think that you throw any light on mine. But most probably you are right, and the whole process of intuition is invalid.'

The sea of clouds was rising rapidly, seeping into and filling crevices and fissures in the rock, expanding progressively its periphery whilst maintaining its density. The young men quickened their step as they saw the roofs of the sanatoria below them becoming obscured, then completely lost, in the swelling, mounting cloud. And as they were descending through a small wood on the slope which led to *Les Alpes*, the mist rippled about their ankles, rose almost instantaneously to their stomachs, then enveloped them completely. A sudden flash of lightning diffused a transient luminosity throughout the thickening folds of cloud; it was followed by a hollow, grotesquely echoing crash of thunder. A few drops of rain penetrated the foliage of the wood; then came the torrent.

Fortunately there was not far to go, and David Bean ran the rest of the way, but Paul, restricted by his limited breathing capacity, managed no more than slightly to increase his pace.

CHAPTER TWELVE

•

The students were dazed with indignation. A letter to the I.S.O., inquiring what progress had been made in respect of the food report had elicited the reply that no food report had been received. And when the matter was investigated, Dr. Vernet admitted good-humouredly that he had not submitted it. 'For,' declared he, smiling broadly, 'what good would the report have done? I have locked it away in my drawer – it is best there!'

The student committee assembled; the meeting was lively but inconclusive. In effect, what fresh action could be taken? Then, the same evening, the management of *Les Alpes* struck the next blow. For several days there had been rumours from the kitchens that fresh, sweeping economies were to be initiated; now, suddenly and drastically, they were implemented. The trays had been brought to the rooms of the bed patients (who ate one hour earlier than those who went down to the *salle à manger*). The meal consisted of the usual bowl of greasy, lukewarm soup; there were some tepid lengths of unflavoured macaroni; there was a portion of limp lettuce floating in salty water (the latter substance being intended, perhaps, as a dressing, a preservative or a token that the lettuce had been rinsed); the dessert was a bruised and turgid apple.

An impromptu meeting took place in the passages – doors opened up and down the corridors. A squat, bearded Italian student had brought his grisly tray with him; those who had not received trays crowded about the exhibits. Suddenly John Cotterell, whose genius it was to translate into action what everyone wished but no one dared, seized the tray and threw it over the lift shaft.

The whole complement of bowls, cutlery and quasi-comestibles described a leisurely trajectory, sank with an impressive hiss and detonated with finality. To M. Halfont, uneasily awaiting in his bureau any audible evidence of the reception of the new diet, it was a sign that actual violence had broken out. '*Mais est-ce qu'il y a de la solidarité dans la maison?*' he cried through the internal telephone system to a clerk discreetly stationed at an advance post overlooking the students' corridor.

Then, without waiting for the reply, he slammed the door, turned the key and lowered the steel shutters of his bureau.

But his fears were extravagant; the students had no intention of repeating their forceful but abortive demonstration of a few weeks earlier. Instead an immediate decision was taken to enter upon a token strike. At seven-thirty some seventy bowls of soup were exposed upon the long tables in the *salle à manger*. No one appeared.

M. Halfont, reassured by the silence and by favourable reports from his spies, had long since left the shelter of his bureau. And now, grasping the implications of the empty dining-hall, he went in search of Dr. Vernet. The latter was in an unhelpful mood. 'You see, you have gone too far, my good Halfont,' he commented. 'If your policy is simply to poison all my patients, then why do you administer the poison in such miserably inadequate doses? My advice is give them one good-sized meal and kill the lot!'

But the matter could not remain as it was. At M. Halfont's instigation Dr. Vernet telephoned to Dr. Hervet, and the latter's reactions were as energetic as M. Halfont could have wished. Within a quarter of an hour both he and his secretary were seated in Dr. Vernet's bureau.

Who was Dr. Hervet, and why should his reactions have been energetic? It is a question which probably could have been satisfactorily answered only by the doctor himself. For Dr. Hervet, although unquestionably Brisset's leading citizen, sought to maintain the anonymity of one of its humblest members.

In Dr. Hervet's house there were many mansions; he owned the five principal sanatoria in Brisset whilst maintaining a controlling interest in a number of others. But he paid rare visits to his establishments, preferring to direct their policies from his own headquarters. The tact with which he dispensed complete medical authority to his delegates, reserving his own talents for matters of administration, had led many who were associated with him to question whether his own doctorate had been awarded in medicine or in commerce.

What took place at the meeting in Dr. Vernet's bureau? It is another question which would have been best answered by Dr. Hervet. But the outcome of the meeting was probably implicit in the fact that next day, just before lunch, the students were summoned by Dr. Vernet to assemble in the *salle à manger*.

'There is a moment in every relationship when leniency and forbearance are mistaken for weakness,' commenced Dr. Vernet, and he went on to state emphatically that the next act of recalcitrance would dissipate this misconception for ever. If he was astonished that another demonstration should so soon follow upon that of a few weeks ago, he was a thousand times more astonished when he reflected on the flimsiness of its motives.

The meal the previous evening had been inadequate – that was obvious to anyone; but the fact that it was obvious presupposed no less obviously that there must have been a reason for it. But instead of waiting to find out the reasons, the students had jumped to conclusions, and passionate, reckless and wrong-headed conclusions they had been! The explanation was simple – supplies which had been ordered from the bottom of the mountain had not arrived. *Voilà tout!*

Another misunderstanding had arisen from the non-submission of the food report: was it possible that anyone was sufficiently crass as to assume that he had gratuitously suppressed it? The truth of the matter was that the whole question was at that very moment being debated at the highest levels; he himself had composed a detailed report which would have far greater authority than anything drawn up by the students.

As soon as the results of the conference were received, they would be communicated to the students. Till then he commended to everyone present the virtues of patience, good breeding and clear thinking.

Dr. Vernet spoke fluently and compellingly, but on this occasion did not appear completely at his ease. The end of his speech was the signal for the serving of lunch, and it proved to be a better meal than any which had preceded it. No one entertained any illusions; no one believed that such a standard would be maintained in the future; nevertheless the meal was really, solidly there, and could be, and was, attacked with gusto.

Paul could as easily have sunk his teeth into the living calf, or, for that matter, the palm of his own hand, as into a slice of animal flesh. The shifting quality of the meat, therefore, did not affect him. On this day, absorbed in thought about the future, and the implications of his returning health, he had paid little attention to what he had been eating. And at the conclusion of the meal he walked quickly out of the *salle à manger*, taking care to avoid the little groups of self-felicitating students which had formed in the corridors and on the staircases.

Opening the door of his bedroom, he remembered that he had intended not to return there, for Kubahskoi had caught a cold and was lying in bed. Then, seeing that Kubahskoi was asleep, he crossed the floor quietly and went out on to the balcony.

It was a fine day in late April: the snow had already retreated far up the mountains, the valley, fragrant and wanton, exposed its nudity to the skies. But the thaw had not reached Brisset and the white meadows and terraces awaited their liberation with the impatience of prisoners-of-war in a compound who can do nothing to modify their condition though they sense the approach of relieving armies. It seemed impossible that the snow could withstand the sun's intensity, that it was not liquidated, translated into a burning, detrital torrent which, tumbling on to the villages of the valley, would turn them into cauldrons; but underneath the snow, and in frozen counterpoint, the earth of Brisset lay as rigid as the surface of a mortician's slab.

Paul leant against the balcony rail, looking out across the great plains to the distant mountains; his secret hopes and desires without limit, his potentialities for implementing them non-existent.

Old appetites had been resurrected with his body; he fell to wondering whether beyond the mountains that encounter would take place which would give point and purpose to his life. But for his bitterness he would have laughed. Neurasthenic, consumptive, penniless, without birth or background, a half-century ago he would have lain in rags in the corner of an alley, coughing his lungs on to the cobblestones. What had he to offer? Patched up, cosseted, restored by a newly-benevolent society, he would soon be fit; fit, that is, to flatten his nose once more against the shop window of life. Perhaps somewhere a drab, a slattern, another human casualty, might drift his way, become attracted to him as independent bits of refuse attract each other on the same dirty patch of ocean…

He heard a sort of music, Looking down he saw making their way towards the front lawn of *Les Alpes* a most remarkable couple, a man playing an accordion, a woman playing a violin. The violin-player was short, agile, about fifty, her hair dyed the colour of copper, her body corseted into the firm outline of a cask. Her companion was older and taller, an ambulant skeleton whose bones were kept together by their covering of skin. On his head he wore a long, pointed cap edged with pendant bells; strapped to his back was a peeling and faded drum surmounted by a pair of cymbals and controlled by cords attached to each ankle. With each pace he took, first the drum then the cymbals made their mocking, psychotically irrelevant contribution to what he was playing.

The couple marched briskly across the snow-covered terrace of *Les Alpes*, stirring a mass of peripatetic *choukas* into a black, blaspheming cloud. Not a yard from where the body of the young woman had struck the ground on Christmas Eve, they came to a halt, suspended their music in the middle of a bar, stood to attention. Then – one, two, three: the woman raised her violin, the man his foot: a twinkling alternation of ribald side kicks and the couple launched into such an extraordinary and vivid burst of melody that heads protruded from balcony after balcony as patients sought visual explanation of the curious sounds.

'Bonne chance! Bonne chance tout le monde!' cried the man, twisting his head with a jingling of bells.

'Bonne chance!' chorused back from some of the balconies.

'Qu'il fait froid ici en-bas! Oh là là!' he cried, kicking vigorously with the foot which worked the cymbals.

A few twists of paper containing small coins fell into the snow.

'Bonne chance les malades!'

'Bonne chance les musiciens!' It was the easy, mutual greeting of the luckless.

Paul wrapped a coin in a piece of paper and threw it to the ground. The violin-player, occupied in the search for other paper screws, failed to notice it; a score of shouted directions came from the balconies.

'Nous avons froid!' cried the man raising his red face to a jangle of bells.

'Allez! Réchauffez-vous ailleurs!' someone shouted in reply.

'On ne rigole pas, c'est pas joli. Bonne chance les malades!'

No more money coming from the balconies, the accordionist brought into play his last remaining faculty. Throwing back his head he started to sing. His voice was light and agreeable; his songs were in French, Italian and German. Though he tempered he did not suppress his own accompaniment, and his complexion grew progressively more vivid.

'J'ai de bons poumons, moi!' he cried, suddenly terminating his recital.

'Ça va, ça va. Vous avez la veine!'

'Et vous alors! Bonne chance et bonne santé à tout le monde!'

'Bonne chance et bonne santé!'

'Bonne chance les malades!'

'Bonne chance les musiciens!'

The accordionist swept off his jangling hat, bowed, curvetted, touched his breast, his forehead, threw out his arms in acknowledgement towards his partner and then towards his audience. Another twist or two of paper. The accordionist replaced his hat. It started lightly to snow.

Turning slowly and playing the same air which had announced their arrival, the musicians started to move off across the terrace. On an impulse Paul threw another coin after them: neither musician noticed it and this time no directions were shouted, for, the recital at an end, the invalids had returned to their rooms. Paul stared after them, tried to call out but could not do so. He climbed up on to the rail of the balcony in order to catch a last glimpse, waving a desperate farewell to the musicians as they passed out of sight. His throat was sore, his eyes burning; because of the depth of emotion which it had provoked, he dared not analyse the strange nature of his reaction.

CHAPTER THIRTEEN

•

The next morning Paul woke in confusion – he had been dreaming that the musicians had returned, that they had greeted him, that they had encouraged him to join them. And in waking, still hearing the music, he had tried to re-wrap himself in his dream, absorbing its validity through the identical sensations in his eyes and throat that he had experienced on the balcony the previous day. Then a violent sneeze and he was awake, and his hand went automatically to his throat.

'Quite a beauty,' commented *Sœur* Jeanne, as she painted Paul's larynx with iodine. He sneezed several times during the day, wound himself tightly in his blankets and by the following morning was in the grip of a very severe chill.

It was really inevitable; for two days Kubahskoi's cold had been at its most infectious and the close contact brought about by sharing a room prevented its isolation. Paul was told that he must remain in bed. After three days the severity of the chill had diminished, whilst his temperature had remained consistently sub-febrile.

On the fifth morning he awoke with a fit of coughing, and as he took his *crachoir* and expectorated, a thin red stream spurted from his mouth. He gazed at the little fillets of blood which, whilst conserving the brightness of their colour, were turning the disinfectant at the base of the *crachoir* crimson. His temperature, which for a long time had been stabilised each morning at 36.2°, was standing at 37.1°.

'Red ink,' commented Dr. Bruneau sceptically on being shown the interior of the *crachoir*. But throughout the morning Paul continued to cough, each time consolidating the texture and intensifying the colour of his initially modest distillation.

The afternoon brought with it a recapitulation of the sort of headache which he had suffered after the induction of his pneumothorax, and in the same way his eyes grew preternaturally sensitive to the light and he was forced to bind them with a handkerchief. By the evening his temperature had reached 37.7°. Dr. Vernet screened him and was moodily reassuring: there was nothing abnormal to be seen, and the blood-spitting was no more than a temporary consequence of the cold.

Towards eight o'clock his headache had diminished and his temperature was little above normal. But when he got out of bed he staggered, and his whole body became lined with a thin sweat; perhaps by tomorrow he would feel still worse.

By the side of his bed there was a large, crude table covered with a cloth lent him by the *gouvernante*. Across one corner was a wooden trough containing some books which he had brought with him from England; in the centre was a portable wireless set – an indefinite loan to the students from the British Consul. There was a pile of newspapers and personal correspondence, a few postcard reproductions of paintings and drawings and a small plant which he had bought on the first occasion he had been allowed out of *Les Alpes*.

If three times each day he was going to receive his meal on a tray, then it was necessary that he should clear the table – up to the present he had balanced the tray on his knees, which was both tedious and a strain. And if by chance all was not well, if, in a word, his state were suddenly and rapidly to deteriorate, then it was essential that he should not be caught unprepared.

He packed up his books and stacked them at the bottom of a cupboard, he carried the wireless set next door to John Cotterell, he folded up the *gouvernante's* tablecloth and put it in a drawer. Some of his clothes were lying on a chair; as he hung them in the wardrobe he wondered what interval would elapse before he would take them out again.

The next morning his temperature had descended to 36.4°, a mere two divisions above normal. He looked long and uncomprehendingly at the level of the mercury, rendered stupid by relief. Then he reflected on and reconsidered each word that Dr. Vernet had said to him the previous day (in the way that invalids subject the lightest utterance of their physicians to intense analysis, often basing their future hopes and fears on certain wholly unintended *nuances* of expression). There had been nothing equivocal or ambiguous in Dr. Vernet's impartment.

On getting out of bed, he became aware of a deep ache centring about his left shoulder on the side of his pneumothorax. It was not painful and resembled an attack of cramp. During the day the ache changed its position. In the evening his temperature stood at 37.2°; Kubahskoi and the British students expressed amusement and relief – a temperature like that could be registered by anyone.

The next few days passed in this way: the ache which had started in Paul's shoulder descended across his back, changing its position with a regularity and thoroughness which suggested that its rôle was primarily exploratory. Morning and evening his temperature measured a bare two divisions above normal. But Paul became obsessed by the significance of his temperature, for it was the only touchstone of his condition. If he were really not ill, why didn't his temperature descend to its accustomed level? If he were ill, why didn't it mount considerably higher?

First thing on waking he would plunge the thermometer into his mouth, snatching it out five minutes later (timed scrupulously to the last cycle of the sweeping second hand of his watch), hoping to see that it was registering 36.2°, fearing that it might register 37°, perplexed and irritated to see that it registered 36.4°.

Nor was he able to wait the whole day, that is to say until six o'clock, before investigating his condition anew; towards mid-morning he would slide his thermometer under his tongue, usually finding that the result was satisfactory, even reassuring. After lunch it would be higher, but this was indication of nothing other than digestive activity. A truer temperature could be measured at three o'clock, and this time the mercury level would be in the region of 36.9°. Still no reason for alarm if only the mercury would climb no higher. Unable to read, without any form of occupation, Paul could think of nothing beyond his immediate condition and its implications: was he or was he not heading for a full-scale relapse? And if he were heading for a relapse, would its outcome be fatal?

The thermometer was his only guide; from three o'clock he would start taking it at intervals of a quarter of an hour, scrutinising each fractional fluctuation. For a period the mercury level would become established on the red line which designated 37°. Was it going to remain there? A quarter of an hour later it would be just a fraction below 37°, and quarter of an hour after that just a fraction above. By five o'clock it would be clearly 37.1°; at half-past five, swelling slightly beyond it.

Half-past five was quite a legitimate time for taking one's temperature. The question now was if 37.1° could be entered on one's chart. It was just too high, but if it remained at that level it would be an improvement on the previous day. At the very thought his spirits became more buoyant: 37.2° the previous night, 37.1° tonight and 37° tomorrow. And so the incident would be closed – closed, that is to say, except for an uneasy memory of the neurotic intensity of his reactions. Then by six o'clock the thermometer would register 37.2°, and a sudden fluctuation would bring it to 37.3°, at which he would take it no more and hesitate no longer, inscribing 37.2° upon his chart.

The fact that Paul was sharing a room prevented his taking his temperature openly: he could not have borne that Kubahskoi should be aware of the precise measure of his agitation. So he would turn on his side with his back towards Kubahskoi, pretending to be deep in a book, whereas in reality he was grasping the thin glass tube between his teeth, obscuring what might be seen of its outline with his hand. And when he had taken the reading, he would shake it down with short but vigorous jerks beneath his sheet.

He affected a complete indifference in the matter, and when, in the evening, John Cotterell or William Davis would come in and demand his temperature, he would contract his brow as though reflecting, and say at last: 'Oh, about the same as last night as far as I can remember.'

Each day there were a few flecks of blood at the bottom of his *crachoir*, and in a column of his temperature chart *Sœur* Jeanne would enter the small red cross traditionally used in a sanatorium to record that a patient is spitting blood.

Paul was also screened far more frequently than was customary. One day he was waiting in the corridor of the *Service Médical* when the door at the entrance was opened and he saw three nurses raising a wheelchair from the outside landing. The corridor of the *Service Médical* was greatly over-heated, the ache in Paul's back had allowed him very little sleep during the previous night, and he was feeling very much more ill than he cared to acknowledge. Now, waiting for Dr. Vernet, he was leaning against the wall, his eyelids falling together.

But the arrival of the wheelchair made him look up. Then he noticed that there was someone in it – what he had first taken to be a pile of clothing was a man almost completely enveloped in a dressing-gown, his chest lying parallel with his thighs. As the chair was pushed past him, Paul glimpsed the drooping face, set, white, and sharp as death.

The cortège passed into one of the rooms of the *Service Médical*. Who was this man? Paul, seeking to identify the features he had seen, considered them, twisting them in his mind, assembling, adding and subtracting, building and reducing, arranging, rearranging, disarranging, exchanging ears for eyes, eyes for lips, lips for a handful of teeth. He revolved the nose beneath the tips of his fingers until it span like a top, reshuffled the features like the particles of coloured paper in the base of a kaleidoscope, shook and twisted the whole until everything whirled like the wheels in a fruit machine. And as feature after feature clicked into place...

That night, as Paul lay in bed, after the light had been extinguished, he became subject to a most curious, semi-physical fantasy. He imagined himself to be in a small, open boat, without oars or rudder, on the belly of a turbulent but silent sea. He felt a preliminary lifting on the approach of a wave infinitely high, sped soundlessly to its frothy apex, hovered, then slid down into a sensual glue of waters. Another wave and he would be raised again, only holding on by inserting his hands, palms upwards, beneath the seat of the boat.

Then he discovered that by regulating the rhythm of his body he could control the size of the waves, and all at once he found himself at large on a black and choppy sea, his boat massaged and cradled within the watery hollows and caverns of its surface. Then with persistent and deliberate agitation he allowed his body to accentuate the natural movement of the boat: it dipped now too deeply into the water, now rose too precipitously from it. The hollows grew larger, and the boat, poised on each clear-cut brink, would race down, hover in the depths as it had hovered on the crests, shudder, groan and then remount. Walls of water re-formed; the boat conditioned its course to the nature of their contours, penetrating them with its prow and the next moment racing up their surface, bound and charted for the skies. Gripping the great seas, gripped by them, it was tossed with reciprocal violence and passion in the spasms which it generated.

Breathing deeply, clenching his teeth, Paul burst the web of his fantasy, turned on his side to ease the murderous ache in his back, and was sucked once more into a vacuum of sensation.

He was now negotiating a narrow ledge which skirted the roof of a skyscraper, maintaining a tenuous balance with his outstretched arms, frightening and exciting himself with stolen glances at the miniature thoroughfares beneath. At the extreme corner of the building he stopped, turned outwards and looked into the great chasm, his toes protruding over the ledge on which he was standing. He leaned forward slightly, then a little farther. As his body began to sway he straightened it whilst he could still do so, at the same time stretching himself in his bed, feeling a sudden tremor of pleasure as the pain-point in his back spread out as swiftly as the black shadow across a flat sheet of paper which has been thrown on a heap of burning coal.

Now he started to cross a tightrope slung from the ledge on which he had been standing to the roof of a neighbouring skyscraper, ecstatically sliding first one naked foot and then the other across its serrated, biting surface. Midway he stopped and looked down; he could wait no longer. Raising one leg waist high, he swung it backwards and forwards in an arc. Still he maintained his balance. Then suddenly he let the rope turn under his foot, and abandoned himself completely to the fall, every part of his body delirious in its own convulsion of weakness and pleasure.

His mouth sagged, saliva fell across his chin and down his neck, but he made no effort to bring his jaws together. He ran one hand caressingly across his back, and the sensation exacerbated still further his delight. He turned his head downwards, his mouth wide open and filled with saliva which gushed across his face and sank into the pillow. All but suffocated, he drifted into sleep.

CHAPTER FOURTEEN

•

He was awakened by the pounding of his heart. Lying very still, he counted the beats – 120 to the minute. He took his temperature; after two minutes it registered 39°. He started to cough; it provoked a small hæmorrhage which filled two-thirds of his *crachoir*.

Kubahskoi, his face covered with lather, his razor still in his hand, rushed out to call *Sœur* Jeanne. They returned just as the hæmorrhage reached its end. Paul smiled, showed her the *crachoir* and his blood-stained fingers. She hurried him to the *Service Médical*. As Dr. Vernet finished examining him, he coughed again; his handkerchief became saturated, and blood ran over his hand and down his sleeve.

The news having reached the British students, they crowded into his room, but were instantly expelled by *Sœur* Jeanne. Kubahskoi offered to prepare a cup of coffee; Paul, lying back on his pillows, shook his head – he did not dare to talk.

Emile entered with the post and put a letter at the end of his bed. Soiled and rumpled, covered with postmarks and amended addresses, it had passed from one Oxford lodging-house to another until, reaching his college, it had been re-directed to France. Kubahskoi slit open the envelope, and handed its contents to Paul.

A solicitor's heading; a letter, typewritten, brief, brisk, self-explicit. His uncle was dead. Paul was a beneficiary under his will to the extent of two-and-a-half-thousand pounds. His instructions for the disposal of the legacy were awaited.

Paul read the letter once, noted with disgust the red imprint of his finger-tips wherever he had touched it, allowed it to slip on to the floor. His uncle dead! A link which he had barely thought to have existed was now irreparably broken. For what reason had his uncle, for whom he had been a disappointment and an embarrassment, included him in his will? He had never felt so grateful, and now there was no one there to thank…

Sœur Jeanne hurried into the room, retrieved the letter and put it on the *table de nuit*. 'Now, listen…' she said. And speaking very distinctly and urgently she explained that during the night he had had a very bad pleural effusion which had caused adhesions to his lung. The adhesions had to be severed immediately. He must now get his clothes on.

With Kubahskoi's aid, Paul got out of bed, and *Sœur* Jeanne helped him to pull his battle-dress over his pyjamas. Seated close to the glass-fronted wardrobe, he caught a glimpse of his reflection. His face was yellow and unshaven. At one moment he must have brushed back his hair with his hand, for his right temple was stained with blood. He seemed to have no shoulders; his back looked as if it were humped. 'Two pips to three, you go first' – he recalled Mr. James's pleasantry as his gaze fell on the irrelevant insignia of his epaulettes.

'Come quickly, they are waiting for us.' *Sœur* Jeanne and Kubahskoi took each an arm, aiding Paul down the passage to the lift. In the sombre, oak-lined entrance hall Emile was standing behind his counter, deep in conversation with two nondescript invalids dressed in tight-belted raincoats and trilby hats. They turned round as Paul entered. They were Dr. Vernet and Dr. Bruneau.

Later, Paul was back in bed. In Dr. Vernet's small Renault he had been driven to a neighbouring sanatorium which was equipped with a far more elaborate operating theatre than that installed in *Les Alpes*. There, stripped to the waist, his arm held rigidly above him by a special apparatus, he had lain for two hours on the operating table. The adhesions had been cut, the wounds made by the insertion of the instruments had been closed by metal clips. He had been wheeled through a lounge filled with patients and their visitors to a room where he could be screened. Dr. Vernet and Dr. Bruneau had gone off in the Renault. *Sœur* Jeanne and Paul had followed in a taxi.

In the early evening Dr. Florent had come into his room and, removing the dressing from under Paul's arm, had inserted a long needle into the pleura; this was a routine injection of penicillin. Dr Vernet called a little later and had said: 'You will pass two disagreeable days. After that you will have to remain two months in bed. But the operation has achieved its purpose – that is what matters.'

And Paul was left with nothing more to do than to wait and to sleep.

It was sleeping that was the difficulty.

Normally Paul slept completely flat. Now, to prevent certain post-operative complications, he had to remain day and night in a sitting position; a permanent back-rest had been inserted behind his pillows. What started as a troublesome innovation rapidly became a torture.

All day, his eyes tightly closed against the light, he would stay propped up, balancing his chin first on one shoulder, then the other, sometimes in exhaustion letting his head fall forward on to his chest. At night the combination of his fever and the back-rest prevented him from sleeping; in the early morning, when his fever was at its lowest, he could not sleep for the coming and going of *sommeliers, infirmières* and *femmes des chambres.*

Even the presence of Kubahskoi became at last a burden. If Paul managed to doze for a few minutes, then the slightest movement would wake him. And although Kubahskoi showed every consideration, he could not remain motionless; nor could he prevent his friends and compatriots from visiting him, and their knocks upon the door sounded with the intensity of a *roulade.*

And at last nothing existed for Paul apart from the desire for sleep.

It was his desire for sleep which led him to send for M. Halfont. He explained that there had been a change in his circumstances and that he wished to leave the auspices of the I.S.O. and become a private patient. He showed M. Halfont the letter which he had received from his uncle's solicitors, and M. Halfont agreed – Paul being too weak – to write to them and to request an initial transfer of part of the legacy to France.

M. Halfont was also willing that Paul should become a private patient immediately. But there was one difficulty. *Les Alpes,* normally half empty, was, owing to the presence of the students, completely full; no single room was available. Paul protested that it was only with this object that he was making the change. M. Halfont walked up and down, his forehead contracted, his hands clasped behind his back. Suddenly he smiled: '*Monsieur* Davenant, it is not impossible that we shall have a room tonight.'

In the late afternoon *Sœur* Jeanne wheeled Paul to his new room. It was square and there was no balcony. The two windows, seen from the bed, hung like pictures; through one Paul could see a steep path climbing up to a little stuccoed church; through the other, a section of a pine forest. There was no sign of the snow. Even the presence of the mountains could be no more than inferred. And – ultimate luxury! – the windows were fitted with curtains. Paul thought of whole nights in which a supple blackness would extrude the sempiternal Alpine twilight; of matutinal slumbers untruncated by the searchlight brilliance of the dawn.

All very good! But there was no immediate respite from the knocks on the door. M. Halfont came to see if Paul was well installed, and to tell him that his personal effects would be moved up the following day. Dr. Vernet hurried into the room, looked at Paul blankly, and hurried out again. The *maître d'hôtel* came in with the day's menu, then the duty floor sister.

A brief interval. A *femme de chambre* entered, abstracted a dressing-gown from the wardrobe, and left without explanation. More knocks. Two porters in green baize aprons. They removed the drawers from the commode (which appeared to be full of clothes) and carried them out (the second porter hooking the door shut with his foot).

Then a full-veiled Sister of Mercy, selling tickets for a tombola ('*Chaque deuxième billet gagne, cher Monsieur!*'). 'One ought to fit a revolving door,' thought Paul, as the Sister of Mercy, going out, almost collided with a priest who was coming in. '*Ah, pardon, Monsieur, je me trompe*,' the priest cried, turning to go. Then, catching sight of an attaché case behind the door, he seized it, glanced at Paul in astonishment and confusion, and left.

Then *Sœur* Miriam, of the *Service Médical*, came to give Paul an intravenous injection. The needle was just piercing the vein when there was another knock at the door. A young girl entered, carrying a bunch of flowers. '*Monsieur* Mercier?' she inquired.

'No longer here,' said *Sœur* Miriam, adding by way of an afterthought: 'He's being buried tomorrow.' Then, turning to Paul and undamming her tinkling cataract of a laugh, she cried: '*Pauvre fille!* She was too late for *Monsieur* Mercier, and too soon for you!'

'*Mais voilà le vrai pessimiste*,' said Dr. Vernet, one hand on his hip, the other designating Paul. Dr. Bruneau, his mouth open, his lips curled back over his teeth, smiled from Paul to Dr. Vernet. '*C'est un monsieur qui pense toujours en noir,*' he said. '*Il attend toujours ses fleurs,*' added *Sœur* Miriam, laughing.

'*Alors, on va ponctionner tout de suite,*' said Dr. Vernet. And, followed by Dr. Bruneau, he walked out of the X-ray room.

Two minutes earlier, when Dr. Vernet had informed Paul that his chest was full of *liquide* and must be drained immediately, the latter had caught his breath, and said: 'But I know about fluid. It never stops.' Dr. Vernet had insisted that a thoroscopy led invariably to the formation of fluid which required to be drained off at once, perhaps twice, after which it returned no more.

So once again Paul found himself stripped to the waist and lying face upwards on an operating table. *Sœur* Miriam removed the dressing from under his arm, and Dr. Bruneau inspected the metal clips, which were still in place. 'I shall slide in underneath them,' muttered Dr. Vernet to himself.

As the anæsthetising needle penetrated Paul's side, it unnerved him. Then Dr. Vernet extracted it, and *Sœur* Miriam handed him a trochar-and-cannula, ten inches long. Paul tensed himself as Dr. Vernet plunged it adroitly between his ribs; it traversed the pleura and sank deeply.

Then Dr. Vernet withdrew the trochar, and fitted a syringe to the end of the cannula; on the plunger being raised, the syringe filled with blood. '*Tiens, tiens!*' he exclaimed. He emptied the blood into a container and refilled the syringe. Again it filled only with blood.

'Something's burst,' murmured Dr. Bruneau.

'That's my opinion,' replied Dr. Vernet.

He now attached a rubber tube to the needle, drew up sufficient blood to ensure a flow, placed the end in a large jar, and put the jar on the floor. Paul turned his head so that he could watch the rising red tide of his blood.

'He's as white as wax!' cried *Sœur* Miriam, suddenly grasping the lobe of Paul's ear between two fingers. 'True enough,' agreed Dr. Bruneau. '*Mais vous voyez, vous voyez,*' repeated *Sœur* Miriam, squeezing and releasing it, and squeezing again to show that no colour returned. '*Ça va, ça va,*' said Dr. Vernet impatiently.

When the jug had filled with blood, *Sœur* Miriam removed it and substituted another. At last the flow decreased to a trickle. Dr. Vernet disconnected the rubber tube and refitted the syringe to the mouth of the cannula. Blood flowed once more; Dr. Vernet moved the cannula up and down in search of the last drop. Paul gasped each time the end of the cannula stabbed into his chest wall. '*Ça gratte un peu*,' conceded Dr. Vernet, 'but now it is finished.' *Sœur* Miriam handed Dr. Vernet the trochar, which she had just sterilised over a spirit lamp, and Dr. Vernet replaced it in the cannula, and extracted the reassembled instrument from Paul's side.

'*Mille trois cents c.c. de sang. Vous vous rendez compte*,' declared *Sœur* Miriam grimly.

'*Il ferait du bon veau. Vous l'avez bien saigné*,' said Dr. Bruneau.

'What did he say?' demanded Paul.

'He said the best veal has the least blood. It is an old French proverb much favoured in the butchery trade. One says, "in the butchery trade", or "by the butchery trade"? English prepositions I find very difficult.' And Dr. Vernet went over to a wash-basin to rinse his hands, whilst *Sœur* Miriam summoned *Sœur* Yvette – the sister in charge of Paul's new floor – to wheel Paul back to his room.

Sœur Yvette was in her early forties, and spoke fluent English. She was intelligent and resourceful; a quarter of a century of experience had enabled her to assess, to adjust herself to, the temperament of whomever she might be nursing. She knew how to discharge her duties zealously but inconspicuously; how to enter and leave a room; how to aid rather than irritate a patient by her presence. And Paul now stood in need of all her qualities, for his condition was deteriorating daily.

No sooner was he back in bed after the *ponction* than the door opened to admit Dr. Vernet, followed by all the personnel of the *Service Médical*. *Sœur* Miriam was pushing, *Sœur* Yvette guiding, a trolley loaded with medical equipment; two porters were carrying a wooden *chaise longue*, which they laid down at the side of Paul's bed. A man Paul had never seen before was stripping off his jacket, and rolling up a sleeve.

'The next proverb, *Monsieur*, this time one much favoured by the French surgery trade,' said Dr. Vernet, folding his arms above his stomach, and bowing slightly, "The veal that bleeds least, lives longest!" *Très pittoresque, n'est-ce pas?* And now we have all come to transfuse you a little blood from a veal who has more than his fair share!'

The following day, Dr. Vernet performed a second *ponction.* With the greatest difficulty he managed to extract 800 c.c.s of a thick and bloody substance so evil-smelling that *Sœur* Miriam removed from the *Salle d'Interventions* each of the containers into which it was syphoned.

A third *ponction*, two days later, revealed the presence of a pus so viscid that it would not pass through even the thickest of cannulas. For two and a half hours, Dr. Bruneau – conducting the *ponction* in Dr. Vernet's temporary absence – pumped industriously, grinned down at Paul, rubbed the sweat from his forehead, swore in German, and twisted the resilient periphery of his coppery hair into a crown of thorns.

In an endeavour to dilute the pus, he introduced distilled water into the pleura, but succeeded in extracting no more than the same quantity, though rendered malodorous and horridly tinted. When at last he resolved to remove the assembled trochar-and-cannula Paul was in a state of coma, and the pus locked within his pleura had not been diminished by a fluid ounce.

Ponction succeeded *ponction;* transfusion succeeded transfusion. The increasing pressure within Paul's chest, caused by the continuous secretion of the pus, necessitated regular *exsufflations*, or extractions of air. In between-whiles, *Sœur* Miriam would come to make intravenous injections or to remove five c.c.s of blood from an artery in order to measure the rate of its sedimentation. The *laborantine*, smelling of ether, would set up her complement of glass-stoppered bottles, phials and rubber tubes on the *table de nuit*, and then prick the swollen ball of one finger after another, in search of sufficient blood to make a count. A dozen intra-muscular injections each day, and his buttocks and thighs became so painful that he felt that he was lying on a heap of embers.

The combination of great fever with the general toxicity of his condition induced an unquenchable thirst. *Sœur* Yvette, murmuring her misgivings in respect of the consequences to his kidneys, acceded nevertheless to his endless requests for the recharging of his water-carafe. Before going off duty in the evening, she would place half a dozen bottles of *eau minérale* on the *table de nuit*, and three urine bottles on a chair by the side of his bed.

Turning convulsively from side to side, writhing, drinking his mineral water, urinating – in this way Paul passed his nights. No sedative that he was given served to ease his condition or to facilitate sleep.

Day and night represented no more than segments in the overall cycle of his fever. Though his lucidity remained unimpaired, his existence was purely physical; an agglomeration of aching, burning flesh, he felt himself to be no more than the sum of its functions and sensations.

Taking practically no nourishment, he soon became incapable of evacuation. Periodically *Sœur* Yvette would set him upon a chamber pot, aiding him to retain his position by supporting his shoulders. But her presence inhibited him. One morning, following the administration of an enema, he begged to be left alone. Such was his weakness, however, that after defecation he fell backwards on to his bed, the contents of the pot soiling his sheets and contaminating his flesh. *Sœur* Yvette came to his assistance, but found him mute and paralysed with horror. Lying quite still, he made no effort to withdraw his limbs from their abominable contact.

He felt that there was nothing more; that life, engaged in his progressive humiliation, had overborne itself; that by this new blow its scope was not enlarged, but terminated, for his spirit was now dead and he could be tormented no further.

Sœur Yvette called for the assistance of another nurse, and with her help Paul was transferred to the *chaise longue*. He lay without movement where he was put, his genitals exposed, his head inclining backwards over a bolster. When *Sœur* Yvette had finished changing his bed, she bathed his limbs, but Paul remained limp, beyond protestation or co-operation.

CHAPTER FIFTEEN

•

The condition of man imposes its own limitations: to an estimate of his significance and of the implications of his existence he can bring no more than the fallible and subjective processes of his capacity for conjecture. Isolated, wedged transiently at a point in infinity, careless of what has preceded his life, preoccupied and obsessed by the thoughts of what may succeed it, shackled and blinded by the problems and prejudices arising from it, his readiness to dogmatise will be proportionate to the intensity of his fears and the deficiency of his imagination.

Whether he chooses to accept or reject some traditional form of belief, modern man is capable of contemplating with some objectivity the chaos of the beliefs and practices of primitive races, and he can rival the ruthlessness and cruelty of their most fanatical members in claiming the prerogative of truth for the religious system to which he subscribes, and which, by its nature excludes all others.

An appetite for faith may be to some extent its justification: it is certainly not its proof – we do not build a fire to prove or disprove the existence of cold, but to keep ourselves warm. A traveller on a perilous journey may draw comfort from the knowledge that he has a pistol in his pocket, though, unknown to himself, his servant has neglected to load it. Like the traveller, we shall only learn whether or not our pistols were loaded when the issue will have transcended speculation; till then we must draw our comfort from whatever we care to believe or disbelieve. Truth, if it exists, will remain unaffected. A starving animal will suck the dug of its dead parent, and a man in extremity can condition himself to believe what he calculates will bring him most consolation.

After *Sœur* Yvette had cleansed his limbs, Paul had lain for the rest of the day in a state of comatose inactivity, ignoring sisters and doctors, paying no attention to their questions, moving his limbs only when the pressure of their weight became unendurable. Dr. Bruneau came in the early evening, but Paul remained staring up at the ceiling, giving no indication that he was even conscious of his presence. Then Dr. Bruneau and *Sœur* Yvette left the room, and Paul heard them whispering together outside the door. Suppressing his breathing, he managed to translate a phrase of Dr. Bruneau: 'There's no hope. His days are counted.'

'Thy will be done,' Paul muttered, closing his eyes in thankfulness.

For he was broken. When the induction of the pneumothorax had brought him near to death he had felt no inclination to revise the tenets of his unbelief. But now, in misery and isolation, he had stood for too long on the edge of the abyss; he felt the need to relate himself to some Vital Principle, not in recantation, not in supplication, but in affirmation. 'Thy will be done.' The desire of the wheel to turn, of the jewel to be worn, of the apple to be plucked, of the mind to equate Atman with Brahman.

Turning in his bed, twisting his burning feet in search of a cool corner of the sheets, he repeated, brought home upon, each proposition of the Lord's Prayer – primarily reverting to it because of its accessibility to his mind, sustaining it because it crystallised the amorphous longings of his spirit, cherishing it because it was free of the dogmas inseparable from the religious system associated with it, in which he had been raised.

'Our Father, which art in heaven, hallowed be Thy name. Thy kingdom come. Thy will be done in earth, as it is in heaven…'

Man the peripatetic anthropomorphist, casuistic but enthusiastic interpreter of thaumaturgies, theogonies and theophanies, hastens to establish himself on an eternal basis by postulating a Protoplast and worshipping It. The Protoplast, obligingly incarnating Itself in human form, short-circuits in a single prayer the whole of its postulator's capacity for whining, flattering, cajoling, berating and self-seeking. The postulator gratuitously devotes the succeeding two thousand years to supplying the lacuna.

'Give us this day our daily bread…'

'Our daily bread' – the free request, freely made. The morning toast, the memory-soaked madeleine, the celestial candy-floss which inspirits us to dare the big dipper and the haunted house. How else oil the wheels *ad majorem Dei gloriam?* Christ did not say: 'Give us this day some bread,' but 'Give us this day *our daily* bread.' Not in abjectness but in joyful kinship, hands across the clouds and cards face upwards on the table. For where the children are responsible *to* the Father, so the Father is responsible *for* the children, and the labourer is worthy of the rod which beats him.

And Paul now saw the splendid great slices of fresh bread, hygienic but unwrapped, piled high upon a platter in the desert, and the earthen pitcher ball-bellied with the iridescent, blessed blood. And drawing into himself the consubstantial, mystic force from material provision, he repeated:

'Forgive us our trespasses, as we forgive them that trespass against us.'

Infinitely subtle. A reminder to man that if he expects to be forgiven, he must forgive; a reminder to God that a man who has forgiven, merits, perhaps, forgiveness.

'Lead us not into temptation, but deliver us from evil.'

There seemed little time left for temptation, but from evil, thought Paul, O good God, deliver me! For the Kingdom was God's, as was the power and the glory and the horror thereof. Nor would God affirm one and deny the other, nor ratiocinate, nor engage in eristic double-talk; for the game and candle, the blood and the wine, the fœtus and the corpse in the allotment were all one, finally, irrevocably, world without end. And facts are facts. Life is hard; belief is harder; total unbelief hardest of all. But too much weeping blinds even the keenest eyes to the Vision of the Presence.

'*Monsieur* Davenant, it is unhappily necessary to perform a *ponction sternale*. I will send a chair for you in twenty minutes,' said Dr. Vernet.

'No,' said Paul. He had decided during the night to refuse any further treatment.

'No what?'

'No thank you.'

Dr. Vernet sighed apologetically. 'My deficiencies of English – we are as usual misunderstanding each other. I said I will perform for you a *ponction sternale*.'

'Yes,' said Paul. His lips were sticking together, his salivary glands seemed to have stopped secreting.

'Good. *A bientôt*.'

'No.'

'Pardon?'

'I said "No".'

Dr. Vernet took a deep breath. '*Monsieur*, you mishear me. I am saying that a *ponction sternale* is necessary. You think that I lose my time?'

'I am not having any more treatment.'

'This is not treatment, it is a test.'

'I don't care, I don't...' In his weakness, Paul's composure was uncertain. Tomorrow he might be dead – there was no one who cared that he was being tortured out of life, that his heart was being driven to a state of seizure.

'Carry out your test at the post-mortem,' he said.

'Are you out of your mind?' cried Dr. Vernet, his great, white-clad figure, fat with health, towering above the end of the bed. Paul turned away, stared at the wall.

Dr. Vernet leant over, clenched his fists on the bed-rail, then released his grip. '*Bon.* We will await developments,' he said, and left the room.

'I will tell you the truth,' said *Sœur* Yvette. And she explained to Paul that Dr. Vernet's hobby was blood, and that where a *ponction sternale* was likely to produce an interesting result even when the result could have no practical application in the case of the patient on whom it was performed – it provided a temptation which he could rarely resist. In refusing it, from whatever motive, Paul had acted wisely. But as for refusing all further treatment! And there were distinct signs that the pus was thinning – just the moment *not* to give up! Paul *must* get into the wheelchair and be taken down to the *Service Médical.* He *must* co-operate. The pus *must* be removed.

'I refuse,' said Paul. *Sœur* Yvette left the room.

'It is like this that one dies,' thought Paul. Lying there, he felt that his body had sunk below the level of his bed, and that his spirit had sunk below the level of his body. So it was that one sank out of life, lower and lower...

Then he heard *Sœur* Miriam's laugh, and the sound of a trolley rattling up the corridor in the direction of his room. The door opened. Dr. Bruneau walked in, nodded, glanced at Paul's temperature chart, grimaced, rubbed his eyes with the back of his hand.

'I refuse,' said Paul.

Dr. Bruneau smiled, started to fill a syringe with anæsthetic.

'I will have no more treatment.'

'Chouk, chouk, chouk,' said *Sœur* Miriam.

Paul drew back in his bed. 'Do not come near me,' he said. Dr. Bruneau slammed the bottle of anæsthetic down on the trolley, smiling no longer. 'The window,' he said, waving his hand towards it. 'When you've had enough of life, jump out! Till then let me do my duty.' And holding a hypodermic in one hand, and pulling the trolley after him with the other, he advanced to the top of Paul's bed.

Paul trembled involuntarily as *Sœur* Yvette approached him with a needle. During the day, as well as Dr. Bruneau's *ponction*, he had had a blood transfusion; this made the fourteenth injection since morning.

A quick stab in his arm, and barely had he gasped when peace swept up the ramifications of veins and arteries like a tidal bore. He turned face downwards, stretched his arms and legs into cool corners of the bed, his body the boss of a wheel, his arms and legs the spokes.

The complete absence of pressure on any part of his body brought to his attention the fact that now he was suspended several inches above his bed. Then slipping horizontally sideways, he passed across the room and out of the open window, in the wake of his detached and hurrying consciousness.

Ecstasy was when he managed to overtake his consciousness and re-confine it in his body; the sensation precluded vigilance, enabling consciousness to re-detach itself and again precede him.

Four or five times he wrenched the ruling faculty back into his body; then, completely outdistancing him, it soared upwards in a tiny golden shower, whilst his husk relapsed into the basic chemicals of its composition and dispersed in the air.

'A visitor for you,' said *Sœur* Yvette.

The price of three morphia-induced sleeps was the mental obfuscation which followed each of them: Paul did not recognise Desmond Beale as he walked into the room.

'Mr. Desmond Beale,' *Sœur* Yvette whispered to Paul.

'I knew him at Oxford,' Paul whispered back to *Sœur* Yvette.

'He's here now.'

'Where?'

'My dear Paul,' said Desmond, walking to the top of the bed and taking

Paul's hand. 'Desmond!' cried, Paul pressing the hand against his forehead. He lay quite still, his eyes closed. *Sœur* Yvette left the room.

'How is it you're here?' Paul asked in a very low voice, his eyes still shut.

'I got a telegram to come immediately.'

'A telegram. From Dr. Vernet?'

'No. Someone called Kibouski.'

'Kubahskoi?'

'Probably.'

The effort was making Paul sweat. He released Desmond's hand, impatiently dried his face with a handkerchief.

It was too complicated to pursue.

'How did you get here?'

'Flew.'

'Flew!'

'Yes. I borrowed thirty pounds. And I've brought enough provisions from the buttery to last me a few days. All I need is a room.'

'I'm glad to see you.'

'I ought to go now,' said Desmond. Paul opened his eyes. Desmond looked down into the white, crumpled face and shuddered. The stench of the sick-room, of purulence, sweat and urine became overpowering. He turned away.

'Oh, no!'

'I'll come back later.'

Paul seized Desmond's hand again. 'Please don't go,' he whispered.

'Dr. Vernet said I could only stay for a few minutes.'

'You've seen him?'

'Yes. He says that your condition is very serious, but that if you have the will to live, you will pull through.'

'I don't want to live.'

'That is what he fears.'

'I'm sorry it's so awful.'

'Is there anything I can do?'

Paul looked up sharply. 'Yes, I was going to ask you.'

'What?'

'If you would… If you were willing?'

'Well?'

'Oh, you know what I mean.'

'Yes.'

'Will you help me?'

'How can I?'

'I think you can.'

Desmond shrugged his shoulders. 'I would first have to have another talk with Dr. Vernet,' he said.

The door opened and *Sœur* Yvette came back into the room. She told Desmond that he had to leave.

'We are discussing something of great importance,' objected Desmond.

'Precisely why you must leave.'

'Very well. I may return later?'

'Tomorrow. If he is strong enough.'

'I see.' Desmond grasped Paul's hand briefly, waved to him from the door, and left.

In the late afternoon *Sœur* Yvette came to give Paul his injections. 'My poor Paul,' she said, 'don't be disappointed, but your visitor has gone.'

'From the sanatorium?'

'No, from Brisset.'

Paul stared at her, comprehension breaking down to panic.

'He found that if he paid for a room here, he wouldn't be able to pay his fare back to England.'

'But I could have given him some money,' said Paul, desperately searching for his wallet on the *table de nuit*, as proof.

'It's too late now. He left three hours ago.'

A sound of laughter and heavy footsteps. The door burst open. Desmond, his hair disordered, his face bleeding, his jacket in ribbons, staggered into the room.

'I've just fallen down a mountain,' he announced, doubling up with laughter. He was rather drunk.

'But you caught the two o'clock train down to Uhle,' said *Sœur* Yvette.

'Yes. And I caught the four o'clock train up again.'

'I've got enough money, Desmond,' said Paul.

'So have I!' Desmond pulled a handful of notes out of his pocket and tossed them in the air.

A bell sounded in the passage. With an exclamation of annoyance, *Sœur* Yvette went to answer it.

Desmond walked across to the wash-basin and stared in the mirror. 'You're drunk!' he exclaimed, pointing severely at his reflection. Then he removed his jacket and stared with interest at his lacerated shirt sleeve.

'That's what happens if you climb up mountains.'

'Why were you climbing mountains?'

'I didn't know I was till I fell down one. No objection if I clean myself up?' He peeled off his shirt and vest.

'*Sœur* Yvette said you'd left.'

'I had. No money, you see.'

'I told you, I've got enough money.'

'And I told you, so have I!'

'But, how – '

'It's a long story. Can't go into it now. But, very briefly, I got in with a drunk in the station buffet at Uhle. He started boasting that he owned the whole of Brisset. I led him on, then challenged him to show me his wallet as proof.'

Desmond stepped out of his trousers and started to rub himself down with a wad of bandages soaked in soapy water.

'But won't he…'

'No. He was absolutely blind, I tell you. Besides, I gave him lots of it back.' Desmond sprinkled his hair with surgical spirit and rubbed it vigorously into his scalp. *Sœur* Yvette came back into the room and gave a cry. Desmond raised his hand in a gesture of acknowledgement, then continued with his toilet.

'Dr. Bruneau's coming. Put your clothes on at once,' *Sœur* Yvette commanded.

'May I visit Paul this evening?'

'No!'

As the door handle turned, *Sœur* Yvette threw Paul's dressing-gown across Desmond's shoulders. Dr. Bruneau came into the room.

'*Bonjour, cher Monsieur*, we have not yet had the pleasure,' he said, affectionately taking Desmond by the hand. 'But it is a rule of the house that new patients remain in bed until they have had their initial examination. Go back to your room now, and I will come and see you almost immediately.' And conducting Desmond to the door and opening it ceremoniously, he bowed him out.

The bedside lamp diffused a luminous, yellow mist about Paul's head and pillows, intensifying the depth of the shadows like a riverside street-lamp in the fog. Antique, modelled in the shape of an oil lamp (in the way that the earliest motor-cars were designed like carriages), it consisted of a brass column with an enormous leaden base, surmounted by a wide-brimmed china bowl, tinted cream and dun, almost opaque. A fringe, perished and brittle, circumscribed the lower edge of the bowl, trapping and absorbing all lateral rays of light.

The lethargic and heavy flies, which in *Les Alpes* survived the winter, centred their existence about the lamp, occasionally making excursions into the far corners of the room, then zooming flatly back. They liked to sharpen their feet, stamp, swarm and crawl about the fringe, using it as landing ground and ambulatory; they transformed the surface of the bowl into a viewing screen for their obscene silhouettes, as they buzzed, crashed, fornicated and expired about the electric globe within.

Desmond returned in the early evening. He was still wearing the clothes he had torn in the afternoon, though he had brushed them and some of the larger rents had been drawn together with wide irregular stitches. He walked steadily, spoke deliberately; with his finger-tips he kept on prising up the edges of the pieces of sticking plaster on his hands and neck.

'You're alone?' he said. 'No nurses with you? Good!' He came across the room and sat at the foot of Paul's bed. 'They've started to persecute me – same old story. But it does not matter.' He looked fastidiously at the gnawed sheaths of his fingernails. 'Air still a trifle voluptuous,' he commented, inhaling deeply.

'Open the window.'

'No. I like it. It smells like a vapour-heated garbage dump. Better than the filthy pure air outside. Are you better?'

'No.'

'How could you be? I'm talking like a fool. Truth is, I'm drunk again, though I don't think it's obvious, in point of fact. I'm rather worried in case any of those bloody nurses come up here again.' He stopped talking, his attention caught by a gross and slothful fly crawling towards him across the counterpane. Opening an empty match box he trapped it inside and closed the tray. There was a subdued buzzing, then silence. Cautiously he reopened the box, but the fly made no effort to escape. 'Christ, even the bloody flies here have lost the will to live,' he cried, throwing the box at the window with such force that he fell off the bed. 'I'm pissed,' he said, getting up, 'thoroughly, legitimately, one-hundred-per-cent pissed. I'd better put my head in cold water.' He staggered across the room, pulled open his collar and lowered his head into the wash-basin. 'That's better, that's much better,' spluttering, scattering water, spitting. 'It's infallible, never fails.' He tripped over a chair and fell full-length. 'Christ, I'll have the whole bloody regiment up here in a minute. Oh God, I'm a fool, I'm a fool.' He got to his feet, staggered to Paul's bed.

'Look,' he said, 'you lie there and you don't say or do a damn thing. Why don't you get the hell out of here?' He pulled a flask from his pocket and sucked at it. 'I had messages for you. Now I've forgotten the lot. It doesn't matter. Perhaps it does, though. Christ!' He drank again from the flask, then rubbed his lips with the back of his hand. 'I want to cheer you up – that's what I've come for. But you won't cheer up. Here, take a drink.' And he thrust the flask at Paul.

'You won't talk and you won't cheer up and you won't drink,' he continued. 'It's all quite clear, all a policy. But you want me to help you – Ah! That makes you prick up your ears. And all before I'd even taken off my metaphorical hat! There's breeding. There's delicacy. Help me and smoke the consequences! All so easy! I just hold your nose while you swallow, then wave my hand at *Sœur* Yvette, flip ten *centimes* to the concierge and heigh ho!, back to Oxford. Then just a little notice in your college magazine: "Our well-beloved, if little known Mr. Davenant retired to the mountains with shop-soiled lungs but somehow managed to terminate his existence by bursting his bladder!" See what I mean! Oh! I know the attitude. *Après moi le foutu deluge*! Charming, *n'est-ce pas*? Not that I blame you at all, in point of fact. Of course, I really don't know what I'm saying. Why am I talking like this? Oh Christ! Oh Christ!' He banged his fist against his forehead, tears coming suddenly to his eyes. 'I'm wrecking everything, I'm abusing you,

I'm making everything ten times worse than before I came. It's typical – I'm not fit to live. Jesus!' He lowered his forehead into his hands and sobbed. Abruptly the sobbing stopped. He raised his head.

'I'm here to cheer you up…' Then craftily: 'To help you cheer up!'

Shaking with laughter, he got up from the bed and started to pace the room.

'Cheer up, old man. Ha-ha-ha! I'm here to help you to cheer up!' he chuckled.

Paul watched him. Outside the area illuminated by the lamp, the extremities of the room could not be seen for the shadows; for long periods Desmond would disappear into them, and then Paul would believe himself to be alone.

Suddenly Desmond threw open a window. The wind tore into the room, and the curtains swelled and tried to free themselves, looking like the rumps of giant birds clamped and held captive by the necks.

Paul drifted in and out of sleep. At times it seemed that Desmond was hovering over him, swollen to the proportions of a barrage balloon; at other times he appeared so small and so far away that until he moved he was indistinguishable from the pattern on the wallpaper. His voice gave no indication of where he was standing; hearing it in one corner, Paul would turn his eyes in that direction. Waving and gesticulating, casting great shadows, Desmond would then emerge from the opposite corner, his face sharp and exsanguineous in the yellow light.

His mood was changing. A series of ecstatic projects had replaced the earlier entreaties and admonitions. When he sensed that Paul was no longer listening, he seized the end of the bed and shook it until Paul's teeth chattered, crying: 'Wake up, wake up! By God, it will be wonderful!'

Suddenly, in his enthusiasm, he tried to force his flask between Paul's lips. Paul coughed. Blood, hastily swallowed back, stained the neck of the flask. Desmond dropped it with a scream and ran out into the passage.

'*Monsieur* Beale!' It was *Sœur* Yvette's voice.

'Come quickly! He's bleeding to death!'

'I told you you weren't to come back.'

'The tourniquets! Get out the tourniquets!'

Sœur Yvette, followed closely by Desmond, hurried into the room.

As she went over to Paul's bed, Desmond twisted a towel into a turban and placed it on his head. '*Voilà un turc!*' he cried.

'Leave at once or I'll send for Dr. Vernet,' said *Sœur* Yvette as she reassured herself that all was well with Paul.

'Leave at once or I'll send for Dr. Vernet!' mimicked Desmond.

As *Sœur* Yvette turned about, Desmond tossed aside the towel, seized the waste-paper basket and inverted it on his head. 'One more of a hundred impenetrable disguises!' he declared. *Sœur* Yvette strode across to him and jerked the basket away, leaving a mousse of rubbish, torn-up paper and apple peel on Desmond's hair.

'You've broken my nose! A doctor! A doctor!'

Sœur Yvette grasped his elbow and guided him out of the room and down the passage.

'He went quite quietly at last,' she said as she returned to give Paul his fourth evening injection of morphia. 'But he is, I'm afraid, becoming too much trouble. This time I must report him to Doctor Vernet, and he will not be allowed to come back into the sanatorium.'

Paul made no reply; his eyes were on the needle as it penetrated the wasted pin-cushion of his upper arm. Deeper, deeper, then, with the depression of the plunger, the subcutaneous, peace-disseminating stab. Vision fragmenting, the room's light and darkness interwoven like strands in a fabric.

Quickly now, quickly to recapture and hold sensation. Groaning slightly with the fiercer pain of pain transmuted into pleasure, he turned on his stomach, stretched out his arms and waited for the take-off. A preliminary, prelusive tensing of the muscles; cigarettes out, safety belts on; a shudder throughout his frame. Then independently, seeking its own ecstasy in the contact of the cold night air upon its feverish surface, a foot slipped out from between the sheets. Error. The truant foot was now the focal point of sensation. Angrily, undrugging his senses by deliberate action, he dragged the foot back between the sheets.

He now attempted to redistribute his weight by contracting the muscles of his abdomen, arching his hips and resting them upon his clenched fists. The hollow beneath his body should aid buoyancy. Abruptly his limbs grew unbearably heavy; the effort of withdrawing his imprisoned hands left him gasping. His position now restricted his breathing, but when he tried to turn over, he found that his arms were too cramped to aid the manœuvre. Believing himself to be suffocating, he twisted, wriggled and rocked until at last he was lying on his back.

Before *Sœur* Yvette had left for the night, she had drawn the curtains. Partially regaining his breath, Paul now noticed how the exact outline of the window, and of its leaded panes, was projected on to the curtains by the moon; when a slight breeze stirred the curtain folds, moonlight swept across the wall beside him like a tide. The sound of the wind brought with it an echo of the sea, the stirring of pebbles, the crackling of dry sand newly saturated.

Paul dismissed these images before they possessed him; there was no sand, no sea, only light on the wall and the wind rustling the curtains. To enforce his control over his senses, he raised himself slightly on his pillow. The curtains blew wide apart. On the patch of wall now illuminated he saw an immense bat, wings extended. The curtains fell back. The room was again in total darkness.

He lay motionless. There was no sound. Had he again been the victim of his imagination and the light? One of the curtains stirred sufficiently to reveal an enormous wing. Another wait in complete darkness, eyes straining, body tensed; the next flutter illuminated – the size of two furry hands clasped in prayer – the whole body of the bat.

Clouds passed across the moon and the outline of the window faded from the curtains. Paul lay waiting. Fully awake, fully conscious, this was now the test. What should he do? The curtains flapped wide and at the same moment the moon shone so brightly through the window that Paul could easily distinguish the design of the wallpaper. And with a wingspan of a yard, revealed in every detail, was the bat.

He must think clearly, must not panic. As the curtains fell back, his hand stretched for the bedside lamp – no, that was wrong. If he turned it on, the great creature would soar up and down the room, crashing into the walls, the curtains, himself.

What was it that people feared from bats? What should he guard against? Bats entangled in the hair. Bats covered with vermin? The teeth? Was it the teeth? The wings wrapped about one's head, the claws fixed in one's mouth, the teeth poised before one's eyes…

The curtains blew wide apart – the bat was crawling across the wall towards him. He gave a cry, pressed the bell for the night nurse, covered his face with his hands.

Silence. Fearfully he withdrew his fingers from his eyes. The edge of one of the curtains had got caught, the light was streaming in. Paul saw that the bat had returned to its original position. Staring at it, conscious of what his act must precipitate, he clicked on the light.

The wall was bare. Paul ducked his head, listened for the flapping of wings. Nothing. At last he scrutinised the wall – there was no trace to be seen. He looked to where he had first seen the body of the bat; there were two electric light points, one above the other. He watched them. They were squat, sinister, but essentially static. Perhaps it had crawled behind some piece of furniture? No, of course there had been no bat. What was happening to his brain?

Exhaustion – perhaps now he would sleep. Then he remembered with dismay that he had rung for the night nurse. She must now be on the way up to his floor to see which invalid was ringing. How could he explain to her what had happened? The only thing to do was to get quickly out of bed and cancel the warning light shining outside his bedroom – in that way she would never know who had rung.

He pulled back the sheets and lowered his feet to the freezing oilcloth. As soon as he tried to stand, however, he fell backwards on to the bed, his heart beating so rapidly that he did not dare move.

Then, easing himself down the bed, he climbed on to a chair and dragged himself across the room, pulling himself from one piece of furniture to the next. He reached the door and opened it. The corridor was empty. Neither the warning light above the door nor the floor indicator at the top of the passage was shining.

He returned to his bed in the same manner, his heart beating so painfully that he had to lower his chest to his knees. What would be the consequences of all his acts of folly? When he turned out the light, he saw that the bat had again taken up its position on the wall. He fell asleep and woke in the morning with the sun shining on his closed eyelids. But on opening his eyes he found that it was not yet dawn – the centre light and the light by his bedside had been shining all night.

CHAPTER SIXTEEN

•

'*Mon cher*,' said Dr. Vernet, taking a chair and sitting down, 'you are an extremely ill man – to tell you otherwise would be to insult your intelligence. But – *et voilà ce qu'il y a d'étonnant* – you remain alive! A few days ago I would have given very little for your chances; today I see one more demonstration of the phenomenal powers of resistance of the human organism. *Évidemment* we cannot yet talk in terms of positive amelioration, still less of convalescence. *Mais vous tenez le coup!*

'As to what the next few days will produce – I cannot say. In the disarming phrase beloved of *notre cher Bruneau*, "I am no prophet!" As ever, it seems to me an equation in terms of quasi-imponderables – the really significant factors we cannot anticipate. Apart from this, on the plus side you have your physical powers of resistance, which are good and for which you are indebted to your fundamentally strong constitution. *Un pauvre malheureux* whose development has been undermined by years of tuberculosis or malnutrition would not survive two days in your condition. On the negative side there is what I am at last forced to recognise as your innate pessimism. In a crisis, when it is least a question of your will, your body and its natural instincts will dominate and help you to survive. But when your good body has extricated you from immediate danger and it is time for your will to play its rôle – then, *cher Monsieur*, I do not know.

'There are moral implications in all this, if one could but seize them. To what extent have you got the right not to will to get better? Ought I to try and keep you alive if you have no very great wish to live? To what extent have I got the right to keep you alive against your will? I don't know, *Monsieur*, and I don't very much care. Perhaps you *would* be better dead, perhaps we would *all* be better dead. Issues like these I leave to more exalted intellects than my own.

'We are here a breakdown factory, and I am the *méchanicien chef*. What is given to me broken, I try to repair. And no questions! *Voilà tout*! It is a practical French outlook, and not a bad one, *en somme*.

'But now you are following me less well – your eyes look past me, as though they were catching glimpses of other shores. It is plain that my presence has become an intrusion. And yet, there is another matter of which I must speak to you.

'Your comrades, *Monsieur*. After you, they constitute my gravest problem. Nothing I do will prevent their trying to use me as a hospital information bureau. Everywhere I go I am accosted and interrogated; fifty times a day I have to refuse some impertinent and temerarious student the authorisation to visit you. And it seems to me that I am now faced with the choice of reconciling myself indefinitely to supporting this nuisance until such time that you are *cent pour cent* restored, or else I must bow to popular pressure, and forfeit for ever my integrity as a man of science. Unhesitatingly, and for the sake of my sanity, I choose the latter. Now outside the door is a first instalment of troublemakers and malcontents, all lined up to pay their probably lethal respects. Any chance of survival would be based on their staying no longer than two minutes.'

Dr. Vernet went to the door and opened it. 'Your comrade is very fragile. You may look, but do not touch. On your honour, for two minutes only.' He stood to one side that they might enter, then with a good-humoured nod left the room. Kubahskoi, most of the British colony, and half a dozen students of various nationalities grouped themselves about Paul's bed.

'Natter, natter, natter!' said William Davis, seating himself on a convenient chamber-pot. 'We risk our heads being bitten off every day by asking Vernet if we can come and see you, and when at last we manage to wear him down and get as far as the door, you both have to spend half an hour whispering sweet nothings to each other!'

'What were you doing? Giving each other enemas?' asked David Bean. 'Or just planning next week's menu?'

'You know there's been a serious outbreak of cannibalism among the Hungarians?' said William Davis.

'Chaps!' said John MacAllister, amidst laughter, 'Vernet's only allowing us two minutes. If anyone's got anything worth saying...'

For a moment there was silence. Then John MacAllister said: 'Paul, this is not a visit, it's a deputation. Will you, for pity's sake, please get better. We've all agreed that we're none of us going to leave Brisset until we can take you along too; but at the same time we don't want to spend the rest of our lives here.'

'Besides,' added Angus Gray, 'life in the sanatorium's come to a stop. There are no nurses – they're all looking after you. There's no food – it's all being rendered down to feed to you in tabloid form.'

'In a word,' interrupted John MacAllister, 'get better!'

'Yes, for Christ's sake get better!' echoed everyone.

Was there anything Paul wanted? Letters written? Reading aloud? Eggs for tea?

The door opened and Dr. Vernet came back into the room. 'Just as I thought – caught the lot of you! Let no one dare to ask for permission to visit *Monsieur* Davenant again! Now quick march, *tout le monde*!'

Kubahskoi alone was allowed to remain a moment longer. He wanted to explain how he had come to send a telegram to Desmond Beale. When it had been known that Paul's condition was serious, Dr. Vernet's secretary had asked him if he knew of anyone whom Paul might wish to see. Desmond was the only friend to whom Paul had ever referred and the name of his college was in the magazine in which his photo had appeared.

'*Tout comprendre, c'est tout pardonner,*' cried Dr. Vernet. '*Maintenant en avant*!'

It was only after they had left that Paul reflected on John Cotterell's absence.

'Then you don't know? No, of course you don't,' said *Sœur* Yvette, as she gave Paul an injection. She went on to explain that subsequent to the discovery that some old lesions had reopened, John Cotterell had had a bad pleural effusion. And – since he refused to admit or to accept that there was anything wrong with him – he was proving a very difficult patient. Nor was Dr. Vernet at all satisfied with his condition. 'You mark my words, he'll be the next one for the operating table!' she concluded grimly.

There was a knock at the door. When *Sœur* Yvette opened it and found Desmond Beale outside, she would have shut it again had not the latter put his foot through the opening. 'Look,' he pleaded, 'I'm absolutely sober and I've only called to say good-bye and give you a present.' And he handed her a half of a salami and a bottle one-third full of gin. 'I'm leaving on the afternoon train.'

Sœur Yvette considered him doubtfully. His features were lost in an ingratiating smirk; his hair had been so flattened that it looked as if it had been painted on his scalp.

'You really are leaving?'

'Yes. Yes. And what is more, I've made a solemn resolution to give up drinking.'

'You have? Well, I hope you'll keep it.' *Sœur* Yvette shook Desmond's outstretched hand and left the room.

He realised now, he explained, that his presence was serving no purpose, and he had made arrangements to leave for England on the afternoon train. But first he wished to make some apology for his behaviour. It had had, however, one good outcome – he was now going to give up drinking. The bottle he had given her was no less a symbol than a present. 'And now I'm sober, and reasonable, and humble, and going,' he said, 'can I not be allowed a few minutes alone with Paul in order to say goodbye?

'Paul,' said Desmond, the smirk disappearing, 'I'm sorry, but I've got to go. In the first place this bloody mountain is sending me round the bend. In the second, that bastard Vernet's sent me a note saying that if ever I cause any more disturbances, he'll call the police. Can you beat it? Of course, it's *Sœur* Yvette who's at the bottom of it. She's a two-faced bloody bitch!' He clenched his fists.

'I don't know what happened last night, but I retain some awful, nagging memories. You asked me to help you die – that is very clear. And ever since I woke up this morning, I've been tormented that like a sot I'd given you false hope. For the truth is that I can't do a damn thing – I'm as helpless and useless in this as in everything else. And I've dreaded having to admit it to you.

'My visit's been a complete failure, though God knows I undertook it in good faith – if the journey had been ten times longer and ten times more expensive, I'd have managed it somehow. And now I'm off again! I'm full of plans and good resolutions – no more drinking, no more debts… It's all very practical – like putting on a mackintosh as the ship goes down.

'But that's not why I'm leaving. The thing is, I've decided to reorganise my life. I'm not going back to Oxford. I want power and money' (each substantive emphasised by the thud of his fist against the centre of the palm of his hand), 'and power and money are just what I am going all out to get. And never mind the means! Power and money,' he repeated rapturously, as he began to stride up and down the room. Then his expression darkened. 'And when I'm rich and powerful – which will be sooner than you may think – there are a few bastards here and at Oxford who will have some very nasty shocks coming to them!' There was a chair in his path: he kicked it across the room.

'And I wasn't shooting a line when I said I was giving up drink. I really am. Why? Not because of *Sœur* Yvette's bloody little bourgeois prejudices, but because it dissipates my powers. And I shall need all my powers to be able to crush my enemies!' His expression became apocalyptic.

'Now don't think that just because I won't be here I'll have forgotten you. As soon as I've got enough money, I'll send you all you want. Here, take this to start with!' He pulled a five-thousand-franc note out of his pocket and flung it on to Paul's *table de nuit.* 'No, keep it. Get someone to buy you wine or flowers or something. A few weeks from now there will be a great smell floating across the Alps – it will be me stinking of money. Till then, keep alive!'

He shook Paul's hand, went to the door, waved and left. The day unrolled. Paul slept and sweated and woke and was injected and fed and slept. Pus was taken out of his body, blood was put into it. His towering fever was artificially reduced by doses of insidious little white pills which made him feel as if he had been dragged by his tongue down a narrow drain-pipe.

In the late afternoon, Desmond returned.

'Thank God I kept just enough money to buy myself a couple of drinks,' he said, laughing. 'If not, I'd have been on that train and I'd never have had the most wonderful idea! My mind's just spinning with it. It's the answer to all our problems...'

He perched on the side of a table, started to swing his legs. 'I just don't know how to tell you about it, it's so pathetically simple. But then of course anything which works always is simple – look at the safety pin! Still, I mustn't give you the wrong idea – its full development will require masterly organisation.' He broke off, his eye caught by the five-thousand franc note which he had tossed on to the *table de nuit.* 'Ah! Have to borrow that back. There are just a few initial expenses...'

'Well now, it's like this. But it's no use – you're going to think I'm joking.

I mean, I admit I'm pissed again, but that's got nothing to do with it. Besides I got pissed after having the idea, not before it. Now listen carefully – this is it. But one point I must make clear before I start – there's not a fortune in it, just a good, comfortable income for one or two people at the top. I mean that's probably why no one's doing it – there's not enough money to attract the real tycoon, whilst it requires too much organising ability to be within the scope of the small operator. But mind you, I say there's no fortune in it… Still, once developed and launched on an international scale there'd be no knowing…'

He glanced at his watch. 'Christ, I mustn't stay here crapping away or I'll miss my train to Chatigny. But I had to look in and tell you I'd be away for a couple of days. I think it'll go all right, don't you? Must admit I feel a bit nervous, like an actor on a first night. He knows the play's all right, he knows it will run for months, but there's always a something, a faint uneasiness, a fear of the unexpected. Difficult to explain, except in the broadest terms. So that's why you're to keep your fingers crossed till I get back. Well, look after yourself and give *Sœur* Yvette the glad news that I am back for good. Brisset's just the right place for our H.Q.'

Two minutes later, and Desmond would have been able to give *Sœur* Yvette the news in person. She came in to puff up Paul's pillows, and to see if he needed anything. 'Ah,' she cried, noticing the flask which Desmond had inadvertently left on the table, 'so he did not even bother to take it back to England! That gives me real pleasure! There is good hope for him. All who sincerely try to reform have access to a special strength. It is part of God's grace to His children!'

She left the room, but returned, very flustered, about forty minutes later. 'Come quickly, there is a telephone call for you from England. I explained that you were too ill, but they said that it was very, very urgent, and no message could be given. I can't ask Dr. Vernet for permission because he's at dinner.'

She helped Paul into the wheelchair and pushed him hurriedly to the telephone box at the end of the corridor.

'Hullo,' said Desmond's voice, 'sorry to get you up, old man, but I'm down at the bottom of the mountain, and I've got twenty minutes to fill in before the train goes out. I bet *Sœur* Yvette didn't recognise my voice just now – I was holding my fingers over my nose! What I'm ringing up about is my plan. I don't think I really gave you the gist of it when I was in your room. Now are you ready for it? I want you to try and get rid of any preconceived ideas you may have on the subject, and try and see what I'm going to tell you with a fresh eye. Well, it's like this – Christ! there's the train coming in. I must have made a mistake with the timetable. Well, can't stop now. Just keep your fingers crossed – that's your side of the bargain. *À bientôt.*'

'I hope not bad news, but do not tell me unless you wish to,' said *Sœur* Yvette as she wheeled Paul back to bed. 'In any case I think it's best if we do not tell Dr. Vernet – he would probably not have let you take the call. Now I think I will give you your morphia and you can go back to your fantasy world, where you are happiest.'

The morphia did not have its customary effect. After the injection Paul turned on his stomach and spread out his arms. His condition grew easier, but he did not become free of his body. Lying very still, relaxing his limbs, he waited.

Minutes or hours passed; the light began to trouble his eyes. It was strange that *Sœur* Yvette had neglected to turn it out. He turned over on his back, just in time to see the flurry at the door as his old and frayed dressing-gown leapt back on to its hook.

Paul stared at it. A fold stirred, then fell back into position. Suddenly, with infinite caution, it inflated and turned completely round on its hook, facing Paul, assessing him. Paul remained rigid, staring at its invisible head, willing it back into inanimation. Sweat broke out all over Paul's face. Then tentatively, and with a slight jerk, it slipped from the hook and came to the bottom of the bed.

There must be no panic – Paul knew instinctively that it was registering his reactions. His breathing was betraying him – the dressing-gown grasped the end of the bed with one hollow sleeve, raised the other in a gesture of eloquence. He drew back in his bed; the dressing-gown stopped as though considering him. On an impulse, Paul lunged at it with his fist – the dressing-gown, assaulted unexpectedly, toppled backwards.

Footsteps sounded in the passage. The dressing-gown leapt back to within a yard of the door, one hollow sleeve raised to where its ear should have been, the other pointed at Paul commanding silence. The footsteps stopped outside his door. The dressing-gown shot back on to its hook, its folds collapsed and hanging, only the sleeves still raised in warning.

A hand touched the door-knob; the dressing-gown sleeves dropped to their full length. But the door-knob did not turn. Whoever was without changed his mind and returned down the passage.

The footsteps had not died away before the dressing-gown jumped from the door and recommenced its address in triumphant frenzy. Previously it had remained at the foot of the bed – now, it leapt back and started a jigging dance of triumph. Then it launched into the mummery of a silent harangue, at the same time grasping the end of the bed with its sleeves. Paul thought: 'I am going to faint. And if I faint, it will be on me.'

Paul braced himself to meet its attack. Sucked down into the whirlpool of his effort, he lost a second of consciousness: his eyes reopened on the dressing-gown, sleeves raised, poised to pounce. He held it rigid with the fixity of his stare. One moment of lowered vigilance and he would be lost; desperately he kept his eyes open, his head painfully propped upon his shoulder. A lessening of his resolution, a mist across his eyes, and then…

It came. Warm and bitter cloth, orifice-filling, all-enveloping. He was suffocating. In a flash of brilliant light, his senses floundered and expired.

When *Sœur* Yvette returned from early Mass, she found him still crouched upon his pillows, fists clenched, eyes open, face bloody. He screamed as she touched his arm, the sound shocking him back to consciousness. 'There!' he shouted, pointing at the dressing-gown which was hanging as usual on the door. *Sœur* Yvette took it in astonishment, demonstrated its limpness, twisted it up, turned it inside out, but when she brought it near him he shrank back in his bed and screamed again. Gabbling, muttering, biting at his fingers, he recounted what had happened; *Sœur* Yvette's protestations and calls to reason were in vain.

And the outcome was a prohibition against the use of morphia for Paul. In the words of *Sœur* Yvette (which she had picked up when nursing a British Army sergeant during the war), he would now 'just have to sweat it out'.

* * *

'*Monsieur*,' said Dr. Vernet equably, 'it may interest you to learn that your amiable friend, Mr. Beale, is now in the hands of the police. In addition to a number of routine statements, he has done me the honour of claiming both that I am his father-in-law, and that I employ him in the rôle of visiting psychiatrist to my sanatorium. My cousin, who incidentally is the head of the police department at Chatigny, and who was hitherto unaware of my British affiliations, has been thoughtful enough to supply me with these details.

'Mr. Beale, it appears, was arrested for begging and threatened assault. His defence is that neither is an offence in England, and that he has deliberately restricted his activities to British tourists. So confident is he in the legality of his actions that he has further confessed that, in conjunction with a partner in the mountains (you, my honoured sir), he has founded an organisation of professional English beggars who operate in all the principal French tourist resorts.

'Mr. Beale's own rôle is what he describes as "softening up" new territory, after which one of his assistants (employed, apparently, on a percentage basis) takes over from him, and he is free to "soften up" somewhere else.

'Had he fallen into other hands than those of my cousin, I hesitate to think in which of our fortresses he would now be languishing. But as it is, he will be given two hundred francs (which sum, *cher Monsieur*, you will kindly remit to my cousin at your earliest convenience), after which he will be ordered to leave the precincts of Chatigny. Further he will be warned that, should he be rearrested, proceedings for extradition will be taken against him.

'Should you be in any form of correspondence with your friend, you would do well to advise him against returning to Brisset. In the first place I could not agree to his paying you any further visits. In the second, Dr. Hervet, who claims that he has been robbed of quite a considerable sum of money, is looking for someone of strikingly similar appearance. Probably, in the circumstances, Mr. Beale would do best if he transferred the whole of his organisation back to England…'

'Quite a diverting story, *cher Monsieur*, and one which demonstrates the value of the French aptitude for compromise. And, *en somme*, there is no real harm. Honour has been vindicated, the status quo maintained, you are a few francs poorer, and I have one agreeable anecdote *de plus* for inclusion in the memoirs which I intend to write *dans le retour de mon âge*.'

The next morning Paul received a letter, which *Sœur* Yvette opened and read aloud:

Dear Paul,

I am back in Brisset, but I haven't the heart to come and see you. The fact is – as you may have heard – everything has gone wrong. I just don't know what to do next.

Did I ever really give you the details of my plan? If not, there's no point in doing so now. But – grossly simplifying – it really amounted to little more than the systematic milking of British and American tourists by telling them hard-luck stories. But good ones – no crap. Missed connections with baggage and money gone on ahead. Currency allowance run out and a wife sick in the hotel, etc., etc. Coupled with a good appearance, courteous manner, educated accent, you'd have said an absolute cinch.

But I hadn't reckoned with the tourist mentality. I swear to you that in all my life I've never seen such a crew of hard-faced, flint-eyed bastards. Three hours' work and not a five-franc piece! I wouldn't even have eaten if a little sod with a crutch (I'd got him pressed up against a corner) hadn't given me a five-hundred-franc note (after which he scuttled away as if I had the plague).

I can tell you that my temper was beginning to wear pretty thin. Then one bloody little jumped-up runt stuck his nose in the air and said: 'It is not my practice to encourage beggars at home or abroad.' I was just going to knock his teeth in when I got arrested.

I first tried to bluff it out by telling the police I was Vernet's son-in-law and a psychiatrist. Then they rang up Vernet and I really thought I'd had it. Then there was a lot of arsing about and suddenly I was given two hundred francs and told to get the hell out of Chatigny.

Well, I managed, one way or another, to get back to the hotel, and now I must rather admit that I've got to the end of my tether.

PS Can't write any more for the moment.

Later

There's a *cabinet de toilette* in my room, and I went out to buy some sausages, and it seems that I left the tap of the *bidet* running, and it's flooded the room, and they talk to me as if I'd done it deliberately. And now something else has happened. In order to heat up the sausages, I put them on a plate on the carpet, and put the electric fire face downwards on top of them. And while I was out of the room, the plate broke, and the fire's burnt a hole in the carpet. This really is the end – I just don't know what to do. I've had nothing to eat, and in case they come in I'm even sitting on the hole as I write this letter.

Evening

I've got to the end of my tether. A maid found the hole and the manager's been giving me absolute hell. Says I've got to pay for a new carpet. I told him that it was probably the maid who'd done it but he said not to give him that crap. Bloody little swine! I just don't see what to do next. I can't go back to Oxford. Then what? Maybe I'll have a shot at the aspirin trick – I've just got enough money left to buy a couple of hundred. If I do I'll leave this letter down in the hall. Somebody will probably post it.

'Goodness!' said *Sœur* Yvette. 'I must telephone his hotel immediately.'

They met on the staircase.

'Can't stop. Train leaves in ten minutes,' said Desmond. He pushed past *Sœur* Yvette. She ran after him, pulling at his jacket. '*Deus ex bloody machina*!' he cried, as he threw open Paul's door.

'Ah, no!' said *Sœur* Yvette, grasping his arm.

'What do you mean "Ah, no!"? I'm catching a train in ten minutes. Let me go.'

'How have you the face to even come here? Didn't you take the pills?'

'Of course I did. How did you know about them?'

'I read your letter aloud to Paul five minutes ago. How many did you take?'

'Dozens.'

'You're not telling the truth!'

'Christ!' said Desmond, pulling himself free, 'I shall go before you say something you'll regret. Besides, you're going to make me miss my train.'

'I'm going off to ring for Dr. Vernet!' shouted *Sœur* Yvette.

'You'd better hurry or he'll miss me!' Desmond called after her. He turned to Paul, his face radiant. 'Look Paul, I'm just off,' he said, throwing open the door, 'and I haven't the time to tell you exactly what's happened, though *Sœur* Yvette will doubtless give you her version when I've left. The point is I'm still alive, and instead of its being a horrible anti-climax, it's all right – there's been an astonishing *deus ex machina*. Do you remember Jack Figgis at Oxford? I knew him when I was in coastal command – he was in a motorboat crew, and specialised in knowing every inch of the south-west coast. Well, I got a *poste restante* letter from him this morning. He says that he's going down from Oxford because he's got a good smuggling contract, and there's also room for someone who can pilot a plane – that's where I come in. It's a big organisation – mainly arms smuggling, and he's given me a rendezvous in Paris in two days' time. Sounds rather my cup of tea, doesn't it? Not of course that I really mind what I'm doing, as long as it's anti-social in some way or other. And who knows what it might lead to? If I get on well, there's no reason why I shouldn't be able to get you a job when you're fit enough.

'Of course I'm dead broke again, can't even pay my bill at the hotel, never mind paying for a new carpet. But – ' he broke off as Paul tried to reach for his wallet on the *table de nuit*. 'Oh, no! Not a *centime*. I'll enjoy fixing the hotel – get into practice again! And of course I'll hitch to Paris. That'll be fun too – I was getting too soft with all this B.E.A. travel.

'Now I'm afraid that it's really goodbye. Still I've seen you through the worst – you're looking better every day. In no time you'll be completely fit. And then – yes, that's it – you could join us. I'll keep a seat warm for you. Six months from now and I guarantee you'll be helping me fly crates of rusty rifles from Argentine to Suez.'

As he was talking he seized Paul's hand and shook it vigorously. Then, picking up and pocketing a thousand-franc note which had fallen on to the duvet, he waved a hurried last farewell and raced out of the room. His footsteps echoed down the corridor, faded, then suddenly grew louder again. His head reappeared round the door. 'Warning – never try the aspirin trick. Just as you're getting the last one down the first starts coming up. They ought to warn you on the bottle. Best thing's to stay alive. Try and grab life by the knackers – it gives you something to hold on to!'

And he was gone for good.

No more blood being available from his particular group, it was necessary for Paul to be given a transfusion from someone whose blood group was universal.

The multifarious transfusions and intravenous injections had hardened his veins and caused them to sink deeply into his arm. Dr. Bruneau had great difficulty in locating the vein and piercing it. At last came the customary spurt of blood. Dr. Bruneau linked the needle by a rubber tube to the little nickel-plated transfusion machine which, when set in operation, would draw the blood from the donor, who was now lying on a *chaise longue* at the side of Paul's bed.

He started to turn the handle. There was a slight hissing from the machine. Paul suddenly felt stifled. 'Stop,' he cried, 'air is getting in. You're pumping air into my veins.'

Dr. Bruneau stopped turning the handle, and examined briefly the connections of the machine. '*Vous avez tort*,' he said at last, and recommenced the transfusion.

Two more revolutions of the handle, and Paul gave a great cry, at the same time pulling his arm away; as the needle slipped from the vein, blood sprayed across the counterpane. His lungs had become rigid. The attempt to breathe contracted his features, puffed his tongue from his mouth, his eyes from their sockets; a series of violent reflexes threw him from one side of the bed to the other. Everyone but Dr. Florent ran from the room, shouting for Dr. Vernet; the former retained his fingers on Paul's pulse, muttering: '*Mon Dieu, mon Dieu*!'

The final reflex threw Paul back on to his pillow. In that moment his vision was brilliant but remote, like the reflection of a well-lit scene in a convex mirror. As Dr. Vernet hurried into the room, Paul heard Dr. Florent cry:

'His pulse has stopped.' Then deafness... then blackness... then...

Waking out of nothing into the nightmare; the white blobs forming into faces, the roaring silence breaking down into speech, the whole act and experience of dying, wasted, thrown away, futilely and wantonly squandered. Dr. Vernet smiling at Paul the smile of warriors and of equals, the smile which dissociates the smiler and the smiled-at from the banal and vulgar *entourage*, the smile of the superior to the superior, the damned to the damned.

'Get out!' said Paul, but his lips would not move. Everyone was crowding round him, he could not breathe, it was all happening again. 'Get out! Get out!' he screamed. And still his lips would not move.

'His pulse is coming back,' said Dr. Florent, his voice very hollow.

'*Monsieur*, you are indestructible. A gift to science,' said Dr. Vernet.

'Get out!' Paul's shout rose barely above a whisper.

'*Il est un peu nerveux. Cela se comprend, d'ailleurs,*' said Dr. Bruneau, understandingly.

'*Oui. On peut le laisser en paix – il n'y a plus de danger pour le moment,*' said Dr. Vernet. Then in English: 'You have no danger, *Monsieur* Davenant. This little incident is closed. And be assured, it will not militate against your prospects of recovery. Now just lie tranquilly and easily. *Surtout, ne pensez pas en noir*!'

'I won't argue and I cannot discuss it. I haven't slept for nights, my fever is burning me up, and the fact is that yesterday you nearly killed me with your leaking machine,' said Paul.

'The machine was not leaking,' said Dr. Vernet.

'The two bloods congealed. It happens once in five thousand transfusions. It is a chance you must take,' explained *Sœur* Yvette.

'And today you take the chance for the last time. Your blood count has improved, and you will not need another transfusion,' added Dr. Vernet.

'I don't care. Besides, you know very well there's no one left in my blood group. And I'm not going to risk – '

'Our *curé* from the village is in your blood group. He has agreed to give you his blood this afternoon.'

'Kindly tell him not to come. He will find that he's wasting his time.'

'He arrives in five minutes.'

'I will not have another transfusion.'

'Good!'

There was a sound of aggressive sneezing from the corridor. The door opened. Paul caught sight of an enormous, black-robed figure which stepped suddenly to one side in order that *Sœur* Miriam, pushing her glass-topped medical trolley, might precede it. The figure then bowed to Dr. Bruneau, offering him precedence. Dr. Bruneau, still sneezing, clasped his nose with one hand and returned the compliment, gracefully and delicately, with the other. Both men began to advance simultaneously, then darted back with more bows, smiles and protestations. Behind them were Dr. Florent and three nurses.

They surrounded Paul's bed. Dr. Florent turned back the blankets. Two nurses started to pull the bed over to the light, another adjusted the *chaise longue*. *Sœur* Miriam began to prepare her needles.

Dr. Vernet was now busy scrubbing his hands. 'Our patient is getting better. He is once again remembering how to protest,' he said grimly.

Paul stared at Dr. Vernet, his lips tightening. *Sœur* Yvette brought the *curé* to the top of the bed.

'I regret *Monsieur* Davenant is not a Catholic, *mon père*,' she said.

'We are all the children of God. It is better to be a good man than a bad Catholic,' replied the large *curé*, inclining his head with gravity and offering Paul an enormous pink hand.

Dr. Florent helped the *curé* off with his black cloak, after which he divested himself of his jacket with the adroitness of a striptease dancer. He had a plump and healthy face, his eyes were cold, but not unsympathetic. As he undid the sleeve of his right arm, rolling it high above the elbow, he revealed pink and tender biceps.

Sœur Miriam removed the dressings from Paul's arms, disclosing the contused and swollen areas where previous transfusions and intravenous injections had been made.

The *curé* lay back on the *chaise longue* and watched with interest as Dr. Vernet inspected first one arm, then the other. '*Bien. On va voir*,' Dr. Vernet said at last, and told Paul to start clenching and unclenching his right hand.

He then rubbed the area of the joint of the arm with a spirit-soaked swab, and plunged a needle half a centimetre below the surface. '*Je crois que j'ai traversé*,' he said, withdrawing the needle slowly, and pulling at the plunger. No blood appeared in the glass syringe. Without removing the needle, but slightly altering its angle, he pushed it deeper into the arm, but still without piercing the vein.

The *curé's* eyes opened wide as, after several more unsuccessful attempts, Dr. Vernet took a second needle and thrust it laterally below the surface of the flesh. Unconsciously he unrolled his sleeve.

Paul watched the detached and spasmodic clutching of his hand as though it were no part of him, a fallen sparrow convulsively expiring. Now it lay rigid, unmodified by his brain's impulses.

'Open and close ze 'and like zis,' cried Dr. Bruneau, making one of his rare excursions into English, and at the same time snatching at the air.

A great effort. The fingers fluttered. Dr. Vernet took another needle and forced it through the flesh at right angles to the first. Paul groaned. Dr. Florent and Dr. Bruneau seized tightly hold of his arm.

'*Mais où est-ce, cette sacrée veine*?' muttered Dr. Vernet, taking a third needle. He prodded, twisted, withdrew, prodded again, and suddenly, eel-like, the vein rose to the surface. '*Voilà! Voilà*!' shouted Dr. Bruneau excitedly, as though drawing the attention of a fisherman to the fact that there was something at the end of his line.

Meanwhile *Sœur* Miriam had been making clear to the *curé* that this somewhat radical procedure had been necessitated by the condition of Paul's veins; in his own case these preliminaries would be effected painlessly and in a very few seconds. And as she was concluding her explanation, she rolled back his sleeve once more, and fixed a rubber tourniquet above the elbow.

When the *curé*'s vein had been pierced and the connection to the transfusion machine had been established, Dr. Vernet took hold of the handle which operated it. At the same moment Paul had an attack of panic.

'I tell you there is a leak in the machine,' he said weakly.

'Nonsense,' replied Dr. Vernet.

'Yesterday I – '

'I know what happened yesterday. Yesterday is not today.' The blood started to pour into his vein, and his body grew tense. 'God,' he said to himself, 'God, it is going to happen, it is going to happen.' There was a pressure in his brain, he felt the restriction of his breathing. 'Stop!' he shouted.

'What is the matter?' cried Dr. Vernet angrily. 'There is nothing at all wrong.'

Nor was there anything wrong. Paul realised the rôle that his imagination had been playing and became silent. Dr. Vernet brought the transfusion to its conclusion.

Sœur Yvette affixed a dressing to Paul's arm. The plump *curé* got up from the *chaise longue* and pulled on his jacket. Dr. Bruneau sniffed loudly, then examined the tip of his nose in the mirror. Dr. Vernet looked at his watch and said: 'And now, *Monsieur* Davenant, with your permission, we proceed to the *Service Médical* and I puncture you.'

'*Mais pas immédiatement après une transfusion, docteur*,' said Dr. Florent nervously. Dr. Vernet turned on him, and speaking rapidly, said: 'I decide when and where what I shall do, but you cause me always to lose my time. First you make his veins rotten, and then I have to come and do your work for you.' In great contrast to the tone of his voice, and the sentiments which he was expressing, he regarded Florent with a genial smile. Florent stared back at him in astonishment.

'Besides,' added Dr. Vernet, directing his smile at Paul, 'Monsieur becomes progressively more difficult, the stronger he gets. Let us profit from the present occasion – in a few days he may refuse to let us torture him at all.' He advanced to the foot of the bed and affectionately patted the outline of Paul's foot beneath the coverlet. 'No, *Monsieur* not quite immediately. I give you two hours to rest and to reflect. Perhaps I will find you then in a more tractable state of mind.'

Then suddenly his voice rose in anger. 'I am tired of being treated as though I were half Gestapo agent, half laboratory assistant.' He stared from face to face, but everyone avoided his gaze. 'Oh, no,' he said, laughing, 'it really is too much. I was not cut out for the rôle of lover, but now, on my knees, I must woo everyone – patients, nurses, my own assistants!' Then his voice rose again, and his face became taut with anger. 'The honeymoon is over, finally, definitively. We will now behave for the rest of our married lives. *Monsieur* Davenant, in two hours I puncture you.' And curtly nodding to the curé he strode from the room.

And during the next two hours, whilst Paul lay motionless, Dr. Vernet expressed his feelings in the most intense activity. Telephone bells sounded *carillons* along all the corridors, *chasseurs* raced up and down the stairs, nurses hurried backwards and forwards between the floors, patients, puzzled, dispirited and apathetic as newly-captured prisoners of war, formed straggling files outside the *Service Médical*, the ancient lift, no less broken in wind than its occupants, groaned so ominously that it seemed that each journey must be its last.

Dr. Vernet darted in and out of his bureau, giving instructions, amending them, countermanding them. '*Maintenant pour les consultations… Maintenant pour les insufflations… Maintenant pour les exsufflations…*' he cried. Patients too weak to walk he plucked bodily from their wheelchairs; the telephone on his desk rang uninterruptedly until he snatched at the apparatus with such force that the connecting lead snapped.

When *Sœur* Yvette wheeled Paul into the *Service Médical,* Dr. Vernet was hammering surgical needles into the false and spongy panelling. 'All blunt!' he shouted, 'the next person who hands me a blunt needle, I shall nail to the wall with it!'

Then seeing Paul: 'Who are you?' he demanded.

'Job,' replied Paul.

'*Ah, comme c'est délicieux, l'humour britannique,*' cried *Sœur* Miriam, tittering.

Dr. Vernet manhandled him on to the operating table. As he withdrew the anæsthetising needle, he plunged the great aspirating needle between Paul's ribs.

'You feel it!' he cried, pushing it deeper into Paul. Paul cried out. 'Then don't move! You feel it because you move!' He took an enormous syringe and fitted it to the needle.

When he could draw no more pus, he made Paul stand, his hand above his head, the needle protruding six inches from his side. *Sœur* Miriam held Paul about the waist, *Sœur* Yvette supported his hips; the trio staggered from the *sale d'attente* to the *sale de scopie.*

On the way back to his room Paul lay slack as a carcass in the wheelchair. Dr. Florent walked beside him, steadying his shoulder.

'*La vie est belle, cher ami,*' he whispered as he helped *Sœur* Yvette put Paul to bed. Paul stared past him. 'Did you hear what I said?' added Dr. Florent.

'The poor boy is discouraged to death,' said *Sœur* Yvette.

'Is there anything you want?' asked Dr. Florent.

Paul's impulse was to say: 'For it to be over.' Instead he shook his head.

'*Mais voyons,*' said Dr. Florent, his eyes suddenly filling with tears. He wanted to sympathise, apologise, encourage, but he lacked the vocabulary in his own language, even more so in one to which, as yet, he had devoted no more than a dozen hours of study.

'We are good friends?'

'Of course.'

'But *very* good friends,' insisted Dr. Florent. On a sudden impulse he seized Paul's hand. He turned to the door. Then inspiration came. He returned to Paul's bed. 'In the future you will permit me to call you Davenant?'

'Yes.'

'And you will call me Florent?'

Paul nodded.

'Thank you.'

'Davenant!' said Dr. Florent, by way of demonstration.

'Florent!' replied Paul co-operatively.

'*A ta santé, Davenant!*'

'*A la tienne, Florent!*'

Dr. Florent walked to the door, springy with pleasure.

The ludicrous nature of the exchanges suddenly made Paul smile. Dr. Florent, overwhelmed, grinned broadly.

'*Bon soir, bonne nuit, Davenant!*'

'*Bon soir, bonne nuit, Florent!*'

Said *Sœur* Yvette somewhat acidly: 'If you would prefer it, I will go out of the room.'

The door shut. *Sœur* Yvette began to arrange the room for the night. 'It must be very gratifying for you,' she said drily, turning down the blankets and straightening them out, 'that when one honeymoon comes to an end, another one so soon commences...'

The man with the purple, heavy-lidded eyes and earthy complexion was John Cotterell. He stood in the doorway, very thin, monk-like in his long dressing-gown. 'Coast clear?' he whispered.

'John!'

'I said, "Coast clear?"'

'Yes.'

'Good.' John Cotterell closed the door very quietly and tiptoed to the foot of Paul's bed.

'Night nurse been round?'

'Half an hour ago.'

John Cotterell sat down. Then he lowered his chin to his knees. 'Had to climb the service stairs,' he explained, when he had regained his breath. 'All the other times I've come to see you, I've always been caught and sent back.' He coughed. As he raised his hand to his mouth, Paul noticed that his formerly well-kept nails were bitten away and his fingertips were ragged. 'You've heard my news?' he demanded.

'That you've relapsed?'

'What do you mean, "relapsed"?'

'I – '

'Get this straight, I've never been fitter. But tomorrow Vernet's going to give me a pneumo. And if the pneumo doesn't work – the knife!' John Cotterell made a hacking, sawing motion. 'Not bad when there's absolutely nothing wrong with me!' His tone of voice was utterly unfamiliar.

'What's gone wrong?'

'I don't know. Do you think I'm scared out of my wits?'

'Of course not.'

'Vernet does.'

'What absolute rot.'

'This morning I told him again that I was absolutely fit and that I would not agree to any treatment,' he continued. 'Do you know what he said?'

'No.'

'He said that it was a classic pre-treatment reaction and that all it meant was that I was in a blue funk. A blue funk! I told him I wouldn't give a damn if I was to be hanged, drawn and quartered, as long as – ' He started to cough, rocked from side to side in his efforts to stifle it. 'Damn it! Damn it!' he repeated.

'As long as?'

'As long as there was a reason for it.' Then, raising his voice, he cried: 'What's the use of giving a fit man a pneumo? Why shouldn't Vernet have one, if I've got to? How can I lie still tomorrow and let that butcher pump air into me?' And as Paul did not answer, he added: 'Well, say something. For Christ's sake say something.'

'What about your engagement?'

'I've broken it off.'

'Why? Why?'

'I can't tell you.' Then, lowering his forehead into his hands – 'My brain feels as tight as a knot.' He started to cough, rocked from side to side to stifle it. 'Damn it, damn it,' he muttered, wiping his eyes.

'Why have you come to see me?'

'I had to. Besides I think that it's the last time we shall meet.' Paul stared at John Cotterell. He felt an overwhelming impulse to ring for the night nurse. Suddenly John Cotterell got up and went over to the window. 'I wish it were lighter,' he said, shading his eyes with his hands and staring out. 'They say the mountains are covered with flowers – they even grow out of the tiniest cracks and crevices in the rock. Angus and David brought back bunches of gentians and mountain violets this morning.' Suddenly he swung round. 'You are a treacherous, bloody spy!' he shouted.

'What are you going to do?'

'Shut up!' John Cotterell shouted, twisting round from the window.

'What!'

'You heard!'

Both men stared at each other.

'I'm sorry.' John Cotterell smiled evasively. He returned to the foot of the bed. 'There are still uncharted islands in strange seas,' he said.

'What do you mean?'

'A new course, new bearings.'

'John!'

John Cotterell leapt to the side of the bed, his face an inch from Paul's. 'You've been speaking to Vernet! Admit it!' he cried.

'I don't – '

'Shut up! You're spying for Vernet. I see the signs. It's written all over your face. I'm glad I know my friends!' He drew back, lips contorted. 'Vernet's a crackpot. He's mad, bad, dangerous to know, ought to be locked up. I watch him, watch him all the time, every moment, every gesture, nothing is hidden.' He glanced over his shoulder. Then raising his hand to the side of his mouth, he leant urgently across the bed. 'There's something in his skull,' he whispered.

He snatched away the hanging bell-push before Paul's finger reached it. 'Easy, old man,' he said, his voice controlled. The evasive smile returned to his lips. 'I've gone too far. I can see in your face that I've gone too far. Can't you see that it's all just an act. If you don't believe me, question me, ask me anything.' He sat down on the edge of the bed and his tone became urgent. 'I came here to warn you. Now listen,' he said. 'When the ogre's eaten me, he'll start on you – you know that, don't you, Paul? This is your last chance to – ' he broke off, coughed and spat into his handkerchief. 'I've got my plans, but I can't trust you – you play both ways,' he said, rubbing his eyes. He got up and went to the door. 'It's all up with me. You could still escape. But you haven't much time. I'll send you a sign, I'll send you – ' he paused and reflected – 'I'll send you gentians, bunches of them. When you get them, put on your pants and don't stop running till you reach the pancake lands. Otherwise – ' he marked each word with the wag of an index finger – 'OUT GO YOU.'

His lips parted. He watched Paul a few moments, then turned and left the room.

'He is not a coward, not at all,' explained Dr. Vernet, smiling, when, at *Sœur* Yvette's request, Paul had related the details of John Cotterell's visit the previous night. 'To tell a real coward that he is a coward serves no purpose, quite the contrary. I taunted John Cotterell in order to make him react.

'All his trouble is that he was convinced that he was cured, and some facet of his brain temporarily refused to adjust itself to the changed situation. Although this is rare, it is not isolated – at bottom it is the reaction of an optimist. Your difficulty, *cher Monsieur*, will be to adjust yourself to being better!

'However, this morning I managed to induce a successful pneumothorax and it has brought with it, as I anticipated, a complete easing of the mental tension. Cotterell is now as reasonable as anyone in the sanatorium.

'As for you, you are looking far less well than yesterday. Kindly forget the whole incident and concentrate on implementing your own *rétablissement.* I am forced to admit to you frankly that if my whole medical reputation were in the balance, I would prefer to be looking after a hundred Cotterells than one Davenant.'

CHAPTER SEVENTEEN

•

Dr. Vernet had no respect for natural obstacles. 'Fishes!' he would cry contemptuously, or *'Des cailloux, des cailloux!'* each time that the cannula became blocked. Syringes lay in graded rows beside him – all sizes from short, slender tubes with a capacity of five c.c.s to the giant clysters of seventeenth-century French farce. Substituting one for another, he would adjust his technique accordingly, either coaxing up the plunger millimetre by millimetre, or wrenching it with a violence which, even though it unblocked the cannula, gave Paul the impression that his very intestines were being drawn up into the syringe. If both methods failed then he would plunge a second cannula between Paul's ribs in order to provide an additional inlet of air. And continually clearing the cannulas with their trochars, tilting Paul from one side to the other, raising and lowering the end of the operating table, he would exorcise rather than extract great quantities of the stinking exudation.

And gradually over the weeks the secretion became less toxic, formed less rapidly, and was easier to aspirate. To set against this, the side effects of the streptomycin were causing alarm; not only could Paul not walk two paces without support, it was even dangerous for him to sit up in bed, for the outcome of any movement which he made was unpredictable. After great hesitation (for whereas the continued use of the drug might lead to the permanent impairment of Paul's sense of balance, its discontinuance could no less lead to a general spread of the tubercular infection) Dr. Vernet decided to terminate the injections.

This did not appear to bring about any ill effects; Paul's temperature decreased progressively and his nights became less troubled. One afternoon *Sœur* Yvette came into his room and found him propped against his pillows, reading a book; her face broke into that sort of archetypal smile which transcends eloquence.

Sœur Yvette's devotion to her patients could not be expressed in terms of nursing; it was her religion, her passion, the essence of her existence. She sublimated her life to the life which she was determined to save, and by so completely inter-relating the two (and by never hesitating to pledge her own), she usually ended by redeeming both.

Now she felt justified in showing a possessive, proprietorial satisfaction in Paul, shaving him, washing him, endlessly brushing his hair – untrimmed for three months – which fell over his forehead like a mane. Sometimes on her afternoons off she would take tea with him, or, sitting at the end of the bed, eat the chocolates he delighted to press on her; sometimes – after lengthy attention to his toilet – she would invite one of her colleagues to his room and exhibit him as proudly as a mother her child.

John Cotterell, too, made good progress. Paul asked regularly for his news, and at last felt reassured.

It was now mid-June, and in about six or seven weeks the I.S.O. scheme was due to come to an end. This meant that all students who were sufficiently fit to travel would be returning to their own countries. Paul could not repress a feeling of relief that John Cotterell would be remaining a month or two longer than the others; suddenly to have found himself alone would have been unendurable.

And before too long it would be possible for John Cotterell to pay him short visits. One day Paul asked for paper and pencil and wrote his friend a short letter to this effect. *Sœur* Yvette conveyed his reply. It seemed that John Cotterell had learned his lesson and was now determined to consolidate his improved condition by complete inactivity. He was not even prepared to write a note.

One of the consequences of John Cotterell's relapse was that the students had lost the initiative in their campaign for better food. The report had at last reached the committee of the I.S.O., and had been read with sympathy. There had been approbation for the patience which the students had shown: there had been fresh promises for an immediate improvement in the diet. And as was customary, these promises had in no way been implemented. And now that the scheme was reaching its end, it was generally acknowledged that, by continual procrastination and resolute bad faith, the authorities of *Les Alpes* had successfully avoided the granting of a single concession.

As Paul was now discovering, the food for the private patients – though an improvement on that provided for the students – still bore the unmistakable stamp of the kitchens of *Les Alpes*. It was of a slightly better quality, and there was more of it, but the preparation indicated both a frugal imagination and undeviating economies. Each morning the *maître d'hôtel* visited all the rooms of the private patients with the day's menu: there were no alternative courses but for a *supplément* it was possible to order a steak, an escalope or an omelette. (But each was so indifferent that few patients – after an initial trial – bothered to make any changes.) Paul soon learned (it was common knowledge among the private patients), how each of Dr. Hervet's sanatoria was exactly graded in respect of the *cuisine*, medical attention and accommodation which it provided. *Les Alpes*, the second most expensive in the chain, provided equivalent medical attention and accommodation to the *Sanatorium Universel*, the most expensive. The considerable difference in price related solely to the quality, quantity and preparation of the food, and if the *cuisine* at *Les Alpes* had been allowed to become tolerable, it would have resulted in the mass-evacuation of the *Sanatorium Universel*. And while there was no compulsion to patronise one of Dr. Hervet's sanatoria, not to do so was to take one's chance medically, gastronomically and sanitarily in any one of the thousand small, privately-owned clinics which, squat and frequently constructed of wood, gave Brisset the appearance of a prospectors' settlement in the early months of a gold rush.

One day Paul asked Dr. Vernet whether he might be allowed a proper vegetarian *régime*, and the latter said that he had no objection but that it was a matter for Paul to settle with M. Halfont. So Paul asked *Sœur* Yvette to arrange for M. Halfont to call on him.

Two days later, after dinner, M. Halfont knocked very formally on Paul's door, entered, bowed, and said with gravity: '*Monsieur* Davenant, I see you are still not well, but you are already on the good route.' He stood very stiffly, bearing his stomach as a bandsman his drum – one part appendage, two parts embellishment. At Paul's invitation he drew up a chair and sat down.

Paul first made reference to his financial situation. He had been informed by his solicitor that an account had been opened for him at a French bank, but that until the transfer could be made, his sanitorium bills would continue to be settled from England.

'*Monsieur*,' said M. Halfont, raising his hand, 'I prefer not to discuss money. For me I like to think that my clients are my guests and that I render them their food and lodgment as gratuitously as I give my services and *bonne volonté*. Besides I have no fears – you are English! I have never been tricked by an Englishman! The other nationalities, yes – all the days. The Persians and the Greeks – *mon Dieu*! And with the French even some of the best families are not, I am ashamed to say, *comme il faut*. The Italians, as you will credit, have few scruples, but still not so bad as the Persians and the Greeks. Monsieur, you would hardly believe… One day when I have more time, I will tell you… However, with the English I have no fears…' And M. Halfont got up to go.

'I wanted to speak to you about food,' said Paul. 'I…'

'Ah yes. You have lost weight, and you must now eat up. It is very good that you mention it. But then it is very English. In England I always say that you are all Churchills, all *bouledogues*. In France we have much courage, but we are not *bouledogues*. Look at the war! We doubted! The English never! In a sense you are our liberators. But we were ready, *Monsieur*. I myself served no less than one thousand and seven days as section liaison courier in the Alpine Resistance unit. I left the Resistance with nothing but my honour!'

'Yes, but…'

'Ah, I know what you say. It is true. But consider, *Monsieur*, for you a war is one thing, for France it is quite another. When a war is over you start life again, but for us, what is left? Always the same geography. Always surrounded by envious, greedy neighbours. Always exploited by unscrupulous politicians and financiers.'

'The question of food.'

'As you say, the question of food. In Spain, in Italy, in Germany they have all. They plant their crops and their vineyards and they leave their cattle in the fields and the sun and the soil do the work. But here in the Alps we work day and night and at the end we have no harvest and our beefs and sheeps are all muscles from promenading on the mountains and we are *kaputt*. You ask then why we do not manufacture watches as the Swiss? But first we must build *manufacturies*, then we must buy primary matters from other countries, and if we sell the watches at an economic price, we make nearly no benefice at all. Life is very hard here, *Monsieur*. It is well known that in the Alps we have the highest suicidal rate in the world, and that explains itself.'

'*Monsieur* Halfont, I wanted to see you – '

'And I wanted to see you, *Monsieur* Davenant. But then I have too much to do, and it is rarely permissible to me to make the calls I want.

But now you are better, and soon it is you who will call on me. From now on it is a matter of *bon moral.* 'Ow is the moral, *Monsieur* Davenant? I hope that you have a good moral, for you it is all-important, it counts the first. With *bon moral* you get well – this all the world knows.'

'*Monsieur* Halfont, I am a vegetarian and I want a vegetarian diet.'

M. Halfont looked confused and indignant. 'But there are special juices in the meat,' he objected uneasily. Paul nodded his head, but gave fresh emphasis to his request by repeating it.

'Well, it is all for you, *Monsieur.* But I counsel meat – it remake you.' As M. Halfont became more disconcerted, so the quality of his English deteriorated. 'You know – 'alf and 'alf is best. 'Alf vegetables and 'alf meat – a good *combinaison.* And it remakes. The juices are good, very good. For me it is *égal.* You do as you like and we talk of it. Yes – at one moment the French were very worried, but the English had *bon moral.* Steak, you know, and English *rosbif. Monsieur*, I wish you *bonne continuation.*' And M. Halfont shook Paul's hand as he spoke, and hurried out of the room.

As Dr. Vernet had predicted, Paul became less tractable as he grew stronger. Everything irritated him – the food, the staff and the climate (it was getting hotter every day).

Two or three times he was disturbed at night by the sound of rowdyism in the village; to his dismay he learned that certain ambulant invalids were celebrating their National Days. Then *Sœur* Yvette warned him that he had best be prepared for another sleepless night, for it would soon be the *Quatorze Juillet*; this was invariably celebrated by a special dinner and ball at *Les Alpes* and a firework display in the village.

The information so obsessed Paul that he could think of nothing else, and his evening temperature rose suddenly by a few divisions.

Sœur Yvette laughed at him, and on one occasion – without his seeing – pinned a small Catherine Wheel to the mantelpiece and set it alight.

The National Day came and went and was succeeded by a heat-wave. Paul lay all day with his bed-clothes rolled back, his pyjama jacket open; doors and windows were adjusted to provide a permanent current of air. By midday he could hardly breathe. Flies and bluebottles were everywhere – they lopped across the room, they cascaded against the windows, they lay buzzing and spinning in circles on the polished surface of the linoleum. The drinking water flowed warm from the taps and the curtains were drawn against the sun until nightfall. It seemed that it would never grow cool again.

One evening *Sœur* Yvette started on a systematic slaughter of the flies, stamping on them with her feet and squashing them against the windowpanes with her bare hands. Paul begged her to desist and then was violently sick; nor subsequently could he bear to look at the windows, where fresh hordes of flies crawled over a stained and adherent debris of wings, legs and flattened vitals.

And suddenly he became aware of the degree of loathing which he felt for his room. Everything in it had the most repellent associations – the dressing-gown hanging from a hook on the door, the double plug in the wall, the *chaise longue* which ran parallel to his bed. The curtains, the bedding, the very floorboards, seemed impregnated with the smell of pus and ether. He could not bear it another day.

Dr. Vernet had no objection to his moving and another room was available in the front of the sanatorium, where *Sœur* Yvette could still look after him. And so, like the aged and ailing leader of a depleted troop of nomads, Paul set out in his wheelchair followed by a miscellaneous body of *chasseurs* who carried between them a chest of drawers with his clothes and the full complement of his shameful and battered cases.

It was a day of dispersal; trunks packed, corridors filled with dirty paper and old magazines, the tramping of feet, banging of doors and the shouting of instructions and last-minute *adieux.* Most of the members of the British party had assembled for the last time in Paul's room, shaken his hand, wished him well. The floor of his wardrobe was covered with cooking equipment; the residue of the common pool had been stacked on the mantelpiece and the window ledges. Only David Bean had not so far called on him, but a few minutes before the party was due to move off he rapped on Paul's door.

'Well, it's goodbye,' he said, grinning.

'Yes.'

'I don't suppose we'll ever meet again.'

'Probably not.'

'Then let's part good friends.'

'As you wish.'

'You don't bear me any grudge?'

'Why should I?'

David Bean laughed and shook his head. 'I don't know. I've always had the impression that you never quite forgave me for telling you so frankly what I felt about your prospects.'

'You mean when you told me I wasn't going to survive?'

'I didn't put it quite like that.'

Paul sat up and inserted a pillow behind his back. 'It doesn't matter now – so much has happened. But if it interests you, you did manage at the time to cause me quite a lot of extra wretchedness and anxiety.'

'I'm sorry.'

'Why? Surely that was what you intended?'

'Not at all.'

'Really!'

David Bean made no reply.

'Did you in fact believe what you told me or did you make it all up?'

'Can't we talk of something else?'

'And there was another besides myself who was not going to survive,' continued Paul relentlessly. 'Who was it?'

'I won't tell you.'

'Probably not, though I don't suppose you failed to tell him.'

'Are you trying to provoke me?'

'At least I'm not trying to demoralise you.'

'Then I demoralised you?'

Paul shrugged his shoulders. Outside the door there was the sound of the last cases being dragged down the corridor. Emile's voice cried: '*Tout le monde dehors, s'il vous plaît.*' David Bean started to button up his raincoat.

'You told me at the time that someone else was not going ever to return to England,' said Paul.

'Must we discuss it?'

'I'm glad that you find it embarrassing.'

'I admit I've made a mistake and I've said I'm sorry.'

'Very well, then. There's nothing more to say.' Paul picked up an open book from his *table de nuit* and started to read.

'We might at least part friends.'

'It makes no difference how we part,' said Paul without looking up.

'That's just where you're wrong. It makes quite a lot.' David Bean's mouth had tightened.

'You think so?'

'I'm sure.'

'What do you mean?'

'I mean this!' David felt in the pocket of his raincoat and tossed a little muslin sack filled with dried leaves on to Paul's bed. Paul took up the sack and examined it. 'Well?' he asked.

'Petals of the common gentian. My *Larousse* says that they're "*apéritives et toniques*", which is probably why invalids leave their beds at night to gather them on mountain slopes...'

'All of which means?'

'That in default of rue, they can serve for remembrance.'

'I won't need either rue or gentians in order to remember you,' replied Paul.

'Oh, they're not in order to help you remember *me*,' said David Bean, laughing. At that moment someone shouted his name in the passage. 'Just coming,' he shouted back. And, nodding ironically to Paul, he hurried out of the room.

'*Sœur* Yvette,' said Paul, 'could you please let John Cotterell have this letter?'

Sœur Yvette took the envelope and looked at it doubtfully.

'And tell him that this time I want a reply. If he doesn't write by return I shall go straight up to his room and ram his pen down his throat!'

Sœur Yvette handed the letter back to Paul. 'It is time for you to know,' she said, 'that your friend is dead.'

It was two evenings later.

'He was a boy of exceptional character. He gave us a lot of trouble and on one or two occasions I had to speak to him severely. But nevertheless I could not help but like him. After the accident I gave instructions both to staff and patients that in no circumstances were you to be informed of what had happened – you were in no condition to assimilate news of such a nature.' Dr. Vernet was seated in an armchair by the side of Paul's bed.

The immediate shock was over. Incredulity had given way to horror, horror had given way to horrified acceptance. And now the bare facts learned from *Sœur* Yvette had been amplified by Dr. Vernet.

The morning after the induction of the pneumothorax the duty sister had found John Cotterell's bed to be empty. A search had been made of the sanatorium, following which the police had been notified. Then a cowman had reported that he had discovered a young man, half-suffocated, on a mountain pass.

John Cotterell had been brought back to the sanatorium. He was wearing flannel trousers, a pyjama jacket and stockings which were shredded and stiff with blood. Under the pressure of the climb, his lung had perforated. He had been given oxygen but had lost consciousness and had died a few hours later.

'On the day of the pneumothorax,' said Dr. Vernet, 'Cotterell had talked disconnectedly about going up into the mountains in order to pick flowers – for you! This idea must have become obsessive, for when we found him his pockets were filled with gentians.'

'Gentians!' exclaimed Paul.

'Little blue flowers that it is strictly forbidden to pick,' explained Dr. Vernet.

'What became of them?' cried Paul.

'What became of them?' Dr. Vernet looked blank.

'I mean – ' Paul stopped in confusion.

'What a strange question. They were thrown away. But – '

'But?'

Dr. Vernet shrugged his shoulders. 'I was informed that they were retrieved by Bean, who morbidly wished to keep them as a souvenir.' Then he smiled. 'But we too are becoming morbid. In a sanatorium each year brings its crop of surprises – irrational, unpredictable, irrevocable. But let us never forget that the main drift goes on, less spectacular but more significant – the reclaiming of dying men and women. And this brings me to my purpose in visiting you this evening. I wish to speak about your condition and your prospects for the future…'

* * *

Condition: convalescent. Consequences of the relapse: the lung has lost its elasticity, the diaphragm was rigid. The pneumothorax would have to be retained for six years instead of the initial two. Prospects for the future: very fair. Davenant could return to England towards the autumn. He should be able to resume his studies at Oxford in the spring. A disagreeable little episode was drawing to its close…

Dr. Vernet left the room. The cathartic information in respect of John Cotterell had canalised all Paul's emotions. Someone had died, someone was going to recover from a serious illness, four young men were returning from a journey on which six men had set out. Shuffle, cut and shuffle again. Re-deal? Perhaps for the time being the Tarot pack could be replaced face downwards on the chimney-piece. Paul yawned and threw a blanket over the camera obscura of his mind.

He turned off the bedside lamp and waited for his eyes to grow sensitive to the faint luminous lines which framed the curtains – a useful, empirical proof that he was not sealed in his coffin. He was in no pain, his breathing was effortless. He felt as detached from the acute period of his relapse as from everything which had preceded it. It seemed to have happened infinitely long ago, to have been necessary and unavoidable – an essential stage in his physical and moral development.

The immature and hostile reactions which he had so often felt towards Dr. Vernet – curious that he should have fallen into so obvious, so emotional a trap. But then immaturity was the mould in which the whole of his previous life had been cast…

The outline of the curtains now delineated, he closed his eyes. Perhaps sooner or later someone would find out that he had played a confidence trick and that the wrong man had died. But even then, what was there left to fear? Once already he had crossed the border – the worst could be no more than to remain the other side. And meanwhile there was time to sleep.

PART TWO

CHAPTER ONE

•

One of the remaining half-dozen students was Kubahskoi. It was over six months since the induction of his second pneumothorax; his analysis was still positive. One day Dr. Vernet sent for him.

'*Mon cher*, we have tried everything. You must reconcile yourself to returning to a Polish sanatorium.'

'Dear God!' said Kubahskoi, covering his eyes.

'You will be able to go on quietly – much as you do now.'

'Please try something else.'

'There is nothing else.'

'Streptomycin, *docteur*. Please let me have a course of streptomycin.'

'I've told you repeatedly that it would do no good, so let us at least leave your sense of balance intact. You don't want to add broken bones to your other troubles.'

'Then an operation. Anything.'

'The risks would be enormous, the chances of success negligible.'

'I will take any risk.'

'I believe you. Happily our surgeons are not equally reckless.'

'Then what must happen to me?'

'Perhaps with rest, good food and a change of scene…'

It was the perennial difficulty of breaking gently to a patient that his case was hopeless.

'Tuberculin, *docteur*. I have never had tuberculin.'

'Nor has anyone for the last twenty years.'

'*Docteur*, please let me have tuberculin.'

Tuberculin – the first of the scientific illusions. When Robert Koch died in 1910, he believed that he had discovered a specific against the bacillus which bore his name. After many years of experimentation its functions had at last been restricted to laboratory tests. But it was a drug about which, in some respects, Dr. Vernet had always retained an open mind. He felt that perhaps in just a few, very limited cases it might provoke sufficient reaction to…

'All right,' he said suddenly. 'Two months of tuberculin. But if there is no change, you must be prepared to go straight back to Poland.'

* * *

Paul was grateful that he still had Kubahskoi's company. Insufficiently recovered to read for protracted periods, too lacking in concentration to listen to much music, too slow at French to listen to plays or talks on the wireless, too dizzy to obtain any satisfaction from his remedial walks in the corridor, he spent most of the day staring at the ceiling, glancing at his watch, taking his pulse and reflecting on what would have been his lamentable state of mind without the visit of his friend to look forward to in the evening.

One day Dr. Bruneau called on him and said: '*Monsieur*, you have one week in which to revise your table manners. Fork or chopsticks as you prefer – but no fingers!' It was one of a dozen jocular formulas whereby a patient was informed that shortly he was to take one meal a day in the *salle à manger*.

'You have no objection to sharing your table with *une belle Anglaise*?' demanded the *maître d'hôtel*, when the day arrived. None at all.

Une belle Anglaise... He had not known that there was another English patient at *Les Alpes*. Then he remembered. In too great a hurry to throw a dressing-gown over his pyjamas, he staggered out into the passage. It was too late – the *maître d'hôtel* had gone. He took up the house telephone and rang through to the *salle à manger*. 'I've just told the head waiter that I was willing to share a table, but I've changed my mind. Please see that I have a table to myself.'

Judy Bascombe! How could he have forgotten? Some weeks previously she had knocked at his door, a very thin, neurasthenic-looking girl. The pretext for her visit had been to inquire after Paul's health, and to present him with a bundle of women's magazines.

She had seated herself. She had been ill for several years. There was no doctor at home or abroad who had not been baffled by her case, almost no sanatorium of which she had not been an inmate. Her memory for detail was prodigious. She had recounted whole conversations as though she had been reading aloud the parts of a play from a text, her native accent always showing as clearly through the great variety of accents she was assuming as the flush at the apices of her cheeks showed through the layers of powder with which they were coated. And she had brought with her a briefcase filled with a representative selection of her X-ray plates...

Sœur Yvette could not have been more co-operative. The visit was never repeated.

There had been a certain passive animosity between the students and the private patients: the *privés* had looked upon the students as social lepers, professional beggars, *gens de charité*, a species wholly beneath their condescension; the students had returned the compliment by regarding the *privés* collectively as morons, individually as hypochondriacs, nymphomaniacs, moneyed wastrels and black marketeers. It was the customary generosity with which one class, race or nationality assesses the characteristics of another.

Paul's change of status had not modified his opinion – he still felt hostility towards the private patients, and had no inclination to become acquainted with them. But there were two occasions when contact with at least the other patients on his floor was inevitable – at the *consultation* and at the *pesée*. The *consultation* was treated as a social occasion. In the tiny *salle d'attente* fifteen dressing-gowned, carpet-slippered invalids, chattering, cackling, full of expectation, attended Dr. Vernet's summons like a group of hens awaiting selection by their cock. Besides Paul, a Greek named Hourmikos showed little relish for these sessions.

Hourmikos, a swarthy, sturdy man in his forties, had been at *Les Alpes* a fortnight. He spoke to no one, met no one's gaze. His luggage comprised no more than a single suitcase. Although not ill beyond the hope of recovery, it was said that he had resolved to die, and that he was refusing any form of treatment. At the *consultations* he wore a raincoat and a pair of galoshes: he did not believe that it was worth his while to purchase a dressing-gown and slippers.

The *pesée* took place weekly before breakfast: women in kimonos with hair tumbling or turbaned, men unshaven, everyone yawning; the tension of the few who, no longer able to bear the spectacle of their descending weight graph, sought a temporary respite by swallowing glasses of water and secreting small metal objects in their pockets; then the advent of *Sœur* Rose, the good-natured, dim-witted night nurse of *Les Alpes*, who wore an eyeshade and whose uniform was a starched calico smock and blancoed tennis shoes. Never having mastered the technique of the weighing machine, her efforts did little to ease the atmosphere. Weights would be added when they should have been removed, adjustments made for kilos instead of for grammes. The weight indicator would swing with the helplessness of a compass needle in a magnet factory. If someone tried to come to her aid, she would cry: '*Ach! Surtout n'y touchez pas, monsieur, dame, je vous prie...*'

Delmuth, a bald and bulky Fleming with a face divided between benevolence and malice, would contrive to be weighed the first, after which he would station himself at the side of the machine, and give a cry of approbation for each gain in weight, a cry of sympathy for each loss.

'*Eh voilà*!' (in clumsy, throaty French). *Vous avez augmenté de nouveau! Mais qu'est-ce que vous faites dans un sana? Vous devez faire du boxe comme Joe Louis*!'

And for a human skeleton whose very bones were shedding their marrow: '*ça va, vous savez. Qu'est-ce que ça peut vous faire de perdre quelques grammes? Gagner, gagner, toujours gagner, c'est très malsain, vous savez.*'

On one of these early mornings Paul tottered from his bed, wrenched at his hair with a comb, dashed cold water in his face, and staggered from his room. In the passage was the *belle Anglaise*, her hair wound in a soiled scarf, her face liverish and unwashed. 'Ow!' she whined, getting into the lift with Paul. 'Ow! Why do they get us up in the middle of the night?'

The lift jerked upwards. At the landing Paul threw open the gilded doors and the *belle Anglaise* flopped out. He followed her, then halted. At the entrance of the *Service Médical*, sitting negligently in the wheelchair in which often he had been a passenger, was a young girl so lovely that her presence illuminated the corner of the obscure passage: a very new, cherry-coloured dressing-gown covered with light polka dots, a pyjama jacket open at the neck revealing a cool, white throat. She smiled, got up from the chair and walked over to the lift. Paul returned her smile, then, suddenly remembering with dismay his matted hair and unshaven face, strode across to the door of the *Service Médical*.

'Well, *Monsieur*,' said Dr. Vernet to Paul at the *consultation* later the same day, 'it approaches the end of a somewhat movemented – is that the word? I mean *mouvementé* – journey. I can now announce quite certainly that your condition is stable. There is no more secretion. The pneumothorax can continue to be maintained by fortnightly refills. In the pocket of the pleural cavity I have left, as you know, a mixture of oil and disinfectant. This must always remain – it serves a number of important functions.

'We are now at the middle of August.' He flicked over the pages of his desk calendar. 'I counsel you to return to England towards the end of September. In this way you will accustom yourself gradually to the English winter. On no condition make any attempt to return to the university before the spring. I will give you more specialised instructions as the time approaches.'

CHAPTER TWO

•

Paul learned that the girl's name was Michèle Duchesne, that she was Belgian, that she was only seventeen years old, and that her room was two doors along from his own on the same floor. One afternoon he encountered her in the corridor, they both stopped, and he asked whether he might visit her that evening. Smiling, she assented. And so, after dinner, carrying a box of chocolate cats' tongues under his arm, he knocked on her door.

Wearing an open-necked shirt and white linen trousers, she was sitting cross-legged on top of a heap of pillows at the head of her bed. Shyly she extended a hand of welcome. Paul presented her with the chocolates. She thanked him gravely and placed them on her *table de nuit*. Then she invited him to sit down.

Paul looked about him. The extraordinary décor. All the walls were covered with posters and pictures cut from newspapers and magazines. There were generals, dictators, film stars and prize-fighters; one section was devoted to fashions, another to jokes, another to cartoons; down the centre of one wall, like the rungs of a ladder, were the banner titles of a dozen different newspapers: the *New York Herald Tribune*, *Le Monde*, the *Continental Daily Mail*, *La Semaine Belge*, *La Gazette de Lausanne*. Across one trousered thigh lay an open, mutilated newspaper, and poised above it a ruthless pair of scissors.

'*Monsieur*,' she said, speaking in French, '*Monsieur* will kindly cut out the titles of any newspapers not at present on the wall and any pictures which he thinks of interest.'

'Of interest?'

'Gay, evocative or sentimental!'

She laughed at his initial astonishment; she lost all trace of shyness.

'*Un peu*,' she replied when asked if she spoke any English; but she would like to learn more. If *Monsieur* would care to, he could teach her – there would be a useful occupation for him. No, *Monsieur* had no need of lessons from her. No, it wasn't a compliment, *Monsieur* spoke French very well *et avec un bon accent – un bon accent anglais*! No, time did not hang heavily and there were often visitors, and, besides, up to now there had been all the pictures to cut out of the newspapers.

Corroborating her statement there came a thump on the door and an immense black-bearded Spaniard entered. He was holding an Air France travel poster in front of his face and chest. '*Voilà!*' he cried, peering round the edge in order to assess Michèle's reactions. '*Excusez-moi!*' he added, catching sight of Paul.

'*C'est gentil, mais c'est pas tout à fait mon genre,*' announced Michèle critically.

'*Mais, Cheli, je viens de la voler au chef de la gare!*'

'*Alors, ne vous en faites pas! Vous irez en prison, c'est tout!*'

The Spaniard gave a cry of exasperation, re-rolled the poster and slapped it down on the epaulette of Paul's battle-dress. '*Hommage à tous les capitaines!*' he roared. '*N'y touchez pas!*' ordered Michèle. '*Pourquoi? Moi qui suis ancien capitaine dans l'armée du Général Franco!*' He turned to Paul and said in English: 'Make attention to Cheli! She say you to steal, and then when you steal, it is not her *genre*! It is the classic type of the young, emancipated, post-war, decadent, new-look pin-up girl without *principes*!' He put on a pair of wire-rimmed spectacles and beamed delightedly from Paul to Michèle. His name was Manniez, and Paul had often seen him in the *salle à manger*. He always wore a grey, roll-necked pullover and corduroy trousers, and his eyebrows were nearly as bushy as his beard. (Paul, inquiring the meaning of 'Cheli', learned that Manniez, discussing phonetics with Michèle, had postulated that Chinese grammars contained the rule that the European 'r' was pronounced 'l'. 'Cheli', the first fruit of his inductive powers of scholarship, had so pleased him that he had henceforward incorporated it into his own vocabulary.)

A tap on the door announced the arrival of the Baron de la Marelle, a short, stout young man with thick spectacles, large features, a dirty knitted sweater and an open dressing-gown trailing its cords. '*Bonjour, chère,*' he said. And, removing his cumbersome pipe, he brushed Michèle's right hand with his lips. She introduced him to Paul, who extended his hand and was offered a crooked and condescending finger. '*Très peu de monde ce soir,*' de la Marelle commented, raising thick eyebrows at Manniez. Then to Paul, whose room was next door to his own: '*Vous habitez la maison, Monsieur?*'

'We all have that honour,' replied Paul.

'But the honour is all mine,' insisted de la Marelle, and as Michèle laughed and Manniez tittered, he quickly added an insolent little bow in case some trace of irony had escaped him.

The door opened and three more visitors arrived. Then came two Belgians, identical twins with identical conditions. '*Bonjour, belle enfant*,' they cried in unison, and then to de la Marelle: '*Bon jour petit baron*!'

'*Quelles âmes vulgaires*,' commented de la Marelle, snorting through his pipe.

The newcomers had brought pictures cut from their newspapers; Michèle considered each impartially, selecting, accepting and rejecting. De la Marelle floated easily from group to group, puffing out smoke, gesturing with the stained and scaly mouthpiece of his pipe, dispensing graciously his opinions. More patients arrived. Michèle, unselfconscious and modest, still seated high upon her piled-up pillows, smiled, shook hands and stacked fresh cuttings and little presents on her *table de nuit*. Under her directions a middle-aged Dutch banker pinned some of her newer acquisitions to the wall.

'*Attention! Le Docteur Glou-Glou!*' someone shouted.

A false-bearded, false-nosed, twittering creature wearing a white gown and carrying a briefcase, tottered into the room. There was a shout of laughter and cries of '*Salut, Glou-Glou!*' It was a Flemish patient who had been ill for many years, and whose medical impersonations had become so compulsive that even without his disguise he continued to play his rôle, forever trembling, stuttering and uttering his diagnoses in high-pitched, senescent tones.

'Oooooo oooooo,' he shrilled at Michèle. '*Quelle sympathique petite consultation nous allons faire toute à l'heure!*' And cooing maniacally he started to wrestle with his hose-pipe stethoscope, pulling it foot by foot from an inside pocket. Another candidate for the strait-jacket, his assistant on these occasions, opened the attaché-case and removed a rusty saw, pliers and barometer.

'*Va-t-en, Glou-Glou*,' cried Michèle, as he advanced on her. He blew out his cheeks and shook them till they wobbled like blancmanges. '*Dites 'glou-glou-glou'!* ' he commanded, putting one end of the stethoscope against her chest and staring lasciviously down the other.

'*Glou-glou-glou!*' everyone chorused.

'*Silence, les oiseaux!*' He jumped in the air in mock rage.

'*Glou-glou-glou!*'

'Aaaaah!' Waving his instruments, tripping over his stethoscope, he curveted round the room, then stopped, arms raised, legs apart. '*Microbe, Bacille, Koch!*' he cried. '*Microbe, Bacille, Koch,*' everyone repeated. '*Microbe, Bacille, Koch, Koch, Koch,*' he chanted, establishing a rhythm by clapping his hands. Then as the refrain came back to him, he started upon an angular war-dance, symbolically reproducing the ritual medical gestures of the consulting-room.

At the same time, Michèle noticed that Manniez, who was seated beside her *table de nuit*, had surreptitiously opened the box of cats' tongues, and had consumed half the contents. '*Vous êtes ignoble!*' she cried, pulling the box away. She turned to Paul to apologise, and the Spaniard leant over and slapped her face. '*Ne dites plus jamais qu'un Espagnole est ignoble!*' he shouted. Her reflex was immediate. She seized a rubber hot-water bottle and threw it at him. His arm was raised too late – it hit his face and burst. He staggered, and to regain his balance grasped at the curtains, which, under his weight, detached themselves from the framework of the window, and he fell to the floor with them piled on top of him.

In the laughter which followed, no one noticed Dr. Vernet come into the room. Suddenly there he was, a white gown over his dinner jacket, standing incredulous with anger at the foot of Michèle's bed. Oblivious of the reason for the succeeding silence, de la Marelle continued to speak: he was lamenting the sanatorium laundry, and inquiring whether one of the poorer patients, a female student, for example, might, for a consideration, be encouraged to care for his personal linen.

'*Mademoiselle*, I abandon your case,' said Dr. Vernet. De la Marelle looked up. '*Docteur*,' he cried cheerfully, 'you've been hiding from me! Do you know that I coughed all night and that this morning I woke up with a headache? I wonder whether – ' He broke off, succumbing to the stare which Dr. Vernet was directing at Michèle.

'Three times I've said that these *soirées* were to stop,' said Dr. Vernet, his voice quivering, 'and this evening I'm interrupted in the middle of my dinner with the information that another is in progress. Well, make still more noise, invite the bed patients, open all the intercommunicating doors and turn the whole floor into a nightclub – it's for the last time! Tomorrow I shall write to your parents to ask them to – ' He broke off. There were gasps of astonishment. Dr. Vernet swung round. Glou-Glou had crept up behind him and had been quietly ausculting his back. For a moment the two white-coated figures faced each other, Glou-Glou standing with his stethoscope poised in the air, his head inclined forward and to one side, his face vacant and very tense. Then firmly and with great precision he placed the stethoscope against Dr. Vernet's chest. '*Dites "glou-glou-glou"!*' he whispered.

Dr. Vernet caught his arm, looked for an instant as if he were going to twist it from his shoulder. '*Venez. Vous êtes surexcité*,' he said at last. Then to everyone else: '*Revenez tous dans vos chambres.*' And he led Glou-Glou from the room.

In fact Dr. Vernet's dinner had been less interrupted than postponed; as was his practice from time to time, he had ordered it to be put back an hour and a half. Besides Mlle. Duchesne (his attack on her had really been directed at her *entourage*), there were a number of other patients scheduled to receive surprise visits. Hourmikos, the Greek, had announced a fast to the death; he was to be caught with his untouched tray and browbeaten into eating. An amateur photographer was reported to be using his room as a studio for pornographic pictures when the day staff went off-duty; a little discretion and one might catch him – and his models. A female patient (who had recently transferred from a neighbouring sanatorium) was said to lock her door at nine o'clock and then to go to bed with her visiting fiancé; give them a quarter of an hour, then make a dramatic entry through the intercommunicating doors between the bedrooms…

A pity Dr. Hervet refused to employ an additional night nurse; a pity that, employing only one, he did not offer sufficient wages to obtain the services of someone more capable and vigilant than *Sœur* Rose. But even *Sœur* Rose (or *Sclérose*, as Dr. Vernet called her to his associates) had formerly been more effective. It was now rumoured that her muzziness was less attributable to natural incapacities than to a supply of cognac in the medical cabinet of the night-duty room. A little on-the-spot investigation might resolve that question one way or the other.

And during the course of it all there would be one or two parties to break up, and probably half a dozen patients to locate, who – strictly confined to bed – would be missing from their rooms. And then, and only then, would it be possible to start to eat a dinner which, with intense conviction and varying degrees of indignation, he would a dozen times have declared to have been abandoned in the middle.

As far as Michèle was concerned, the upshot of it all was a night tormented by the thought of repacking her cases, of the long train journey back to Liège, of the explanations to her relatives and parents. And although for the next few days she desperately waved away all the heads which protruded round the door, the situation would soon have been the same as before but for the co-operation of *Sœur* Yvette.

If Paul's visits were less discouraged than those of the other patients, it was partly because of the sustained inoffensiveness of his conduct over a long period, partly because, owing to his solitary existence, he invariably arrived unaccompanied. A similar privilege was allowed to Manniez, who specifically claimed the right of access to a co-religionist; and henceforth he never entered Michèle's room without a missal held in his hand like a special visa from the Holy See.

Michèle seemed incapable of remaining in bed. First thing in the morning, at the conclusion of her toilet, she would change her pyjamas for an open-necked shirt and white linen trousers. Whenever Paul called on her, he would find her engaged in sorting out a drawer, rearranging her photographs on the *table de nuit*, or pinning new *images* on the wall. When her meal was served, she would sit at the side of her tray on the bed, one leg crossed over the other, occasionally stabbing at morsels of food with her fork. And at the least pretext she would be up again, searching for a letter, drawing the curtains against the sun, dusting the mantelpiece ('*Ah, je ne sais pas supporter la poussière*'), and the food, tepid on arrival, would become rigid and congealed. When Paul remonstrated with her, she would either pay no attention, or laugh and say: '*Alors, vous avez fini?*'

She had brought with her a number of board-games – ludo, draughts, snakes-and-ladders – and a purposeful selection of school textbooks. One evening Paul found her with a pencil tucked behind her ear and an algebra primer before her on the bed table. 'Ssh! I'm working out a problem,' she said severely, and continued counting aloud on her fingers, muttering her calculations, elaborately inscribing algebraic symbols in a notebook, until Paul said: 'Very well. Since you're busy, I'd better leave.' At which Michèle gave a little cry, announced the problem to be resolved, and bundled her books into a drawer.

Manniez, no less than Michèle, contrived to keep the *décor* of the room in a constant state of flux. He stuck her photographs on to improvised cardboard mounts and suspended them in rows by her bed; he shifted whole sections of *images* from one wall to another in order to permit the greatest possible concentration. It was also Manniez who had provided the three great posters. One, six feet square, advertised a coffee powder by representing a steaming cup of coffee the size of a zinc bath. The second, on the interior of the door, bore the words '*Loterie Nationale*' superimposed on an enormous plane tree from the foliage of which were fluttering hundreds of bank-notes. The last hung opposite her bed, a French travel agency poster, with a view of the Alps and the laconic invocation: '*Passez vos vacances dans les montagnes!*'

Usually Michèle seemed in good spirits, but one day when Paul called on her it was evident that she had been crying. And as they talked she suddenly turned her head away. '*Excusez-moi*,' she said. '*Je suis tellement bête.*'

There was a long silence. 'If I were capable of any spontaneity of feeling, I would know just what to do and say,' thought Paul. He stared awkwardly at the collection of little objects on Michèle's *table de nuit* – the carved ebony negro from the Belgian Congo about whose neck Michèle had hung a medallion of the Virgin; the photographs, as precariously supported, each by the other, as the walls of card houses; the worn missal bursting with the slips announcing the First Communion of her friends; the little circle of lead at the end of a ribbon which, when Michèle held the whole in the air, would answer questions affirmatively or negatively by circling or swinging like a pendulum.

And Michèle, regaining some measure of composure, explained how the isolation, the transition from *pensionnat* to sanatorium, the longing she felt to see her parents, the continual injunctions she received to remain in bed, the uncertainty as to what was going to happen to her, had all, suddenly, and at the same moment, become too much.

'I'm very ashamed, *Monsieur*,' she said, wiping her eyes. And she added: 'But I'm only seventeen.'

'*Monsieur!*' repeated Paul. 'For the rest of our lives I forbid you ever again to call me *Monsieur.*'

'Then like a *poilu* I must call you "*Mon Capitaine*",' she said, giving a little salute, and smiling, though the tears still glistened in her eyes.

Encouraged by Paul, who wished to distract her, she spoke of her early life, of her childhood and upbringing in Liège, of her parents, to whom she was devoted and for whom her stay at *Les Alpes* was ruinous. It appeared that her health had never been robust; there had been pleurisies, two bouts of pneumonia, and several months passed in a preventorium in the Ardennes soon after her tenth birthday. And it was at a *pensionnat* at Lausanne, where she had been studying, that, two months previously, it had been discovered that she was tubercular.

Michèle had never before spoken of her condition, and Paul had deliberately avoided any inquiry, choosing to infer from her appearance and energy that very little was wrong. Now he let his gaze wander from her pale, oval face, with its delicate and sensitive features, to her arms, as slender, shapely and subtle in movement as the necks of swans. And grudgingly he conceded to himself that so slight and graceful a frame was unlikely to be concomitant with high physical reserves.

'I suppose there's not really very much wrong with you,' he said as casually as possible.

She shrugged her shoulders. 'I saw Dr. Vernet this morning, and he asked me if I had a lot of courage. Imagine, *Monsieur* – ' She broke off, correcting herself. 'Imagine, Paul, how much his question frightened me.'

'Did you ask what he meant?'

'Yes. He only smiled and shook his head.'

'There has never been any talk of treatment?'

'Only at first. Dr. Bruneau said I should have a pneumothorax.'

'And then?'

'That was all. He didn't speak of it again. What do you think will happen to me?'

'Oh, nothing much. I'm sure you're not very ill.'

'I would be very frightened to die,' said Michèle. She was leaning forward in her bed, her chin cupped in her hands.

'There is no question of that.'

'Paul, I know I'm very ill.' Michèle looked steadily into Paul's eyes, her own eyes very wide.

'How do you know?'

'I saw a medical report. It was in the drawer of my father's bureau. It said that my condition was grave and that some form of treatment would have to be attempted.'

Paul avoided her gaze. 'I must go,' he said, looking at his watch. 'It's time for the *cure*.'

'Paul, how much longer are you staying at *Les Alpes*?'

'About another month. Long enough to see you well on the way to recovery.' And he smiled at her and left the room.

CHAPTER THREE

•

'Is so bad, the food. Please to sign the declaration.'

Mayevski, a Pole, accompanied by Manniez and Glou-Glou, was visiting all the rooms in search of signatures.

'This will be the sixth petition that I've signed since I've been here,' said Paul with a smile. And as he wrote his name, he added: 'And it will be my last.'

'Because we will get better food?'

'No – because I'm leaving here in a month!'

New patients invariably believed that corporate action must lead to an improvement in the diet. It took a long time before they gained some insight into the workings of the organisation to which the sanatorium belonged.

Initially M. Halfont never failed to accord each complaint and petition his sympathetic attention. Sometimes, as had been his custom with the students, he would expound the difficulty of providing a satisfactorily international cuisine; sometimes he would blame the chef and claim that he was scouring the whole continent for a suitable replacement; sometimes he would say (as once he had said to Paul): 'Always please remember, before complaining, that this is the cheapest sanatorium in the Europa!'

On one occasion when a whole deputation had come to complain about some particularly offensive rissoles, he had said: 'I do not deny that they tasted a little strange, but listen to the explanation. The chef – he's a good fellow really – wanted to give you all a special treat. He chose a celebrated recipe of Escoffier which required prime beef, truffles, fresh cream and abundance of three-star cognac. If anything was wrong, then the fault was Escoffier's – probably the ingredients were far too rich!'

'We never got near enough to taste them,' replied the leader of the deputation. 'Our complaint was about the way they stank!'

When the relatives of patients wrote letters of protest, M. Halfont would reply that there were no real grounds for complaint, at the same time discreetly pointing out that consumptives were notorious grumblers, and that their attitude was a recognised facet of their disease.

And now the close of Paul's stay at *Les Alpes* was marked by a total loss of appetite and a consequent decrease in weight. In order to tempt his palate he went, one day, to a restaurant in the village, but found to his dismay that he could eat barely anything that he had ordered. In Michèle's room he sat silent and still: sudden movement or speech made him feel very sick.

Dr. Vernet correlated the symptoms which Paul at last described to him, and said: '*Monsieur*, you are sickening for a cold or a *grippe* – it will be very interesting to see which.' Two days later, the symptoms having intensified, Dr. Bruneau said: '*Monsieur*, as ever I incline before the opinion of my esteemed *patron*, but I humbly advance the opinion that it is less a question of a cold than of a good bout of 'flu.' In the afternoon of the same day Paul visited the sanatorium dentist, who took one look at him and said: 'My poor *Monsieur*, you are quite yellow. Has no one told you that you are suffering from jaundice?'

'Cold or *grippe*?' Dr. Vernet demanded cheerfully in the evening.

'According to the dentist, jaundice.'

'*Tiens!*' said Dr. Vernet, genuinely surprised, at the same time raising Paul's eyelid with his forefinger. 'In future, when in doubt, I'll send my patients to have their teeth examined. Did he advise you about treatment?'

'I urged him to.'

'But he feared a breach of professional etiquette?'

'I suppose something of the sort.'

'A pity. I am sure you would have found his ordinances more agreeable than mine.'

Jaundice – probably of an infectious nature. Sentence: back to bed, solitary confinement, diet of unseasoned, unthickened, strained soup and boiled, unflavoured rice or macaroni.

When Michèle heard the news she hurried to Paul's room, but was turned back by *Sœur* Miriam, who had just pinned '*Visites Interdites*' notices to the inner and outer doors (that on the inner door being emphasised by the addition of a skull and cross-bones). And on narrow tables between the doors were the lugubrious concomitants of suspected infection – spirit stoves, bowls, soap, basins of water, towels, gowns, masks and hoods.

There then occurred one of those changes which, under any circumstances, leave an invalid breathless with incredulity and indignation – *Sœur* Yvette was suddenly transferred to another sanatorium of the *Société.* To replace her came *Sœur* Valérie, a small, sluttish bigot who was lazy and officious. She irritated everyone – staff and patients; she rampaged up the corridors, she slammed the doors, she abused the *femmes de chambre.*

The tedium of personal disinfection soon discouraged the doctors from visiting Paul more than once or twice a week. The *femmes-de-chambres*, fearing contagion, gave up cleaning the room. *Sœur* Valérie rarely called to make the bed before midday, and a waiter would periodically remove from between the double doors one tray of unspeakable, untasted food, and substitute for it another.

Each morning Paul looked at himself in the mirror. Yellow eyes blinked from yellow sockets at a yellow chest, a yellow stomach and yellow genitals from which flowed yellow urine. And when *Sœur* Miriam came to carry out a sedimentation test, the syringe filled with yellow blood.

He slept and woke, lay for hours in the same position. Dust lined the tables and chairs, the battle-dress (which, days before, he had tossed on to the marble-topped commode), the interior of his nostrils, of his throat, and of his lungs. It radiated at him out of the wireless set, out of his blankets and pillow-cases, settled on his food and crammed the hollows of the macaroni. With each breath all the dust in his area of the room rose and redistributed itself. Where it had become adherent it preserved in outline the base of any object which had been moved or displaced.

Impossible to work, impossible to read – the least movement and he vomited. And in under two weeks he was supposed to be returning to England! He began to wonder whether he had ever really anticipated returning. He had made no plans, had given no thought to where or how he should live.

By his bedside he kept a small photograph of Michèle (abstracted without her knowledge from her album). He sought no information about her condition from visiting doctors, because in isolation he could not have borne bad news.

His one regular visitor was *Sœur* Rose, the dim-witted night nurse.

She would pad up the corridor at six o'clock each morning, wearing tennis shoes, smock, mask and hood, and carrying a tumbler of *Sels de Carlsbad.* Paul would drink the lukewarm water, the *'sels'* undissolved, congealed, hard as rock, remaining fixed to the bottom of the glass to do service on each subsequent occasion. And in the last days of September, when he should have been packing his bags, he was yellower than at the outset.

Even within the enforced limitations of the *régime*, the food was trumpery. The soup was the lachrymal secretion of empty heads and empty larders; the *pasta*, in its centimetre of cloudy exudation, looked like a dish of etiolated, disintegrating octopus; the permitted daily ration of fruit was composed solely of grapes of the size and rigidity of small marbles, testicular pellets taut with a surfeit of seeds set in a glutinous and bitter fluid.

He wrote intemperately to M. Halfont; he had skirmishes with Dr. Vernet; he tried to dust the room with an old pair of pyjamas, till, retching and exhausted, he collapsed upon his bed. All he had achieved were fresh, crazy dust patterns, faces, shapes and every nuance of symbolic physical allusion, a trap for the eyes and, when he was drowsy, an additional source of disorientation.

And all his despair lay in the conscious recognition of the fact that in some way the situation was as native to him as wellbeing to another; not to be yellow, unshaven, sick, isolated, unable to work, deficient in physical and moral resources, was to counterfeit, to cheat, to court and merit retribution.

This was a life which should be ended, should be over, it marched on its knees, it was trash. A few more weeks and the dust would rise above the level of the bed and he would be suffocated; a few more weeks and he would have excreted himself into his bed-pan; a few more weeks and he would dispose of himself as waste *pasta*, no longer consumptive because unfit for consumption. He would run amok, throw the sterilisers out of the window, spread contagion like yellow butter up and down the arteries, alleyways and bolt-holes of the sanatorium mad-house.

He found some outlet for his feelings by systematically indulging a fantasy which had dominated his mind since the beginning of the new illness – the total destruction of *Les Alpes.* Utilising what he remembered of his artillery training, he planned the gun positions in the surrounding countryside from which the sanatorium could best be assailed; he reviewed in detail every aspect of the sanatorium's architecture in order to determine the most telling points at which to direct his fire.

Assuming three medium field guns with only two rounds apiece, where and in what order should they fire? Assuming no artillery, but a troop of men with grenades, where and what should they attack? Assuming neither artillery nor troops, but one reckless partisan armed with charges of dynamite and a knife... The unconvincing problems set in O.C.T.U. test papers now provided infinite scope for his obsession.

Closing his eyes he saw the collapse of pillar after pillar, wall after wall, the main staircase blocked, the liftshaft full of rubble, the corridors and bedrooms strewn with the debris of fallen ceilings, of corpses, fragments of corpses, blood, hair and teeth.

'Of course you may well not be contagious at all,' said Dr. Vernet reassuringly.

'Not contagious!' cried Paul incredulously.

'On the other hand you may be contagious.'

'You mean it's possible that all these precautions were unnecessary?'

'Oh yes, quite possible.' Dr. Vernet flicked the corner of the window-ledge free of dust and leaned up against it. 'To tell you the truth, the liver has never been my *forte* – it is the one organ in the body which has failed to capture my imagination. I prefer something one can get at easily, and take out if necessary. Kidneys aren't bad like that – you take out one and the other swells to twice the size and compensates entirely. And lungs will be the next to come out, you mark my words... '

'And if the liver had managed to capture your imagination, then I might not have had to spend six weeks of isolation?'

Dr. Vernet laughed. 'I told you you should have entrusted your case to the dentist. No, but seriously, your jaundice has gone on for too long, and I begin to suspect other complications. Now I've arranged a little test for tomorrow – not painful but extremely disagreeable. We will insert a tube into your stomach and take an extraction of your gastric juices. And at the same time we'll clear up the little matter of whether you are or not contagious.'

'I'm not going to have any more tests.'

'This is our stock conversation. If you were writing a novel about our relationship you would have difficulty in sustaining much interest in the dialogue.'

'I would concentrate on descriptive passages.'

'Then you would make it still more tedious. Why ever don't you try to get better?'

'I'm told that jaundice is the consequence of bad food.'

'And of about twenty other things. In your own case it is probably attributable to some of the medicaments you received during your relapse. Or then again, it may be the symptom of a spread of the disease to the liver. But whatever the apparent cause, let us not overlook a certain psychosomatic proneness to infection. Still, we shall know more about it tomorrow. Test at half-past nine!'

'Have you any idea what these six weeks have been like to me?'

'I don't know,' said Dr. Vernet, going to the door. 'You must have had a lot of time for reading.'

CHAPTER FOUR

•

The test revealed both that Paul was not contagious and that there were no specific complications; the severity of the attack, nevertheless, would require the maintenance of a restricted diet over a considerable period. The notices disappeared from the doors, the prophylactic bric-à-brac was re-assimilated into the anti-icteric reserves of the *Service Médical*. Paul was once more a freeman of the sanatorium.

Out into the centrally-heated passage shining with the reflection of first snows on polished floors; warmly clad, ambulant invalids passing through the swing doors; Emile delivering mail; the *laborantine*, unselfconscious as a pleasure–boat waiter, balancing a tray of six specimen jars of foaming urine; *Sœur* Valérie, pen in mouth, a report form on the table in front of her, staring thoughtfully at a stack of temperature charts and a bundle of clothes (clean laundry, a suit, a raincoat and a pair of shoes) neatly tied with cord and labelled: *M. Hourmikos.*

The first visitors – Kubahskoi, Glou-Glou, Manniez and certain of the nurses. The missing weeks resumed and restored in a few phrases, gestures and grimaces.

Kubahskoi, arms puffy and contused, condition unchanged, had been granted an extension of a further two months of tuberculin injections. The set of his features, the intonation of his voice, were dry of hope; it was evident that he was adjusting himself to the prospect and the implications of sooner or later returning to a sanatorium in his own country.

Glou-Glou, relatively lucid and controlled (for his mental health was always inversely related to his physical health), had had a relapse. He sat coughing quietly at Paul's bedside, his little, trapped eyes twisting in all directions as though seeking a breach in the cornea through which to escape. Stripped of his medical accoutrements, he looked like a market-place charlatan on the run, one whose stock had been seized, but whose inside pockets were bulging with a residue of unguents, potions and specifics.

He spoke sensibly, coherently; when a cough forced him to raise his portable *crachoir* to his lips, he hurriedly sounded his chest with knuckles and crooked fingers, at the same time whispering barely audibly: '*Glou-Glou, dites: "glou-glou-glou"*.'

Manniez, very satisfied with himself, announced his condition to be comfortable, almost consolidated, not worse, certainly in no way worse, better if anything, better, that is to say, in so far as it could be better, for inasmuch as it was almost consolidated there was little scope for betterment, and it had now been almost consolidated for – and he broke off to count the months in Spanish on his fingers. 'I am now almost consolidated since nearly six months!' he said proudly, and his beard expanded an inch on either side, the only visible symptom and symbol of the smile which it concealed. And now, did Paul want (or did he not want?) to buy a second-hand accordion in splendid condition at a throw-away price? There was no more therapeutic or melodic way of gently re-conditioning all the muscles of the upper half of the body. 'Buy now,' he advised, 'a real occasion. Today you learn to play and tomorrow you make Cheli dance!'

And Hourmikos, whose clothes were awaiting disposal, had accomplished his modest purpose. It was the nurse who had attended him who recounted to Paul the course it had taken. He had resisted every attempt to make him eat; nevertheless he had been basically so strong a man that it had taken a relatively long time before his fast had taken effect. Each day he had had violent disputes with Dr. Vernet and Dr. Bruneau; on one occasion when Dr. Vernet in a fury had ordered him to take his temperature, Hourmikos had snapped the thermometer in two and had tossed it at the doctor's feet.

On the day that he had died, his nurse had made a last attempt to get him to take some nourishment. Hourmikos had smiled slyly and had replied that he would do so on one condition – a condition which he could only whisper in her ear. 'I will eat,' he murmured very weakly, 'I will eat if you will be so good as to let me put my fingers up your skirt.' The nurse had slapped away the skeletal hand prematurely raised. 'Wicked man,' she had cried. 'God will punish you for your evil thoughts!' But her admonitions had had no effect, and each time she had gone near him he had persisted in obscene gestures and demands. And as he had died, he had cursed her, saying: 'Only the Queen of Bitches would refuse a dying man the right to touch it for the last time.'

* * *

Michèle. Every sound in the passage, every knock on the door, and Paul asked himself: 'Is it she?' His thoughts had so often turned to her during his weeks of isolation that he had had to suppress them as aberrant, anachronistic. But now that at any moment she might be calling on him, he so feared her reaction to his deplorable appearance that he would have given anything to have reverted to the circumstances of his former putative contagion.

To make himself more presentable, he had shaved off the beard he had grown, realising only too late how well it had served to conceal the glabrous, yellow contours of his cheeks.

Then when she didn't come, he became the prey of another sort of panic. Perhaps she had forgotten him. Perhaps she had formed an attachment elsewhere. Perhaps the whole concept that any feeling had ever existed between them had been no more than the wishful elaboration of his imagination.

And when at last she did come (which was immediately on learning that the isolation notices had been removed) she ran without knocking straight into the room, stopping abruptly and raising her hand to her mouth in confusion as she suddenly reflected on the indiscretion of her mode of entry. But as she looked at Paul her confusion turned to dismay, and Paul, who had been holding his bedclothes about his chin, now pulled them above his nose.

She insisted that he bare his face, and when, protesting, he did so, she considered it gravely. (And when on subsequent occasions he would grip the top of his sheet and pull it upwards in nervous concealment, she would laugh and say: '*Ce n'est plus la peine, pauvre Chinois, j'ai déjà tout vu. Songez donc que je suis une fille chinoise, douloureusement frappée d'une vilaine blanchisse!*'

She looked in even better health than formerly and utterly free from anxiety. This, coupled with the fact that it appeared that she was no longer confined to her room, led Paul to assume that her condition had greatly improved. She laughed, however, when he gave expression to this opinion, and replied that Dr. Vernet had done no more than relax his initial severity, allowing her to get up for half an hour each evening on the understanding that she did not stir from her bed during the remaining twenty-three-and-a-half hours. And carelessly she added the detail that two or three weeks earlier she had had the induction of a pneumothorax, and that soon Dr. Vernet would be performing an operation for the cutting of the adhesions.

Unfortunately it was not so straightforward as all that. Whenever Dr. Vernet screened Michèle, he commented with a groan: '*Mademoiselle*, you have so many adhesions that whether we shall ever manage to cut them, God alone knows.' The reiteration of this remark at last so distressed her that one day, after a consultation, she rushed to Paul, crying: 'I know that there are lots of adhesions, but why must he keep on telling me?'

And then one afternoon on a medical round Dr. Bruneau asked whether she had been told that as there was practically no possibility of a thoroscopy being successful, Dr. Vernet had decided to abandon the pneumothorax. And a little later Dr. Vernet sent for her, apologised that he had not given her the news himself, and then confirmed the substance of what she had already learned from Dr. Bruneau. She was at first incredulous (for in her own mind she had never doubted that she would have the operation, and that its outcome would be successful). And then, when Dr. Vernet thought that he had brought the matter to a close, she started to protest, to plead; but he was adamant, reasserting that the chances of the operation's success were not remotely commensurate with its risks. 'There are thick, multiple adhesions, *Mademoiselle*, between your lung and the main artery. There are even adhesions to your heart…' There was nothing to be done and no other treatment to be attempted. He had acquainted her parents with the facts, and it was now up to them to decide whether they wished her to remain in Brisset or to return to Liège.

'Believe me, *chère Mademoiselle*,' he concluded, 'if it were the question of my own daughter, I would be forced to make the same decision.'

'*Soit!*' said Michèle, getting up from her chair and offering her hand to Dr. Vernet. 'So it's really all up with me,' she added.

'We never think or speak in such terms, *Mademoiselle*.'

'But is it not the truth?'

'You have every chance of recovery. Rest, good food – ' Dr. Vernet broke off, realising that for once he had failed to introduce into his voice the requisite note of conviction.

In Paul's room, Michèle's courage temporarily deserted her. Her entry woke him from an afternoon dream so horrible that for some moments he was unable to orientate himself; when, however, he made a movement to turn on the bedside lamp, she begged him to leave the room unilluminated.

She sat at the foot of the bed, waited till she had proper control of her voice and of her breathing, then repeated what Dr. Vernet had told her. And suddenly her control broke down, and she wept, covering her face with her hands. Paul, tense with horror, tried to comfort her, reassure her, stumbling grotesquely between the clumsy locutions of consolation and the outraged realisation of his most veiled and secret fears. At one moment he stretched out his hand to touch her shoulder, but she shuddered and drew away from him. Her sobbing stopped, but she remained with her head buried in her hands. 'Michèle,' whispered Paul, 'I swear to you everything will be all right.' She got up and went towards the window, looking out for a moment across the mountains, her tear-stained face just visible in the reflected glow of the setting sun. Then, without a word, she left the room.

The next morning, coldly, almost hostilely, Dr. Vernet said to Michèle: '*Mademoiselle*, I have decided to look inside your chest.' Before she could smile, before the preliminary movement of her lips, he raised a cautionary hand. 'Do not misunderstand me – there is no question of a thoroscopy, no question of cutting any adhesions. It is – and I repeat it – merely that I have decided to look inside your chest.' And again, because he saw that she was about to speak, he silenced her: 'Do not erect any false superstructure of hope, do not exaggerate in your mind anything that I am saying. My intention is to satisfy my curiosity (causing you in the process a certain, inevitable degree of pain) and I offer you no further recompense than the fee for my services.' And with a quick nod, and a curt '*Bonjour, Mademoiselle*,' he strode out of the room.

Laughing with excitement, Michèle ran to tell Paul the news. All Dr. Vernet's recommendations and reservations had been in vain; she neither considered nor contemplated them an instant. 'I knew he would do it, I knew he would do it,' she repeated. Her happiness was overwhelming, her confidence in life was both vindicated and restored. Her enthusiasm was so infectious that it disarmed Paul's critical faculties, and it was not until she had left him that he reflected on how an operation too dangerous to perform one day had become in her eyes no more than a formality the next.

Michèle's visits to Paul increased progressively, and no member of the sanatorium staff had the heart to reprove her. Doctors and nurses behaved towards her with extreme mildness. De la Marelle sent her delicacies out of the hampers which he regularly received from his home in Normandy. Glou-Glou brought her a phial of the notorious Erlinger serum (which he claimed both to have invented and to be currently employing in re-establishing his own health), and Dr. Florent presented her with his school edition of Molière, explaining – with some confusion – that though the volumes did not look much, it was what they contained which mattered.

And Michèle, the hem of her cherry-coloured dressing-gown swirling about her calves as she hurried down the corridor, or darting into Paul's room wearing no more than her open-necked shirt and white linen trousers, seemed unaware of the abnormal, the exceptional, degree of anxiety and solicitude which her situation was attracting. Her slender, boyish figure fitted sideways into an armchair, her trousered legs trailing over the arms, she would talk easily, light-heartedly, with Paul, to all appearances no more disturbed by the prospect of the future than she was by the present or the past. And when Dr. Vernet (fearing the state of mind which might follow upon disillusion) felt impelled to repeat his initial strictures concerning the operation she interrupted him, saying: 'I know, I know, you're going to cut me up just for your own amusement and to make a bit of money.'

A date for the operation was announced; it was cancelled on the evening before it was due to take place and put back by a couple of days. Michèle, who had been psychologically and physically prepared, reacted to the news with nervous impatience. 'It would have been almost all over now,' she protested to Paul, clenching and unclenching her fists. Then she made a conscious, almost visual, adjustment to the revised situation, and made no further comment on what had occurred.

On the actual evening before the operation she was delayed in reaching Paul's room by certain pre-operatory treatments and preparations; when at last she arrived, she looked so alone, so young and so menaced that Paul closed his eyes. A large swelling under one arm indicated the presence of a preliminary dressing: her slender neck looked as if it had been bared for the guillotine.

She had brought with her her draughts board, and without a word she set it up on the table by Paul's bed and drew up a chair. They played several games with the nervous intensity of the occupants of a condemned cell, till at last Michèle tossed a handful of the pieces she had won on to the duvet and said: 'I can't go on playing any longer.' She went over to a table and sat on it, swinging her legs. Then she walked about the room, looking at books, straightening objects, flicking away dust.

'Oh! I'm so tired of this sanatorium,' she said. 'I will be glad to get back to my *pensionnat*.'

'You'll be back there very soon.'

'Why do you say that when you don't believe it?'

'But I do believe it.'

Michèle picked up a magazine and started to turn over the pages.

'You know, a thoroscopy is not so terrible,' said Paul; 'I had quite the wrong idea before mine. I – '

'Oh! do stop!' she broke in, tossing the magazine on to the bed. 'I can't bear another word. No one here ever talks about anything else.'

'I'm sorry.'

'This morning in the *Service Médical* I overheard *Sœur* Miriam talking to one of the sisters. She said: "*La petite Duchesne* believes in miracles. But in fact there's not one chance in a hundred that her thoroscopy will be a success." You understand – "not one chance in a hundred"!'

'Michèle!'

'Michèle!' she echoed. She came close to him. 'Do you think like everyone else that I'm so naïve that I don't know my life is in the balance and that all the odds are against me?'

Paul stammered, and shook his head.

'Then you do!' she cried.

'No. No, I don't.'

'*La petite Duchesne!* So childish, so moronic that she believes everything that she's told! You see! And that's the reason why you dare say that you believe I'll soon be back at my *pensionnat!*'

'That's not the reason.'

'Then what is?' she demanded furiously.

'I can't tell you.'

'You can't tell me!'

'No.'

'Why?'

'Because it's a bad reason, hopeless, futile, pathetic, of interest and significance only to me,' cried Paul, his own anger suddenly rising.

'You mean?'

'Nothing.'

'Of course you mean nothing!'

Paul turned from her gaze. 'I believe what I've told you and I believe it because I've got to believe it.'

'Why? Why?'

'Because I must. Because – '

'Because?'

'I won't tell you.'

'Because?'

'Because I love you.' He turned back to her savagely. 'Don't say anything. Don't reply. I'll be mocked no more by you, Michèle. I love you and I've loved you since first we met. Don't look at me as if I'm mad. I'm sorry if I distress you, but I had to make it clear that I was not talking idly. I'm committed. And because I'm committed, I've got to believe that the thoroscopy will succeed.'

He reached out to take her hand, but she drew away from him as she had done several evenings before. 'I must go now,' she said, glancing at her watch, 'Vernet must already be sharpening his knives.' She turned at the door to wave good night, then seeing the expression of pain on Paul's face she ran towards him. He clasped her desperately, held her face in his hands, covered her features with kisses, pressed his lips against her lips until the pain made her gasp, and under his teeth thin fillets of blood spread from her lips to his mouth.

CHAPTER FIVE

•

The next morning he crossed her briefly in the passage outside the *Service Médical.* An ill-natured, middle-aged female patient, knowing that Michèle was to be operated on during the day, demanded of her: 'Are you frightened, *Mademoiselle*?' 'Certainly I am very frightened,' Michèle replied quietly. Then seeing Paul, she handed him the envelope, and returned down the passage to her room.

Back in bed, he opened the envelope.

3 heures le matin

Mon cher Paul,
C'est avec le sourire et avec joie que je vais à la thoroscopie, car d'avance j'ai tout offert à Dieu pour votre guérison, qui, croyez-moi bien, Paul, m'est mille fois plus chère que la mienne. Excusez-moi de vous le dire, mais je sais que la vie n'a pas été très gaie pour vous. Cela doit changer, vous le méritez tant. La vie est belle, Paul, il faut l'aimer de toutes ses forces et lui sourire malgré tout.

Pardonnez-moi toutes ces parôles – je me mêle sans doute de ce que me regarde pas. Vous savez, peut-être, que mes parents ne peuvent pas venir. Vous avez été si gentil pour moi. Je n'avais aucun droit de vous avoir parlé comme j'ai fait tout à l'heure – j'espère seulement que vous ne m'en voulez pas. Votre intérêt pour moi m'a fort touchée, m'a beaucoup émue.

Au revoir, Paul. Je pense à vous,
Michèle.

At midday Paul learned from the *femme de chambre* that Michèle had just been taken from her room. A little later Dr. Bruneau called on his morning round. 'You are still very yellow, *Monsieur.* You must keep very strictly to your diet,' he commented. Then he added gratuitously: 'The little Duchesne is having her operation today. What a state everyone is in!'

Waiting. He lay very quietly, eyes staring at the ceiling, ears no less alert for each step in the passage than during his first weeks in the sanatorium. Lunch came and he sent it away again. In the whole world only two factors at this moment mattered – Dr. Vernet's skill and Michèle's powers of resistance. He had no rôle. He was an omnivorous mouth, a digesting stomach, a Pavlovian heart pounding to no effect on its static base. 'The little Duchesne is having her operation today…' At this moment, at this precise and awful moment.

Perhaps Dr. Vernet had seen that nothing was to be done and had given up the operation. Perhaps Michèle had already been taken back to her room. Paul got up hurriedly and went along the passage. Standing outside her door, he knew the room was empty. Nevertheless he knocked and went inside. The bed was prepared for her return – the sheets were turned down and a back-rest had been inserted beneath the pillows. Newly fixed above the bed, surmounting a newspaper reproduction of a Flemish *pietà*, was an ivory crucifix.

He returned to his room and walked up and down until he was exhausted. Michèle, nude to the waist, strapped to the operating table, instruments protruding from her side, her whole slender body… Crack across his thoughts came the memory of a young girl whose heart had failed during the course of a long, complicated thoroscopy some months earlier. Panic. He went to the door and pulled it open. The passage was deserted, except for *Sœur* Valérie.

'Sh!' cried *Sœur* Valérie. 'It's still the *cure de silence.*'

'*Mademoiselle Duchesne* – ' started Paul.

'The operation is still going on. What do you expect? Now go back to bed!'

Paul sat down on his bed, re-read Michèle's letter.

Three hours had now passed since she had left her room. What was happening? Most thoroscopies took no more than an hour or an hour and a half. He waited another twenty minutes. He heard *Sœur* Valérie leave the passage, then there was the sound of whispers and a door opened and shut. Able to control himself no longer, he set off once again for Michèle's room. It was still empty. Flowers which he had ordered for her had now arrived. And lying on the writing table, in *Sœur* Valérie's childlike hand, was the unfinished notice: PAS DE VISI…

The door opened and in came *Sœur* Valérie, carrying a case of sterilised needles and some phials of morphine. 'Ah, no!' she cried. 'This time you've gone too far. I'm going to report you to the doctor.'

Chased back to his room, Paul waited, watch in hand, for the end of the *cure*. At four o'clock the doors along the landing started to open and waiters began to serve tea. Paul went into the passage. There was still no sign of Michèle.

On an impulse he went to call on Manniez in case somehow news had reached him. Manniez, wearing a roll-necked, check pullover and a woollen cap, was in bed studying catalogues of goods which he ordered singly or in small quantities from Spain and resold in the sanatorium and the village.

'You wish to buy one very good under-garment?' he said, jumping out of bed and pulling a large carton out of the wardrobe.

'I came to see if you had any news of Michèle. She has been away for more than four hours...'

'No. No. I have no news. You have any news?'

Paul shook his head.

'Look, Davenant,' said Manniez, 'I ask you only fifteen hundred francs for this undergarment. Here you pay six times this. She fit you to ravish.'

Paul found himself feeling the quality of the pants which Manniez was thrusting at him. 'No, thank you,' he said. He turned to the door.

'Well, twelve hundred francs just! The lowest yet. The tissue is without equal for keeping hot!' Manniez, believing Paul's departure to be a feint aimed at further lowering the price, pursued him into the passage. 'A thousand francs,' he cried, 'and I voluntarily lose my benefice!'

He visited Michèle's room twice during the next hour. Returning just before the five-thirty *cure*, he was about to knock when he heard the sound of people moving about and smelt ether coming from under the door.

Too sick to go forward or back, he leant against the framework of the doorway. With Michèle less than five yards away, the result of the operation seemed as inaccessible as ever. To knock at the door would lead to ignominious dismissal. But to continue in suspense, when all was resolved, was unthinkable. He turned away and walked up and down the passage; he knew that for the moment he was too distraught to face the finality of the news. Suddenly Dr. Vernet came through the swing doors. He was wearing a smart, well-pressed suit, looked alert, purposeful, fresh, in brilliant health, his hair newly brushed, his face shining from the toilet he had just completed. And yet for five hours this man had been leaning over an operating table…

'*Bonjour, Docteur.*'

'*Bonjour, Monsieur.*'

And Dr. Vernet passed down the passage and out through the service exit, and the question which he could have answered better than anyone had not been posed.

Cursing his shame, his sickly appearance, his wretched, patched dressing-gown, his capacity in life to do no more than lounge up and down the passages of institutions, Paul went back to his room, slammed the doors and climbed back into his ruffled bed. He felt that he had as much hope that Michèle would return his love as that she would fall in love with the concierge. He stared at his discoloured hands. 'Every external part of the body turns yellow except the hair and the nails,' Dr. Vernet had explained to him at the inception of his jaundice. But his nails showed as yellow as if the flesh beneath had been stained with nicotine. Oh God! Oh God! He should have died during his relapse. He should never have been born.

A knock at the door. It was *Sœur* Juliette, the elderly nurse who cared for patients in the immediately post-operative stages.

'*Monsieur* Davenant?'

'Yes.'

'Please come to the room of *Mademoiselle* Duchesne.'

Paul hurried after her, pulling tight the cord of his dressing-gown. 'What is the result?' he called out desperately. 'The operation has succeeded,' said *Sœur* Juliette, 'but the consequences are in the hands of God.'

CHAPTER SIX

•

Dr. Vernet had never done better. (Later he was to write in Michèle's *carnet*: '*Chère Mademoiselle, vous êtes, pour moi, une cause de "péché d'orgueil"; mais aurai-je dû l'avouer?*') At a medical conference on the morning of the operation he had exhibited Michèle's X-ray before a number of his colleagues, and they had been unanimous in declaring the case inoperable. He had reserved his own opinion; of those present, only his personal assistants had been aware of his intentions.

The first direct view of the interior of Michèle's chest had shown the condition to be even more complex than had appeared from the X-ray plate. Dr. Vernet had been tempted to abandon the whole project *sur-le-champ*. What was the purpose in cutting a great mass of adhesions, of running considerable operational risks, of inflicting a formidable degree of pain, if the outcome was to be a post-operative pleural effusion which would lead to the re-adherence of all that he would so laboriously have detached?

He had allowed his assistants to look through the thorascope; their expressions, the shakes of their heads, had shown that they did not anticipate that their *patron* would proceed with the *intervention*. Then suddenly the fanaticism which opposition invariably provoked in him, which gave every obstacle the appearance of a challenge, had begun to dominate his reactions. Reinforced in his attitude by the knowledge that his patient had no other hope of survival, he had taken up his instruments, and, to the incredulity of everyone present, had set to work.

Initially he would not even have contemplated the operation if he had felt any doubts in respect of his assessment of Michèle's character; nevertheless her display of *sang froid* surpassed his expectation. Five hours of intensive, often agonising, manipulation, and she had borne all in silence.

At the close of the operation, each assistant had seized his hand; he had rebuked their enthusiasm. 'Await the consequences before congratulating me,' had been his whispered comment. But he knew that he had never worked to better effect.

Péché d'orgueil... In England it was generally held that multiple adhesions could not be cut: provided all went well, he would send off copies of pre- and post-operatory X-rays to the principal British medical journals. In America the practice of the pneumothorax was falling into disrepute owing to the reluctance of American surgeons to commit themselves to the performance of extended thoroscopies; documentation of his latest achievement addressed to the right quarters could not fail to make its impact. And in Stuttgart, where next month he was to address the Medical Council on the principle of the application of collapse therapy, the case would serve as a dramatic postscript. Provided, always provided, that all went well…

Michèle was brought back barely conscious to her room. Her pulse-beat was irregular; she was in a high fever; loss of blood necessitated an immediate transfusion. During the operation she had made *Sœur* Juliette promise that on returning she would be allowed to see Paul. When all the doctors had left the room, *Sœur* Juliette, dismissing the objections of *Sœur* Valérie, kept her word.

Paul stood by the side of Michèle's bed. She smiled at him, her face as white as that of the ivory Christ on the wall above her. He took the hand which she opened on the counterpane but had not the strength to lift. *Sœur* Juliette left the room, and Paul dropped to one knee, kissed her hand, raised it to his eyes and his brow. Then he gazed at her with the intensity of one who does not dare believe the validity of what he sees.

In the way that an outrageous gamble, when it does succeed, sometimes succeeds outrageously, so Dr. Vernet ended by sweeping all the winnings from the board. Not merely were there no major complications, but even the minor, routine complications associated with the most straightforward type of thoroscopy did not occur. Three days after the operation, Dr. Vernet felt sufficiently confident to pronounce it as having completely succeeded.

Nevertheless, he hastened to qualify his statement. For two months Michèle must remain in bed; any imprudence, any relaxation of self-discipline, and she might still provoke the pleural effusion which would lead to the undoing of all his work. 'Your future is in your own hands,' he said severely. 'Try to deal with it as circumspectly as I did when it was in mine.'

Within a few days what had initially appeared miraculous appeared miraculous no longer – it was implicit in everyone's attitude that the operation could have had no other outcome. The general interdiction on visitors was raised. Patients drifted in to offer their *félicitations* and good wishes; they stayed to discuss their own conditions or the gossip of the sanatorium. Manniez re-established himself with his missal; de la Marelle, unwholesome pipe between his teeth, thick eyebrows arched in permanent surprise, found only too many pretexts for visiting Michèle's room.

Michèle regained strength with astonishing rapidity. Schoolbooks, maps and geometrical instruments reappeared from cupboards; the white, open-necked shirt and linen trousers replaced the more conventional night-dresses of the immediately post-operational period.

Glou-Glou, who had now taken to his bed, made repeated requests to be allowed to see her. One day *Sœur* Juliette, taking Michèle back from the *Service Médical*, wheeled her into his room. But Glou-Glou, engrossed in the dissection of a deceased pet goldfish, claimed first that he did not know her, then insisted that she had called on him for a consultation. Then when, in exasperation, *Sœur* Juliette wheeled her away, he wept for the rest of the day, declaring that he had been tricked, that his visitor had not been Michèle, that the sanatorium authorities, aware of his love for her, were deliberately and callously abusing him with counterfeits.

Paul attended upon her, shopped for her, spent hours in her room. His visits began early. The breakfast coffee which was served to the patients was invariably tepid; for some time past he had taken to reheating his own on the portable stove left him by the students. Now, since the operation, he collected Michèle's coffee and reheated it at the same time.

He quickly discovered that he had insufficient reserves of energy with which to discharge his new commitments. The reflection of his sickly morning face in the mirror above the wash-basin made him dread the moment when he would have to show himself to Michèle; the quarter of an hour earlier which he had to get up in order to complete a partial toilet before collecting coffee, seemed to sap his strength for the remainder of the day. Accordingly he relaxed all his habitual occupations: during the morning and afternoon *cures*, instead of reading or studying, he slept.

In the evening he would always feel better. He would sit at the end of Michèle's bed, and when the other visitors had left and the sanatorium had become still, he would sometimes lie at her side. Once, in this way, they both fell asleep, and Paul tiptoed back to his room at two o'clock in the morning, thankful that he had had the good fortune to wake up before the arrival of the *petit déjeuner*.

CHAPTER SEVEN

•

Sœur Valérie had appointed herself guardian of the sanatorium's morals, and her first foray on their behalf was with Mayevski the Pole. At no time had their relationship been easy. Mayevski, who had become the friend and table companion of Manniez, had a poor grasp of English (the language in which each linguistically corrupted the other) and absolutely no grasp of French.

Sœur Valérie disposed of one word of English – 'yes'. For imponderable reasons she substituted this word for *'oui'* in her ordinary conversation, quite irrespective of the language group of the person to whom she was speaking. This concession apart, she worked on the assumption that the French language, if spoken slowly and with sufficient distinctness, was intelligible to anyone. She would call on Mayevski and, in a tone of voice which penetrated the double doors, would repeat: '*Vous-devez-être-chez-vous-à-partir-de-dix-heures. Si-vous-êtes-encore- une-fois-absent-de-votre-chambre-je-parlerai-à-votre-sujet-aux-médecins.*' Mayevski would be heard to laugh heartily and to reply: 'You silly old bitch. I do not understand one word of what you say.'

One evening *Sœur* Valérie went to Mayevski's room at ten o'clock and remained there until he returned four hours later. He said: 'Now I see what you want. But you are too late. I've just done one, and I'm too tired to do another.'

The next morning *Sœur* Valérie demanded Mayevski's summary expulsion from the sanatorium. If she had had wider experience of private sanatoria (she had previously worked in a state sanatorium) she would have acted less precipitately.

At *Les Alpes* – as in most private sanatoria – sexual licence was discouraged, but not prohibited. (Prohibitions were the prerogative of State institutions. Managements of commercial sanatoria were well aware that the most significant attraction which they had to offer was a relative absence of restrictions.) Love, and its course, were facilitated by the provision of intercommunicating doors between the bedrooms. Sometimes chance provided an auspicious neighbour; more often it was the consequence of a discreet change of apartment.

At the sisters' table, discussion of the patients' morals was the theme of every meal; bitterness and tension were engendered by the fact that liaisons between sisters and patients, and even between doctors and patients, were not infrequent. The elderly and preternaturally ill-favoured were unshakable; they formed a tight-lipped alliance for the suppression of vice. Where no doctor was involved, they harried the offenders in their charge, visited their rooms at the times they considered least propitious, submitted endless reports and protestations to Dr. Vernet – (with the probable outcome that a patient thus victimised would eventually move to the floor of a morally less exigent sister).

Dr. Vernet's reactions depended upon his private feelings towards the offender, and upon the degree of authority he was able to exercise. The irregularities of certain patients, whatever their circumstances, would be passed over; towards others he would behave ruthlessly. Where a patient was sponsored by an organisation, where a wife was financed by her husband, his power was often considerable, and he did not scruple to use it. Initial warnings, if disregarded, were implemented; organisations, scandalised parents, husbands would receive graphic reports of the behaviour of their *protégés*. On Dr. Vernet's advice, pocket money would be withheld, visits suspended, divorce actions threatened; every variety of punishment would be advocated but that of the removal of the offender.

Patients who financed themselves – and these constituted the majority – were less pregnable. And Mayevski did not merely finance himself, he occupied the most expensive corner suite in the sanatorium.

Dr. Vernet being engaged in the operating theatre, *Sœur* Valérie took her plaint to Dr. Bruneau, who, before she had made much progress, regarded her sourly and said: '*Sœur Valérie, fichez-moi la paix avec vos histoires.*' Spitting with indignation, she trapped Dr. Florent, and harangued him in the corridor. Dr. Florent, who for a long time had been shocked by Mayevski's behaviour, reacted uncharacteristically. Believing that later he would be able to justify his action to Dr. Vernet, he went straight off to Mayevski and informed him that his conduct had rendered his continued presence undesirable. 'Ho! Ho!' laughed Mayevski, 'then I depose myself in a magnifico, nothing-barred sana in the Swiss Alps!'

The news reached M. Halfont. M. Halfont, horrified at the prospect of the further depletion of his half-empty sanatorium, hurried off to Dr. Vernet. Dr. Vernet, who had just finished operating, listened to his story unemotionally. He had absolutely no interest in Mayevski, either as a person or as a case. He knew the extent of his activities. Mayevski slept in rotation with three sex-hungry women – an excessively corpulent sister, a sub-normal Italian *femme de chambre*, and a smooth-skinned Maltese patient whose fear of conception was so great that the precautions she imposed upon her lovers constituted sufficient punishment for the offence. If Mayevski left, the Maltese would find another lover. As for the fat nurse and the half-witted chambermaid, if they found no one else, they would, for all Dr. Vernet knew or cared, go to bed with each other. It all just didn't matter. The only moral of the story was that Florent must be censured; he must be informed that his initiative was no more to be exercised in respect of the organisation of the sanatorium than it was in the consulting-room.

M. Halfont, reassured, hastened to tell Mayevski that he had been accorded another chance. Mayevski, who was feeling indignant and humiliated, replied that he did not want another chance. He explained that he had come to the sanatorium for the surveillance not of his morals, but of his health. M. Halfont warned him of the dangers of interrupting his *cure*, of the intensive discipline enforced in Swiss sanatoria, of the climatic advantages of the location of *Les Alpes*. He urged on him discretion and a change of floor. Little by little, persuasion reinforcing tact, tact reinforcing persuasion, the consequences of Dr. Florent's rash intervention were avoided.

It was Paul and Michèle who now provided the topic of conversation at the sisters' table. The situation, they all agreed, was made worse in view of Michèle's youth; they speculated grimly on the actual clinical limits of the affair. They were unanimous that the time had come for Dr. Vernet to intervene.

Sœur Juliette, the elderly nurse in charge of post-operational cases, called on Paul and asked whether she might speak to him frankly. The frequency of his visits to Michèle, she explained, was attracting malicious attention. She wished neither to encourage nor to discourage the affair; she only wished to protect from unnecessary pain and disillusion a young girl for whom she felt deep affection and whose courage she admired.

What, in a word, were his intentions? If they were not serious, if he regarded all that had passed as no more than a flirtation, then she begged him to leave the sanatorium, or at least to discontinue his visits.

It was then the turn of Dr. Vernet. He sent for Paul and told him bluntly that the time had come for him to leave the sanatorium. His pneumothorax was working satisfactorily; the condition of his liver required no more than the maintenance of his present régime. There should be no delay. Adjustment to an English winter necessitated progressive acclimatisation throughout its initial stages. It was now the end of October. Another fortnight, and he would have no option but to remain in France till the spring.

At almost any earlier period of his stay, this curt dismissal would have represented the summit of Paul's hopes. Now its pronouncement sounded as ominous as the initial diagnosis of his illness.

It was not that it was unexpected; the question of his departure had preoccupied Paul since the day that he had been declared non-contagious. He knew that he should leave Brisset at the first opportunity. A recent bank statement showed that he had spent more than half his uncle's legacy; it was obvious that he should conserve as much as possible of what remained to aid him through the long period of re-adaptation and convalescence ahead. But offsetting this, offsetting every other consideration, was the knowledge, progressively more certain each day, that his love for Michèle was all that counted in his life.

Michèle clapped her hand over Paul's mouth. He pulled it away, looked at it in the palm of his own hand. White and beautifully shaped, it seemed at that moment the most precious thing that he was renouncing.

'Don't reply – nod your head,' she said. 'If you speak I'll cover your mouth again with my hand.'

'I – '

Up came the hand. The nod which Michèle required was to signify agreement that the topic would be dropped. (She had discovered that it was the only way of avoiding lengthy and abortive discussions about the future which wasted entire evenings and left them both in a state of nervous exhaustion and despair.)

'You've got to listen,' said Paul, pulling the hand away and securing it to the other which he was already holding. 'We always knew it would have to end like this, we never pretended otherwise. I've got to go, there's absolutely no alternative. And anyway, Vernet's throwing me out…'

'End like this? What will be ending? You don't think that just because you go that we will stop loving each other?'

'No.' Paul released her hands.

She leant forward in her bed, grasped the tip of Paul's tie and pulled at it (as was her custom) until he leant over and their lips met. 'Then if you must go, take me with you,' she said. She was now kneeling. Her hair had fallen about her shoulders, her white shirt was unbuttoned where, some minutes before, Paul had pressed his lips against her chest.

Paul cupped her face in his hands, looked intently into her eyes. 'Take me with you,' she repeated 'I could work. I wouldn't be a burden to you. Only let us stay together.'

'We're ill,' he replied bitterly. And he thought: 'If I could dig ditches or cut down trees I'd take you with me, steal you by force if you didn't want to come. But, as things are, what hope have we? How shall I ever be able to earn a living when I've got no connections, no experience, no talents and no health?'

'If you go, I shall die,' said Michèle.

'Of course you won't die.'

'I shall have a relapse – it will be the same thing.'

Paul got up from the bed and in great agitation paced up and down the room. 'But what other decision is there to make?' he demanded. And when Michèle did not reply, he went on: 'Of course it should never have happened. We're both to blame.'

'For falling in love?'

'Yes.'

'How can you say that? How can you speak in such terms of our love?'

'They're the only terms I know.'

'Terms of defeat?'

'Of course.'

Michèle turned away. 'I can't answer you,' she said. 'I didn't know that it had all meant so little.'

Paul stared out of the window, his shoulders drooping, his hands thrust deep into the pockets of his dressing-gown. He recognised with disgust his weakness for projecting the bitterness of his situation into some form of personal recrimination. But what was to be done? Even his own immediate, single future posed difficulties which had in no way been resolved. Physically he felt little better than when he had arrived at the sanatorium nine months previously. He did not know to what he was returning, where he would go for his six months of convalescence and acclimatisation, or whether in the spring he would qualify for the resumption of his university grant. Nor had he occupied himself with these matters, for, once separated from Michèle, he cared little what became of him.

He turned. Michèle held out her arms and he ran to her bed, kissed her face, her lips, her shoulders, explained himself in tortuous, stilted phrases, affirmed and reaffirmed that nothing had significance beyond his love for her. Then he lay beside her, his eyes closed but his legs on the edge of the bed, his whole body ready, at the first sound from outside, to resume an upright position.

Michèle passed her fingers through his hair. 'You remember how before your jaundice you said that you were going to leave in a month?'

'Yes.'

She was silent a moment, then continued: 'The afternoon that Vernet told me he couldn't operate I came to your room and wept. Did you ever realise why?'

Paul opened his eyes but did not answer.

'It wasn't because I was afraid to die but because I knew that long before I would be dead you would have left me.'

'Michèle!'

'And if you went now I really would be ill again. Vernet says I can get up at Christmas. Wait till then, wait just two months and I promise I won't try to make you stay any longer. Everything's easier to bear if one can get up…'

Paul held her in his arms. It was the sort of indeterminate, negative decision to which his nature was the most prone – he acknowledged it and at the same time felt only relief. And he wondered, even as he kissed her, to what extent, a quarter of an hour ago, he would have insisted on leaving if he had not been secretly sure that whatever his arguments Michèle would successfully circumvent them.

CHAPTER EIGHT

•

'Well, *Monsieur* Davenant, you have made your decision?' demanded Dr. Vernet.

'Yes.'

'Ah!'

'I am staying till Christmas.'

Dr. Vernet's face grew rigid. His eyes looked as if they had been removed with ice-tongs from a refrigerator.

'In fact I probably won't be leaving much before the New Year,' Paul added. If there were to be an explosion, it might as well be of spectacular proportions.

For a moment Dr. Vernet appeared to be contemplating a reply. Then without a word he left the room and slammed the door. Paul swallowed a small glass of neat cognac which, in anticipation of Dr. Vernet's visit, he had concealed beneath an upturned cup on his *table de nuit*. The door flew open again. 'Don't think that because you choose to turn my sanatorium into a residential hotel, you will be able to behave as you like. Also I refer you to the rule that the consumption of spirits in patients' bedrooms is prohibited.' This time the force with which he slammed the door blew open the french windows.

Dr. Vernet's mood, that day, reacted upon everyone else. *Sœur* Valérie came to him to complain that Mayevski, her old enemy (now installed on a different floor), had had the effrontery to call on Michèle during the evening *cure*. Dr. Vernet instantly sent for Mayevski and forbade him to pay Michèle another visit during the remainder of his stay (which stay, he commented, Mayevski might now terminate as soon as he liked, and without fear of medical opposition).

He stormed at everyone within reach. A patient reported that M. Halfont had entered a medical prescription on his bill as though it had been a dietary supplement. '*Encore de votre escroquerie*,' Dr. Vernet shouted at M. Halfont over the intercommunication system. '*La prochaine fois j'avertis la police!*'

Experienced patients and members of his staff recognised the signs and kept away from him.

* * *

Sœur Valérie now started to cultivate the intolerable habit of calling on Michèle with her knitting, and discussing with her the benefits of a religious life, the desirability of renouncing the world whilst still very young, and the spiritual advantages conferred by an early death. She would sit at the bottom of Michèle's bed, short legs apart, garters visible, pricking the rumps of passing devils with the shuttlecock points of her knitting needles. When Paul came into the room, there was nothing to be done but to sit down, to hold *Sœur* Valérie's skein of wool, and to listen to the holy discourse.

He confided his difficulties to Glou-Glou, who very civilly agreed to ring for *Sœur* Valerie at a prearranged time, and to keep her occupied with a number of requests. Glou-Glou took to this new rôle with zest. Improvising brilliantly, he would demand in succession bed-pans, bed-baths, inhalants, massages, sedatives, lotions, drops for his eyes, nose and ears, the re-making of his bed, the refilling of his hot-water bottle, the preparation of a hot drink. At the same time he would present *Sœur* Valérie with bars of chocolate, admire her biceps, interrogate her on certain details touching on the nature of the divinity. *Sœur* Valerie, indignant and flattered, sweated, gobbled the chocolate, and attempted to answer Glou-Glou's curious questions, whilst the latter, quacking compulsively, would time his pulse by the second-hand of his alarm clock, or consult one (or compare both) of the thermometers which he kept permanently under each arm. For a little while, Paul and Michèle would be left in peace.

At last, as soon as the bell would start to ring (at the same time each evening), *Sœur* Valerie would throw down her knitting and jump off the bed, crying: '*Mon Dieu, c'est le fou qui sonne. Il est sympathique, mais qu'il est exigeant!*' And she would run out the door and down the passage, knowing from experience that Glou-Glou's finger would remain on the bell-push until she had actually reached the door of his bedroom.

It was less easy to dispose of Dr. Vernet. He re-imposed the restrictions prevailing before Michèle's operation, he enforced a religious observation of the times of the *cures*, and made no attempt to disguise the irritation which Paul's presence caused him.

If Dr. Bruneau and Dr. Florent were present when he was giving Paul a refill of air, he would refer to him sarcastically as '*ce monsieur byronique*'; if he were unattended by his colleagues, he would conduct the whole operation in silence, neither greeting Paul on arrival nor saying the customary *au revoir* when he left. One day, encountering Paul in the company of the priest who months earlier had given him a transfusion of his blood, he commented: '*Mon père*, you would never guess the uses to which *Monsieur* Davenant has put your innocent blood!'

Most patients discerned a new moroseness in Dr. Vernet's demeanour. He frequently gave the impression of being preoccupied, whilst at the same time he seemed to have lost interest in the general routine of the sanatorium. He abstained more and more from medical rounds, procrastinated over diagnoses and appeared in no hurry to conduct the initial examination of new arrivals.

There was an incident which everyone felt could not have occurred some months earlier. One afternoon, in the passage of the *Service Médical*, twenty patients were awaiting their turns for the *consultation*. Suddenly there was an uproar from the *sale de scopie*. The door opened. Dr. Vernet emerged, pulling by the hair a female patient who was aiming kicks at his ankles. '*Petit salaud*!' she cried. And she added by way of explanation to the spectators: '*Il a couché avec moi hier soir, mais aujourd'hui il veut de nouveau faire le grand médecin*!' Struggling, they passed down the corridor of the *Service Médical*, through the doors at the bottom and out of sight. It smacked very much of the recklessness of a dictator in the decline of his *régime*.

Early in December Dr. Vernet summoned Kubahskoi to his bureau and informed him that the tuberculin treatment had failed and that it was to be abandoned. He should now make arrangements to return to his own country before Christmas. However, if – as once he had claimed – he were really willing to run any risk, there was an elderly surgeon at Brisset who practised (when he could find a patient) an operatory technique which, like tuberculin, had generally fallen into disrepute. It was radical and violent; it had virtually no advocates.

'I cannot recommend it,' said Dr. Vernet, 'but if you care to take a chance, I will not dissuade you.' And he added casually that if Kubahskoi were to decide in favour of the operation, he would do best to leave *Les Alpes*, for administrative changes which were pending were likely, before long, to lead to the complete reorganisation of the sanatorium.

* * *

There were days when Michèle was obsessed by a desire to get up; nothing then would console her. Paul would bring her books; she would thank him and leave them uncut on the *table de nuit*. Manniez would try every way of cheering '*la petite gosse*', as he termed her; it would be without avail. She lay in her bed as if in shackles, her eyes turned desperately towards the window, symbol of the world to which she now wished to return.

She had failed to regain the weight which she had lost at the period of her operation; Dr. Vernet ordered a bowl of porridge and an omelette to be supplied as daily supplements to her *petit déjeuner*. One day Paul opened her wardrobe: on the top shelf was a row of porringers, whilst the omelettes were stacked, one on top of the other, like loofahs in a chemist's shop window.

Four weeks, three weeks, two weeks to Christmas and to the first legitimate occasion when she might leave her bed. Time passed, but time stood still. The six months that she had already been in bed, the danger, the suspense, the suffering – all were more endurable than the two weeks still to be got through.

Manniez started to re-decorate her room for Christmas. Michèle's neighbours complained about the hammering; the *gouvernante* complained about the damage to the walls; the *femme de chambre* complained that the floor was always charged with debris. No arrangement satisfied him; the holly, the mistletoe, the paper chains which he put up one day would be taken down the next. He fused all the lights whilst installing a row of Chinese lanterns, and alienated *Sœur* Valerie by disguising Mayevski in the costume of Saint Nicholas and trying to smuggle him into Michèle's room one evening after supper.

Paul was not looking forward to Christmas. Indeed, at no moment during the previous year had he even contemplated a second Christmas at *Les Alpes*, believing that by then either he must have left or be dead. And with Christmas would come the absolute necessity of making some decision in respect of the future.

Taking stock: he got up for meals, he went out for walks, he was allowed to miss the morning *cure* on Sundays. He led what Dr. Vernet termed 'a normal sanatorium life'. Indubitably it was an improvement on what had been his condition when first he had arrived at the sanatorium. But nevertheless he made no movement without effort; when he stood he wanted to sit down; when he sat down he wanted to lie down; when he lay down he wanted to sleep.

As the days passed, his anxiety and depression increased. Manniez was arranging the names of the people who were to sit at his table for the dinner on Christmas Eve: Paul, de la Marelle, Glou-Glou, Mayevski and Delmuth. And a place would be kept for Michèle. (She had to eat in her room, but she was to be allowed to come down for an hour afterwards). More than anything Paul wanted to be with Michèle, but alone and in very different circumstances.

At last, within a few days of Christmas, the whole idea of the meal became so intolerable that Paul decided to eat in his room. The decision, which to everyone else appeared merely petty or bloody-minded, was in reality an act of despair. Either the aftermath of the jaundice or his psychological state had caused a rash on his scalp. This had started to spread to his face. Shaving was made difficult and ineffective; hairs were enclosed by spots which became septic. As soon as one spot started to diminish another would develop elsewhere. It was perplexing and humiliating. And now the associative complications of Christmas had the effect of exacerbating the condition. Paul dreaded all encounters, especially those with Michèle.

A protestation from M. Halfont. He sent a message to Paul that all the waiters would be needed in the *salle à manger*, and that except in the case of patients too ill to get up there would be no room service. Paul replied that he did not mind forgoing the Christmas meal, as he had done the year before. Manniez, however, refused to take Paul's resolution seriously, and persisted in reserving his place.

The finishing touches were put to the decorations in halls and passages; the great tree was erected in the *salle à manger*. Almost every patient capable of climbing out of bed would be present at the dinner. Normally on these occasions the sisters sat with the patients; this year, however, they were informed that the exigencies of the kitchen required that they should dine at their communal table an hour or so in advance of the main meal.

Paul had long since stopped writing or receiving letters. Of the great mass of cards and parcels arriving at *Les Alpes*, none was delivered to his room. The only remaining contact he still possessed with England was the irregular statements of his shrinking bank account.

The day arrived. 'Listen, Davenant,' said Manniez at lunchtime. 'Or you come, or you don't come. Say now please.' The *maître d'hôtel* was standing at the table, seating-plan in hand. '*Puisque vous vous levez tous les jours, pourquoi pas ce soir?*' he demanded. The situation was, of course, ridiculous.

Back in his bedroom, Paul looked in the mirror. Spots with white heads; emplacements where spots had been amputated by his razor; inflamed patches of scalp visible through the extremities of his hair. His whole face looked on fire. It was too obscene. If only he could manage to look merely ill, to look yellow, grey or green. He felt suddenly too exhausted to undress.

He awoke, sweating, at the end of the *cure de silence*, took his temperature, pulse, and timed his breathing. A light fever was already beginning. So much the better. His fingers crept to his scalp which was irritating. 'Oh, Christ, my life,' he suddenly cried aloud, 'my filthy, pustulous, neurotic life.' He jumped from his bed. He must start afresh, start again from the beginning. How? How? How? The useless body, the shop-soiled lungs… With shaking hands he started to tie up the presents he had bought for Michèle.

Seven o'clock. In front of each sister was a plate of spaghetti. One sister was weeping, the remainder were eating in silence. M. Halfont came into the *salle à manger* and, smiling, wished them the compliments of the season. There was no reply. 'What is the matter with you all?' he demanded. Then: 'Is it possible? No! Ah, but I think so!' He looked accusingly from face to face. 'You are sulking because this year we are not paying you to sit and gourmandise!'

Suddenly he clapped his hands together. 'Listen to me! There is a bad spirit in the sanatorium. What right have you to complain? We are here to serve, not to blow out our stomachs! When will you realise that the true message of Christmas is not stuffing but self-sacrifice? You are eating good, second-quality spaghetti well prepared – in Germany or behind the Iron Curtain they would change their politics for it. Where else would you be gratuitously provided with such a meal?'

The sisters began to tell him. 'Stop!' he shouted. 'I've been asked to deliver a special invitation to you from the management, but you won't listen!' The sisters stopped talking. 'You are invited to come down to the *salle à manger* at half-past nine...'

'For supper?' demanded one of the sisters.

'For the lighting of the candles on the Christmas tree.' He smiled uneasily. 'It will be a splendid sight! And there will be music, too! And that is not all,' he added quickly, for his words had caused a gasp of astonishment. 'Should any patient invite you over to his table to drink a glass of wine, the management hereby gives you full authorisation to accept.'

At eight o'clock Manniez and Mayevski came to Paul's room and stripped the sheets and blankets from his bed. Paul resisted, half joking, half in anger. They gave him five minutes in which to get dressed. Paul re-made his bed and got back into it. They returned, reinforced by Glou-Glou and de la Marelle. The bedclothes were again stripped back. De la Marelle opened the wardrobe and took out the only suit. Paul struggled abortively with Mayevski – for a moment he was on the verge of losing his temper. Then he laughed and submitted. They refused to leave the room until he had finished dressing.

In the main hail, which was full of patients, they were joined by Delmuth. Emile had been stationed outside the entrance to the *salle à manger* with instructions to admit no one; he was arguing with a group of patients who were insisting that they were too tired to remain standing. At exactly half-past eight the doors were opened from within by the *maître d'hôtel*, while Emile stood to one side. The *salle à manger* was in darkness but for small clusters of candles on the tables; *Heilige Nacht* was playing through an amplifier. When everyone was seated and the record had come to an end, the main lights were turned on and M. Halfont, speaking through a microphone, asked that, as a safety measure, the candles should be extinguished.

Paul looked about him. Dr. Vernet, wearing a blue suit, winged collar and bright red tie was sitting with a few guests at a table at the head of the dining-room. At some tables there were patients whose appearances were so changed by the substitution of day clothes for pyjamas and dressing-gowns that at first Paul failed to recognise them; there were even some he had never seen before, men and women who, in the course of the year, would only be allowed out of their rooms to attend the Christmas or New Year dinner.

The music started again – a selection of carols. The waiters began to serve the *hors d'œuvre*. 'Gentlemens,' said Delmuth, smiling confidently and leaning forward across the table, 'gentlemens, we are all known to each other, but to avoid embarrassment, and as a gesture to the season, and to put us all at our ease, let us announce in order our names, ages, nationalities and occupations. I will voluntarily start. Hans Delmuth, thirty-nine, Flemish, a civil engineer.' He got up and bowed.

'We know each other,' said Mayevski, 'and I think we lose our time in talking so.'

'Good – as you like. It is true I make the suggestion in the hope of encountering a brother engineer, for I am lonely and at Christmas I specifically seek out the company of a brother engineer. And what is your profession, Sir?' Delmuth demanded, turning towards Paul.

'None.'

'Is not possible, please.'

'Then I am a professional invalid.'

'Ho! Ho! Very good! That is British humour, gentlemens. "A professional invalid!" Very good indeed. I depict we shall much laugh this evening. Now I am wondering, gentlemens, how many languages we all speak between us. That must be very interesting. I speak thirteen – Flemish, French, Dutch, German, English, Russian, Italian, Greek, Spanish, Portuguese, Finnish, Swedish and Croat. Say, please, who speaks more than this?'

The question was ignored.

'You speak Cockney?' Delmuth asked Paul.

'No.'

'Pity. I next wish to learn Cockney.'

The service was very slow. Glou-Glou refused to eat his *hors d'œuvre* or to let the plate be taken away. He was dressed in professional black, with a clean pyjama jacket instead of a shirt. He kept one knee crossed over the other, and periodically tested his reflexes with the handle of his fork.

'On Christmas Eve one thinks where one was the year before,' said Delmuth, showering pepper into his soup. 'Let us, to pass the time, recount what we were doing this day one year ago. For me it is very simple – I was here. But I have a strange story to relate…'

Suddenly all the lights went out, leaving the great Christmas tree as a blazing set piece. There were cries of approbation. The '*Marseillaise*' was played over the amplifier, and everyone rose to his feet and started to clap. A waiter dropped a heavily charged tray. The lights were turned on again.

'Quite a ghost story,' continued Delmuth, as though there had been no interruption. 'How do you think I spent last Christmas? In the company of a suicidal woman, a dying English pauper and a beardless Sikh! Not bad! But why do I specify "beardless" Sikh? It is the key to my story, which I now name "The Story of the Beardless Sikh".'

'Michèle, she will soon be here, and we still eat the soup,' said Mayevski. He tried to attract the attention of a waiter.

'It was like this. I had just arrived at *Les Alpes.* Think, gentlemens, to arrive at a sana for Christmas! From Dr. Vernet I had the authorisation to get myself up for the repast, but I concluded from induction that it was more wise to stay in bed. But I made the compromise to visit my neighbour, who called himself an emancipated Sikh, emancipated because the previous evening he had cut off his beard. Is that not picturesque? You see, the Sikh is not permitted to cut off his beard.'

Paul swallowed the rest of his wine. 'The English pauper?' he demanded.

'Oh, a pauper student.'

'You mean a student studying to be a pauper?'

'Yes. No! Ha! Ha! Very good, a play on compound nouns, or do I confound?'

'Let him finish the story or he never stop,' said Mayevski, glaring at Paul.

Delmuth recharged his glass and swallowed the contents like an oyster. His rudimentary face was growing pinker. 'The Story of the Beardless Sikh,' he repeated thickly.

'*Misericordia!*' cried Manniez. 'I can no longer hear this rubbish.'

'It was the night of the anniversary of the matriculate contraception of Our Lord, and I, Hans Delmuth, engineer…'

'*Qu-est-ce qu'il raconte? Comprends pas l'Anglais,*' complained de la Marelle.

Dr. Florent came over to the table. He was making a circuit of the dining-room, shaking hands with all the patients. Glou-Glou seized the proffered hand excitedly, tested the pulse, and forced Dr. Florent to sit down. '*Comme ordonnance, un bon verre de vin*,' he shouted, rising to his feet. A waiter took the opportunity to remove Glou-Glou's *hors d'œuvre* and soup and to serve the next course.

'*Ça va, Davenant?*' inquired Florent.

'*Ça va.*'

'*Vous allez quand même mieux qu'il y a un an.*'

'*Oui, oui, je vais mieux.*' The wine was increasing Paul's habitual streptomycin dizziness. He looked at his watch. It was nearly time for him to fetch Michèle.

'This so-emancipated Sikh was now fearful for the consequences of his beard-cutting. For this reason he would not anger his god more by attendance at a Christian celebration. I said him that one floor below there was an English pauper who was dying, *kaputt*, no hope, *finito*. I said: 'Why you worry? Here is someone nearly dead, but you are nearly well.' Then as I am still saying there came terrible screams!'

To offset the slowness of the service, two patients got up from their table and started to dance. It was a test case – everyone awaited the official reaction. The dancers passed quite close to Dr. Vernet. He gave no indication of having noticed them. Immediately a number of couples left their tables and began to circle the *salle à manger*.

Paul got up, staggered badly and sat down again. 'Will you fetch Michèle? I'm too dizzy,' he said to Manniez. Mayevski and de la Marelle joined in the dancing. Dr. Florent excused himself and went to visit another table. Glou-Glou hummed tonelessly to himself and scraped his knife across a plate in time with the music.

Manniez returned with Michèle. Paul stood up. 'But you didn't call for me,' Michèle protested. 'Can't walk – I'm drunk,' Paul replied. She stared hard at him before she sat down. 'I've swallowed half a glass of wine,' he went on, laughing, 'but you know what my sense of balance is like. Oh! You look so lovely!' He reached for her hand, but she drew it away. De la Marelle came over and asked her to dance. She smiled and refused. He sat down beside her and started to flirt.

'Do you like my story, *Monsieur* Davenant?' shouted Delmuth across the table.

'No,' said Paul.

'Ha! You joke again!'

'No. I'm not joking.'

Delmuth shot out his hand and grasped Paul's wrist. Paul jerked his wrist free and a bottle of wine fell off the table and shattered on the stone floor. Conversation suddenly stopped. Everyone looked up to see what had happened. 'Gentlemens, please silence, gentlemens!' There were calls of 'Sh' and 'Silence'. 'Gentlemens,' Delmuth shouted above the sound of the loudspeaker, 'gentlemens, fill your glasses. *Hommage au passé! Hommage aux thoracés! Hommage aux détraqués!*' '*Taisez-vous, espèce d'imbécile*,' called out a waiter. '*Hommage aux foutus!* It is my pleasure to wish you Happy Christmas in thirteen different languages! *Joyeux Noël! Auguri per Natale, Huggelig Jul...*' His greetings were lost in cries of approval and emulation. Everyone kissed or shook hands with everyone else. Some climbed on to chairs and tables. Glasses were raised. Toasts were drunk. The health of each doctor was individually called. Dr. Vernet replied on behalf of the staff with the toast: '*De tous à tous!*'

The dancing was resumed. Delmuth sat down, smiled impassively at Paul, and ordered some more wine. Michèle reached out and removed Paul's glass, at the same time continuing to talk to de la Marelle. Mayevski came back to the table, a peculiar smile of anticipation on his lips. There was a series of reports. *Sœur* Valérie, who had come down with the other sisters, ran screaming across the *salle à manger*, a squib attached to the hem of her skirt. After initial consternation, patients and sisters laughed and applauded. Dr. Vernet sat smiling broadly, *Sœur* Valérie was led away weeping.

The meal was over. Tables were pushed back to widen the area of the dance floor. A popular American tune. Manniez pulled Michèle to her feet and they joined the dancers. Paul drained his glass, refilled it, then drained it again. The lights were lowered. Delmuth was dancing with a fat Swedish patient. 'I accept your apology,' he called out to Paul as they passed the table.

Paul watched Michèle and Manniez as they steered their way into and through the dancing throng. It was nearly midnight. Under M. Halfont's direction, waiters started to bring up crates of champagne from the cellar. The music changed. Delmuth returned to the table, but

Manniez and Michèle continued dancing. 'Listen,' said Delmuth, 'you want to hear the end of my story?' Paul paid no attention. He was watching *Sœur* Thérèse, who had crossed the floor to speak to Michèle. 'Your hands were trembling, you are very drunk,' said Delmuth. 'Shut up!' said Paul. He was trying to catch what *Sœur* Thérèse was saying. 'Davenant, you will hear my story!' shouted Delmuth, beginning himself to tremble. The music stopped. M. Halfont beat the strokes of midnight on a brass gong. A line of waiters marched in with armfuls of balloons. At the same time there was a rapid distribution of streamers, squeakers and coloured paper missiles. The *maître d'hôtel* opened the first champagne bottle. There was a cheer. Popping corks then sounded a broadside. The music started again.

Manniez came back to the table. 'Where's Michèle?' demanded Paul. 'Ordered from Vernet to bed,' said Manniez. 'I must go to her,' said Paul. He tried to get up, but found that he could not co-ordinate his movements. 'Christ! I really am drunk!' he said to himself.

'Come!' shouted Delmuth to Mayevski, who was now sitting at a neighbouring table, 'champagne for everyones!' He signalled his instructions to a waiter. Patients were aiming the paper pellets at each other. The streamers were dividing the *salle à manger* into multicoloured segments. A volley of missiles from the next table landed on the face of the waiter who was about to set down the champagne glasses. He dropped the lot. In retaliation Delmuth hurled back handfuls of cold potato. There were cries of protestation.

'Now I finish my story,' said Delmuth, pouring the champagne when fresh glasses had been brought.

'But we know it,' said Paul. 'The woman jumped out of the window. And that's the end of the story.'

'Is not the end!' cried Delmuth, banging his fist on the table. 'She jump, but you don't know why! It was directly because the Sikh run into her room. She scream. The nurse who anæsthetise her turn round. In this moment she escape from her bed and jump from the window. Now you see! The Sikh then go nearly mad, fall on his knees and swear it is a warning of his god for shaving his beard. From that day he never shave again!'

'Who cares?' said Mayevski, pouring himself more champagne.

'He cares! The pauper student!' shouted Delmuth, lunging at Paul across the table. '*Sale petit homme de charité!* Why too did you not jump out? You live on charity, you take money. I am an engineer. I am ill since twenty years, but always I pay for myself. I work, I relapse, then I work again. While I am ill, I work. In bed during one year I work and keep myself. I speak thirteen languages and you speak not two. What are you? An artist? You despise engineers. We despise you. When I hear of artists who starve and die, it lights a fire in my heart. All my story was to expose you, and now is all gone wrong.' In exasperation he looked for something to throw. Then he seized the edge of the table and turned it over.

Paul pushed back his chair just in time. Crockery, cutlery and glass cascaded all round him. Delmuth's voice sounded above the crash. 'Gentlemens, an error! I slip, gentlemens! Make no attention! No one is hurt!' Dr. Vernet stood up. The dancers crowded round to see what had happened. '*Enlevez tout! Le plus vite possible!*' said Delmuth, handing a thousand-franc note to each staring waiter. 'Good! You see, it is nothing!' he said, smiling on all sides. 'I settle all. I pay for all.' M. Halfont came up. 'Please – on my bill, all, everything. One, two, three times the value. I liquidate all my indebtedness!'

The table was righted, re-laid. 'More champagne,' cried Delmuth. 'I pay! Please have the pleasure, gentlemens, to join me. Sit down! No more stories, I think! Where were we all this night, two years ago? That must be very interesting! For myself I was in a sana in the Bernese Oberland! Pull up, please, your chairs. Quite different from here, and not a little special! *Garçon! Garçon! Le champagne!*'

He changed his seat in order to be next to Paul, put his arm around him, called him 'dearest friend', inquired about his mathematics, wrote formulæ on the table-cloth. Paul drank two more glasses of champagne, then lowered his head on to the table.

When next he raised his head, it was two o'clock in the morning. The dance was still in progress. Dr. Vernet was leading a conga reel between the tables and in and out of the doors. Glou-Glou was performing a solo in the middle of the floor. Delmuth was retelling his story in German to a drunken Hungarian.

Paul got up and edged his way out of the *salle à manger*. At the entrance to the lift there was another reveller. After a confused discussion, each claiming that the other had the true right of precedence, they entered the lift together. Paul pressed the button for the floor of his companion. The lift mounted. They both began to sing. When the lift stopped, the reveller refused to get out. He insisted that Paul should press the button for his own floor. The lift set off again, both occupants singing uninhibitedly. At his own floor, Paul felt impelled to return the gesture. The lift remounted. It descended and re-ascended several times before Paul's companion at last staggered out. Standing with his arms threaded through the wrought-iron lift shaft, he sustained a duet with Paul as the latter descended.

'*Chagrin d'amour*,' chanted Paul, as he left the lift unsteadily. A door opened. Michèle, wearing her cherry-coloured dressing-gown, shot out into the passage. 'Oh! You're so drunk! Go straight to your room!' Paul was so startled that he nearly lost his balance. He clung to her for support. 'Don't touch me! I hate you!' She guided him as far as his door. He entered, stumbled and fell on to the bed. Michèle went away. She returned almost immediately with the presents he had given her a few hours earlier, and tossed them on the bed. Then she left, slamming the doors.

Paul tried to get up, but slipped off the bed to his knees. He lowered his dizzy head on to the *duvet*. To Michèle, who returned at that moment, it looked as if he were trying to pray. 'Oh! Hypocrite!' she cried. She pulled him up roughly and started to remove his clothes. He tried to explain, to protest his sobriety, but his speech was at the same level as his condition.

She put him to bed, turned out the light and left the room. In the darkness the bed heaved and rolled. He sat up and felt for his bedside lamp. Under his fingers it crashed to the ground. He tried to pick it up but cut his hand on the shattered bulb. He lay back. The end of the bed was rising and dipping. There would be no question of sleep.

He woke up very startled, his mind clear and aghast. It was still dark. The village clock struck five. There was not a moment to be lost. He threw aside the bed-clothes. He must go at once to Michèle. Everything must be explained. He must induce her to take back the rejected presents.

He opened his door very quietly. All the lights in the corridor were out. A floorboard creaked. He turned sharply. The sound of heavy breathing. He stepped quickly back into the room and shut the door.

Muffled footsteps and the handle turned. Emile stood in the doorway, a torch in his hand and a figure in a white sack balanced across his great shoulder. 'Sh! Don't make a sound!' he said. 'This is only the old woman out of forty-six. Have you got a sip of cognac?' He came into the room and shut the door carefully. He had a pair of socks pulled over his boots. 'You're looking green, *Monsieur* Davenant. You shouldn't come out of your room at this time in the morning if you don't want to see some queer sights!' He guffawed. 'Did you say you had a sip of cognac?'

'Cognac,' repeated Paul. Unable to withdraw his gaze from the draped figure, he backed towards the cupboard in which he kept his provisions.

'Didn't you know this was the way we did it? The lift's too narrow for a coffin,' said Emile, guffawing again. 'But they don't like me to be seen on the job – that's why I stood up against the wall when your door opened. Then I said to myself: "*Monsieur* Davenant won't mind – he's an old hand now!"'

Paul removed the cap from the bottle and passed it to Emile, who wished him *Bon Noël* and raised it to his lips. 'They say I drink,' he said. 'Well, they're right! In my time I've carried out more than three hundred stiffs on my shoulder!' He took two more gulps at the bottle. 'That's better. That's a lot better. I'd best go along now or I'll be meeting some more early birds!' He chuckled insinuatingly.

At the door he stopped and turned as if struck by a sudden thought. (After having delivered a patient's mail, he would often stop and turn in the same way, demanding: 'Have you heard the one about the Jew and the farmer's daughter?') '*Monsieur* Davenant,' he said, fixing Paul with his watery eyes, 'I hope that one of these days I'll not be carrying you out like this over my shoulder!'

CHAPTER NINE

•

As soon as Christmas was over, Kubahskoi went to Dr. Vernet to tell him that he had decided to risk the operation. 'Too late!' said Dr. Vernet, raising his eyebrows. 'If you had made up your mind when I first spoke to you, your fate would now have been decided. As it is, you will have – wait till tomorrow,' he said, dismissing Kubahskoi. 'I shall be addressing the whole sanatorium.'

The next day it was announced that all patients who could leave their rooms were to assemble in the *salon des privés* at twelve o'clock. The morning *cure* was ignored. Patients visited each other, exchanging rumours, seeking authentic information. What had happened? Had war been declared? Had a specific been discovered? Had the franc been devalued?

A little before midday, doors opened up and down the corridors, and the dressing-gowned, carpet-slippered battalions, still speculating, converged on the *salon des privés*. Paul and Michèle went there arm in arm. Apologies had been exchanged. Presents had been re-accepted. They were more united than ever.

A few minutes after twelve, Dr. Vernet, wearing a lounge suit, came into the *salon*. He was about to speak, when some more patients arrived. He looked at his watch, then ordered that the doors be locked to prevent the entry of any more latecomers.

'Well,' he said, speaking very quietly, 'it is my privilege to inform you that you have all been given one fortnight's notice to quit!'

'*Comment?*' and '*Qu'est ce qu'il dit?*' demanded patients on all sides. Someone at the back called out: '*Docteur, nous n'avons rien entendu.*' Dr. Vernet repeated his statement in a voice barely louder than before. There was immediate consternation. Dr. Vernet raised his hand for silence.

'Let us not get too animated,' he said. 'We are now approaching the end of the era of the private sanatorium. For a long time it has been inevitable that the *Société*, which has been consistently losing money, would be forced to close one or other of its leading establishments – *Les Alpes* or the *Sana Universel*. I have done everything possible to prevent the choice settling on *Les Alpes.* I have failed. Two weeks from today all your rooms must be vacated.'

He went on to explain that accommodation had been reserved at the *Universel* for all patients currently under treatment. Other patients wishing to remain in Brisset and under his medical supervision were advised to make immediate application to the management of that sanatorium. Separate arrangements for the few students still remaining at *Les Alpes* would be made in due course by the I.S.O.

A patient got up and inquired whether a joint protest might lead to the *Société* reconsidering its decision. 'No chance whosoever,' replied Dr. Vernet. Would Dr. Vernet and his staff be remaining indefinitely in Brisset? 'Just so long as I have any patients.' Dr. Vernet's simple statement was acknowledged by applause. 'Would it not have been possible for the *Société* to have given longer notice?' asked a Belgian. 'Quite possible!' replied Dr. Vernet. 'If there are no more practical questions, then the meeting is at an end.'

In England there were floods, blizzards, snow-storms, hailstorms and three distinct varieties of influenza germ. Even had he wished to, there could have been no question of Paul's leaving France before the Spring.

To his dismay he found that even the cheapest rooms at the *Universel* were appreciably more expensive than those at *Les Alpes*, he decided that he would have to find alternative accommodation.

'I can't possibly stay there. I shall have to find a room in a *pension*,' he said to Michèle the same evening. 'No!' said Michèle, sitting up sharply in bed.

'But you said yesterday that we'd be together till the Spring.'

'We shall be together. We shall see each other every day.'

'No!' repeated Michèle. She wound her arms about Paul's neck. If he left, everything would be changed, everything would be ruined. They must both remain under the same roof. 'It's no use,' said Paul. 'It's either that, or I will have to leave Brisset altogether.'

During the next few days he called at a number of hotels and boarding-houses. He was aware that his appearance did not recommend him to the proprietors of these establishments. (Each displayed a board with the name of the *pension* and the warning: *Seulement pour les Bien-Portants.*) Whenever he asked for a room he was scrutinised with suspicion and turned away with the information that the house was full.

The days passed and with less than a week in which to find accommodation, he was forced to intensify his efforts. Climbing and descending hills in the heavy snow, his army greatcoat buttoned to his chin, his shoulder-blades running with sweat, he visited the outlying *pensions* of the settlement. 'No rooms,' he was informed everywhere. 'No rooms and no vacancies before the spring.'

Many of the *pensions* were cold and ill-kept – by comparison the *Universel* seemed to possess every advantage. With only four days left, Paul decided to discontinue his search. He would take a room at the *Universel* and make some attempt to offset the high bills by intensive economy on all other forms of expenditure.

The fact of having made a decision raised his spirits. He set off for the *Universel.* At the reception bureau he learned that the last remaining room had been let that afternoon.

The next morning he awoke exhausted. All trunks and cases had been taken from the storeroom and delivered to their owners. Paul looked at his own shabby collection with distaste; he could well have dispensed with seeing them again. There were the labels which he addressed in his room at Oxford. Why, on each label, had he underlined France three times? Had he imagined that by doing so there was less likelihood that his baggage would go astray, or that it would reach its destination more quickly?

He opened one case and found it full of screwed-up sheets of year-old newspaper which he had used in packing his clothes. Every crumple revealed some phrase or headline which caught his eye and compelled him to unfold and flatten the paper to examine the context.

What was he doing wasting time in this way? With a sudden shock of horror he reflected that if he did not find accommodation within the next two days, he would either have to leave Brisset or attempt to gain admission to another clinic. Another clinic! New Vernets! New Halfonts! New Emiles!

He cancelled the lunch which he had ordered in bed, and got dressed quickly. He must revisit all the main hotels and *pensions* in the hope that since he had last called, a vacancy might have occurred. As he passed in and out of the swing doors, meeting always the same refusal, he felt like a sickly commercial traveller with a case full of patently unsaleable products.

Two days to go. 'Well?' demanded Dr. Vernet.

'A *pension*,' replied Paul. 'I shall be able to convalesce and come to you weekly for consultations.'

'*Monsieur*,' said Dr. Vernet, 'you do me too much honour.'

Paul buttoned up his greatcoat and set off once more for the village. He had no plan. He studied the local paper and called abortively at half a dozen new addresses. He made a series of small purchases, each time inquiring whether the shopkeeper who served him could recommend any lodgings. In the late afternoon he began to acknowledge that his task was hopeless.

What now? He went to a tea-room and ordered a cup of chocolate. A waitress came over and greeted him – she had formerly been a *femme de chambre* at *Les Alpes*. He told her of his difficulties. She said that she knew of a small *châlet-pension* in a wood just above the *Universel*. It was very simple, but clean, and the food was good. Because of its location very few people knew of its existence. Paul finished his coffee and set off there immediately.

He climbed up past the *Universel* and followed a narrow path into the wood which led him after several minutes to a clearing. There, small, trim, part wood, part brick, was the *châlet*. On a board was printed *Châlet Anniette*, and underneath, half-obscured by drifted snow, the words: *Pension. Chambres.* Paul knocked at the door. He had decided in advance that whatever the nature of the accommodation, if any were available he would take it.

Paul returned in great excitement to the sanatorium. Without bothering to remove his coat he went straight to Michèle to tell her the news. He recounted briefly his earlier disappointments and the way in which he had learned of the existence of the châlet. Everything connected with the châlet appeared propitious. It was close to the *Universel*; it was very cheap; the *patronne*, Mme. Anniette, was willing to provide a vegetarian diet.

He described what he had seen of the châlet. It was on three floors and contained seven or eight rooms which by eccentric partitioning could be equally considered a dozen. Paul's room was approached by a separate entrance. The partitions provided an inner and an outer room, the windows of the inner room – which contained the bed – opening on to the interior of the outer room. There was a wonderful and unbroken view across the Arve valley. He had arranged to move there the next day.

When he went to bed that night, one thought dominated all others: 'Whatever else happens, this is the very last night I shall ever spend in *Les Alpes*.'

The next day the move was accomplished. The path leading to the châlet was too narrow for a car, and Mme. Anniette collected Paul's luggage in a horse-drawn sledge. In a very short time he was installed, and able to return to *Les Alpes* to help Michèle with her own packing.

Michèle's room. The cherry-coloured polka-dotted dressing-gown had gone from the door, the *petit nègre* with his holy medals from the *table de nuit*. The photos, the books, the scarves used as tablecloths were all packed and hidden from sight. Only the *images* and posters remained to distinguish it from any other room in the sanitorium.

And the *images* and posters would soon be gone – Michèle was unpinning them one after the other as Paul entered the room. She turned and ran into his arms.

'You've been crying,' said Paul, looking into her eyes. Michèle shook her head, smiled and returned to her task.

'Leave them,' Paul said. He pulled Michèle away from the wall and embraced her again. 'I will buy you some reproductions for your new room.'

'I couldn't leave them – someone would come and tear them down.'

'But it will take hours.'

'No, it won't – not if you help me.'

'It's such a waste of time and energy,' said Paul. Reaction from the whole awful week. Suddenly dejected and morose, he sat down on the edge of Michèle's bed. Why earlier had he felt elated?

Michèle was struggling with a recalcitrant drawing-pin. 'Please help me get it out,' she said.

'But I don't understand why you're going to all this trouble.'

Michèle looked up in amazement. 'You don't understand why! After all that's happened in this room.'

'I don't feel much sentiment for anything that's happened in *Les Alpes'*.

Michèle did not reply. She prized up the drawing-pin with a nail file.

'I can't stay here if you go on,' said Paul. He got up and started to pace the room; at that moment it seemed as though there were no other issue in the universe. 'Well, if you must have them, tear them off. For goodness' sake don't try and take out every pin.'

Michèle continued to remove the pins, but she took care to keep her face averted.

'Well, I shall go then.' He strode resolutely to the door and grasped the handle. Michèle ran and caught his arm. He freed himself, face set, nostrils distended. She turned away, but not before he had seen her face.

'Michèle,' he said. 'Are you satisfied now?' a voice in his brain demanded. 'Michèle,' he repeated. On entering he had received sufficient indication of her emotion at vacating her room – why, therefore, had he persisted in tormenting her? Why, in the intervals of being tormented, did one invariably assume the rôle of tormentor? 'Oh, my darling,' he said, hugging her, 'I was teasing you. Please don't cry,' he repeated, 'I'm not worth it. I hurt you because you're vulnerable and the only person who cares. I'll unpin all your *images*, pull the pins out with my teeth, anything, if only you'll stop crying.'

And as a gauge of the sincerity of his words he applied himself to the drawing-pins, setting about each with the care and urgency with which an experienced picker plucks ripe blackberries from a bush when the first heavy drops of rain prelude the onset of a thunderstorm.

CHAPTER TEN

•

To wake in the little enclosed room with its dark, stained walls was to wake in the cabin of a sailing ship. No early nurse to drag in the day's anguish on the heels of her institutional shoes. Only Mme. Anniette (or her assistant Pierre) with a tray of scalding, aromatic coffee, toast and home-made cherry jam.

Mme. Anniette was small, broad and meridional, with generous eyes and wide features. The death of her father (a carpenter in the employ of a sanatorium) had forced her, many years earlier, to turn the family châlet into a *pension*. Pierre, tall, timid, ragged and fleshless (a doctor had once said: 'Don't put him in the X-ray cabinet – just hold him in front of a strong light!'), had passed five years in bed and five years convalescing in the *Châlet Anniette*. Money spent, health unrestored, he had continued a further twenty years in the châlet, aiding Mme. Anniette in return for his keep.

Besides Paul there were two other lodgers – an ex-army sergeant in his fifties and a young German-speaking electrician from Alsace. Both were former invalids who had subsequently found work in the mountains. At lunch and dinner the three men shared a rexine-topped table in the small *salle à manger*.

Paul kept very much to the routine which he had learned at *Les Alpes*. Mme. Anniette was enthusiastic and co-operative. '*Faut bien vous reposer*,' she would say, coming to ask him, as he lay on the divan, what he wanted for lunch or dinner. First he must get completely fit – there would be time enough to look for light work in the mountains. 'And when that day comes,' she would tell him, 'though I've not got two sous to rub together, *Monsieur* will find that I have *le bras long*.' When she had agreed with Paul the modest sum which she asked for board and lodging, she had omitted to mention that it included flowers, plates of fruit, chocolate, glasses of port, cups of coffee and indeed anything which lay to hand whenever she encountered him. '*Il faut manger*' was the phrase most constantly on her lips.

For Paul and Michèle nothing mattered except the visits which each paid the other. Initially they felt strangely inhibited – for the first time since they had known each other there was no danger that the door would suddenly open and a nurse or doctor walk into the room. ('It's like a hut on the edge of the world. One feels a million miles from anywhere,' Michèle had said when first she had looked out of the window across the darkening valley.)

She came to the châlet each morning (at the end of the *cure*), always – as Mme. Anniette daily attested from her window – running the last twenty paces to the side entrance which led to Paul's room. Her straight, slender body superbly moulded by ski-jacket and trousers, her skin glowing and her eyes bright, she looked now as if she had never been ill in her life. If Paul were lying reading on his divan, she would put a hand over his eyes, toss aside his book and throw herself beside him; if he were looking morose she would simulate his facial expression, press two fingers in imitation of the muzzle of a gun to her forehead, say in English, 'It is the end,' then roll her eyes and fall over sideways; whatever Paul's mood he would never be able to restrain himself and both would burst into uncontrollable laughter.

They went for long walks beneath the burning February sun, penetrating ever more deeply into the surrounding countryside, reaching vantage spots which to Paul, from his bedroom at *Les Alpes*, had seemed as unattainable as the mountains of the moon.

In the village they never failed to encounter someone whom they knew. Joining up perhaps with one couple, they would go to drink hot chocolate in a café and there discover, grouped about a table strewn with sunglasses, cigarette packets, ashtrays and aperitifs, another half-dozen former inmates of *Les Alpes*.

Once every two weeks Paul called at the *Universel* and Dr. Vernet, taciturn and unsmiling, put a needle between his ribs and injected him with air. From the day that he had announced to his patients the decision of the *Société*, Dr. Vernet had reverted to his former standards of thoroughness and efficiency; many suspected that up to that moment still graver issues had been in the balance. Perhaps the *Société* had even been contemplating the total relinquishment of his services. Nevertheless, though still faithfully attended by *Sœur* Miriam and his two assistants, he was finding life less congenial. At the *Universel* he had no official status. No attention had been paid to his request that all his patients should be accommodated on the same floor, and so when he made a medical round with his assistants, he was forced to travel from one extremity of the building to another, often encountering and re-encountering the *Universel's Médecin Chef* and *his* assistants, also engaged in the same practice. Sometimes both sets of doctors became confused as to which rooms contained their respective patients, and not infrequently a patient just recovering from the effects of one concerted visit would find his door flung open for a second time and himself subjected to another.

The days were accounted for. After his evening meal Paul would return to his room and either read or listen to the wireless. Although he was invariably tired and fit for nothing more arduous, the solitude induced in him an indefinable uneasiness – it was as though in the preceding year he had developed a faculty for anxiety which now, though no longer relevant to his situation, continued to exercise itself on its own account. Accordingly he tended not to hurry his dinner, and when it was at an end he often passed the remainder of the evening in Mme. Anniette's little bed-sitting-room in company with the other members of the châlet.

At times his sleep was very troubled. He had a recurrent dream that something was standing at the side of his bed, and he would try desperately to scream, and – as one day Mme. Anniette was to confirm to him – frequently succeeded in screaming to his full capacity. Trembling, he would wake and turn on the bedside lamp and often rush in his pyjamas to the side door of the châlet, throw it open and draw up incredulous when he saw that instead of the tracks which he had anticipated, the surface of the snow was smooth and unbroken.

It was not in Michèle's nature to resist, to assert her will in opposition to her love, to cavil or to refuse. The caresses which she repulsed were also the caresses which she sought, and all her desire was to give herself completely. And yet there were reasons for abstention, reasons most valid to a young girl's heart, compacts with God, promises and resolves, concepts which could not be repeated to a man without belief and a decade older than herself.

There were times when she tried to explain herself to Paul. Their common future, their continued well-being (as had been true of their meeting and of their survival) depended upon their faith and their capacity for keeping faith. To err or to retreat from this condition was wantonly to put all in hazard. 'Faith with what?' Paul would demand, only refraining from pursuit of the question when he saw the distress which it caused Michèle. However, the situation was one which by its nature could not be protracted indefinitely.

They saw each other twice a day. At the end of the morning *cure* Michèle came to Paul at the châlet. At the end of the afternoon *cure* Paul called for Michèle and they would go out for tea. On Sundays Michèle was excused the morning *cure* and went to mass in the village. After mass she climbed up to the châlet and she and Paul would go and explore the mountain paths.

On the last Sunday in February there was a blizzard with freezing winds from the east. Michèle came into Paul's room after the mass, her snow-boots in one hand, her missal in the other. They sat together looking out of the window until the panes became frosted over.

Paul insisted that Michèle should not leave the châlet until the wind had dropped. At midday she tried to telephone the *Universel* to say that she could not get back to lunch, but the storm had put the system out of operation. Mme. Anniette very willingly laid an extra place at table. At the end of the meal Michèle said that she must get back to the sanatorium in time for the *cure de silence.*

But the wind had grown more violent – it was with difficulty that they forced open the front door. In the few yards to Paul's entrance the snow penetrated their hair and clothing.

They removed their jackets and dried themselves in front of the stove. Paul argued that for Michèle to be seen returning immediately before the *cure de silence* was to direct greater attention to her absence from lunch. The compulsive need for afternoon rest (intensified by having missed the morning *cure*) began to possess them. They lay down beside each other on the divan. In a moment both were asleep.

Paul woke the first. It was already dark. In order not to disturb Michèle, he lay motionless, listening to the soft, sweet sound of her breathing. Then he stretched his arm about her waist. She smiled, half opening, then closing her eyes. He pressed his lips first lightly, then crushingly against her own. She made no effort to restrain him as he got up to turn the lock in the door.

CHAPTER ELEVEN

•

One of Michèle's Christmas presents had been a *carnet* with the word '*Poésie*' written across the highly decorated cover. She had asked a number of patients to write their favourite poem on one of the coloured pages with the result that there were verses in Turkish, Arabic, Persian, German, French and English. Then a charming and shy young Frenchman called Marcel Duplessis wrote (with the modest parenthesis: '*Inspiré de Ronsard*'):

Quand vous serez bien vieille
Au soir, à la chandelle,
Direz chantant mes vers
En vous émerveillant
Marcel me trouvait belle
Du temps que j'étais jeune.

There was an alteration in the tone and nature of the subsequent entries. '*De l'Amour et de l'Amitié à travers les Siècles – A Mon Amie Michèle Duchesne*', wrote one patient, quoting a dozen disparate couples which related to the impression which Michèle had made on him.

A female patient wrote archly: '*Tout mon souvenir à la petite Michèle qui par son courage et sa gaité s'attira toutes les sympathies* (*sympathies masculines tout particulièrement*!)'

A middle-aged Dutch banker: '*Cordial souvenir à la belle et gracieuse Madamemoiselle Michèle – Ton entrain juvenil, ton rire frais et joyeux furent pour le moral de tes compagnons d'infortune un précieux réconfort.*'

An elderly Englishman: 'How nice to be always gay! You bring a ray of sunshine with you when you visit your friends.'

A young Irishman, newly married: 'My daughter is fifteen days old today and should she grow to be like you, Michèle, I would be very happy.'

A Belgian who knew both Paul and Michèle: '*Comme tous j'ai entendu votre rire, et peut-être ai-je mieux compris que d'autres quelle somme de franc courage il représente. Lutter contre la matière est grave, mais avoir à lutter contre l'esprit est beaucoup plus difficile...'*

The last entry to date was by Dr. Florent. An infantile drawing of a house with a cat outside and then the message: '*Bon courage pour encore quatre semaines.*'

In four weeks it would be Easter, and Michèle's parents had obtained permission for her to return to Liège for ten days' holiday. The four weeks diminished to three, to two and at last to one.

When the Baron de la Marelle realised that the reason why Paul had refused to make an entry in the *carnet* was because he did not wish to include himself in the category of Michèle's friends, he tore his own entry from the book. For a long time he had honoured Michèle with his lofty attentions, had addressed her in epithets of condescending devotion, had discoursed on his friends and connections, on his family château and estates and on the subtle and innate distinction conferred by high birth.

One of the principal consolations in the lives of the majority of patients, he frequently assured her, was that illness and enforced residence in a sanatorium afforded them the unique opportunity of associating on terms of relative intimacy with a restricted and exclusive élite. Nor were the members of the élite entirely without consolation – de la Marelle let it be known that the balance between his *rente* and what he had actually spent during the past year was equal to several times the annual income of the President of the Republic.

Sustaining the disparity between the two sums was, in fact, his dominant activity. Any additional incidental expenditure – an X-ray plate or a course of vitamin injections – provoked him to initiate compensatory economies. At last, to provide a fund from which these vexatious expenses might be met he moved to a smaller room, ordered no supplements to the menu and abstracted the magazines, periodicals and newspapers (to which formerly he had subscribed) from amongst those provided for general use in the sanatorium library.

He kept no account with the concierge (who added a service charge of ten per cent to the disbursements made on behalf of patients) preferring to station himself in the hall and to importune anyone going out of the sanatorium to make his purchases for him. Whenever possible he prevailed on Michèle to dispatch his commissions. At the end of the subsequent examination, enquiry and veiled accusation of theft until each franc had been accounted for, he would develop one of his favourite themes.

'What greater satisfaction than that of bearing by inalienable right one of the historic names of France? What more propitious destiny for a young girl than the right to share that name?' he would demand rhetorically, and in the style of the Comédie-Française. Then scratching the crown of his head with the mouthpiece of his pipe, and watching Michèle obliquely: 'What future more spectacular than that of being allied and affiliated to a man whose style and patronymic are to be encountered between the pages of the principal court memoirs?'

One day he called on Michèle with a bundle of soiled handkerchiefs which he asked her to wash through for him. She refused with vigour. He shrugged his shoulders and stuffed the handkerchiefs into the torn pocket of his unsavoury dressing-gown. Then he asked her to marry him.

'Understand,' he said, 'that but that I am ill, I would not contemplate such a union – on your own admission your background is wholly unsuitable. Nevertheless your good looks and your air of natural breeding suggest to me that for the purposes of documentation it won't be too impossible to ferret out some sort of ancestry. My mother is visiting tomorrow, and though inevitably the news will be a major disappointment to her, I am sure that with tact and understanding we will be able, little by little, to accustom her to the idea. In any case, leave all that to me! For your own part, behave as naturally in her presence as you do in mine, and at the same time, take care to act towards me with excessive solicitude – nothing, in the final count, could be better calculated to gain her good opinion.' Then raising his voice in a sudden pettish aside, he shrilled: 'Besides it's time that mother began to face the facts – my illness has completely upset all my matrimonial prospects!'

De la Marelle took Michèle's fascinated silence for assent and advanced to embrace her. Michèle stepped back until she was blocked by her bed. 'Have your prospects really sunk so low?' she questioned.

'That will all depend on your future behaviour and deportment,' replied de la Marelle gallantly.

'But your noble background. Your ancestors...'

'One or two of them made marriages that were very little better.' He stepped forward again, eyes gleaming. Michèle tried to step back, stumbled and fell on the side of her bed. De la Marelle, believing it all to be a ruse, flung himself on her. She eluded him with ease and he sprawled across the bed.

'Conceited, presumptuous little baron!' she cried, laughing so much she could barely stand.

'You are emotionally unsettled. I do not demand an immediate reply,' said de la Marelle, sitting up on the bed.

'But I will give you an immediate reply. I wouldn't – '

'Say nothing rash! Reflect on my offer!'

'I wouldn't – '

'Your judgment's impaired. Don't say what you'll regret later.'

'I wouldn't marry – '

'No one else of my rank – '

'Let me speak!' cried Michèle. 'I wouldn't marry you if you were ten barons or twenty barons or a detachment of barons. I wouldn't marry you if you were the King of France or the King of the Solar System or the King of the Universe. I wouldn't marry you – ' she sought unsuccessfully for fresh images. 'I wouldn't marry you,' she repeated finally.

'You wouldn't marry me!' declared de la Marelle incredulously. He got up from the bed.

'No!'

'Why?'

'I don't love you.'

'But I don't ask you to love me. My mother didn't love my father and she was the daughter of a duke.'

'You might have been very different if she had!'

'Well, as it happens. I don't love you either!'

'Then that solves everything!' Still laughing, Michèle took de la Marelle by the elbow and led him to the door.

'Will you marry me?' he demanded, wrenching his elbow free.

'Go back to your room and put your handkerchiefs in the laundry basket.'

'Will you marry me?'

'And at the same time it wouldn't be a bad idea to send your princely sweater to the imperial, coroneted wash-house.'

'Oh, you're so impenitently plebeian!' said de la Marelle, stamping his foot.

As he left the room Paul was coming up the passage to call for Michèle. '*Bonjour, M. le Marquis*!' Paul called out cheerfully. De la Marelle stared at him furiously, gave a curt and insolent bow, and strode on to his room.

Mme. de la Marelle proved more amenable to the proposed union than her son had anticipated. She called on Michèle on the evening of her arrival, regarded her from the door, and said: 'Mademoiselle, you are even prettier than my son had led me to believe.' Then she shook hands graciously with Michèle, and drew a chair to the side of her bed.

'I know all your secrets – you have nothing to conceal from me,' she said smiling. 'My son has done you a great honour which you, with commendable restraint and modesty, have declined. Nevertheless I have little doubt that you will change your mind when I tell you that subject to a satisfactory report on your health (for we don't want two invalids in the family), and on your unimpaired capacity for child-bearing, I am not, in principle, opposed to the union.' She sat back, the better to admire the effect of her words.

'But Madame, there is no question – '

Mme. de la Marelle leant forward again and took Michèle's hand in her own. 'I know precisely what you are going to say, but please put it out of your mind. What my son really needs is a good, clean girl who will look after him, attend to all his needs and console him for the brilliant future and marriage of which his illness has deprived him. The question of social background is absolutely of secondary importance – besides (and if my husband were alive, he would agree with me), my son has blue blood enough in his veins for both of you!'

'Madame,' said Michèle, withdrawing her hand, 'you have made a tremendous mistake. What you have taken for modesty is in reality disinclination and distaste.'

'Disinclination?'

'And distaste.'

'Distaste! For my son!' declared Mme. de la Marelle, opening her eyes very wide.

'Yes, and I have made it very clear to him that there could be no question of marriage. Besides he knows perfectly well that I am engaged to someone else.'

'To someone else!' Mme. de la Marelle could now do no more than echo Michèle's words.

'And so there is really no point in our discussing the matter any further.'

'No point! There is every point!' cried Mme. de la Marelle, rallying and returning to the attack. 'When it is a matter of my son's happiness, I put that before everything else. As for whosoever you say you're engaged to – I know all about him!'

'From your son, I suppose.'

'Of course not – my son wouldn't acknowledge the existence of such a person. Dr. Vernet spoke of him when I was making some preliminary enquiries about you.'

'So you have been making enquiries about me?'

'Yes. And it may interest you to know that whilst Dr. Vernet speaks well of you, he also thinks you can be very stubborn and self-willed. As for the man in the châlet – '

'Please don't say anything. My affairs do not concern you, Madame.'

'They concern me inasmuch as they concern my son.'

'Nor, I assure you, do they concern him. You say that you are looking for a good, clean girl, who could look after your son and console him for the marriage that he might have made – I suggest that you start the search for her in the vicinity of your own kitchens!'

'*Mademoiselle*,' said Mme. de la Marelle, getting up from her chair, 'your insolence surpasses anything that I have ever experienced. I shall do my best to make it clear to my son that he has had a more fortunate escape than he will probably ever realise.'

At that moment the door opened and de la Marelle came into the room, his dressing-gown unfastened, the cords, as usual, trailing behind him. 'Is everything settled?' he asked.

'My poor boy,' said Mme. de la Marelle, darting towards him.

'Oh! don't fuss, Mother.' He took his pipe from his pocket and started to light it. 'Vernet's just shown me my new X-ray. There's been absolutely no improvement since the last,' he muttered between puffs.

'No improvement! What ghastly news!' Mme. de la Marelle shot a tortured, accusing glance at Michèle.

'Oh! sit down, Mother – you're getting on my nerves.'

Mme. de la Marelle resumed her seat and her son placed himself moodily on the end of Michèle's bed.

'Are you in pain?' whispered Mme. de la Marelle.

'No.'

'Come and sit in the armchair – you'll be more comfortable.'

'Do stop chattering. You're giving me a headache.'

They all sat in silence. At last Michèle picked up a book from her bedside table and started to read. Suddenly Mme. de la Marelle got up from her chair.

'What are you doing?' de la Marelle demanded angrily.

'I'm just going out for a moment.'

'Why are you going out?'

'I must.'

'Why must you?'

'I have to go to the toilet.'

'To go to the toilet! You've got all day to go to the toilet! Sit down and stop trying to irritate me.'

'But – '

'Sit down.'

Mme. de la Marelle did as she was told. De la Marelle continued to glower and to puff at his pipe. Michèle continued to read her book. Half an hour later a waiter came to announce that M. le Baron's dinner had been served in his room and that it was getting cold.

Michèle arrived at the châlet. 'How are the Marelles?' demanded Paul when he had embraced her.

'*Ils m'embêtent. Mais parlons d'autre chose – nous n'avons pas longtemps*.' She lay at Paul's side on the divan.

Paul lowered his head on to her check-shirted shoulder, pressed the whole length of her slender body against his own. What would it be like, he wondered, when each morning did not end this way?

Their long-term plans had been formulated. Paul would remain in the mountains until such time as Michèle was definitively recalled to Belgium. Then he would return to England and look for work, whilst Michèle would seek parental sanction for their marriage. As soon as possible she would rejoin him, and, if necessary, she too would take a job.

Paul took her face in his hands, scrutinised its every facet, obsessed by the knowledge that before his eyes it was changing with the imperceptible inevitability of an hour-hand circling the face of a clock. In this face where all was perfection, all change must be decline. He wanted to possess her eternally, but eternally in the present. It was *now* which mattered. It was always *now* which mattered.

His hands passed beneath her shirt, under her shoulder-blades, the nails penetrating the cool, sweet-smelling flesh. Usually, the more tightly he held her, the more she seemed elusive. But now, inexplicably, miraculously, the pulsations of her heart ceased to echo the passing seconds, responded instead to a deeper organic rhythm in his own body. And suddenly he knew with the force of revelation that his life had entered upon its optimum phase. This was both the meridian and the point of eclipse. In terms of time they could never again be closer.

This time there could be no question about it. Paul was lying face downwards, his head buried in the pillow. The sound of breathing, of muffled movement was very close. A spanner? An iron spike? To move, to cry out would be to precipitate the blow and impair its accuracy. Better to lie still and let the skull be cleanly crushed. Paul tensed as he felt the rush of air across his neck. The instrument skimmed his hair. He could no longer control himself. Scream after scream. He woke up.

Complete darkness. This was the way the mind snaps. This is the way the mind snaps. Yes, this is the way… 'My dear friend…' Paul was drinking port, after dinner, in the junior common room of his college. 'My dear friend…' Laughter, 'Joan of Arc and her voices…' More laughter. 'If that were all *I* heard… I – ' He broke off as the duvet slipped from his bed. 'Now watch what will happen!' he murmured in a confidential aside. To retrieve the duvet he stretched out his hand to the floor. Under the tips of his fingers, in a sudden glow of light, something inert shot into instantaneous, threshing defiance. Paul recoiled, then propelling himself on his arms, he tried to throw himself over the side of the bed on whatever was there. But he could not open his eyes – he tried to tear back the lids. With screams on his lips, he awoke a second time.

The curtains now showed transparent against the windows. 'Oh God, what can I do, what can I do?' he repeated, sitting up and holding his head in his hands. What caused these hallucinated nights? He drank nothing, he avoided before sleeping the sort of reading that might tend to stimulate bad dreams. Was there still somewhere in his body a pocket of treacherous morphia discharging itself, drop by drop, into his brain. How long had passed between his two wakings? Paul stared at the hand which had sought to retrieve the duvet. What had it nearly touched? Then he shuddered with the sudden conviction that what had passed had not been the product of his imagination. He got out of bed and started on the search of his room which would lead, finally, to the outer door and the untroubled, immaculate surface of the snow.

CHAPTER TWELVE

•

It was the last Sunday before Michèle left for Belgium. Mme. Anniette had prepared and packed a picnic lunch. Paul and Michèle set off from the châlet as soon as Michèle had returned from mass.

The previous day, Mme. de la Marelle, tearful and distracted, had left Brisset at the request of her son – he had declared that her congenital lack of tact had been responsible for the failure of his suit. She had intercepted Dr. Vernet during the course of his medical rounds and having described the unhappy situation, and demanded whether in his opinion she should go or stay. 'You should go!' Dr. Vernet had replied with conviction – he had grown tired of interminable interviews about the Baron de la Marelle. But her son was inconsolable, he neither ate nor slept, she had insisted. Dr. Vernet had refrained from comment. 'And' – she had hesitated – 'And every day he meditates on suicide!' 'Tell me who,' Dr. Vernet had replied, examining his nails with interest. 'Tell me who, in this sanatorium, does not!'

'He never wants to see me again and it is all your fault. You have come between a mother and her son!' she had shouted after Michèle, whom she had encountered in a passage. Then she had followed her to her room and had alternately abused and cajoled her until Michèle had agreed to accompany the Baroness to her son's bedside to explain that she alone had been responsible for her decision. De la Marelle, however, had received the double visit with such a display of invective, with such cries of '*Traitresse*!', '*Ingrate*!' and *Espèce de chipie*' that Michèle had left immediately. Eagerly Mme. de la Marelle had confirmed the justice of these epithets, at which her son, goaded beyond coherence, had seized a bocal of aperient syrup and had discharged it in her face.

De la Marelle saw no virtue in discretion. Whilst doctors injected his pleural cavity with air, whilst nurses propelled calcium up his veins, whilst waiters brought fresh table linen and *femmes de chambres* polished the handle and outer surface of his chamber pot, he expounded and extended on his unreciprocated passion, on Michèle's infidelity, on Paul's unworthiness and on the criminal blunders and inadequacies of his mother… His application disseminated the details of the affair throughout the sanatorium and reinstated the association between Paul and Michèle as the primary topic of conversation at the sister's table.

It was partly to be temporarily free of this atmosphere, partly because it would be their last walk for some time and partly because they were already over-familiar with the environs of their own sector of Brisset, that they had decided to descend by the *crémaillère* to the lower village, and from there to penetrate into the surrounding countryside.

'What are you thinking?' asked Michèle, as they walked in silence down the slope from the châlet.

'Nothing.'

'Are you in a bad mood?'

'No.'

They passed the shuttered façade of *Les Alpes*, as predacious, brooding and derelict as the Colosseum, and as they drew level with the main entrance they saw that standing just inside the portal, like three dehiscent grotesques from a Leonardo cartoon, were Dr. Bruneau, M. Halfont and Emile.

'*Bonjour!*' called out Dr. Bruneau. 'Sanatorium for sale. Do you want to buy one?'

They stopped. The three men, wearing raincoats and slouch hats, left the portal and surrounded them.

'Caught!' cried Dr. Bruneau, playfully seizing Paul and Michèle by an arm. 'Where are you escaping to?'

'Where is there to escape to?' replied Paul.

'Nowhere. Why don't you learn to adapt yourself to your circumstances? Your health compels you to stay in the mountains. Good! Be like Roosevelt, the deaf Beethoven, the arthritic Renoir – treat your situation as a perpetual challenge. Teach yourself, *cher Monsieur*, to react.'

'I am quite alone in the sanatorium,' said M. Halfont, addressing Michèle and screwing up his eyes. 'Ten years of hard work and when the sanatorium is sold I have no job. Emile stays with me temporarily as caretaker.'

Emile guffawed and winked at Paul. 'There's less of this,' he said, flexing his knees and staggering a few paces under the weight of an imaginary body. 'And there's more of this.' He raised an invisible glass to his lips.

'Learn to take your opportunities where you find them. The sanatorium is for sale – why not buy it? Seriously, *Monsieur*, why not consider buying the sanatorium?' demanded Dr. Bruneau, raising his voice to command everyone's attention and at the same time exchanging sly smiles with his companions. 'You have here your nucleus staff – a *médecin chef*, a *directeur* who is also an acknowledged authority on international invalid cookery, and a celebrated multi-lingual *concierge*.' He put a persuasive arm about Paul's shoulder. 'Write to your distinguished friends in England and borrow enough money to pay the deposit on a mortgage. Then reopen the sanatorium section by section, undercut the *Société* and before you know what has happened you will have become one of the reigning princes of Brisset!'

'We must be going. We're catching the train to the village,' said Paul.

'Make your time here count for something,' continued Dr. Bruneau, still clasping Paul's shoulder. 'Have you no hidden talents to develop? Can't you paint or compose music? Or perhaps there is a secret work of which we know nothing but which, when it appears, will make us sit up in astonishment that we were all so blind!'

'No, I'm afraid not. I've got absolutely no talents. If I had my life over again, I think I'd study medicine,' said Paul. Emile grinned.

'Well, at least apply yourself to something,' cried Dr. Bruneau, squeezing his arm round Paul's neck. 'When I was ill I composed a thesis on lymphadenitis. There's an example for you. Why aren't you doing something? What sort of student are you meant to be?'

'With students I like always very much to discuss the distinctions in economicals between the countries – is a very nice digression,' said M. Halfont.

'Take a correspondence course, anything. Study semantics, bee-keeping, boot-repairing. Prepare yourself to become a Doctor of Commerce at an American university.'

A grinding, groaning sound from the direction of the station announced the arrival of the *crémaillère*. Paul disengaged his neck from the imprisoning arm. 'We must go now. Thank you for all your advice.'

'Come one day to tea – the passages of an empty sanatorium are full of ghosts, it is very interesting,' said M. Halfont. 'You can go anywhere, re-see your old rooms, the *salle à manger*, the *Service Médical*. And whilst it's not in use you ought to visit the refrigerated mortuary – a most expensive installation.'

'If you are not able to study do something practical, make artificial flowers, cut out leather purses, address envelopes for *Monsieur le Curé*,' shouted Dr. Bruneau as Paul and Michèle hurried down the hill.

They caught the train, and eight minutes later arrived at the lower village. They set off from the station, following the mountain road until the main settlements of sanatoria were out of sight.

'Sois gentil. Je pars demain,' said Michèle. It was very strange, thought Paul, as he took her hand. He had dreaded her departure. Nor had he overlooked the danger that once she was back in Belgium her doctor might decide that her condition was sufficiently consolidated and that there was no need for her to return to the mountains. And the extraordinary thing was that without loving her any less, without his love being in any way modified, he felt suddenly, walking at her side in the hard, thin, clear air, emotionally detached and uncommitted. 'Could it be that now that we are both better, we no longer need each other?' he wondered. It was an idea which even a few hours earlier would have been unthinkable.

The sun was very strong – the snow had gone from the roads, its periphery was shrinking in the fields and meadows. They passed through a wood, turned up along a path and soon found themselves in a remote and uninhabited area where the only buildings were crude, low-built byres that were used when the cattle were brought to graze in the mountains in the summer. A little after midday they stopped at a ridge above the Arve valley and ate their meal.

'Bruneau is pathological,' said Paul. (It was essential to speak – unquestionably Michèle had registered his malaise.) 'Thank God we're both free of him,' he added as an afterthought.

'You think we are?'

'Well, *I* am. I can't say I'll never have a relapse, but I can say it will never be Bruneau who'll treat me for it. Why, if I had to choose, I'd prefer Halfont or Emile – neither could do worse than Bruneau. What a trio! Do you think they all sleep together in the refrigerated mortuary?'

There was another silence.

Then Michèle said: 'I wish I'd already been home and that this was my first Sunday back.'

'You won't feel like that when you get there.'

'Of course I will.'

'You'll see,' said Paul. He got up from the boulder on which he had been sitting and went to the edge of the ridge. 'There is something strange about this place,' he said, looking up the valley in the direction of Brisset. 'We all adapt ourselves to it far too easily.'

'What do you mean?'

'I mean that it ought to be the most terrible upheaval to come and live in the mountains, to leave everyone and everything one knows and loves, but instead one accepts it, one forgets that one ever lived in any other way and finally one doesn't even seriously think in terms of leaving – it's as though one's past life were something one had once read about in a half-forgotten novel.'

He paused, but, as she interposed no comment, he resumed: 'The fact is, of course, that it's all part of some compensatory mechanism. The day comes when one is better and suddenly, in a flash, one realises that it isn't the past which is unreal but the present.' He turned about and faced her. 'You'll see the truth of what I say when you get back to your own people. Brisset and all that has happened will seem like an episode from a queer, receding dream.'

Michèle did not reply. 'We ought to go now,' said Paul, looking at his watch. He cleared away the paper bags and cardboard cups, stuffing them into an army haversack, which he then slung over his shoulder. In silence, preoccupied with their thoughts, they set off back to the village. After several minutes they found that they had taken the wrong path, but as it appeared to be leading in the right direction, they continued along it. It twisted about the mountainside, in and out of the undergrowth, the village appearing at times to be nearer, at times to be farther away. At last they felt that they were making no progress and that they would do better to turn back.

Suddenly they came out of a wood into a clearing. Like banks of seats in an antique theatre which had been constructed with the Arve valley as its stage, row upon row of tombstones rose above and fell below the path, covering whole acres of the mountainside. And as Paul and Michèle continued, so the vista extended; tombs had been built into every niche, recess or fissure.

So it was here, discreetly beyond the range of any but the best walkers, that they were accommodated, the former comrades of the *salle de consultation* and of the *salle de scopie*, of the *salle à manger* and the midnight corridors; the comrades with good morale, the comrades with bad; the comrades with temperature graphs, weight graphs, pulse graphs, respiration, sedimentation and evacuation graphs, with everything, in fact (except their personal feelings), neatly charted, calculated and calibrated as they shuffled and snuffled their way to the grave.

Paul and Michèle glimpsed the threnodic, brief descriptions of the nearest stones. '*Né* Calcutta 1905. *Décédé* Brisset 1935'. '*Né* Milano 1920. *Décédé* Brisset 1945'. '*Né* Camden Town 1915. *Décédé* Brisset 1938'. '*Née* Lyon 1895. *Décédée* Brisset 1912'. '*Né* Hamburg 1901. *Décédé* Brisset 1912'. Holland, Sweden, Hungary, Greece, Canada, Java, New Zealand – multifarious places of origin, a common place of decease. Ultimate League of Nations – chatterboxes, wise-wives, cretins and saints, the whole tubercular crew, formerly united, rotting in the banality and tedium of a sanatorium existence, still united, rotting undividedly in death. Brisset, known narrowly in every European country as '*le cimetière de l'Europe*', was in reality '*le cimetière du monde entier*'.

The size not of the graveyard but of the graves abruptly diminished as if the patients who had coughed themselves in two had been buried each half separately. Paul and Michèle had reached the toy-town cemetery: cute, lilliputian graves surmounted by permanent wreaths as derelict and as bare as the little skeletons beneath; still, sagacious rows of the *locataires en perpétuité* of the inexpensive boxes in the children's amphitheatre; little ones who had come from far to breathe the Alpine air and who had terminated their journey in three feet of Alpine soil.

Ideal extension of a sanatorium. Here prognosis hugged diagnosis; here every patient was *sage*, observed scrupulously his *cure*, committed no *imprudences*; here were the model, the absolute patients, the *nonpareils* of the whole tubercular world. Was there not in Brisset one doctor, composed, conscientious, white-bloused, stethoscope in hand, to make token rounds, from time to time, of all the graves? To ask: '*Et comment ça va, cher Monsieur?*' To praise the *bon moral* of one and the *sagesse* of another? Did not they deserve at least this tribute, these mute graduates of the Alpine academies?

CHAPTER THIRTEEN

•

'What do you do now that you are a widower?' demanded *Sœur* Miriam as Paul put on his shirt after a refill. What indeed?

He went for walks. He sat inside and outside cafés. On two consecutive afternoons he attended the showing of the same indifferent film in the village. One evening at his invitation Pierre, Mme. Anniette's assistant, came to drink a glass of port in his room. Handkerchief gripped between his teeth, tears rolling down his cheeks, he related the story of his life, an odyssey of relapses, of *défaillances*, of slender ambitions ever thwarted by the condition of his health. '*Une fois tutu, Monsieur Davenant, on l'est pour toute la vie,*' he concluded, wiping his eyes.

'*Ça ne va pas avec le moral, ça ne va pas du tout,*' said Mme. Anniette after lunch, the fourth day after Michèle's departure. Paul lay back on the divan in her little bed-sitting-room, sipping the coffee she had just given him. '*Il faut faire quelque-chose,*' said Mme. Anniette. There was, she explained, a little hotel on the lake, not far from Annecy, which was clean, attractive, and where special terms were allowed for clients whom she recommended. There would be no effort required from Paul – she would reserve the accommodation, buy the ticket and pack the cases. A few days '*en plaine*' and he would return invigorated and refreshed.

Mme. Anniette did all that she had promised and more. She pressed Paul's clothes for the journey, relined his jacket and bought him a copy of *La Symphonie Pastorale* to read on the train. And the next morning she and Pierre accompanied him to the station and stood waving until the *crémaillère* had disappeared from sight.

The same evening, just when supper was over, Paul reappeared at the châlet; he offered no explanation for his return other than the drawn and desperate cast of his features. Mme. Anniette quickly laid a place between the sergeant and the Alsatian electrician and cooked an omelette. When Paul had finished eating, he went at once to his room.

* * *

The sergeant was in excellent spirits. (An *ancien thoracé* in his early fifties, he had lost nine ribs and was as thin as a filleted eel. He worked in the local garage.) Hat on the back of his head, shirt-sleeves rolled above the forearm, chair tilted, he cried: 'Shut up, Fritz, and eat your sausages!' He shot a glance at his *petit chou*, a plump, half-witted, middle-aged *femme de chambre*, who called for him in the evenings. Too timid to come to the dining-room with '*toutes les grandes personnes*', the *petit chou* sat on the sergeant's bed, and watched the scene through the half-open door. The sergeant opened and closed his hand at her – she burst into smothered laughter.

'*Mais c'est pas joli*,' said Fritz. (Ten years younger than the sergeant, he walked with a limp and lacked a kidney. He boasted that he had had T.B. in every part of his body except the lungs.)

'Eat, I tell you!'

'Ah, no!'

Mme. Anniette had killed a chicken and had served it with rice. Fritz was disconsolate that because he had only just arrived and because, moreover, he had said that he would not be back for supper, all the chicken had been eaten.

'I like chicken. When have I said I didn't like chicken?' he demanded, though no one had suggested the contrary. He slipped off his jacket and rolled up his sleeves.

'Eat! Eat!' The sergeant was ecstatic.

'He never tells you what he's going to do, and then if things don't go as he planned he howls like a spoiled child.' Mme. Anniette forked some more sausages on to Fritz's plate. Fritz stared at them disconsolately.

'Oh, là, là! He's still thinking of his chicken,' chuckled the sergeant, shaking from side to side and tugging at his moustaches. '*Le brave* Fritz is still thinking of his chicken!' He again opened and shut his hand at the *petit chou* and she collapsed face downwards on the duvet to stifle her laughter.

'I'm very fond of chicken,' muttered Fritz, stuffing the sausages into his mouth.

'And was it good? Oh, la – la!' The sergeant smacked his lips, rubbed his stomach and raised his hat.

Fritz masticated loudly the last of the sausages.

'I want some more. I'm still hungry.'

'You eat enough for five people,' protested Mme. Anniette. She piled his plate with potatoes.

'He's not a Fritz – he's a pig!' cried the sergeant, winking at Paul.

Fritz snorted, guzzled and lowered his face into the plate as though it were a trough. The *petit chou*, who had just recovered her poise, let out a shriek and re-buried her face in the *duvet*.

'That's enough, Fritz,' said the sergeant severely. There were times when he resented Fritz's success with the *petit chou*.

Paul got up from the table. '*Bonsoir, M'sieu*,' said the sergeant and Fritz together. The *petit chou* peered out at him, then crouched back behind the door. He heard her laughter as he closed the front door.

He went to his room and to bed. There was no object in trying to read; he took a sedative and turned out the light. Michèle. By the end of the first long, solitary afternoon he had known that he loved her without reserve or reservation. How had he believed even for a few hours that his feelings had changed to indifference? What was this demon of perversity which even the worst rigours of his sickness had failed to exorcise? And his despair and loneliness had mounted during the succeeding days until at last he had become incapable of any degree of objectivity, believing that deliberately, calculatedly and progressively he had alienated himself from her love. What chance was there, he asked himself, that she would return? Her health was restored and her parents could ill afford the sanatorium fees. What would become of him? He could not contemplate life without her. He must not think about it, it was no good thinking. He turned on his side. The panic in the station and in the streets of the little town near Annecy, the suspicion, hostility and insight into his condition in the shops, restaurants and hotel... Was he, like Pierre, going to be forced to pass the remainder of his life in the mountains? Again he turned. There must be a position in which the mind as well as the body could be rested. Where was there any rest? Perhaps he and Michèle should return to England whilst he had still the balance of his uncle's legacy. Perhaps he should try and take his degree and then find employment. Could he ask Michèle to wait? What was the use of asking Michèle anything, since he had lost her? His hand went up to his forehead.

* * *

The side door to the passage which connected with his room opened and shut – his brain registered the sound but not the implications. Then suddenly he sat upright in his bed. He had not been dreaming, he had not even been to sleep. He listened, suspended his breathing. Nothing. Trembling slightly, he lay down again. A board creaked outside his door. He seized his torch, which he kept by his bedside.

The door opened. There was more creaking of boards. He shone the torch. The beam illuminated the sickly face and disorderly red hair of Dr. Bruneau.

'Turn off that torch, you're blinding me,' said Dr. Bruneau.

'What do you want?'

'I happened to be passing.' Dr. Bruneau found the switch for which he had been groping. 'Ah! That's better,' he said. He took off his raincoat and shook it over the floor. 'It's snowing – the winter's started again.' He looked about him. 'Very much as I'd expected – wooden walls, a few *bibelots* and hessian curtains. Is there very much noise?'

'Very much noise?'

'I mean from one room to another.' Dr. Bruneau tapped one of the walls with his knuckles. 'Tight as a drum, and thin as paper. A very primitive piece of construction. It's my guess that one would hear every sound. Is there anyone next door to you?'

'No. Why do you ask?'

'Who else is here besides you? The *patronne*? A servant?'

'An assistant and two lodgers.'

'*Anciens malades?*'

'Yes.'

'The *patronne* must have a thriving business! On a quiet night do you hear voices from the other rooms? Or sounds?'

'Sounds?'

'Sounds, *cher Monsieur*,' said Dr. Bruneau impatiently, waving his right hand and clicking his fingers. 'If someone gets in or out of bed, and the bed creaks, do you hear it?'

'I don't know. I never really – '

'Or if they knock over a chair or kick their slippers across the room.'

'I – '

'Sh!' Dr. Bruneau put his ear against the wall and raised his hand. 'I can't hear anything. Are they all in bed?'

'I expect so.'

'Who sleeps above you?'

'The *patronne*.'

'And how many rooms are vacant?'

'Three or four.'

'Sh!' Dr. Bruneau again applied his ear to the wall. 'I can hear breathing. I can distinctly hear breathing.'

'It's probably my own.'

'Well, stop breathing.'

Dr. Bruneau at last appeared satisfied. 'I may be joining you here – that is, if I am really convinced there is no noise,' he explained. Then, as Paul gave a slight gasp, he added quickly: 'No, it's unfair of me to raise your hopes. The thing is that the *Société* has given me notice to quit my room in the autumn, and by then you'll probably be far away.' He sat down on the end of the bed and playfully seized one of Paul's blanket-covered feet and wagged it. 'Now tell me truthfully, are you pleased to see me? We meet less often than we used to, don't we? Oh, before I forget, I had a funny dream a few nights ago. It was that you'd relapsed and were back again at *Les Alpes*, and I was looking after you. Quite nostalgic, really. But they say dreams go by opposites, don't they?' He grinned, showing his gums. 'Now tell me what you're doing. I hope that you are using your freedom profitably – *les beaux jours* won't last for ever. What are you reading now?'

He got up and examined Paul's shelves. 'Same old books – Proust, Stendhal, Dostoyevsky. Not precisely what I would call *avant-garde*. You're a century behind, *cher Monsieur*. You see yourself in front of a *décor* of samovars and racing droshkys or dining by candlelight *chez de Princesse de Noailles*, whereas in reality you're just another of Chekhov's dreary, eternal students. Can't you grasp that you are living in the world of a romantic young boy still in his *lycée*?

'Develop, grow up, *cher Monsieur*,' he exhorted, throwing his arms apart. 'Make yourself understand that you are separated from all these nineteenth-century neurotics by two wars and your own nearly mortal illness. Do you study politics? Have you any knowledge of political institutions? Are you preparing yourself for the future in order that you may be of service to the world as I, in my humble way, have been of service to you and many others?'

He put on his raincoat and buttoned it up to the neck. 'Why do you lie with the light out at only ten o'clock? It's your body which needs resting, not your mind. Think of Pasteur, think of Koch, think of Einstein. What would they have done if they had not kept their minds supple and receptive? Be encouraged by the example of great men – you too have your mite to contribute, however slight and insignificant.'

He went to the door, then turned. 'There's no need to mention my visit to your friends,' he said smiling candidly. 'In any case I am sure that we are both men of the world. Good night.'

The new client would be staying for only one night – a brisk, pretty girl in her early twenties. Where had she come from? Who had recommended her? Was she visiting friends or relations? To all Mme. Anniette's questions, the girl had made non-committal replies.

At supper there was a lot of passing of dishes and '*Après vous's*'. Fritz had so flattened his hair that it looked as if it had been painted on his head. The Sergeant was wearing his Sunday hat, and when the *petit chou* arrived he shut the door of his bedroom in order that she might not be seen.

When the meal was over, the girl remained at the table. Paul went back to his room. The sergeant joined the *petit chou* who could be heard sobbing behind the bedroom door. Fritz, when he could offer no more to eat, tentatively offered himself. He was rejected. Disenchanted, he left the dining room.

A little later Mme. Anniette started to lock up for the night. '*Laissez Madame*,' ordered the girl, coming out of the dining room. She was expecting a visitor. If Mme. Anniette would go to bed, she would make herself responsible for bolting the door.

At two o'clock Paul was woken by screams which he was pleased to note were not his own. He sat up and turned on the light. There was a lot of stamping, some shouting, the sound of breaking glass and the slamming of the door.

Then someone left the main entrance of the châlet and came to the side. There were footsteps in the passage which led to his room. Dr. Bruneau came in. He was wearing pyjamas, his feet were bare and his forehead was bleeding.

'Did you hear any noise?' he demanded.

'No.'

'Good.' Dr. Bruneau looked about him. 'I've come to spend the rest of the night on your divan – the door of my room's clicked to. You're quite sure you didn't hear any noise?'

'Not a sound.'

'Why was your light on?'

'Since your advice I now read late.'

'Ah!' Dr. Bruneau seemed satisfied. 'Well, I would like one of your blankets and a pillow. And you'd better let me have your overcoat.'

'Adaptability is our primary aim,' said Dr. Bruneau didactically, as Paul helped him make up a bed, 'we must adjust ourselves as a preliminary to mastering it.' He folded back the blankets and got between them. Paul returned to his own bed and turned out the light. As his head touched the pillow he heard Dr. Bruneau's last sighs change to first snores.

Paul was wakened by Dr. Bruneau shaking his shoulder. 'For God's sake pull yourself together, they're bringing in your breakfast. I'll step into the wardrobe,' he said.

There was a knock at the door. Mme. Anniette entered cautiously with the breakfast tray. She raised an enquiring eyebrow and Paul pointed to Dr. Bruneau's place of concealment. Mme. Anniette clapped a hand over her mouth and nearly dropped the tray. There was a cry of '*Merde*!' from the wardrobe. Mme. Anniette set down the tray and ran from the room. Dr. Bruneau emerged red-eyed and frantic. 'You fool,' he cried, nursing one foot after the other, 'you've upset a box of drawing pins on the floor of the wardrobe.'

'I'm sorry.'

'Did the *patronne* hear me shout?'

'Probably not – she's a little deaf. Besides, it was muffled by the clothes.'

'She suspects nothing?'

'Nothing.'

Dr. Bruneau looked at the breakfast tray. 'Why did she bring in two cups?'

'I can't imagine.'

Without pressing the point, Dr. Bruneau poured himself a cup of coffee, drank it, poured himself another. 'That's better,' he said, wiping his lips with his thumb.

'Now I want you to do something for me. I have had a little *malentendu* with the young lady who had dinner here last night, and unfortunately my clothes are still in her bedroom. Will you, therefore, under the pretext that they are your own, go and collect them?' Paul put on his dressing-gown. 'And don't forget my shoes,' Dr. Bruneau shouted as he went out the door.

A pretext was unnecessary – all Dr. Bruneau's clothes had been flung into the passage after him, and had remained there until they had been picked up by Mme. Anniette. She had just finished pressing them when Paul came into the hall. '*Ça ne va pas pour un grand psychologue de porter des vêtements aussi chiffonnés*,' she said.

When Paul returned Dr. Bruneau was biting a croissant and shaving in hot milk. 'Probably very good for the complexion – you should try it,' he said, redipping Paul's shaving brush in the milk jug. He glanced at his clothes. 'She didn't give you a small whip with them, did she?'

'I'm afraid not.'

'Pity.'

Dr. Bruneau began to get dressed. 'Women are strange creatures. They know how to arouse appetites, but not how to satisfy them. Yet if one points the way, they often tend to react violently.'

'It can all be difficult.'

'Difficult!' repeated Dr. Bruneau, 'difficult!' He started to put on his raincoat. I assure you, *cher Monsieur*, that if that girl had pushed me any harder out of the door, I'd have entered your room via the ceiling!'

Mme. Anniette had read two books in her life and had read them alternately throughout her life – a biography of Beethoven and a biography of Napoleon. They had furnished her with more exact knowledge than the majority of people possess on any subject, and she would draw on it to provide Paul with advice or to point out the consolations of his situation. '*Pensez au pauvre Beethoven, vieux, sourd et sans le sou*,' she would say, or '*Pensez à Napoleon, traqué, trahi et jeté sous les griffes de ses cruels ennemis*!'

She urged him not to remain alone in his room. On the evenings when there was a broadcast of a play all the members of the châlet would, as a matter of course, assemble about her wireless set, Paul lying on the divan, the sergeant opening and shutting his hand at the *petit chou* (who preferred to listen from behind his bedroom door), Fritz and Pierre on the floor (the latter with his head within three inches of the speaker). Mme. Anniette, whether unravelling her knitting, her accounts or her thoughts, would follow and commentate the play's action, saying: '*Mais écoutez-moi ça!*' or '*Mais quel salaud, celui-là!*' Every sentiment expressed would be approved or disapproved; she would retort to unsympathetic characters in their own coin or, more ominously, content herself with saying '*Attendez, mon vieux! Est-ce que vous allez attraper quelque chose tout à l'heure!*'

And when Paul was alone, she would call on him and seek to distract him by relating anecdotes of her childhood or by discoursing on the background and history of Brisset's prominent citizens. Sometimes seeking to alleviate his depression she would succumb to it. A discourse in praise of human nature would become progressively modified during its delivery until at last she would cry: '*Tout le monde est vil. Il n'y a que des escrocs. On vous roule partout!*' And at times, as she developed her theme of resignation and acceptance, her own feelings would break out in a cry of: 'Work! Work! Work! Why? What for? To earn money to protract still further this *sale comédie* of existence? *Monsieur* Davenant, I swear to you that if I believed my body contained still five years of life I would hang myself from that hook in the ceiling!' And, her stance Promethean, her shoulder-straps straining, she would point dramatically to a small metal plug that would not have borne the weight of a bird-cage.

With Michèle's return no more than a few days distant, Paul's sense of anticipation was equalled only by his apprehension – her single communication since her departure had been a brief and non-committal card. He feared that each post might bring news that she was not returning to France, and once she obtained access to her room at the *Universel* to reassure himself that her belongings were still there, that they had not, at the order of her parents, been packed and sent back to Liège.

CHAPTER FOURTEEN

•

The *crémaillère* had arrived ahead of time. As Paul hurried up the hill the first passengers were leaving the station. The enormous, bearded figure of Manniez (who haunted the station on the days when he was expecting a consignment of merchandise from his own country) came out of the main entrance. At his side, and arm in arm with him, was Michèle. She detached herself from Manniez, ran down the hill, and threw herself with such force into Paul's arms that he nearly lost his balance.

'Tell please the truth,' said Manniez, panting after her. He turned to Paul and beamed, his open mouth a suggestive clearing in the undergrowth. 'Cheli and me are arrived from Paris. Do not believe when she say she have been in Belgique.'

'Oh, you're back, you're really back,' said Paul. He felt as if he had stepped from winter into the sun.

'Is true,' persisted Manniez, leaping between them and taking the arm of each as they started off down the hill. 'We went together anywhere, me carrying my elegant smoking with silk facings, Cheli carrying a grass skirt, the most existentialist couple in the most scandalous *boîtes de nuit*!'

'*Oh, mes valises*!' Michèle's hand went to her mouth. She turned pleadingly to Manniez.

'*Sois gentil. Reviens à la gare et demande au concierge de les faire descendre.*'

'Ah! my little *maîtresse*. She depend on me for everything.'

'*Et dépêche-toi*!'

Manniez turned to go, then stopped. 'Listen, Davenant, you want to buy one electric *raseur*? Half the price and twice the accomplishment of any *raseur* in the *monde*. For you I make yet cheaper – one quarter the price!'

'And four times the accomplishment?'

'Oh! C'est toi qui est raseur,' said Michèle to Manniez, stamping her foot. '*Allez, cours…*'

'My little *maîtresse* have but to command…' Manniez brushed

Michèle's hand with the tip of his beard and hurried back to the station.

On the way back to the châlet Paul urgently declared his feelings to Michèle. 'I can never again be separated from you, my life just stops, or rather, what is worse, goes on…' Her smile both mocked and encouraged him. 'It's true,' he protested, taking her hand. She smiled again. 'I will show you how true it is,' he said very seriously.

'*Oh, Mademoiselle, grâce à Dieu que vous êtes de retour,*' cried Mme. Anniette, putting her head out of the window as they reached the châlet. '*Je vous jure que Monsieur n'a pas eu le sourire aux lèvres depuis votre départ…*'

'It's always like this,' said Paul desperately, 'we're always on the verge of having to leave each other.'

'But what did you expect?'

'Not that you would be leaving in a few weeks.'

'I only said I might be. My doctor in Liège said I ought to spend the whole of the summer in the mountains.'

'Thank God for your doctor in Liège.'

'Yes, but it isn't he who pays the bills. As it is, my father owes the *Universel* for the last two months…'

Paul had been quite unprepared for such news. The next few days he passed in a state of great despondency, fearing that at each meeting with Michèle he would learn of her recall. Then when this did not occur he reapplied himself to resolving the problem of the future.

It had taken him a long time to understand and acknowledge that Michèle had never been discouraged by his situation but only by his reaction to it. (In much the same way de la Marelle had never grasped the extent of his error in assuming that he might dazzle Michèle with the prospects of wealth and rank. She had no conflicts in the matter – de la Marelle's world, the world of café society, of low-slung, powerful cars, of glossy magazines and the people whose pictures they contain, filled her with incredulous amusement but little curiosity; the social ambitions which her attractions could legitimately have nurtured had no more relevance to her than the claims of quietism to a debutante in the middle of her first season.)

Undeniably, Michèle's needs were minimal. For several weeks her father neglected to send her pocket money and she, knowing too well the reason, neither commented nor complained. In the corner of her red ski trousers was a single twenty-franc piece, and she conserved it jealously. When Paul would dip his hand in her pocket and produce the coin, she would laugh delightedly and cry: '*Voilà mon dot!*'

To her the future presented no very great complication. If Paul could not find work, then she would work (a touching if unrealistic assessment of their difficulties). '*Pourquoi te tourmentes-tu quand au fond c'est si simple?*' she would demand. And often when she was lying beside Paul, she would say: '*Tous vois comme je prends peu de place!*'

At last, instead of re-reviewing and re-rejecting a dozen different forms of employment which several weeks earlier they had both agreed to be out of the question, or staring desperately at the 'Appointments Vacant' column or writing to an ex-serviceman's organisation and enquiring whether its directors could help him in his search for employment. In this way he learned of a scheme for training ex-servicemen (who had no degree) as teachers. The period of training lasted a year, and subject to the satisfactory outcome of an interview when he returned to England, there was no reason why he should not join the course which was due to start the following September.

It appeared as a miraculous solution to Paul and Michèle, and even the prospect of a year's separation was mitigated by the certainty that they would be together at its conclusion.

With practically no intermission of spring, Brisset changed from winter to summer. The tinkling of cowbells, the light bright dresses, the vicarious sensation of being *en vacances* – the Alpine sun bred euphoria as it bred flowers from the face of the rock. For no more valid reason than the absence of specific news, Michèle's departure, and the time when it would be necessary to set in motion the whole machinery of adjustment to new circumstances, appeared progressively less imminent.

The afternoons, split by the *cure de silence*, seemed without beginning or end. Half-way through the *cure*, at three o'clock, Paul would get up and go to the village to make some purchases either for Mme. Anniette or for one of his friends at the *Universel*. All the patients and many of the shop-keepers (of whom the majority were *anciens malades*) would be still in bed; Brisset had the air of an outpost suddenly abandoned by its inhabitants before the advance of the enemy. Sometimes as he tiptoed down the silent streets Paul would encounter Emile slipping into a bar for a *fine*; sometimes, passing the house in which the *petit chou* had her room, he would glimpse her watching him from behind the window. But if he turned to wave, she would instantly slam the shutter. At half-past three he would catch the *crémaillère* to the *Universel*.

Usually Michèle was sitting up in bed waiting for him. One afternoon, however, he found her asleep, one naked arm hugging a teddy bear, by her side one of Dr. Florent's paper-bound volumes of Molière still open at the page where she had been reading. Paul closed the door very quietly. A sound from outside disturbed her. She stretched herself lightly, squeezed the teddy bear, kissed its black cotton nose, closed her eyes as if about to sleep again, opened them, glanced at her watch, frowned slightly, and, still unaware of Paul's presence, recommenced to read.

It became generally known that Paul arrived at the *Universel* a little before the official end of the *cure*. One afternoon he was sitting on Michèle's bed, when he heard the turning of the handle of the outer door. (Oh, admirable institution of outer doors with their split seconds of grace!) But although Paul was on his feet when Dr. Vernet entered, Michèle's bedding was awry, her hair disordered, her face flushed.

'*Bon*!' said Dr. Vernet. The monosyllable, pronounced like a judgement, implied all that was contrary to its meaning. He turned and left the room.

Paul hesitated, then hurried after him. As he stepped outside the door, he saw that Dr. Vernet was turning the corner at the end of the passage. 'Dr. Vernet!' Paul called out. By the time he had reached the corner, Dr. Vernet was half-way down the corridor which led to the main staircase. 'Dr. Vernet!' Paul shouted again. Dr. Vernet started to descend the staircase which spiralled the liftshaft. Paul followed him and Dr. Vernet increased his pace. As soon as Dr. Vernet reached the ground floor he got into the lift which was waiting there; Paul was halfway between the first and the ground floors when the lift shot up past and stopped at the seventh floor, where Dr. Vernet had his *bureau de consultation*. Paul descended the last few stairs and pressed the button on the liftshaft. The lift remained stationary. Dr. Vernet had left the gate open.

The village clock struck four: the end of the *cure de silence.* Two waiters pushed a large trolley of tea-trays from the kitchen to where Paul was standing; patients came out of their rooms into the previously deserted corridors. Paul rattled the gate of the liftshaft. '*Ascenseur!*' shouted someone on another floor. One of the waiters kicked the shaft and shouted: '*Ascenseur, s'il vous plaît.*' '*Ascenseur! Ascenseur!*' was taken up by a variety of accents. Then a patient on the sixth floor climbed to the seventh and got into the lift. It descended in a tantalising series of rushes, picking up fresh passengers at every floor.

Designed to hold eight passengers, it contained at least a dozen; the additional weight caused it to sink a few inches below the level of the ground floor and it was impossible to open the church gate. There was a lot of laughter. One of the passengers stretched out his hand to press the second-floor button, miscalculated owing to the crush, and the lift quivered, hesitated, then slowly ascended to the sixth.

'*Nom de Dieu!*' cried the waiter who had originally kicked the liftshaft. He rattled the handle and shook the gate. '*Ascenseur! Ascenseur!*' cried other patients who were still waiting for the lift on their own floors. The lift redescended to the ground floor and, this time, before it could sink too low a passenger pushed open the gate and, laughing hysterically, the occupants burst out like shrapnel.

'*Davenant! Mon cher ami!*' It was Glou-Glou. The waiters pushed the trolleys into the lift. '*Ah, non! Il n'y a pas de place,*' they protested, as Paul tried to follow them. The lift set off again.

'*Voulez-vous me donner votre pouls?*' cried Glou-Glou, seizing Paul's wrist as the latter gazed helplessly up the shaft at the disappearing floor of the lift. '*Pas de ralentissement, pas d'intermittence,*' went on Glou-Glou, pulling out his watch. '*C'est bon signe… Vous n'avez toujours pas de vertiges? Bon encore. Vous m'entendez bien? Oui… Pas d'oppressions? Pas de nausée? Etat stationnaire, donc favorable. Mon prognostic reste le même: touts les chances de guérison. Du repos. Encore du repos. Toujours du repos.*'

The lift arrived and discharged another load of passengers. Paul got in and pressed the button for the seventh floor. His heart suddenly started to beat very quickly. What, in actual fact, was he going to say to Dr. Vernet?

He could have spared himself. 'The chief is busy. He can't see you today,' said *Sœur* Miriam severely, intercepting him before he had time to knock at the door of Dr. Vernet's bureau.

With a shameful sensation of relief, Paul returned to Michèle's bedroom. To his surprise, she was not there. She came back a few minutes later, her polka-dotted dressing-gown loosely over her shoulders. Her face was white.

'Where have you been?' demanded Paul.

'With Vernet.'

'But I was standing all the time at the bottom of the liftshaft. I didn't see you go up.'

'He sent *Sœur* Miriam for me. She took me up in the side lift.'

'Well, what happened?'

'I've never seen anyone so angry.' She sat on the side of the bed in order to regain her composure.

'What did he say?'

'He said that it was only because he knew that I would soon be leaving that he wouldn't send me away, but that in any case he now considered both our cases to be out of his hands.'

'Both our cases?'

'Yes. And he also said that if ever he again caught you here during the *cure*, he would send for the police!'

'What a funny thing,' said Dr. Vernet, with amusement. Paul, stripped to the waist, was lying on his side, and Dr. Vernet was seated next to him, a refill needle between thumb and forefinger. 'When we say that a case is out of our hands we mean that a patient is better and that he no longer needs us.' With the tip of a finger he felt for a convenient inter-costal space and swabbed it with iodine.

'I took it that you wanted me to find another doctor.'

'You are at liberty to take it like that if you want.'

'I don't.'

'Good!'

The needle descended. It penetrated and, with a crunching sound, traversed two inches of coriaceous tissue. 'Our relationship is that of *garagiste* – is that the word? – and client.' Dr. Vernet connected the refill machine to the needle. 'When you want air you stop at my garage and I pump.'

'You said that you would send for the police if you ever found me again at the *Universel*.' Paul spoke quietly and cautiously – he always feared that talking during a refill might lead to undue expansion and subsequent perforation of the lung. As if he had divined this, Dr. Vernet pushed in the needle a little farther.

'I said that that was what I would do if I found you there during the *cure*.'

'I see.'

'Besides, the information was for *Mademoiselle* Duchesne, not for you. In France it is a custom that when we want to caution a delightful but occasionally recalcitrant child we threaten to send for the police.' Dr. Vernet jerked out the needle and dabbed iodine on the puncture.

'And when the child has grown up?'

'We still sometimes threaten to send for the police.' Dr. Vernet motioned Paul into the X-ray cabinet. 'All right,' he said, a minute later. Paul got out of the cabinet and put on his vest.

'Do you consider that you are behaving honourably?' asked Dr. Vernet.

'I'm sorry?'

'I said do you consider that you are behaving honourably?'

It was hard to answer questions of that order with dignity whilst tucking in one's shirt tails. 'I can't say,' Paul replied brusquely.

'You don't labour under any set of exacting moral standards?'

'In certain things.'

'How very convenient for you.'

Paul did not answer. Dr. Vernet could have the next move if he wanted it. He went over to the mirror and threaded his tie through his collar.

'You are in good circumstances, *Monsieur* Davenant?'

'No.'

'You will have to earn your living when you leave here?'

'Yes.'

'Then it is not unreasonable to deduce that a marriage is not precisely imminent.'

'I prefer not to discuss it.' Paul took a comb from his pocket and pulled it through his hair.

'You prefer not to discuss it! Very well! What do you prefer to discuss?

May I ask, for example, whether you ever have the intention of returning to your own country?'

'Yes, I have.' Paul replaced the comb and turned away from the mirror.

'When?'

'In a few weeks.'

'When *Mademoiselle* Duchesne leaves?'

'Yes.'

'Thank you for keeping me so exactly informed.' Dr. Vernet sat down at his desk and, to show that the interview was at an end, he started to sort some papers.

Paul put on his jacket. 'It's over six months since I have had an X-ray plate,' he said.

Dr. Vernet did not look up.

'And you haven't examined me since I left *Les Alpes*.'

'No?'

'Nor have I had a blood or sputum test.'

'*Tiens!*'

'And you have expressed no opinion as to my condition.'

'I told you last autumn you could return to England.'

'Yes – and nothing since.'

Dr. Vernet gave no indication of having heard the remark. Paul hesitated a moment, then said: 'I think that after all you would prefer me to go to another doctor.'

Dr. Vernet put down the papers which he had been sorting. '*Monsieur* Davenant,' he said, his whole voice dangerously controlled, 'you can do what you like and you can go where you like. If you want another doctor, tell me and I will hand over your dossier. Until then, have the courtesy not to examine me respecting my methods.'

CHAPTER FIFTEEN

•

It was nearly the end of July. In his current report to her parents Dr. Vernet had declared Michèle's condition to be consolidated; in consequence both she and Paul feared that any day she would receive a letter summoning her back to Liège. When at last her father wrote, it was to say that on the advice of her Belgian doctor he had decided to let her remain in the mountains until the beginning of September.

Ecstatically Paul informed Mme. Anniette that he would be staying for at least another month. She nodded approvingly.

'You should be looking much better,' she commented. He ought to remain in Brisset for the whole of the autumn, if not for the winter. If he would consider doing so, the room he could have for nothing. ('Why not, *cher Monsieur*? In any case it will be empty.') His only expense would be food and heating.

For their peace of mind, and in order that the month might be as happy as possible, Paul and Michèle agreed to avoid all reference to their departure until the very last days. Little over a week had elapsed, however, when, one afternoon, Michèle, her face white, ran into the châlet.

'What is the matter?' cried Paul, jumping up from the divan.

Too breathless to speak, Michèle handed Paul a letter.

Paul glanced helplessly at the closely-written pages in Mme. Duchesne's all but indecipherable writing: a mass of endearments, banalities and exclamation marks.

'I can't read this. What does she say?'

Michèle took back the letter and read the relevant part of it aloud. It was to the effect that her father had grossly miscalculated his *situation financière*, and that on this account she would have to return to Belgium early the following week.

'Oh, my God!' cried Paul. And as he took Michèle in his arms and hugged her desperately, he wondered for just how long, in fact, they would be separated. And what would happen if he couldn't find work, or if Michèle couldn't obtain parental sanction for their marriage? Suddenly feeling very weak, he sank down on to the edge of the divan. In some terrible, inexplicable way the letter appeared to presage the collapse of all their most cherished plans.

Paul decided that at all costs he must leave Brisset on the same day as Michèle. With a reaction of revulsion (which he preferred not to analyse) he despatched a reply-paid telegram to a Bayswater hotel. A few hours later came the answer that all the rooms were taken. A second, third and fourth telegram to progressively more expensive hotels produced replies which differed textually but not in content. In the debilitating Alpine sun he laboured up and down the hill to the post office, throwing himself at each return on his divan and falling instantly into a short but heavy sleep from which he awoke sweating and dry-mouthed. And the next day, with another half-dozen telegrams despatched and not one favourable reply, he would have sought accommodation at Claridge's or the Ritz, had he not feared that the doormen, on seeing his clothes and his luggage, would have barred his entry. 'Very well,' he told himself at last, 'I shall return even though I have nowhere to go.' Better, in fact, that he had no room reserved; better that the next year's difficulties should start even before he had set foot out of Brisset; better anything than circumstances which would allow him time to think… All that mattered was that he should leave Brisset at the same time as Michèle.

And trunks had to be packed, *adieux* had to be said, railway reservations had to be made. '*Comment? Comment?*' cried the scandalised clerk at the booking office. Four days' notice and *Monsieur* really expected to obtain a second-class sleeper through to Calais! 'But I must,' said Paul. 'Must!' mocked the clerk, echoing Paul's tone of voice. 'Well, please see what you can do.' 'Well, please see what you can do!' cried the clerk over his shoulder. To catch Paul's accent he was imitating an American trying to speak French.

'And I shall have a trunk, two cases and a crate of books.'

'A trunk, two cases and what?'

'A crate of books.'

'*Des livres sterling ou des livres à lire?*'

'Books for reading.'

'Books for reading,' repeated the clerk contemptuously. 'What's the size and weight of the crate?'

'I don't know. About this size.' Paul indicated the length, height and breadth with his hands.

'About this size!' The clerk whirled his arms like the sails of a windmill. 'Why didn't you find out the size and weight before coming here and wasting everyone's time?'

'I shall let you know the size.' (*This is all just part of the nightmare*, thought Paul.) 'Can the crate travel with me in the sleeper?'

'No, it can't travel with you in the sleeper.' The clerk got wildly to his feet and looked as if he was going to summon a *gendarme*.

'Well then, it can go separately,' said Paul quickly.

'Separately?'

'Yes, separately.'

'You mean separately?'

'Yes, I mean separately.'

'Good!' The clerk, with the air of a magistrate completing a deportation order, wrote a number of details on an official form. Then he looked up maliciously at Paul and said: 'You will inscribe a list of the titles, authors and values of each book on a customs declaration form, and any you miss will be confiscated and you will be liable for prosecution…'

'That can't be necessary,' said Paul, appalled by the thought of the task.

'Can't be necessary! I have just said that it is necessary!'

'I would like to see the stationmaster.'

'I am the stationmaster.' The clerk seized a gold-braided hat from the desk and clapped it on his head.

'Oh, all right,' said Paul.

'When will you know about the sleeper?' The question had transcended presumption; the stationmaster stared at Paul with an expression of incredulous fascination. 'You will know about the sleeper,' he repeated slowly, controlling his voice, so it seemed, less on his own behalf than on that of the railway company and of the whole French nation. 'You will know about the sleeper at a given period of time after I shall know about the sleeper. *Bonjour, Monsieur!*' He got up and walked out of the office.

Paul hurried off to the village carpenter. Not only did he not know the size and weight of the crate of books, as yet there was not even a crate…

And after the carpenter, he had an appointment for an X-ray to be taken, and after that a test of the sedimentation rate of his blood and of the vital capacity of his lungs. And as he had had no sputum for several months, he had to attend the following morning before breakfast at Dr. Vernet's laboratory for a tube to be inserted down his throat in order that a specimen might be syphoned for analysis.

The X-ray, Dr. Vernet informed him, at a hurriedly arranged consultation, was in order, his sedimentation was normal and his vital capacity was what was to be expected. The result of the *tubage* would not be known for a day or two because the specimen had been sent to an outside laboratory for analysis; still, there was no need for any misgivings in that connection. The pneumothorax was working satisfactorily; it would have to be maintained with regular refills of air for at least another four years. 'The oil at the bottom of the pleura?' inquired Paul. 'As I've always told you – not to be interfered with,' said Dr. Vernet. And as he shook hands with Paul for the last time, he said: 'I will not worry you, *Monsieur* Davenant. Your condition is stabilised – you have no more chance for a relapse than I have.' And more from a love of precision than from a desire to provide Paul with further illumination, he added: 'Not that the analogy is exact. As I have never been ill, it is obvious that I am precluded, *ex hypothesi*, from the possibility of relapse.'

And between times, and at every opportunity, his heels together, his elbows tucked into his sides, his face grey with physical and emotional exhaustion, Paul stood in the sun taking photo after photo of Michèle. Within two days he had taken a dozen rolls; their development and printing in London would comprise the one event to which he could look forward on his return.

It was when everything that could be accomplished had been accomplished, when the last goodbye had been said and the last case had been packed, when Paul and Michèle could only cross the room in the châlet by stepping over the trunks and the crate (inside which all the books had now been secured) that Paul reached a state in which he could neither reason nor think clearly. 'You don't know what my life was like before I met you. I can't go back to it,' he repeated helplessly to Michèle.

It was in this context that he suddenly conceived the idea that to reduce his own tension and the strain that he knew he was imposing on

Michèle he must lop off the three days which remained to them, that he must – thereby circumventing the whole anguished preamble of elaborate and final leave-taking – quit Brisset that very evening. (It was the reaction of the hydropic who, *in extremis*, plunges a knife into the heart of his swelling.)

At the end of the afternoon he accompanied Michèle back to the *Universel*, then telephoned her on his return to the châlet to tell her of his decision. It was, he insisted, the best thing that could be done. He would go to Chatigny for the three days and return to Brisset just to collect his baggage. And because, as Michèle protested, the sound of her voice became as poignant to him as her physical presence, he interrupted what she was saying with: '*Mon amour, comprend-moi et pardonne-moi – je ne peux pas en discuter, je ne peux plus entendre ta voix qui me déchire.*' Michèle made no reply but the line remained alive; Paul could hear the sound of her breathing. '*Au revoir*,' he whispered, and replaced the receiver.

On the way to Chatigny he had no doubt as to the wisdom of his decision; doubt only started when he had selected and installed himself in a hotel. To tire himself beyond the capacity for further reflection he walked for miles about the deserted, midnight town, but when at last he returned to bed he could not sleep, his mind a beleaguered fortress to the battering ram of his thoughts. He heard the chiming of each hour, each half, each quarter; he saw the dawn rising against the curtains.

Progressive illumination delineated first the outline, then the substance and finally the texture of each object in the room; by a similar process each particular facet of Paul's situation became subject to the same systematic clarification. And when every object had achieved optimum visibility and – by subsequent integration into the commonplace pattern of the room – had become invisible again, Paul jumped from his bed with a cry, overwhelmingly convinced only of his folly in having truncated by an entire evening the time still remaining to himself and Michèle.

He was back in Brisset by the middle of the morning, and he telephoned Michèle as soon as he reached the châlet. Although she came at once, by the time she had arrived he had fallen asleep, and when he awoke at her entry and held her in his arms it seemed as if the period of separation had miraculously passed and that he would never again be parted from her. Then over her shoulder he saw the crate and the trunks; his body stiffened and Michèle turned quickly, believing that someone had entered the room.

Paul sat up and swung his legs to the ground and Michèle sat beside him; she asked for no explanation and Paul offered none. He stared intently at the opposite wall as though a film was being projected on its surface. It was as if the pressure of his emotions had produced a spontaneous pre-frontal leucotomy, for suddenly he felt nothing and wanted nothing and even the presence of Michèle appeared superfluous.

The condition proved to be transient. Paul slept during part of the afternoon and awoke with his nervous system refreshed, restored and susceptible to instantaneous laceration. It was in this state that he conceived a plan which appeared so reasonable and so obvious that he could not understand why it had not previously occurred to him. He would return with Michèle to Liège and persuade her parents to consent to an immediate marriage. He got dressed rapidly. Before telling Michèle, he would have to hurry to the station to amend his booking.

The stationmaster was in the booking-office. '*Vous avez eu de la chance,*' he said gruffly, assuming that Paul had come to inquire about his reservation.

'I've come to change my booking,' said Paul. Each word was an effort – the rapid walk in the sun had made him feel sick.

'Your reservation,' said the stationmaster. 'I have succeeded in making it.'

'I've come to change it,' repeated Paul. He leaned on the counter and closed his eyes. Liège and Michèle's parents. He would be courteous but very firm. If only she had not been under twenty-one and had not required their consent. 'A ticket to Liège the day after tomorrow. I want a new reservation…'

The stationmaster decided that it was some sort of joke and best ignored. 'Here are your tickets,' he said, producing a paper wallet. 'There is a voucher for your sleeper and for the Channel crossing. You will also have to pay the cost of two calls to Paris. It has all been a great deal of trouble.'

'Listen,' said Paul, 'I said I didn't want it. It's got to be cancelled – my plans have changed.' The stationmaster gazed at Paul, his eyes widening. 'A seat has already been reserved for a *Mademoiselle* Duchesne. I want to reserve the seat nearest to it.'

'You are not going back to England?'

'No.'

'*Nom de Dieu!*'

'I am sorry for the inconvenience.'

'Inconvenience!' The word touched off the fuse and like a rocket the stationmaster shot under the counter and up beside Paul. 'And you want me to make another reservation?'

'Yes.'

'*C'est de la saloperie*,' he roared, jumping with anger. He seized Paul's wrist and abused him in a gathering frenzy which Paul, in another sort of frenzy, cut short by wrenching free his arm and banging his fist so hard on the counter that it scattered the wallet and its contents and a mass of travel brochures. In silence both men stared at each other, each registering the impression that the other was mad. The stationmaster ducked back under the counter.

'Then you will make the reservation for the day after tomorrow?' said Paul.

'I'll see what I can do.'

Paul left the office. The stationmaster rallied and became himself again. '*Vous allez payer. Cela je vous jure*,' he cried after Paul, defiantly striking the counter and sweeping from it the few objects that remained there.

Paul went straight back to the châlet, where he knew that Michèle would be waiting for him. Half-way up the hill he felt faint, and he sat down for some minutes by the roadside.

'*Mon amour, qu'est-ce que tu as?*' demanded Michèle, when Paul entered the châlet.

'Good news, the best and only news,' he said, sitting on a trunk and lowering his chest to his knees to regain his breath. 'I'm going back with you to Liège. I'm going to ask your parents to agree to our immediate marriage…' He started to cough, his eyes watered and he could not continue.

'*Tu es malade… Tu es malade…*' cried Michèle. She took his hand, stared distractedly at his face.

'Yes,' said Paul. He smiled. 'But soon I shall be so well.' He cleared his throat. 'We shall get married and go back to England. I don't know how I ever thought that I could live apart from you, even for a short time. There's still some of my uncle's money, we won't starve, and what else matters?' He lowered his face on to Michèle's shoulders and closed his eyes. 'It's just in time,' he thought, 'in a few more days I should really have been ill.' And he reflected on that curious element of luck which had never quite deserted him, which had brought him through an all-but-mortal illness to a love which he had never dared anticipate, and which now was preserving him from breakdown by setting him decisively upon a path which, with greater courage and confidence, he would have chosen long before.

To help pass the last afternoon Paul and Michèle had decided to go to the cinema in the village – they were to leave for Liège by the eight o'clock train the following morning. Paul arrived at the *Universel* a little before the end of the *cure de silence*, and having nothing better to do he went to the laboratory to see whether the result of the *tubage* had been received, and if so to confirm that it was satisfactory.

The door of the laboratory was open; there was no one inside. Paul took the lift to the *Service Médical* and asked *Sœur* Miriam whether she knew the result of the analysis. No, said *Sœur* Miriam. If the result had arrived it would be in the laboratory.

Paul returned to the laboratory. Still no one there. On a table there was a sheet of paper torn from a squared exercise book. It was a list of names marked with ticks or crosses. Paul looked down the list: his own name was marked with a cross.

Pondering the significance of the marking, he went to Michèle's room to say that he would have to wait a few minutes until the *laborantine* had returned. Michèle was just getting dressed – Paul embraced her as he had so often embraced her at similar moments, his hands penetrating the folds of her underwear.

The third time he went to the laboratory, the door was shut. He knocked. The *laborantine* was seated at a table, examining a slide under a microscope. She looked up as he entered.

'You've come for the result of your analysis?'

'Yes.'

'I've given it to Dr. Vernet.'

'What is it?'

'You must ask Dr. Vernet.'

'But can't you tell me?'

'I can't remember it.'

'You haven't a copy?'

'No. I'm sorry.' She smiled and turned back to the microscope.

In the *Service Médical* Paul learnt that Dr. Vernet was away from Brisset for the day. He went straight back to the laboratory.

'Dr. Vernet is away. You've got to tell me the result. I'm leaving Brisset tomorrow.'

'I can't tell you. I don't remember it.'

'But don't you see that I must know it at once?'

'Yes, I do, but I can't help you.'

Paul suddenly felt extremely uneasy. 'Do you think it was positive?'

'I don't know.'

'Do you think that it might have been positive?'

'It might have been positive or negative – I can't say.'

On the way back to the *Service Médical*, Paul passed Michèle. 'I think something is wrong. No one will tell me anything,' he murmured.

This time in the *Service Médical* Paul encountered a young doctor whom he had never seen before, but to whom, nevertheless, he explained the urgency of his situation. The doctor agreed to telephone the laboratory. He went into his bureau and put the door to, without closing it. Paul heard snatches of conversation. '*Oui… Monsieur Davenant… Non, Davenant, D-A-V-E, oui, c'est ça… C'est qu'il part demain… Bon… Oui… Oui… Bien. Merci.*'

The door opened. '*Monsieur*, I'm sorry to tell you…' The doctor paused. Paul leant back against the wall. 'I'm sorry to tell you that your analysis is positive.'

'Thank you. Thank you for finding out.'

'I am sorry.'

'Am I very positive?'

'Very positive.'

'What should I do?'

'It is up to you. If you want you can go back to England and have further treatment there…'

'Yes, but…'

'Or you can stay here. Dr. Vernet will be back tomorrow.'

'I had better stay.'

'Probably.'

'*Merci, Monsieur.*'

'*De rien, Monsieur.*'

Paul went to break the news to Michèle.

There was nothing very much to be said. Paul and Michèle left the *Universel* and went down the hill to the station.

'Mais dites alors, c'est trop fort ça,' said the clerk at the booking office.

'I am ill again. I only learnt five minutes ago.'

'But it's too late. You can't cancel it.'

'*Qu'est-ce qui se passe-t-il?*' The stationmaster had heard the voices and had come into the booking office. '*Ah, c'est vous!*' he cried when he saw Paul.

'He wants to cancel his ticket,' explained the clerk indignantly.

'Jésus!' cried the stationmaster, breaking straight into the middle of his repertoire. 'It's here you're ill, not in the lungs,' he shouted, stubbing his thumb against his forehead. 'You ought to be locked up. This time you will pay in full, I promise you…'

The combination of events had partially anæsthetised Paul. Ill everywhere but for the moment nowhere, only dull and slightly drowsy, a hollow head on a hollow body. No grief. Michèle would leave tomorrow and alone.

Later in the evening, amidst the trunks and cases, the room bare, the curtains undrawn, the scattered drawers, like open coffins, gaping at empty shelves, Michèle made an affirmation of her love.

'I am not sad,' she said. 'This had to happen, there was no avoiding it, I've known for months that you were not well. We may be separated for some time, but we know that nothing will change our feelings and that as soon as you have recovered we will be together. This knowledge will be the strength for you to get better quickly, and for me to be able to go on living without you.'

Yes, agreed Paul, he would get better quickly, and all his strength, as she said, would be his knowledge of their love. And he thought to himself, as he lay with his head on her shoulder and eyes tightly closed, that they would never meet again.

It was ten o'clock, the doors of the *Universel* were locked at ten-fifteen. 'We must go now,' said Paul. He got to his feet. The light dipped. There was a sharp detonation and suddenly the room was in darkness. 'Paul!' cried Michèle. 'It's all right,' said Paul. He groped his way along the wall to his bedroom door and felt for the switch. The light shone through the door into the outer room.

The bulb in the lamp over Paul's desk had burst, leaving only the holder and twisted filament; a framed photo of Paul and Michèle (which Paul had intended to pack only just before leaving) had blown face downwards and the glass had smashed.

There was a sound of knocking from above. '*Qui a-t-il?*' came Mme. Anniette's voice. 'Nothing,' called back Paul. The room, illuminated only indirectly from the side, looked menacing and sinister in its bareness; the mute hostility of the trunks, the uncurtained windows. '*Mais qu'est ce qui s'est passé?*' cried Mme. Anniette again. Paul paid no attention.

He took Michèle in his arms and their bodies momentarily integrated, each limb, each bone pressed against its counterpart as though engaging in its own private leave-taking. The opening of the outside door precipitated the end of the embrace. They hurried out of the room as Mme. Anniette came into the passage, torch in hand. 'What was it? I thought I heard a shot,' she said.

'It was nothing,' repeated Paul.

And when he had taken Michèle to the door of the *Universel*, had kissed her and had instantaneously turned away (as they had arranged beforehand), he returned to find Mme. Anniette seated on one of his trunks and staring at the broken bulb.

'You are not superstitious, *Monsieur*,' she said as he came in.

'No.'

'Then thank God for it.' She crossed herself. 'The last time I saw a bulb burst like that, my sister was found hanging from the ceiling of her bedroom.'

CHAPTER SIXTEEN

•

Paul woke as abruptly as a pane of glass is shattered; his hands flew to his face as though to protect it from flying fragments. Six o'clock. Michèle was still in Brisset. In a single movement he sat up, threw aside the bed-clothes, projected his legs to the floor.

Then he remembered that he had become positive again. A sudden access of horror parted his lips. He fell back on to the pillow.

Not merely positive, but very positive. Which lung? Another pneumothorax? Ribs out? Or nothing? Nothing, no further treatment possible, just rest, good food, fresh air... what then? Permanent hospitalisation in a state clinic in England? He must see Dr. Vernet immediately. Paul made another automatic movement to get up.

This thought now checked him: he was never going to see Michèle again. And she was still in Brisset. He could get up, shave, dress, go to her... Perhaps he could persuade her to catch a later train. Perhaps he could persuade her to stay a week, a month. 'My head will burst,' thought Paul.

He lay back and closed his eyes. But the intense morning light like twin incandescent bullets pierced the lids, hollowed the sockets and exposed the surface of his brain, which bubbled like a new coat of paint in the sun. And when he opened his eyes – the mockery of the stripped room and the piled baggage. Should he unpack? Unpack! Probably he had passed his last night in the châlet. Tomorrow he would wake in a sanatorium bedroom. How was he going to pay? A balance of a few hundred pounds and after that...

He stumbled from his bed and hurriedly washed his face and brushed his hair. Michèle might call on him before she left, perhaps at this moment she was nearly at the châlet. Seven o'clock – one hour until the departure of the train. How could she come? And if she did come, what then? No, better that she did not come.

Back in bed Paul listened for every sound. Up to half-past seven she might come. After that what would he do? What would he think of? What would he hope for? Twice he grew rigid and stopped breathing, mistaking a sound elsewhere in the châlet for the opening of the side door. Then, at twenty-five past seven, the side door did open.

'Michèle,' Paul cried, throwing aside the bedclothes. The door of his room opened and in came Mme. Anniette with the breakfast tray.

'I have been thinking about you all night,' she said. 'Do not worry, *cher Monsieur*. What does it mean, to be positive? Pouf!' And she shrugged her shoulders and turned her eyes to the ceiling. 'In Brisset we are breathing bacilli night and day; take an analysis of anyone at a given moment and the result will be positive. Why, if you sent some melted snow to the municipal analyst that would come back positive!' She set down the tray on Paul's bed. 'As it is, you will now spend the winter in the châlet and in the spring you will go back to England completely consolidated. And six months from now you will realise that this whole little episode has been a blessing in disguise.'

One hour later Paul arrived at the *Universel*. He went straight to Michèle's room. Until he had actually opened the door he had not lost the secret hope that by some miracle he might find her there. A *femme de chambre* had already made some attempt to prepare it for its next occupant, but the bed linen had not yet been changed (the impress of Michèle's head was still visible on the pillow) and there was a pile of debris in the corner. Paul looked through the debris and found underneath a pair of Michèle's bedroom slippers which she had discarded; he instantly took possession of them. There was nothing else.

Dr. Vernet was not in his bureau. Paul walked up and down the waiting-room. It was two years since he had been dressed and shaved at eight o'clock in the morning – he had the curious impression that his pending interview with Dr. Vernet was in respect of taking up some sort of employment in the sanatorium. He suddenly saw himself always dressed and shaved at this hour, helping the waiters with the breakfast trays, distributing library books and magazines to the patients, seeking Dr. Vernet's advice concerning small matters of administration… At half-past eight Dr. Vernet arrived.

'You!' he cried.

'Yes.'

'But you're leaving today.'

'No. I mean I was.'

'Well?'

'Then you haven't heard the result of my analysis?'

'Of course I have – it was positive.'

Paul stared at Dr. Vernet in amazement.

'It's of absolutely no significance, just probably a part of the healing process. You're not going to change your plans for that!'

'Then I'm not ill again?'

'How you love to torture yourself,' said Dr. Vernet, laughing. 'Your X-ray is good, your sedimentation is good – what more do you want?'

'But – '

'Eighteen months and you have been consistently negative! And now just once you're positive.'

Paul followed Dr. Vernet into his bureau. He felt too dazed by Dr. Vernet's wholly unanticipated reaction to follow more than the drift of his argument. Already new plans were forming in his mind. He thought: 'If I really am all right I will go straight on to Liège.' Then an apparent fallacy presented itself. 'But how do I know that I've been consistently negative? It's over six months since I've had an analysis,' he objected.

'Well, that doesn't mean that you've been positive for six months!' Dr. Vernet laughed again.

'No, but nevertheless...'

'Besides, it's probably the consequence of a cold.'

'I haven't had a cold.'

'Well then, the consequence of not having had a cold.' Dr. Vernet sat down at his desk. 'Now are you going to return to England?'

'But if I'm positive...'

'I'll give you a slip explaining all that to your doctor in England.'

'I mean that it's no use going back if I'm not cured.'

'Then you want to stay here!'

'I want nothing more than to be able to leave. But like this...'

'I see.' Dr. Vernet regarded Paul in silence. Then he said: 'Very well, we shall make fresh tests and analyses, after which I hope to be able to convince you that you are perfectly all right to return to England.' He wrote some notes on a memorandum pad, then got up from his desk. 'You are looking yellow, *Monsieur*,' he said critically. 'Is your liver troubling you again?' And before Paul could answer, he added: 'I know a very good test which always produces interesting results – it takes a whole day to perform! You must have nothing to eat after dinner tonight and you must report to the *laborantine* at eight o'clock tomorrow morning. And you will need to swallow a special cachet before you go to bed.' He wrote a prescription and handed it to Paul. 'Now goodbye, *Monsieur*, and *à bientôt*.'

Paul returned to the châlet in a state of great confusion, new hitherto inconceivable hope jostling with the feeling that logically his hope could have no foundation.

Mme. Anniette was discouraging. 'If he says you should go back to England he should have his head examined,' was her comment. And she added: 'You may be very sure that it's not for your benefit that he wants you out of the way!'

The absurdity of Mme. Anniette's suggestion encouraged Paul to dismiss her point of view and he wrote at length to Michèle to tell her of the new development. 'So if only Vernet is right we shall be together before the end of the week,' he concluded. When he had finished the letter he again became disturbed by doubt and to reassure himself he added a postscript: 'You are still in the train as I write this and every second is taking you farther from me. Oh! I would be in complete and final despair if I were not sure that I would soon be with you. Vernet never sought to spare me in the past, so there can be no question that he is doing so now. He must believe what he has said or why should he have said it?'

In the afternoon he went down to the village to post the letter. As he was leaving the post office he encountered Kubahskoi whom he had not seen since the closing of *Les Alpes*. At the latter's suggestion they went to have tea in a nearby café.

Paul attempted to excuse himself for his long neglect. 'The truth is I spent every available moment with Michèle,' he explained. Kubahskoi asked for news of Michèle and Paul related the events of the past few days, dwelling in detail on the denouement that had occurred that very morning. 'Vernet is absolutely convinced that I am all right, as long as the results of the new analyses are favourable, I shall leave for Liège at the end of the week,' he said in conclusion. And he reflected to himself: 'It is strange. This morning I woke up thinking everything was over, whereas now, just a few hours later, I can think and talk in terms of my plans...'

Kubahskoi expressed confidence that the analyses would prove satisfactory, but he added the qualification that in his experience Dr. Vernet could be extremely erratic. And he described how, when *Les Alpes* had closed (just ten days before he had been due to undergo the operation which Dr. Vernet had arranged for him), he had found accommodation in a clinic which was supervised by Dr. Dubois, the head doctor of the *Universel.* The latter, after a preliminary examination, had declared the proposed aspiration too dangerous to attempt; he had initiated instead a course of streptomycin (the drug which Dr. Vernet had invariably refused him). At the end of three weeks Kubahskoi's analysis had been negative for the first time in several years. Then Dr. Dubois had abandoned the second pneumothorax which Dr. Vernet had induced the previous year, observing that it had never been necessary. Now he had been negative for six months and was due to return to Poland in two weeks' time.

As he finished speaking, two other former patients of *Les Alpes* came over to the table – Delmuth and a Dutch doctor (who now that he was better was himself practising in one of the clinics). 'Ah, Davenant!' cried Delmuth. 'We have not encountered since last I had the honour of upsetting a table on you at the Christmas!'

The Dutch doctor shook hands with Paul. 'I knew you at *Les Alpes, Monsieur*, but at that time you were in no condition to know me. I left there some months before you had recovered.' Both men drew up chairs to the table. Delmuth turned his about, sat astride it and rested his chin on the back.

'Gentlemens,' cried Delmuth, 'Davenant is my number-one favourite comrade of Brisset but I was divided from him by a *sort barbare.* But now we are brothers reunited and nothings will never part us!' He seized a plate and a knife and shielded Paul with the first whilst with the knife he drove back imaginary assailants.

'And what has happened to you since?' demanded the Dutch doctor. Paul repeated his story much as he had related it to Kubahskoi.

'And Vernet's advice is that you pay no attention to the result of the analysis but just return to England?' said the doctor when Paul had finished. Paul nodded.

The Dutch doctor attracted the attention of the *garçon* and ordered tea for himself and Delmuth, then he said laughingly: 'Vernet has become a faith healer – to each of his patients he now says: "Take up thy bed and walk!" By the end of the month he won't have any patients left at all. For Brisset it is a most commendable development!'

'What do you mean?' asked Paul uneasily.

'Well, in a word and strictly between ourselves (though it is already pretty widely known), the *Société* has decided that it doesn't require two doctors at the head of the *Universel* and it's dispensing with – Vernet! You can imagine how Vernet feels about that. But his contract has expired and there is nothing he can do about it, nothing that is beyond the limited revenge of ensuring that none of his patients remain to swell the coffers of the *Société*.' And the Dutch doctor laughed.

The *garçon* brought the tea and Delmuth poured it.

'And so I would advise you,' pursued the Dutch doctor, 'to treat anything Vernet says in the light of what I have told you. If his cures are on a heroic scale, the same is surely true of his errors. And again, if you don't mind my saying so, I think that you shouldn't wait until he has left before you consult a new doctor. You look very toxic to me and I think you ought probably to be in bed. Tell me, have you a temperature?'

'No.'

'How do you feel?'

'All right.'

'You don't look it.'

'I never do.' Paul only wanted to get away, to lock himself up in his room in the châlet.

'My friend Davenant,' said Delmuth, as Paul got up, 'I am now one philistine converted – I give up being engineer and become artist. Tell me please where I find beautiful young girls to take off their clothes for me to paint them.'

'Think of what I have been telling you,' said the Dutch doctor.

Paul shook hands with each of the three men, but Delmuth, the last, would not release his grip. 'Sorry. Is locked,' he explained.

'Let me go. I must catch my train.'

Delmuth pressed the tip of his nose, then the dimple in his chin. Then, as if suddenly remembering the right combination, he pulled and twisted the lobe of his left ear, and his great grocer's hand shot forward and open like the till of a cash register.

Paul passed the whole of the next day in the laboratory undergoing tests which made him retch physically and mentally, and, the morning after, he went to the *Universel* to learn the results.

Dr. Vernet greeted him reassuringly. 'Although there are still a number of results to come in, I can tell you, *Monsieur*, that there is absolutely no reason for you to stay in Brisset.'

'Then I'm negative?' said Paul with sudden hope.

'No. Now don't have that tortured look in your eyes – I've explained to you that it doesn't mean anything.'

'It means everything,' said Paul. 'I was going to get married… I was going to work…'

Dr. Vernet sat down at his desk, stared for several seconds at an inlaid paper knife. 'Well, what do you want to do?'

'What should I do?'

'I've told you.'

'You mean I should go back?'

'Yes.'

'And work?'

'No, not at first.'

'When?'

'That will depend on your progress.'

'Then you agree that I am not well.'

'You are well enough to return to England. But that is not my only reason for wanting you to leave Brisset.' Dr. Vernet looked up and gave Paul an open and candid glance. 'You see, my work here has come to an end and I would not wish to leave you in incapable hands.'

'So you *are* leaving!'

'You knew?'

'I had heard a rumour.'

'Well then, you will understand my feelings in the matter.'

'What about Dr. Dubois?'

'Dubois!'

'Yes.'

'Wholly unsuitable!' Dr. Vernet leaned back in his chair. 'With your temperament you require someone who is experienced both in psychology and in general medicine. If you are determined to stay, there is only one doctor whom I could unreservedly recommend. Have you heard of Dr. Bertin?'

'No.'

'He is exceptionally gifted and I am happy to say that he has consented to look after such of my patients as will have to stay on after I have left. I will arrange for the three of us to meet some time next week.'

As Paul was leaving the *Universel* he encountered a nurse whom he knew and he asked her whether she had heard of Dr. Bertin. 'Bertin!' she exclaimed. 'Why do you want to know about him?' 'Dr. Vernet has recommended him to me.' 'You are joking,' she replied. Then, when Paul insisted that he was not joking, she said circumspectly: 'You must speak to someone else. I'm afraid that I can't tell you anything about him.'

'Bertin!' cried Mme. Anniette, when Paul had returned to the châlet. She led him by the arm into her kitchen, where a friend of hers, a nurse from one of the clinics, was sitting. '*Monsieur* has had a little relapse and Vernet has told him to become a patient of Bertin!' 'Bertin!' exclaimed the nurse incredulously. 'Why, he isn't even a T.B. doctor!'

Together the two women enlightened Paul. Dr. Bertin, it appeared, had no connection with any clinic or sanatorium and his practice was of a notoriously dubious character. In addition, he was both a drunkard and a drug-addict and a few months earlier his well-known habit of injecting himself by passing a needle through his clothing had all but led to his death from blood-poisoning. '*Mon cher Monsieur*,' said the nurse, 'rather than go to Bertin, I would counsel you to buy a home encyclopædia of medicine and to learn to treat yourself.'

Mme. Anniette had often spoken to Paul of Dr. Dubois. A former invalid, he was the titular head of the *Station* (in addition to his appointment at the *Universel* and the supervision of a number of private clinics). He had looked after Mme. Anniette, her father and Pierre, her assistant (though he had never charged for his services).

Outraged by Dr. Vernet's recommendation, Mme. Anniette now got in touch with Dr. Dubois and arranged a consultation for Paul, only informing the latter of what she had done when the matter had been concluded.

The same day Paul received a letter from Dr. Vernet which informed him that an error in the analysis of his gastric juices would necessitate the repetition of the tests which had been carried out two days before, and that accordingly he should report to the *laborantine* at eight o'-clock the following morning. Paul, without periphrasis or explanation, replied that he would not be attending the test and that he wished all his documents, dossiers and X-rays to be sent to Dr. Dubois.

But was it in the charge of Dr. Dubois? Would Dr. Dubois, in fact, accept his case? And what was it that he expected or hoped to learn from Dr. Dubois? He had already rejected the advice that he should leave Brisset but equally he could not accept the advice that he should stay. But Dr. Dubois was well known to be sympathetic and understanding; the thing would be to reveal everything, his emotional condition and mental state, to depute unreservedly to Dr. Dubois the solving of a problem that patently excluded the possibility of solution.

Such resolutions as Paul had made in this respect did not survive his initial handshake with Dr. Dubois – the latter (a large man in his late fifties), received Paul courteously but with a degree of coldness which indicated both that he possessed prior information concerning his new patient, and that what he knew he did not like. Undoubtedly Dr. Vernet had submitted a damaging report in respect of his conduct, damaging, that is, though probably containing nothing that was not true. Paul saw again very clearly the utter hopelessness of his situation.

'*Eh bien, Monsieur, qu'est-ce que vous voulez de moi?*' he demanded, his face expressionless, his demeanour uninviting.

Paul summarised dispassionately the salient details of his case history as though he were relating a series of events in the life of someone who was dead and whom he had never known. 'What am I doing here?' he asked himself. He looked with distaste at the chromium steriliser, the rack of pneumothorax needles, the surgical instruments display case, the X-ray cabinet and the couch on which patients would lie down for their refills. (On entering the door he had registered the presence and position of these exhibits in the same way that when, summoned at school to the prefects' room, he used to register the location of the hard-soled gym slipper and the ominous disposition of the furniture.)

'Dr. Bertin!' ejaculated Dr. Dubois, interrupting Paul's narrative.

'Yes.'

'Do you know Dr. Bertin?'

'No.'

'Go on,' requested Dr. Dubois, looking curiously at Paul.

When he had come to the end of his account, Paul looked at the floor and said: 'I can't think why I didn't leave.' And he continued half to himself: 'I was a fool, an absolute fool. If I had taken Vernet's advice I would have been miles away...' Dr. Dubois made no comment, but picked up and started to read a letter which Paul saw had been signed by Dr. Vernet.

'If Dubois shows the least tendency to agree with Vernet, I shall leave Brisset tonight,' thought Paul.

Dr. Dubois looked up from the letter. 'Dr. Vernet is of the opinion that the change in the analysis was brought about by a cold. Did you have the cold immediately before the analysis?'

'I have not had a cold for over a year.'

'Then why did you tell Dr. Vernet that you had had a cold?' demanded Dr. Dubois, raising his eyebrows.

'I didn't. I told him that I had not had a cold.'

Dr. Dubois stared at Paul, then referred again to Dr. Vernet's letter. 'There is a lot which isn't clear to me,' he commented. And he added: 'In any case you have an enormous dossier and a lot of X-ray plates and I have not yet had an opportunity for studying them. Now tell me – you have a room in the *Châlet Anniette*?'

'Yes.'

'Are you comfortable there?'

'Very comfortable.'

'And Mme. Anniette looks after you well?'

'Very well.'

'Then for the time being you can stay on there.' Dr. Dubois reflected a moment. 'There is nothing more,' he said. 'Carry on quietly and come and see me again three – no, four – days from now, and I should be able to express an opinion on your condition. *Bonjour, Monsieur.*'

CHAPTER SEVENTEEN

•

Four days of tension and apprehension amidst the trunks and cases, packed, locked but unlabelled. At one moment Paul would decide categorically to refuse to enter a sanatorium, at another he would make up his mind to request immediate and radical treatment, anything which would conduce to the early restoration of his health. Sometimes his body broke into a sweat when he thought of Dr. Dubois proposing heavy surgical treatment; sometimes it broke into a sweat when he thought of Dr. Dubois telling him that there was nothing more to be done. 'But it's always like this,' he thought helplessly. 'For two years I have done nothing but wait for medical decisions, for the results of tests, analyses and X-rays, for the outcome of one form of treatment or another.' Was there any reason for assuming that it would ever change?

He arranged for the development of the films which he had planned to have developed in London – suddenly he found himself in possession of fifty new pictures of Michèle. For two days he looked at nothing else, examining them, studying them with lamps and magnifying glasses, crudely projecting them on to an improvised screen, dozing and sleeping over them until at last the fixed visual image which he possessed of each provided an hallucinated impression of her presence. 'I see you with my eyes open or shut,' he wrote to her; 'you are here in everything but yourself; I find myself stretching my arm about you and only understanding when it contracts about nothing that in reality you are a thousand miles away.'

When Paul got up on the morning of his second interview with Dr. Dubois, he wondered once again whether he had passed his last night in the châlet. Dr. Dubois received him as him as impersonally and distantly as on the first occasion – there was no gauging in advance the nature of his impartment. He glanced unhurriedly through the leaves of Paul's dossier, opened and closed a drawer (without inserting or removing anything), cleaned his rimless spectacles with a special cloth, coughed, and was about to speak when the telephone rang and postponed what he had to say by another five minutes.

'*Bien, Monsieur*,' he said to Paul, the call over but the receiver still in his hand. He replaced the receiver very deliberately on the hook. 'It is impossible for me, or for anyone, to assess the condition of your lung – it is obscured on the X-ray plate by the shadows that have been caused by the thickening of the pleura, by your protracted pleurisy and by an extensive bronchiectasis,' he said. He clasped one hand in the other. 'Nevertheless a careful comparison of the X-rays taken during the previous year has not revealed any visible evidence of deterioration, and therefore it is not unreasonable to hope that the change in the analysis will prove to be transitory.'

He went on to say that in his view there could be no question of Paul leaving Brisset, but that equally there was no reason for him to enter a sanatorium. He recommended that Paul should take a course of a new antibiotic in tablet form; if the trouble were not extensive there was every hope that no more vigorous form of treatment would be required.

'Then there is a chance that I may be able to leave before the winter?' demanded Paul. Dr. Dubois reflected for a moment. 'It is not impossible,' he conceded.

So shifting is the scale by which good and bad fortune are measured that Paul's relief was no less than that with which, a week ago, he would have received the news that the initial analysis had been an error. He thanked Dr. Dubois as if the latter had been responsible not merely for the diagnosis but also for its leniency. He went straight from the *Universel* to the nearest chemist's shop so that he might start the treatment within the hour. He wrote to Michèle to express his confidence in Dr. Dubois and his certainty that he would be joining her before long. He unpacked one of his cases (deliberately not touching the remainder of his luggage in order to maintain the impression that he was on the verge of imminent departure). He settled down to wait.

His reaction of relief sustained him through the first few days, but at last their length and emptiness, the intensity of his loneliness, the uncertainty of his situation, the uneasiness of his sleep and the panic of his wakings prompted little by little a return to that state to which, in whatever circumstances, he all too readily reverted, where hope had no footing and his cerebral pressure was registered by the emergence from his psychic weather house of one or other of the trim, twin figures, dread and despair.

Mme. Anniette continued to visit him and to send her representatives; sometimes he passed an evening with the sergeant and the *petit chou*, sometimes with Fritz, whose room resembled the refuse dump of a radar station. Delmuth called on him and occasionally stayed for a meal. ('Is a nice walk with æsthetical benefits at the conclusion,' he would explain.)

First Kubahskoi, then Dr. Florent, who had been looking for a suitable post ever since the closure of *Les Alpes*, then Dr Vernet left Brisset. Dr. Bruneau (who because of his health could not quit the mountains) remained in charge of the small residue of Dr. Vernet's patients, none of whom had agreed to accept Dr. Bertin as medical adviser.

At last, reluctantly and with infinite precaution, Paul prised open the lid of his crate and removed half a dozen of his books.

To Mme. Anniette's dismay Delmuth at last cultivated the habit of calling daily at the châlet. When she caught a glimpse of him through Paul's window, she would cry: 'There's the werewolf!' (a reference to Delmuth's manner of eating) and hurriedly leave the room.

Whatever Paul's state of mind, he did not anticipate Delmuth's visit with pleasure, whilst Delmuth himself never had any clear idea why he had come and would regularly declare that it was for the last time. Nevertheless when Delmuth failed to arrive at his usual hour, Paul would become ill-at-ease, even an unwelcome visit being preferable to the prospect of an afternoon's introspection.

Delmuth's preoccupation was alternately to reassure or to alarm Paul in respect of his condition. 'If Vernet say you not ill, then you not ill,' he would insist, but then a little later he would point contemptuously at Paul's large bottle of antibiotic tablets and cry: 'Why you bother? For you, two stage ten rib *thoraco* with double *drainage* top and bottom!'

Paul's baggage always provoked a reaction. 'Unpack!' Delmuth would sometimes cry, aiming a kick at a trunk. 'Is now quite clear you have to spend the whole winter in the châlet.' But another time he would approve the fact that the trunks were still packed, for he would declare that it was equally 'quite clear' that Dr. Dubois would shortly be sending Paul to a sanatorium. But whatever the nature of his views, the summing-up would be invariable: 'For you the tragedy is that Vernet have left Brisset!'

There were times when Delmuth could not bear to remain in the châlet and would force Paul out for a walk. On these occasions he would speak of his wife (who was shortly to join him in Brisset), of his mistress at home ('a frivolous and sexual young girl for whom I am the life') and of his mistress at Brisset, a local shop-girl who received him in a kimono and whom accordingly he had christened 'Lotus Flower'. 'Or a mans is attractive to womens or is not. I am!' he would explain.

And when on this subject he would refer to Michèle (of whom he did not approve). 'A mans need a wife very much older than himself and not at all pretty.' Had Paul ever really imagined that Michèle would have married him? Had it escaped his notice that she flirted with everyone? 'I tell you now in conference,' said Delmuth, 'that Michèle was most of all attracted by me, but I make it quite clear from the first that I am too old a monkey to be caught so easily.' And he added complacently: 'It cause her much pain, I think. Is why she had to choose you.'

When his wife did arrive, Delmuth brought her to the châlet. Mme Delmuth fulfilled very generously her husband's two basic requirements in a wife, adding by way of good measure an immense bulk, a limp and a voice like the grinding of a gear box. From the first encounter she assumed her husband's ambivalent attitude towards Paul, attacking him for his outlook on life (which he never expressed), for not asserting himself, for not taking up some small manual occupation which would bring him a little money. (It was Delmuth's constant boast that when necessary he could maintain himself from his bed.)

Sometimes the Delmuths would invite Paul to spend the evening with them in their bare, chilling *pension* room, where the single assertion of their presence was a large, flat, metal cross which Mme Delmuth had nailed above the bed. When Paul arrived she would straightway expound her views on life, religion and the upbringing of children ('*Il faut qu'un enfant aie une crainte, Monsieur*') and if she observed her husband on the point of speaking she would eye him malevolently and rebuke him in advance for the folly and presumption of anything he might be about to say.

Paul visited Dr. Dubois fortnightly. He finished first one, then a second, bottle of the tablets, but there was no change in his analysis. The skies grew overcast. '*Ah, ça y est*,' said Pierre gloomily, taking brooms and brushes out of the woodshed and putting them in the front porch of the châlet. Within the week Brisset was under the first snow of a new winter.

Winter, that is to say, in Brisset, but autumn anywhere else. 'But what is happening?' wrote Michèle. 'It is over two months since I left you. Are you no better? Is there no chance of your getting away before the bad weather starts? What does Dr. Dubois say about the future?'

Dr. Dubois said nothing about the future; he limited himself, after each of Paul's fortnightly examinations, to the single observation: '*Pas de changement*.' And whilst Paul always hoped that Dr. Dubois would express the opinion that he was better, he was nevertheless reassured to learn that there was no fresh evidence of deterioration. He would repeat to himself Glou-Glou's consolatory maxim: '*Etat stationnaire, donc favorable.*' 'Dubois appears satisfied,' he wrote back to Michèle, 'and – I am certain I will get away before the end of the year.'

In fact he *was* certain, though his certainty was the consequence of a decision which six months ago would have appeared unthinkable – but then so would the situation which had prompted it. He had at last adjusted himself to being positive; indeed he now suspected, probably not incorrectly, that he had never been negative, but that earlier analyses had failed to reveal the presence of the bacilli. A new cosmogony had replaced the old. He was positive, but he was not chronically ill. Life was not necessarily over, nor was there any obligation to pass what remained of it in the ward of an institution. There were people who were positive all their lives but who, nevertheless, earned a living, married, reared families. In a word, he had resolved to stay in Brisset until the next analysis and then, irrespective of the result, to go.

To this end he determined to get as fit as possible. He got up early, worked and went for remedial walks with Delmuth. He was grateful for Delmuth's company on these walks. Everywhere he went, everything he saw, recalled Michèle, and the immediate sense of separation became unendurable when he was alone. The return of the snow intensified these reactions, for it was with the snow that Paul most associated Michèle, and during a few days in which Delmuth had been indisposed he had not had the courage to leave the châlet.

Probably because he was imposing on himself a heavier day he found that he had to rest for longer periods. His cheeks were permanently flushed. '*Comme Monsieur Davenant a de belles joues rouges*,' cried the *petit chou* when, one afternoon, at the sergeant's request, he was taking her photograph. 'Well, why should it not be a sign of returning health?' he asked himself. He had had a gravestone pallor for long enough. When he returned from a walk he would lie on his divan and fall immediately asleep, a peculiar sleep, a sleep from which waking was difficult, which invaded the whole of his body like a general anæsthetic and retained his limbs prisoner after waking so that he would have no alternative but to lie motionless for another hour.

Posters appeared in the village announcing an evening excursion by motor-coach to a town at the bottom of the mountain where there was to be a representation of Rossini's *Barber of Seville*. '*Voilà ce qu'il vous faut*,' declared Mme. Anniette.

On the day of the opera Paul remained in bed until the late afternoon; he knew that without preparatory rest he would be too tired to enjoy the performance. But the effort of getting up was as considerable as if he had not rested at all, and when he had finished dressing he lay down again on his bed until it was time to leave.

The sense of tiredness diminished as he climbed into the coach and left him completely, replaced by a sensation of anticipatory excitement, as the driver pressed the self-starter, the lights dipped and the ancient vehicle trembled, then nosed cautiously forward. 'I feel as well as at any time in my life,' he told himself. But half an hour later, the slow descent still uncompleted, his hand pressed between his head and the vibrating window, he was reflecting with dismay that the evening had barely started and that at the end of the opera there would still be the prospect of the long journey back.

The whole of the next day he remained in bed (the coach had arrived back at half-past one). And four days later when he next called on Dr. Dubois his temperature graph had four times infiltrated the red line of the chart. '*Mais pourquoi?*' demanded Dr. Dubois. He listened in silence to Paul's explanation, then ordered him to remain in bed until the temperature had returned to normal, and to visit him weekly instead of fortnightly.

The days were rapidly shortening, the snow was falling more thickly. There being no external window to the little bedroom, the light was poor. After deliberation (was it worth it for a day or two?) Paul and Mme. Anniette rearranged the room with the top of the bed protruding through the door of the partition. And to assert the innocuousness of his condition Paul lay during the afternoon on the divan.

'Why, is nearly no fever at all,' cried Delmuth, outraged, at the same time tossing back on to Paul's bed the temperature chart which he had seized with such enthusiasm. 'Wait!' said Paul lightly, though secretly he was not without apprehension. When, since his illness, had a temperature not had sinister implications? 'Wait!' echoed Delmuth. 'I wait since nearly three month. Please be interesting. Please ravish me with a little spectacle.'

Mme. Delmuth too came to the châlet; sometimes one parting Delmuth would encounter the other arriving. She would sit at the end of the bed, her bulk preventing Paul from stretching his legs, causing the mattress to sag and creating such havoc with the bedclothes as to suggest that the bed had not been made for a month. 'You did not thank God for your health when you had it: by what right do you complain now that He has taken it away?' she would demand. And since Paul rarely replied (in any case, he knew that to talk increased his temperature), she would continue: 'Throw yourself at His feet, implore His pardon and meekly accept His punishment, knowing that whatever its severity it will be less than your desserts.'

The snow was not yet thick enough for a sledge; Paul, wrapped in rugs and blankets, paid his next visit to Dr. Dubois by horse and cart. Dr. Dubois expressed concern at the persistency of his temperature. 'You must remain in bed. There can be no question of getting up until it is normal.'

The same evening his temperature increased appreciably, a consequence, Paul thought, of the journey to the *Universel.* (He always found an empiric reason for each variation – a heavy meal, too many blankets, a troubled sleep.) Nor did it descend during the night. When he woke it registered (five times within a half hour) the highest morning temperature since he had left *Les Alpes.*

'This is it,' thought Paul, acknowledging at last that which up to the present he had refused even to fear. Mme. Anniette brought the breakfast, lit the oil-stove, and as usual asked his temperature, but he did not reply, only asking her not to make up the bed.

Up to the previous evening he had disciplined himself not to take his temperature more than twice in twenty-four hours, but now, supine, the bed in the same heroic disorder in which Mme Delmuth would leave it (sheets, blankets and duvet integrated into a camel's hump which any movement would threaten to precipitate on to the floor), he relapsed into the nerve-wracking habit of taking it every quarter of an hour.

During the subsequent days he relaxed all occupation, no longer attempting to read, no longer leaving his bed to lie on his divan, but subordinating everything to the taking of his temperature. And as this was undoubtedly affected by movement and by speech, he would lie for hours in the same position, feigning sleep or replying in whispered monosyllables when any one called on him.

The course of his temperature graph (which was also the graph of his mental state) was erratic and diabolic, sometimes conceding him a whole day of hope, revealing its duplicity by a heady upward dash in the latter half of the afternoon, sometimes damning the day from its inception. He consulted his pulse no less than his thermometer, counting and correlating at last so automatically that at one moment he found that he was timing the tolling of the church bell.

One morning he woke up feeling too sick to eat; it was the sickness which provided the clue to his condition. Was it not a fact that the antibiotic pills (which were large and of which he swallowed sixty a day) were so frequently the cause of such severe digestive disorders and nausea that in many cases their administration was impracticable? And he realised (in a moment of revelation), that he had discovered the real reason for his temperature.

He took no pills that day. The heightened significance of each temperature reading now produced a state of such anxiety that he could not bear to remain in ignorance of the general trend of his temperature during the five minutes in which the thermometer was under his tongue; accordingly (for continually to remove the thermometer was to invalidate the final reading), he held an inverted mirror above the thermometer, drew back his upper lip and watched with fixed and fascinated gaze the jerky expansion of the mercury. A six o'clock his temperature was two divisions lower than at the same hour on the previous day. He was too excited to sleep; in this minor diminution (the temperature registered was still excessive) he saw the re-establishment of his hopes and projects. On both the second and third day his temperature fell by a further two divisions respectively.

On the fourth day, drawn but triumphant, he handed his temperature chart to Dr. Dubois. On his next visit, the latter shook his head and commented that the situation had now become unsatisfactory. Paul hurriedly drew Dr. Dubois' attention to the improvement which had taken place during the last few days and explained that it was to be attributed to his having stopped taking the pills. Dr. Dubois conceded that it was not impossible that there was some connection, but that it was unlikely; he added that, if his temperature had not become stabilised by the end of the week, Paul would have to enter the *Universel.*

On the way back in the cart Paul determined that his temperature would become stabilised, but when he took it that evening it had risen by nine divisions. 'It is because I had to go to the *Universel*; otherwise it would have been no higher than yesterday,' he thought in despair.

In the morning he awoke shivering and in confusion, having dreamed that he had passed the night in an army hut with a leaking roof and that his bedding had been soaked: an experience which he had had as a recruit. Then he saw that his pyjamas and sheets were drenched and that his whole body was running with sweat. He took his temperature and consulted it after two minutes; the reading demonstrated that the period of speculation was at an end, that his day need no longer be spent in frenzied and ceaseless recourse to his thermometer.

Mme. Anniette changed his bedding, at the same time reluctantly insisting that she should get in touch with Dr. Dubois. Paul requested her not to do so but to wait one more day, not through any hope of amelioration, but in order that he might adjust himself to what he now acknowledged was inevitable.

Mme. Anniette had brought with her a letter from Michèle but Paul did not open it (he had not disclosed to her the deterioration in his condition). At last even the sight of her writing on the envelope caused him such an intensity of emotion (he was once more possessed by the certainty that he would never see her again) that he shut it away in the drawer of his *table de nuit.*

He could not eat, his fever made it difficult for him to lie still, but nevertheless each hour which he still contrived to pass in the châlet appeared an hour of respite. Delmuth called. 'Is, I think, the last time we meet together here,' he declared, eyeing Paul appraisingly. 'I shall be here a few more days,' insisted Paul. Delmuth shook his head. 'Is over,' he said, with finality.

In the evening his fever decreased and he took a little nourishment. Again he felt the awful stirring of hope, again began to associate his condition with his having left the châlet the previous day. 'If I am no worse tomorrow I shall not get in touch with Dr. Dubois,' he resolved.

He opened Michèle's letter and was comforted by what he read. 'Perhaps even yet it will finish well,' he reflected as he settled down for the night. Michèle's letter, the diminution of his fever, a new change of bedclothes and pyjamas, induced a sudden feeling of well-being; he drifted easily with the current between the parallel banks of waking and sleeping.

Persistent sounds from the other side of the wall wove in and out of his consciousness; he was aware of them, then not aware of them, then aware of them once again. Then suddenly he was wide awake. There was a muffled laugh and the creaking of a bed. But the next room was empty. Then he remembered that two days previously the sergeant had changed rooms and was now his neighbour.

He tried to settle down, but the sound of another laugh jerked him back from the edge of sleep. He lay very still. Again the creaking of the bed, then the unmistakable cackle of the *petit chou*, followed by more laughter, which resolved itself into a whispering which rose and fell to the distinct and unremitting accompaniment of a hand patting bare flesh.

Paul sandwiched his head between the pillows, but this did little to muffle the sounds. Then the whispering dropped to a murmur, and then there was silence. Paul, very relieved, took a deep breath and fell asleep almost instantly. A little later he was woken by more laughter, and at the same time he became aware that his fever was returning. A series of alarm-clock cackles from the *petit chou*, the hoarse, indulgent laugh of the sergeant and the resumption of the terrible patting. Paul again thrust his head between the pillows, but withdrew it, stifling, a few moments later. He wiped his face and forehead. He knew that only sleep would arrest his rising fever which, if unchecked, would in its turn preclude the possibility of sleep. Resolutely he reclosed his eyes and kept them closed.

His feet were burning. He moved them to the other side of the bed, and when, again too hot, he moved them back, he found that the sheets were moist and clinging. The noise of the love-making continued. 'God,' thought Paul, 'it will go on all night!'

A new hazard – the contents of his stomach were rising to his throat, and the effort to keep them down was leaving his runaway fever without course or rider. From next door the character of the sounds indicated development. The sergeant (owing to his restricted breathing) and the *petit chou* (either equally broken in wind or else in moronic emulation) were emitting alternate, raucous gasps which, with the metallic grinding of the bed springs, sounded like an ancient steam train setting out on its last journey.

Paul's whole body broke into a heavy sweat and, swearing, he tore off his pyjamas. He groped for the towels and knocked over the stand. An interruption, two gasps long, as the sergeant and the *petit chou* each retained a single breath, then uninhibited resumption. Paul pulled a towel from the floor and started to wrap it about his middle, when, like claws dividing tissue, pain tore his chest. He remained rigid till it had subsided, then lay back on the pillow. A new exudation formed about his thighs and seeped into sheets and blankets. 'Christ!' he muttered, raising a sweating hand to a sweating forehead.

His fever bounded forward, relating him organically to the train now flat-out across open country. The volume increased, the rhythm became swifter. Paul was now on the running-board, now stoking, now swinging great boulders of coal from the open tender. More fuel. More fuel. Flames leapt backwards from the furnace, searing, roasting his naked arms and chest.

A climacteric cataract of cries, the train over the edge into the river and the furnace out. Paul lay still. His body had taken over and every pore was vomiting.

Paul had woken in his vomit. As he sat up a familiar movement in his chest had shown it was full of fluid. He had renounced all further resistance, succumbing to the comatic element of a high fever, lying waiting for the sledge which would soon be taking him away, not caring what would happen, taking consolation from the knowledge that at least his destination was the *Universel* and not *Les Alpes*, that in having severed his connection with Vernet he had at the same time cut loose from Bruneau, Halfont and Emile.

He speculated briefly on whether he might be given Michèle's old room, whether the chef would make any concessions to his vegetarian diet, whether he was going to live or die, but then his mind relapsed, he re-emerged into his boyhood, recalling the sequence of the shops in the street in which he had lived, the names and faces of the boys at his first preparatory school, the collections of objects he had made, the cigar-box which he had filled with two rows of cut-out transfer butterflies transfixed with pins and which had brought on him such contumely for not having resorted to killing-bottle and net.

He heard the arrival of the sledge. In came Dr. Bruneau. 'Come on. Get ready. You're not so sick you can't get out of bed.' Paul stared at him uncomprehendingly. Dr. Bruneau pulled back the bed-clothes.

'I'm Dr. Dubois's patient,' Paul whispered.

'That remains to be seen. The *Universel* closed down yesterday and the *Société* has reopened *Les Alpes.* For the time being I am looking after all those who are patients of Dr. Vernet. Now come along – I can't wait all day.'

PART THREE

CHAPTER ONE

•

THE familiar entrance hall, the combined and particular smell of cooking, dust, floor-polish and ether. Paul, head bowed, dizzy, near collapse, steadied himself at the concierge's counter. M. Halfont came into the hall.

'*Vous êtes le bienvenu!*' he cried, taking Paul's arm.

'*Laissez!*' ordered Dr. Bruneau. '*Il sait très bien marcher.*'

Sœur Rose, gaping and edentate under her eye-shade, waited at the liftshaft. The wounded, snail-pace lift groped upwards; through the arras, at the intersection of floor and ceiling, Paul glimpsed Emile's massive, uniformed body, face pink and contented, emerging from a lavatory.

Sœur Rose led him to his room, helped him off with his clothes.

'No!' she cried, as he tried to get into bed. 'I must weigh you first.'

Paul shook his head, bent double to regain his breath.

The door opened and in came M. Halfont. 'What have you, *Monsieur* Davenant? Have you fever?'

'*Monsieur* doesn't want me to weigh him,' protested *Sœur* Rose. Then to Paul: 'How do you expect to get better if you don't get weighed?' The telephone rang and she shuffled out into the corridor.

'She is simple,' explained M. Halfont. 'When we get more sisters she relapse back into night nurse. Till ten days you are our one guest, then we receive guests from the *Universel* and at the same time new guests from a scheme. Everything here is altered – new politics, new policies. *Le Docteur Bruneau* will look after you. He is a very good medicine. Vernet is of course too a very good medicine, but in my mind – ' he glanced over his shoulder and lowered his voice – 'in my mind Bruneau is still better.'

Sœur Rose came back into the room.

'*On vous demande au Service Médical*,' she sang out. In the darkened *salle de scopie* Dr. Bruneau was seated on the music stool, his head bent, his hands over his eyes; solemn re-consecration of the cathedral into which Paul had first blundered two years previously.

Sœur Rose supported him as he stood inside the X-ray cabinet; as usual he endeavoured to overhear Dr. Bruneau's comments, as usual they were inaudible in the buzz of the mechanism. As he climbed out of the cabinet, Dr. Bruneau left the room.

'What did he say?'

'Little poems. Tiny little poems,' said *Sœur* Rose soothingly. Back in bed he fell instantly into a poisoned, toxic sleep, waking with froth on his lips as Dr. Bruneau entered the room.

'*Monsieur*, I have come to set your mind at rest.'

The concept 'Then I am all right,' impressed itself as irresistibly on Paul's mind as a view on a viewfinder. Dr. Bruneau continued:

'I mean – don't misunderstand me – I mean I am willing to take complete charge of your case. Anyway I have been appointed by the *Société* to look after Dr. Vernet's former patients. You would only be able to have Dr. Dubois in a supervisory capacity, and there is no need for that. I am expert in Dr. Vernet's methods. I will treat you as he would have done.' He grinned, curled back his lips. 'All right? Agreed?'

'How – ' Paul stopped, held his breath to prevent himself from retching. 'How ill am I?'

'We shall see. Puncture tomorrow.'

'Fluid?'

'A tank full. Can't you feel it? Now have you made up your mind?' Dr. Bruneau took out a pencil and notebook and looked at him expectantly. 'Well?'

Dr. Dubois was the rope ladder out of the pit, the light at the end of the tunnel, the safe-conduct out of enemy territory.

'I am Dr. Dubois's patient,' said Paul weakly.

'That is just the point. You need not continue to be.'

'I must continue with him.'

'There is no must about it.'

'I – '

'Well?'

The effort to talk made Paul retch violently. He lay back panting on his pillows.

'Right. We will discuss it again tomorrow,' said Dr. Bruneau. 'Do you need anything?'

Paul shook his head.

'*Sœur* Rose will give you something to help you sleep. Good night.'

Good-night. Fluid. The adherence of the lung to the chest wall and the loss of the pneumothorax. The reopening of the lesions in the lung and relapse into his former condition… A *femme de chambre*, middle-aged, her scalp showing through her thinning hair like the sun through clouds, brought the dinner tray which demonstrated that in respect of food the 'new policy, new politics' were none other than the 'old policy, old politics'. *Sœur* Rose fussed and hobbled inquisitively about the room.

'A bit of a set-back?' she asked repeatedly, or: 'What could have accounted for it?' Then through association of ideas: 'Have you any news of the little Duchesne?'

She handed Paul one sleeping pill and, forgetting she had done so, returned a quarter of an hour later with a second. Paul swallowed both. He slept until the arrival, next morning, of *Sœur* Miriam.

'*Alors, nous recommençons,*' she said. She bound a ligature about his arm and extracted some blood for a sedimentation test. He fell asleep again. Half an hour later, unwashed and unshaven, he was summoned to the *Service Médical.*

'It's like old times to be puncturing *Monsieur* Davenant,' said Dr. Bruneau nostalgically as Paul lay, chest bared, on the operating table. *Sœur* Miriam nodded agreement, covering Paul's chest with the rug which had served on so many similar occasions in the past.

'Ten days of our undivided attention for *Monsieur* Davenant,' said Dr. Bruneau, filling a syringe with water and discharging it into the air.

'What day are they coming from the *Universel*?' asked *Sœur* Miriam.

'Friday week.'

'And the scheme from Holland?

'The following Monday.'

'How many will there be altogether?'

'A hundred. A hundred and thirty. One never knows till they come.' Dr. Bruneau fitted a needle to the syringe. 'What does it feel like to be our only guest, *Monsieur*?' he asked. Paul turned away his head as Dr. Bruneau forced the anæsthetising needle, then the cannula, between his ribs. 'It's like pushing a pin through india-rubber,' complained Dr. Bruneau. He removed the trochar and attached a syringe to the mouth of the cannula. Paul twisted his chin to his shoulder and watched the syringe.

'This will be interesting,' said Dr. Bruneau, easing the plunger. Nothing happened. 'No good!' Dr. Bruneau detached the syringe and tossed it into a bin. *Sœur* Miriam handed him a new syringe and this time a brilliant, emerald-coloured pus oozed into the container.

Dr. Bruneau held the syringe to the light. 'Opaque and iridescent,' he said dreamily. 'Packet-boats gliding down Ægean waters…'

'It must be crawling,' *Sœur* Miriam's voice rebuked the poet in Dr. Bruneau.

'Crawling,' agreed Dr. Bruneau, discharging the syringe into a receptacle and then refilling it. 'Green Ægean waters lapping golden beaches of pestilence in the sun… What have you been doing, *Monsieur* Davenant?'

'Look at the oil!' cried *Sœur* Miriam as Dr. Bruneau discharged the contents of another syringe.

'That's where the microbes have been evoluting.'

'*Ça alors!*'

'A lot of the oil appears to have integrated with the pus, but it will separate later.'

'To get like that it must have been going on for months.'

'Certainly.'

'What will it have done to the pleura?'

'What indeed!'

'And Dr. Vernet said it was never to be touched!'

'*Sœur* Miriam, stop giving away state secrets!' Dr. Bruneau smiled conspiratorially at Paul. '*Monsieur*, ignore what we have been saying!'

'But he's not a fool. He knows quite well.'

'You hear, *Monsieur*, *Sœur* Miriam says that you are not a fool! You have made an impression on her – she's never said that about a patient before.' He stopped syphoning the pus, and massaged the fingers of his right hand. 'It's hard work,' he complained; 'you must have a mayonnaise mixer inside you to make it so thick.'

'So he's back again with a new pleurisy,' said *Sœur* Miriam.

'It's not a new pleurisy, it's a continuation of the old.'

'You mean, the old one never stopped.'

'Precisely.'

'Then – well how will it ever be stopped?'

'Evidently not by sealing it up with oil and disinfectant.' He turned to Paul. 'Do not trouble yourself, *Monsieur*; in these enlightened days there is always something we can do. If necessary we could strip down your ribs on the affected side and collapse the chest wall on to the lung: that would surely arrest the secretion.' Then to *Sœur* Miriam: 'Kindly prepare a litre of distilled water. I will now wash out the pleura.' And whilst *Sœur* Miriam searched among the bottles in the medical cabinet, Dr. Bruneau, smiling down at Paul, rubbed the numb tips of his fingers up and down the flesh and ginger parting in his hair.

Dr. Bruneau tore into the room. 'Are you strepto-resistant?'

'What?'

It was evening. Paul had fallen asleep over his supper tray. Under his arm, where he had been aspirated, a plover's-egg bruise was forming.

'Strepto-resistant. Strepto-resistant. S-T-R-E-P-T – '

'I don't know.' Paul rubbed his eyes.

Dr. Bruneau tossed his head with impatience. 'How many grammes of strepto have you had?'

'I can't remember.'

'Think, *Monsieur*. Try and remember.'

'I have no idea.'

'You can't not know.'

Paul did not reply. Dr. Bruneau gave a cry of exasperation. 'I'm asking for your sake, not for mine. How long were you given it?'

'A few weeks.'

'A few weeks! A few months! A couple of years!' Dr. Bruneau waved his hands in the air.

'It had to be stopped because it was affecting my sense of balance.'

'That was only because it was administered intra-muscularly. What I want to know is how much you had.'

'Can't you see from my documents?'

'If I could, would I be here? Dr. Dubois has got your documents.'

'Can't you ask him?'

'There is no need to bother Dr. Dubois.' Dr. Bruneau took three short steps towards the door, turned, and took one long step back.

'How are you feeling since the aspiration?'

'Better.'

'Less sick?'

'Yes.'

'Temperature?'

'Lower.'

Dr. Bruneau seized Paul's temperature chart. '*Zut!* Down seven divisions! That's quick service!' He looked at Paul intently.

'*Monsieur*, there is something I would like to do.'

'What?'

'I would like to put you some strepto in the pleura whether you are resistant or not. Get your dressing-gown and follow me.'

Paul followed Dr. Bruneau down the overheated passage to the *Service Médical.* Dr. Bruneau switched on the lights.

'Get up on the table,' he ordered, at the same time unlocking the medical cupboard. 'Strepto... Strepto... *Ah, voilà*,' he muttered. He picked up a phial, snapped off the top and drew the contents into a syringe.

Paul lay on his side, his forearm at ninety degrees, his hand resting on his head. Dr. Bruneau turned, syringe in hand.

'How did that get there?' he demanded, fingering the bruise below Paul's armpit. 'Now don't go saying that I did it,' he added banteringly, then, changing his tone: 'On your back, now – this won't be pleasant. I can't get in under your arm. I will have to go through the top of your chest...'

'*Secouez le bocal!* Shake ze bot-tel!' It was the following morning. Dr. Bruneau had just given Paul a second inter-pleural injection of streptomycin.

'*Secouez le bocal?*'

'Like zis!' Dr. Bruneau dropped on all fours and shook himself like a dog which has just scrambled out of a pond. Then reverting to French: 'Do this twice a day, your head lower than your body, your face first to the ground then to the ceiling.' He rolled over on his back, supported his buttocks with his hands and wagged and wriggled his trunk. 'In this way the strepto will wash all round your chest wall,' he explained, getting to his feet and rubbing the dust from his clothes.

'I'm to have more injections?'

'One every day.'

'Then I am not strepto-resistant?'

'It turns out that you have never been tested. I am arranging for cultures to be grown.'

'If I am resistant the injections will do no good.'

'None.'

'What then?'

'*Monsieur*, you are always looking ahead. Wait till you hear the result.'

'How long will that be?'

'Three weeks.'

'Three weeks!'

'Now don't complain. Your temperature is much lower, you're feeling better...'

'How long will I have to stay here?'

'I don't know. Nobody knows.'

'Was the fluid positive?'

'You are asking me seriously?'

'Yes.'

'*Monsieur*, the bacilli were standing on each other's shoulders.'

Paul turned away; he resolved that he must obtain Dr. Dubois' assessment of his condition without delay. On the way back to his room he came upon the *femme de chambre* with the thinning hair and she took his arm.

'I am all right,' he said, freeing himself. She laughed and followed him into his room. As he lay in bed, reflecting on how best he might get in touch with Dr. Dubois, she dusted and polished the furniture that was nearest to him. Suddenly, leaning forward, she tapped the top of his thigh with the tip of her broom. Paul looked at her in astonishment. She laughed and left the room.

Dr. Bruneau had made no further reference to the question of whether or not Paul intended to be supervised by Dr. Dubois; did this mean that Dr. Bruneau now assumed that he himself was in sole control? This was a matter about which there could be no procrastination; he would go down to the foyer and telephone Dr. Dubois immediately. As he threw aside the bedclothes there was a knock at the door and in came Delmuth.

'Back to bed, sick mans,' he cried heartily. 'How are you? Yesterday they tell me you are not receiving. Is true? Still, is no matter. Wait! I have a present for you from my wife. Is not much.' He searched in the lining of his overcoat. '*Voilà.*' He handed Paul a copy of *Hymns, Ancient and Modern.* Inside was stamped: *English Church. Brisset.*

Paul got back into bed. Delmuth looked at him critically.

'You are better or you could not walk, but your cheeks are ever too ripe. What is with your fever?' He sat down in the armchair.

The *femme de chambre* re-entered the room without knocking, looked from Delmuth to Paul, laughed and went out again. Delmuth clicked his tongue and slapped the arm of the chair which turned to flesh under his fingers. 'Good-looking. Not much hair but very good-looking.' Then: 'I was right about the location of our next meeting place. Is my trouble – I am always right.' He smiled complacently.

'Now what will they do to you? Have you thought? What do you think they will do to you?'

'Bruneau drew off fluid yesterday.'

'Was just fluid?'

'No. Pus.'

'I know.'

'How do you know?'

'I have already spoken with Bruneau of you.'

'What did he say?'

'Now you are interested!'

'What did he say?'

'That you were very well.'

'Will you tell me what he said?'

'That you surely represent England at the next Olympic Games.'

'Delmuth!'

'What do you want to know?'

'What he told you.'

'He was silent – like the pyramids.'

'What did he say?'

'Nothing.'

'Did you speak to him or not?'

'No.' Delmuth shook with laughter.

Paul stared at him in horror. He thought: 'This man is my only friend in France.'

'Listen, old mans, you know the saying: "You die if you worry, you die if you don't, so why not worry?" Ho-ho-ho! You see? Why not worry? Ho-ho-ho! Why not die? I tell you now my treatment guide to the T.B.C. Is simple. First time ill – bed rest. First relapse – pneumothorax. Second relapse – thoracoplasty. Third, fourth, fifth and sixth relapse – pleural, lobectomy, pneumonectomy and pleuropneumonectomy. Then for the morale and to stop worry – pre-frontal leucotomy. You see? Easy. Fifty thousand francs, please.' Out came the grocer's hand.

Delmuth's expression changed. He got up, sat at the top of Paul's bed and held Paul's arm.

'Look, old mans – is all just a joke. You know this. Or we joke or we go mad. I was ill all the war – bombardments, German occupation, no food. And in this time I had still to support myself and my wife. You see? I know what it is to relapse. But for you is not so – you have no one, you are alone. One day you have no money. All right. Good. Your country has free welfare. You go back there and you still have bed and food!'

Paul got out of bed.

'Why you get up?'

'I must go down to the hall.'

'Why?'

'To telephone.' Paul put on his socks and dressing-gown.

'Who you telephone? Your mistress?'

'Never mind.'

'Who you telephone?' Delmuth barred Paul's way to the door.

'Let me pass.'

'You telephone Lotus Flower! Since my wife is come she have someone else.'

Paul pushed Delmuth aside; in his present state of tension he would not have a moment of tranquillity until he had spoken with Dr. Dubois. Once outside his room, he realised that he was weaker than he had thought; his fever was returning; his pyjama jacket was adhering to his back. The lift was in operation. He steadied himself at the head of the stairs, then started to descend. The rapidity of his heartbeat forced him to sit down. When he got up again a movement inside his chest showed that the secretion was re-forming.

There was no directory in the telephone booth. Cursing his luck, Paul went in search of Emile. Emile was not to be found. Paul's heart was again beating too quickly to allow him to remain standing; he shut himself in the telephone booth and sat on the chair. Then he noticed that someone had written the number of the *Universel* in pencil on the wall.

'Dr. Dubois is not here. Who is calling?' came the voice of Dr. Dubois's secretary. Then: '*Monsieur* Davenant! But Dr. Dubois left here a quarter of an hour ago specially to see you before catching his train. Hurry back to your room or you will miss him.'

Paul replaced the receiver and returned as quickly as he could to his room. Delmuth was still there.

'Hello, sick mans.'

'Has Dubois – ' Paul leant against the wall. 'Has Dubois been here?'

'Yes.'

'Where is he?'

'Gone. He could not wait.' Delmuth followed Paul into the passage. 'You lose your time. He is in the train to Paris,' he shouted after him. 'He say he will see you when he come back in one week...'

Dusty, slothful flies like miniature hedgehogs, the oviparous philoprogenitive, all-season nurslings of the primitive central-heating installation, were emerging from their places of concealment, dipping stridently across the room to Paul's bedside lamp and, like their forebears eighteen months earlier, transforming the glass bowl into an illuminated, transparent hive. Eviction was complicated and purposeless – the swarm would return as to a carcass.

Paul's supper tray lay in front of him; delivered at half-past six and now, at half-past ten, still uncollected, it would inevitably remain for the night. A book by Mauriac (open at a page on which the author asserted the belief that the virtual sum total of terrestrial unhappiness was the product of illicit sexual relationships) was supported against a tureen of grey, greasy soup. Intermittently Paul read a page, half a page, a few lines.

Delmuth had left at midday. Ten and a half hours gone; nine and a half hours to go. Then the arrival of the breakfast tray, the making of the bed, the summons to the *Service Médical*; then a further twenty hours to devote to Mauriac. When for a few seconds the flies were silent, Paul could hear the ticking of his watch.

The moment when the crags and valleys of past and future are flattened into the infinite desert of the present; the moment that in company, in mirth or in grief, seems non-potential to the human condition; the moment when the soul looks at itself in the mirror and sees there is no reflection. If Delmuth, Bruneau or Emile could have walked through the door, Paul would have wept with relief.

CHAPTER TWO

•

Next morning, after the injection, Paul told Dr. Bruneau that he must speak with him; Dr. Bruneau led him into the bureau formerly occupied by Dr. Vernet. Without preamble Paul demanded that Dr. Bruneau should reveal to him the precise implications of his condition; the latter, with ill-concealed exasperation, replied that he had nothing to add to what he had already said. Paul, having anticipated this reaction, asserted that Dr. Bruneau had told him nothing of significance; he now wished to be told definitively whether the relapse would entail the loss of the pneumothorax. Dr. Bruneau retorted that the problem was incidental to the main problem, which was to stop the pleurisy; he added tartly that since Paul had elected to be supervised by Dr. Dubois, he should govern his curiosity until the latter's return.

Paul got up to go, hesitated, then said:

'You told me that these days there was always something which could be done.'

'I said that? About what?'

'My condition.'

'You mean something more radical?'

'Yes.'

'That could only be as a last resort.'

'It would be so very drastic?'

'Probably.'

'What?' Paul tried to sound casual and unconcerned.

'I can't say; time enough to talk in such terms when everything else has failed.' Dr. Bruneau looked at his watch and, to show that the interview was over, made the movements preliminary to getting up.

Paul raised his voice to retain him. For two years, he said, every variety of substance had been pumped in and out of his body. When and at what point would it be decided that everything else had failed? Dr. Bruneau replied that the finer shades of the question could be debated indefinitely: the short answer was that everything would be said to have failed when local treatment had ceased to produce adequate results. There was a moment, said Paul, beyond which this sort of existence could no longer be endured. Dr. Bruneau denied this. He said: 'Everything this side of death can be endured.'

Both men were silent.

'You must have learned by now that the body and the mind speak with different voices,' Dr. Bruneau said at last. He got up.

'That is all that you have to tell me?'

'That is all that there is to tell you.'

Paul remained a few seconds in thought, then turned and left the room.

'The sleeping pills you give me are not strong enough, *Sœur* Rose.'

'They would send an elephant to sleep.'

'Elephants probably sleep more easily than I do.'

'Well, you can't have anything stronger.' *Sœur* Rose proffered the capsule between her trembling, foreshortened fingers, dropped it, raised her eyeshade like a visor and looked about her. '*Ah, voilà!*' She picked up a small piece of cotton-wool, held it to her left eye, then threw it angrily to the floor. Paul watched her intently. Was he going to get a double supply? *Sœur* Rose hesitated, then got protestingly to her knees. '*Ah, enfin!*' She polished the elusive capsule on the hem of her skirt, then handed it to Paul. As soon as she left the room, Paul put the capsule in an empty matchbox, which he then placed inside the drawer of his *table de nuit*. He was resigned to passing a bad night; he was resigned to passing thirty bad nights.

The decision eased his mind, but sleep eluded him. As it grew later, so he became more confused. At times it seemed to him that he had already collected sufficient capsules and this impression became so persuasive that once at midnight and once at two o'clock he turned on his bedside lamp and examined the contents of the matchbox. When at last he slept he dreamt of Michèle, a muddled, anxious dream in which their past re-developed in terms of the future, a dream which left him, in the first moments of waking, with the feeling that in some way time had resolved their difficulties and that they were together again. Then as his mind cleared and in the moment that he realised that he had been dreaming, this concept was replaced by another. He pulled aside the sheets; he had over-slept, he must hurry; Michèle was occupying the room two doors down from his own and he had not yet started to reheat her coffee.

The door opened and *Sœur* Rose shuffled into the room.

'*Bonjour, Monsieur Davenant*,' she said, setting down his breakfast tray on the bed-table. 'Eat your breakfast quickly – Dr. Bruneau will be puncturing you in under an hour.' Her face puckered, she was trying to remember something. 'Oh, and he said be sure that you remembered to shave under your arm.'

Paul drank half a cup of coffee, then got out of bed. As he lathered his cheeks he wondered whether he could endure thirty more days. What was the alternative? He stared at the reflection of the taut, extended surface of his throat and ran his thumb over the blade of his open razor. Two minutes' work as against a month's. How deep did one go? Did one cut or stab? What were the chances of success? Irrespective of whether or not he had the courage to cut his throat, he had to acknowledge the fact that capsules probably offered less scope for failure. As far as he knew, fifteen grains of pheno-barbitone constituted a lethal dose, and each capsule contained a single grain; as a precaution he had arbitrarily doubled the estimated amount. If life became intolerable he would allow himself the bonus of a few days right at the end.

He shaved his armpit. The plover's egg was now little more than a black-and-yellow inset in the surface of the skin, but the marks of the trochar and of the subsequent penetrations were clearly visible. He raised both his arms; the single, shaved armpit looked like the mark of some penal confraternity.

His toilet completed, he returned to bed and awaited the summons to the *Service Médical*. He heard *Sœur* Rose walking down the corridor towards his room. This was it. He swung his legs out of bed and started to pull on his socks. 'No, no,' cried *Sœur* Rose as she came into the room. 'I have only come to make the bed.'

Five minutes later he was again lying back on his pillow. 'Thank God no one knows how agitated I get,' he thought. And he reflected how the whole of his life had been the attempt, sometimes more, usually less, successful of concealing the true nature of his feelings from those about him.

The house telephone rang in the corridor. Paul sat up, but awaited additional confirmatory sounds. Silence. He lay back. Rapidly approaching footsteps. He pushed back the bed-clothes, put his feet to the ground. The door opened and in came the *femme de chambre*. Paul hastily took his Mauriac from the marble-topped commode.

'*Ça va bien? Oh, oui, ça va bien,*' she said. She brought in a broom, shook it over the floor and then attempted to sweep up the débris which fell out of it. 'How is your good-looking, well set-up friend who visits you?' she demanded. And as Paul replied non-committally, she added: 'One would never guess that he wasn't well. I'm sure he knows how to make his wife a happy woman!' In whatever part of the room she was working, she was attracted to Paul's bed as though by centripetal force; she interspersed her other tasks with the flattening and puffing up of his duvet, the tucking in of his sheets, the straightening and aligning of his pillows. 'I must go now,' she said. 'I hope you don't think this is my ordinary work.' She smiled, winked, and tapped Paul's thigh. As he smiled back at her, she laughed and said: 'And I also know what's underneath your sheet…'

The telephone rang again. As *Sœur* Rose entered the door, Paul pulled free the sheets which the *femme de chambre* had just tucked tightly into place.

'No,' she cried, raising her arm like a traffic policeman, 'Dr. Bruneau only wants your temperature chart. Where is it?' Up went the eyeshade and she peered about her. Paul pointed to the chest of drawers.

'Ah!' *Sœur* Rose hurried over to the chest of drawers and snatched up a newspaper.

'No, next to the newspaper.'

'Ah!' *Sœur* Rose located and seized the chart, carried it with the newspaper to the door, stopped, scrutinised both objects and tossed the chart on to Paul's bed.

'But you want the chart,' said Paul.

'Don't muddle me,' said *Sœur* Rose, going out of the door. She was back in five minutes.

'I told you not to muddle me and now you've gone and made me make a fool of myself in front of Dr. Bruneau,' she wailed.

'When is he going to aspirate?'

'Soon. Any minute. Be patient. Where is your chart?'

Paul handed it to her.

'Ah!' she said accusingly. 'If it was on your bed, why did you tell me to look on the chest of drawers?'

Paul lay and waited. The moment before the insertion of the needle; then the moment when the needle jagged its way through the flesh, probed relentlessly beyond the area that it was anæsthetising, stabbed a nerve, or with dull sound struck a rib… Would the trochar slide in easily or would it encounter channels of calcified tissue through which it would not pass?

Emile came in with two envelopes addressed in Michèle's bold, clear handwriting – they had been brought down from the *Châlet Anniette*. Paul took them with great eagerness, first opening the one which bore the later postmark. Absence of news, she wrote, was rendering her imagination as sombre as his own; he must know that she had no one to confide in, no one to turn to; she begged him to have pity on her and to reply by return of post. Below her signature (and just above the faint imprint which she had made to form the outline of lips) was the message: 'Have faith in our love! It is stronger than anything which can oppose it! The future is ours!' Paul then opened and read the earlier letter.

He was about to write a reply when *Sœur* Rose came into the room with his temperature chart; an entry had just been made of twelve different kinds of bacillus and streptococcus which had been identified in his pleural fluid.

Paul lay down his pen. What, in such a context, could he write to Michèle? His eyes closed.

Forty minutes later he awoke, looked dully at his watch, then realised with sudden panic that his summons to the *Service Médical* must occur at any moment and that after the aspiration he would be in no condition to write; thus Michèle would be subjected unnecessarily to an extra day's suspense. For the time being, expedience must resolve the issue; with a combination of weary self-disgust and of relief he wrote consolingly and optimistically of his condition. Then he folded the letter, sealed it, and took it down to Emile.

When he returned to bed he lay face downwards, his head under his pillow, indifferent to telephone bells and footsteps in the passage.

'Wake up, *belle au bois dormant*,' grumbled *Sœur* Rose as she shuffled in with the lunch. She set the tray on the bed-table. 'Puncture this afternoon. Be ready,' she said as she went out. Paul sat up, rubbed his eyes, then removed the cover from the *réchaud* – a mixture of fat meat and beans. He separated a dozen of the beans from the meat and ate them with a spoonful of floury potatoes.

He fell asleep immediately after lunch but woke when *Sœur* Rose returned to collect the tray. '*Bonne cure,*' she said, drawing the curtains. He fell asleep again, waking (more with his body than with his mind) about an hour later; he groped for his watch, but was able neither to interpret the position of the hands nor even to be sure that he was holding it the right way up. Was it morning, evening, afternoon or night? Then he realised the significance of the light beyond the curtains, and he looked again at his watch. An hour until the end of the *cure de silence* and the aspiration, then after that the balance of the afternoon and the whole of the evening. Automatically his thoughts turned to his razor, to the length of cord which secured his dilapidated trunk, to the drop which separated the balcony from the ground.

At the end of the *cure de silence* he once more abandoned himself to listening for every sound in the corridor; there was a succession of footsteps and the telephone bell rang so frequently (though no one came to his room) that at last he got out of bed and went into the passage. Doors were open up and down the corridor; the staff was occupied in preparing the rooms for the patients whose arrival was anticipated towards the end of the week.

A little later there was a knock at the door and in came Mme. Anniette, crying: '*Des salauds! Des salauds, je vous dis!*'

'*Madame* Anniette!' cried Paul, sitting up. She took his hand, then with a single movement divested herself of her cape and swung a heavy suitcase on to a table. And as she opened the case and took out some of Paul's clothes and some food which she had prepared for him, she related how, when she had arrived five minutes ago, Emile had had the impertinence to tell her to use the back lift.

'I told him, *Monsieur* Davenant, that lifts were for those whose feet could only carry them to the nearest bar, and I climbed the stairs.'

Then, suppressing her indignation, she came and sat down by Paul's bed. Good wishes from all the occupants of the châlet, good wishes from the postman, good wishes from the lady who collected the laundry – Mme. Anniette ticked off each with her fingers.

'Ah, *Monsieur*, if wishes could heal…' His room, she told him, would be ready for whenever he wished to return and any other lodger temporarily in occupation would be '*foutu dehors!*' At last, with the promise that she would call again soon, she took her leave.

'*Bonne cure*,' said *Sœur* Rose at six o'clock.

'The aspiration?'

'Ah!'

'When is it to be?'

'Soon. Any moment.'

At seven o'clock *Sœur* Rose brought in the supper tray.

'*Bon appétit*,' she said, setting the tray on the bed-table. Then a thought occurred to her: 'Wait! Don't eat! I will first find out about the puncture!' Three-quarters of an hour later she returned to collect the tray. 'What! Not eaten? How does *Monsieur* expect to grow up into a big, strong man?' she demanded with mock severity: Then: 'Ah! The puncture! Wait! I will telephone *Sœur* Miriam!' She went out of the room and returned smiling serenely, her eyeshade perched above her brow like an inverted coronet. '*Sœur* Miriam says you are to enjoy your meal. Dr. Bruneau went down to the village before dinner but he said he would puncture you when he got back at nine.' Paul opened the *réchaud* – it contained an omelette.

Half-past eight. Nine o'clock. Half-past nine. The door opened and in came Dr. Bruneau.

'*Comment cela va-t-il?*' he demanded. Without replying, Paul drew back the bedclothes and reached for his dressing-gown.

'What are you doing?'

'Getting up.'

'Why?'

'For the aspiration.'

'For the aspiration! At this time of night?'

Paul looked at Dr. Bruneau with sudden misgiving. '*Sœur* Rose said you were going to aspirate at nine o'clock.'

'At nine o'clock,' repeated Dr. Bruneau in a puzzled tone of voice. Then he suddenly laughed. 'So I am, *cher Monsieur*. At nine o'clock tomorrow morning.'

CHAPTER THREE

•

The *femme de chambre* continued to pay Paul her curious attentions, one evening smuggling him some extra food, another evening drawing up her skirts, kicking her legs in the air, laughing and going out of the room. Delmuth and Mme. Anniette called for a short period each day. Everyone said: 'It will be better when the patients arrive from the *Universel*.'

Whatever the time of day, it seemed as if it was always that time of day. The hour after breakfast barely glanced across the abyss of the middle morning to the hour before lunch; the remaining hours conceded at best a funeral pace with many halts, each, as it were, in mourning for its own passing. Each day, as with ephemera, seemed as long as life.

The wretchedness of this cycle of days and nights became in some way apparent to Dr. Bruneau. One evening, making his routine visit, he felt constrained to try to divert Paul by demanding his opinion of modern painting; his motive was so explicit that Paul felt too embarrassed and self-conscious to reply. Good-naturedly implying by his attitude that the next quarter of an hour was to be devoted to Paul's pleasure whether or not the latter had the capacity to appreciate it, Dr. Bruneau proceeded to describe canvases which he had seen, outlining rapidly and with nervous, impatient gestures the nature of each composition, the technique employed, the degree of anatomical distortion (and the organic disorders it would provoke), the deviation from established laws of perspective, the disregard of accepted criteria in respect of the balance of masses, the texture of the paint surface and the method of its application. In this way he appeared to re-create rather than to describe each painting, an illusion which he sustained consciously, for when at the close of a description he indicated the canvas's height and width, he retained his hands in the position in which they had demonstrated one or other of the dimensions, curled his fingers as though about a frame and proudly suspended the completed picture before Paul, who, staring between Dr. Bruneau's hands at his white-draped chest and stomach, felt compelled to murmur: '*Comme c'est étonnant*,' or '*Oui, oui, très, très bien…*'

One evening *Sœur* Rose thought she saw a ghost in the linen cupboard (it was the inevitable bolster) and ran screaming down the passage; *Sœur* Miriam declared that *désœuvrement* was sending her as dotty as *Sœur* Rose; the *laborantine* caught a cold and, her hair in curlers, was to be encountered half a dozen times a day swinging along from her bedroom to the laboratory with a bottle of her own urine for analysis. (In the latter context *Sœur* Miriam declared that, whilst she had heard of people living by taking in each other's washing, it was the first time she had heard of people living by taking in their own.)

The overall function of each of Paul's days was the sum of its immediate activities – the morning injection or aspiration and the evening garnering of another pill for his matchbox. There had already been a difficulty: as if he had penetrated Paul's intentions, Dr. Bruneau had forbidden him any more sedatives. Paul's protestations having been disregarded, he had been forced to ring for the night sister (who, like the day sister, was *Sœur* Rose) at two o'clock in the morning in order to re-demand the pill which he had been earlier refused. *Sœur* Rose, understandably outraged by the prospect of potentially broken sleep every night, had contracted secretly with Paul to maintain his supply.

Most of the day and night at least one of the levels of his mind would be occupied with Michèle, and in consequence he frequently had an hallucinatory impression of her presence – that moment in a waking dream when the light becomes many times more brilliant and the cerebral image, three-dimensionally solid, emerges into independent existence. When he went out of the door of his room (there was nothing to distinguish the passage from the passage of his former floor and his new room corresponded with the one which had then been occupied by Manniez), it was as though he had just visited Manniez and was now returning to his own room or to Michèle's. And, once in the empty passage, he could not repress the conviction that Michèle had preceded him by a moment, that as he had opened his door her own door had closed, or that, the hem of her cherry-coloured, polka-dotted dressing-gown swirling about the calves of her white linen trousers, she had, a few seconds earlier, passed through the swing doors half-way down the passage.

This impression, co-existing as it did with the acknowledgement of its utter falsity, was so painful that Paul looked forward to when it must be dissipated by the arrival of the patients from the *Universel*; indeed frequently he would have welcomed an additional summons to the *Service Médical* for the relief that the incidental company would have brought him. When at the end of the week, and by chance on a day when both Mme. Anniette and Delmuth had failed to visit him, he was told that the arrival was to be delayed still longer, he relapsed into so palpable a state of despair that on his evening round Dr. Bruneau felt constrained to interrogate him.

'What have you in mind, *Monsieur*? What are you thinking of?'

'Nothing particularly.'

'No thoughts that you should not have?'

'No.'

'Then what, *Monsieur*, is the matter?'

'Nothing.'

'You are sure?'

'Yes.'

'Good.' Dr. Bruneau went over to the door, then stopped. 'You are not telling the truth,' he said, returning to the foot of the bed. He studied Paul's face whilst Paul stared expressionlessly at the bottom of his bed.

'Well, what is it? What are you planning?'

'I've told you. Nothing.'

Dr. Bruneau walked up and down the room, glancing about him for unfamiliar objects. 'Let me see your temperature chart,' he said suddenly. Secure in the knowledge that *Sœur* Rose had not marked down the sleeping pills, Paul handed it to Dr. Bruneau.

'So you are managing without sedatives,' said Dr. Bruneau,

'You stopped my having them.'

'Are you sleeping?'

'No.'

'Why haven't you complained?'

'What would be the use?'

'It would be no use.'

'That is why I haven't complained.'

'I should think not. You've lived on sedatives – for two years they've been your daily bread.'

'I have never needed them more than at present.'

'Have you ever asked *Sœur* Rose for any?'

'Yes.'

'And?'

'She refused.'

'Of course she refused – she's under orders!' Dr. Bruneau went over to Paul's bed-table and pressed the bell for *Sœur* Rose; a minute later he re-pressed it, retaining his finger on the bell-push. *Sœur* Rose stumbled angrily into the room like a diver hurrying through water.

'What's the matter?' she demanded. 'I gave you your – '

'Dr. Bruneau wants you,' interrupted Paul hurriedly.

'Dr. Bruneau! Where?'

'What did you give him?' cried Dr. Bruneau, stepping forward and seizing *Sœur* Rose's arm.

'Ah! Ah!' *Sœur* Rose raised her eyeshade and gaped at Dr. Bruneau.

'What did you give him?'

'Ah! You're hurting my arm.'

'I said, what did you give him?'

'Nothing.'

'You're lying.'

'No.'

'What did you give him?'

'I gave him – ' She swallowed. Paul held his breath.

'What?'

'I gave him a vitamin pill.'

'A vitamin pill!'

'Yes.'

'You mean you gave him a sleeping pill!'

'I didn't! I didn't!'

'You did!'

'Never!'

'If you have given him sleeping pills you will be out of here tomorrow.'

'I didn't! I didn't!'

'Tell the truth!'

'I am telling the truth!' *Sœur* Rose started to sob. Then she pointed accusingly at Paul. 'He drives me mad, it's always pills, pills, pills – he wakes me up at two in the morning asking for them. But I won't ever give him one, not a single one.' She hid her face in her hands.

'All right,' said Dr. Bruneau suddenly. He reflected a moment, then added: 'Well, take care you never give in to him – he can sleep perfectly well if he wants to.' His tone changed and he smiled from *Sœur* Rose to Paul.

'Always remember that *Monsieur* Davenant is our number one patient, in fact our only patient. We must not lose him.'

'He always gets me into trouble. When you asked for his chart he handed me a newspaper,' wailed *Sœur* Rose.

'There! There!' Dr. Bruneau winked at Paul.

'He's sending me mad.'

'That's enough, *Sœur* Rose. Go away and don't forget your orders.'

Sœur Rose scowled at Paul and left the room. Dr. Bruneau resumed his pacing.

'*Monsieur!*' he said at last, pleadingly engagingly. Paul looked up. Dr. Bruneau stopped at the bottom of the bed, leant confidentially forward with his elbows resting on the bedrail, his chin on his clasped hands; his sickly face looked as white as a stage moon.

'Your condition is a little better: your temperature is down and the pus is definitely thinner. Why are you getting up to your tricks?'

'I am not.'

'No?'

'No.'

'Well, I hope not; it would be bad for you, bad for me, bad for the sanatorium and – it wouldn't work.' Dr. Bruneau's index fingers reached and elevated the corners of his eyes, transforming his face into an Asiatic mask; his chin sunk forward until it rested on the bed-rail.

'Put it all out of your mind,' he said. He closed his eyes. 'Look upon the treatment we are giving you as sport, *cher Monsieur*, as a gamble in which you stand to win or lose everything. And if you don't like to see it in those terms, then consider yourself an experiment of the gods in what a man can endure.' The eyes opened. He stood up and straightened his jacket. 'Are you a believer, *Monsieur?*'

'A believer?'

'Yes. Do you believe?'

'No. Not really.'

'I thought not. Then if you intended to kill yourself, you would have no special little scruples or doubts?'

'I don't know.'

Dr. Bruneau laughed.

'Everyone agrees that the idea of another life is ridiculous, but, like Talleyrand, no one ever quite cares to close the door. Still, it doesn't matter, one has very little to lose.'

'To lose?'

'I mean one has no need to shout one's credulity from the housetops.'

'No.'

'No.' Dr. Bruneau sat down on the edge of the bed. 'Have you reflected much on these matters? Have you ever reflected, for example, that the idea of another life is really no more ridiculous than the idea of this one? If one, why not another?'

'I see what you mean.'

'But of course we can equally argue that our view of what is or is not likely does not necessarily correspond to the opinion or working of the Absolute.'

'That is so.'

'Obviously it is not so simple as all that.'

'No.'

'Nevertheless we can isolate and identify certain general principles in respect of life itself. Let us do so.' Dr. Bruneau's brow creased into the external pattern of relentless inner dialectical activity. 'The primary principle, the governing principle, the over-riding principle, in a word the principal principle – ' He broke off to give greater emphasis to what he was going to say. 'The principal principle is – ' He paused again, puffed out his cheeks: 'Blind will!' His cheeks went hollow. 'Blind will, *Monsieur!* Blind will, the core, the central pivot of the philosophy of Schweitzer – '

'Schopenhauer.'

'Schweitzer, Schopenhauer, whoever you like. Where was I? Blind will! Do you doubt it, *Monsieur*, do you doubt it?'

'No.'

'If you ever do, reflect on the battle for supremacy going on night and day in your own chest – ravenous hordes of rudimentary organisms gnawing their way to survival! The outcome could change the whole trend of evolution! We compliment ourselves that we are the end-product of evolutive life – look at the fate of the double-brained

Diplodocus who lorded it over the earth for ten thousand times the length of historical time! For all we know, we are mere sports, mere temporal detritus, mere homeoecstasic projections of some of the lesser amphibia washed up on the Devonian and early Carboniferous beaches. For all we know – ' Dr. Bruneau paused to take breath – 'the future of the world will be bacterial, and I, in bringing my science to your aid, am being retrogressive and anachronistic.' He laughed in uninhibited delight at his capacity for intellectual paradox. 'Do you ever spare a thought for Judgement Day?' he added.

'Judgement Day!'

'I mean if you kill yourself. There is an old superstition, *Monsieur*, that one is best advised to live out one's life. Or don't you mind running the risk of having it all over again? In any case why is it that when people think in terms of another world they always assume that it will be governed on different principles from those which God – if He exists – saw fit to establish in this one?' He paused for comment, but received none. 'Don't bring up the Fall of Man!' he cautioned (unnecessarily). Then as if Paul had brought it up: 'Man could not have fallen if he had not been equipped to fall, and one does not install equipment where one does not intend it to be used.' A sudden suspicion occurred to Dr. Bruneau. 'What am I talking about?' he demanded.

'About there not being another world,' said Paul with a start.

'Absolutely not! The exact contrary, in fact,' said Dr. Bruneau tartly. 'Does this sort of thing not interest you?'

'It interests me very much.'

'Would you prefer me to stop?'

'No. Not at all.'

'Very well, then. I was urging you, *Monsieur*, to consider that inability to adapt yourself to this world was perhaps not the best recommendation for prematurely moving on to the next. Can you not see that if there is a grain of truth in the Scriptures it is in the assessment of life as a test? What do you think the next world will be? Harps? Angels?' Dr. Bruneau dismissed the idea with a wave of his hand. 'Believe me,' he continued very warmly, 'the next world won't be all that different from this one, and the man who gets on will still be the one who knows where to look for his opportunities. In a word – same set-up, bigger scale.'

'Yes.'

'Or same set-up, smaller scale, size being purely relative. Yet how many people, divines and theologians included, have ever conceived of a heaven the size of a pin-head?'

'Very few.'

'Very few! *Cher Monsieur*, none! And whilst heaven may be neither microscopic nor gargantuan, the faculty for formulating such concepts is apportioned to the humble man of science!' He bowed. 'I think – ' he resumed, but broke off as he caught sight of the time. 'I must go,' he said hastily. He stopped at the door. 'There are people who claim that scientists have no capacity for abstract thought. Yet what is science?'

'What is it?'

'I am asking *you*, *Monsieur*.'

'I can't say.'

'Then pay attention. Science is the alliance of four distinct qualities: the ability to think theoretically; the ability to relate theoretical thought to practical application; the courage and conviction to follow blindly wheresoever truth points the way.'

'You said there were four.'

'Those are four – the courage and conviction to follow truth blindly count as two.'

'I see. Well, it is a very comprehensive definition.'

'The least modification and it would be less than the truth.' Dr. Bruneau glanced at his watch. 'The world, *Monsieur*, is not well run.'

'No.'

'You agree!' Well, take it from me it would be to no one's disadvantage if it were governed by a select committee of doctors!'

'Yes.'

'It's a state of affairs unlikely to come about in our lifetime!'

'Yes.'

'Is that your opinion?'

'No. Not at all.'

For a moment it appeared that Dr. Bruneau was on the point of further elaboration. Then he shrugged his shoulders in humorous resignation. 'Goodnight, *Monsieur*.'

'Goodnight.'

'And spare a little thought for what I have been telling you.' Dr. Bruneau closed the door. Whilst the latter had been discussing the problems of adjustment in this world and the next, Paul had only been concerned in attempting to adjust himself to his revised situation. What now? He knew that he had six sleeping pills but after what had happened, would *Sœur* Rose supply him with any more pills? Instinctively he reached for the matchbox in which he kept his present stock, in order to recount them. Then he realised that he had not heard the sound of Dr. Bruneau's departing footsteps. He withdrew his hand and waited. The door shot open.

'What are you doing?'

'Nothing.'

Dr. Bruneau stared at Paul's hand, which the latter opened. 'You are going to settle down and sleep?'

'Yes – if I can.'

'Why shouldn't you be able to?'

Paul shrugged his shoulders.

'*Monsieur* – on your honour you have no pills?'

'None.'

'I don't believe you.'

'Why are you so concerned?'

'Because I'm your doctor.'

'Once you told me I could jump out of the window.'

'That was different. I wasn't in charge then.'

'Isn't Dr. Dubois in charge?'

Dr. Bruneau smiled mysteriously. 'That is another matter,' he said. He gazed round the room. 'You haven't your books here,' he commented.

'No.'

'Why not? Have you stopped reading?'

'Yes.'

'You ought to do something with your hands.'

'Yes.'

'Can you paint?'

'No.'

'Would you like to make a rug or a basket?'

'Not really.'

'Have you ever made a leather purse?'

Paul shook his head.

'Why not try?'
'Perhaps I will.'
'You do nothing to help yourself.'
'No.'
'Well, goodnight.'
'Goodnight.' This time the footsteps resounded down the corridor.

Paul woke up at three and lay without sleep for the remainder of the night; when he heard the first sounds of the new day – the banging of a door, a snatch of shouted conversation, the distant moan of a vacuum cleaner – he got up and sponged his body. The death mask of the mirror stared incuriously back, then disowned itself with a cursory shake of disapproval. 'I am not yet thirty,' he reflected involuntarily. Then he drew apart the curtains and glanced at the moonlit landscape with which he associated all his troubles; so to the damned, he thought, must appear the mountains of hell. He returned to bed. The brief, physical activity had restored his mental circulation; his nocturnal misgivings dissolved with the night before the prospect of the day's evil. He resolved that before the day was over he would have determined both the time and manner of his end.

CHAPTER FOUR

•

After breakfast he was summoned to the *Service Médical* for his injection. Dr. Bruneau was in a good mood.

'New long needles specially for swollen pleuras! Now I won't have to drive it right up to the hilt!' he cried, waving a packet in the air. After the injection he gave his drenched-dog shimmy and demanded in English:

'You shake always ze bot-tel two times a day?'

Paul nodded gravely.

Towards the middle of the morning *Sœur* Rose came into the room to change the handtowels.

'*Sœur* Rose,' said Paul. She paid no attention. '*Sœur* Rose,' he repeated, raising his voice. She left the room.

When she came in with the lunch her eyeshade was so low that in order to see where she was going she was forced to walk with her tortoise neck thrust forward and her head thrown back. '*Sœur* Rose,' said Paul very urgently. Because she still took no notice, he seized her wrist as she set the tray on the table. 'You've got to listen to me,' he said.

'Ah! Let me go.'

'I'll let you go if you listen to me.'

'What is it?'

'You're not going to stop giving me my sleeping pills because of what happened last night?'

Sœur Rose freed herself with a sudden twist of her body, and fell sprawling to the floor. She scrambled to her feet and ran out of the door, her scream marking each stage of her progress down the passage.

'God! I've done it now!' he thought. Three minutes later, still howling, she returned at a jog-trot with Dr. Bruneau, whose face had turned the colour of his hair.

'Out!' he cried, waving his hand at the door.

'What!'

'Out! Today!'

'Let me explain – '

'Not necessary. Out!'

'Look!' howled *Sœur* Rose, rolling up her sleeve and exhibiting the marks on her arm to Dr. Bruneau. She burst again into her neurotic, self-pitying wail.

'Be quiet, *Sœur* Rose. *Monsieur*, you will make other arrangements. Today! This morning!'

'But just listen – '

'Don't waste your time. You're not going to kill yourself here and you're not going to assault my staff.'

'He nearly broke my arm! Ahhhhh!'

'Stop that noise or get out!' cried Dr. Bruneau, clapping his hands over his ears.

'He said that if I didn't give him pills he'd pretend to you that I'd given him a pill every night last week! Ahhhhh!'

'You hear, *Monsieur*! You hear!'

'That's not true.'

'Ahhhhh!'

In exasperation Dr. Bruneau gave *Sœur* Rose a push. She staggered and her eyeshade fell over her nose.

'What did you say?'

'I said it wasn't true.'

'Ahhhhh!'

'Get out!' cried Dr. Bruneau, waving his arm at *Sœur* Rose.

'He lies all day without moving – I'm frightened to come in the room for what I may find. Ahhhhh!' The last cry came as Dr. Bruneau bundled *Sœur* Rose through the door.

'Now, *Monsieur*,' he resumed, kicking the door shut, but controlling his voice. 'Now decide your arrangements. Emile will do your telephoning for you.'

'But listen – '

'I won't listen!' Dr. Bruneau's voice soared.

At that moment *Sœur* Rose's head appeared round the door.

'He asked me – Ahhhhh!' She broke off and slammed the door as Dr. Bruneau turned and strode towards her, fist raised.

'You see! You see what you've done!' he cried, turning back to Paul.

'What I've done?'

'Who else?'

'I only asked her for a sleeping pill because I can't sleep at night.'

'I don't believe you. Why shouldn't you be able to sleep at night?'

'Can't you think?'

'No.'

'Because I lie rotting here, day after day, year after year.'

'Have you ever thought what it's been like treating you?'

'I know which I would have preferred to be doing.'

'Well, it's all over now.' Dr. Bruneau turned to the door but stopped, outraged.

'Is it my fault that you're lying here?' he demanded.

'I didn't say it was.'

'I've told you to occupy yourself. I've told you to take up handicrafts.'

'Yes.'

'I've taken you into my confidence. I've discussed by the hour the things which interest you.'

'Yes.'

'I've given you devoted medical attention. Did Dr. Vernet ever do any more for you?'

'No.'

'Well?'

'But don't you see – '

'No!' cried Dr. Bruneau, again raising his hands to his ears. 'I don't see and I don't know and I don't understand and I don't listen and YOU LEAVE TODAY!' The last words were shouted from behind the slamming door.

Paul lay against his pillow, breathing rapidly. Another sanatorium? Would Mme. Anniette take him back in the châlet? The rate of his breathing increased; his chest rose and fell. The window! He looked towards it. This was the moment! No more thought! Quickly! Now! Now! He drew back the duvet and swung his legs to the ground, but the sudden effort made his heart beat too quickly for him to stand; he lay sideways, his hand pressed against his chest. The door opened and in came Delmuth.

'Hello, sick mans!' he cried enthusiastically. Then: 'What have you? You go mad?'

Paul sat up, gasping.

'Leave me, Delmuth! Leave me!' He tried to get to his feet.

'Leave you? *Dieu merci!* What have you? Daymares?'

Delmuth seated himself placidly at the side of Paul's bed. 'What happens? Tell, please.'

'Not now. Leave me for three minutes.'

'Ho-ho! You make pi-pi in the wash-basin! Don't bother for me!'

'No, I – ' Paul again tried to get to his feet.

'Your face is dripping.'

Paul took out a handkerchief and dabbed his cheeks and forehead.

'And I can hear your heart!' Delmuth went over to Paul and placed his hand on Paul's chest. 'Is displaced. Is much displaced by the fluids,' he announced censoriously. 'Now say please what is with you.'

'I can't. Not now.'

'Say, please.'

'Do go away.'

'I not leave till you say.'

Dully Paul recounted what had happened; Delmuth listened in a sort of ecstasy.

'This Bruneau say you must go today?' he said when Paul had finished. Paul nodded.

'He will not change his intentions?'

'No.'

'You are sure!'

'Yes.'

'Perhaps he will. I go see.'

Delmuth left the room. Paul looked across to the window, but the fit, and with it the strength, had gone. He lowered his head in his hands. Delmuth returned several minutes later.

'Is true what you say. Is all true.' He stood with his buttocks pressed against the rim of the wash-basin.

'Of course it's true.'

'Yes. I had thought perhaps you exaggerate.'

'What did he say?'

'He say is all true.'

'I must go today?'

'No. No. He say you must go today.'

'Today?'

'No. No. Today!' He smiled encouragingly. 'Is a good thing I see him,' he added.

'A good thing?'

'Yes. I think otherwise he let you stay. Is not a cruel man, Bruneau.'

'What did you say to him?' cried Paul.

'No. No. I not tell you.'

'Delmuth!'

'No. Is private. Is our secret.'

'Delmuth, for God's sake!'

'Well, all right. I tell him you kill yourself one moment to the next!'

'You told him that!'

'Yes.'

'And that is why you went to see him!'

'Yes.'

Paul stared at Delmuth, who started to pick at his thumbnail with his teeth. An initial reaction of outrage and anger was qualified before it could develop by the realisation that what had happened was implicit in his relationship with Delmuth and the inevitable penalty of having confided in him.

'Why did you do it?' Paul asked, after a brief pause.

'You see, I know Bruneau have plans. Yes.' Delmuth nodded significantly as though agreeing with what he had said.

'Plans? For me?'

'No, for him. He plan to propose himself against Dubois as candidate for *Médecin Chef.* If something happen now like you killing yourself, the *Société* say he have no control.' He examined with interest his moist and shining fingertip. 'Is logical,' he added reasonably.

'I see.'

'Is nothing personal,' resumed Delmuth hurriedly. 'In fact Bruneau tell me just now is probably best for you if you do go out of the window, but not while he is in charge.'

'He said that?'

'Yes. He say if Dubois was here, very good, but Dubois is already retarded three days, and how he know you wait till Dubois come back?'

'What did he mean when he said it would be best for me to go out of the window?'

'You not know, sick mans?'

'No.'

'Yes, you know. You joke again.'

'I tell you I don't know,' cried Paul desperately, the palms of his hands growing moist.

'Everyone know, Emile, *femmes de chambres*, all… Your pleura is *foutue!*'

'But – '

'No buts, is *foutue*. Always now you make *liquide* till your lung pops!'

Paul closed his eyes. The colour mounted to his cheeks.

'Now is time to pack. You like me to help you?' Half of Delmuth's thumbnail came adrift and he spat it on to Paul's duvet.

'No. Please leave me, Delmuth.' The urge and the strength to destroy himself sent vivid messages of collaboration up and down his arteries.

'Come! I prepare your cases.' Delmuth opened the wardrobe.

'Please go away.'

'Silly mans!'

'I mean it. Go!'

'You've said that.'

'If you don't, I'll ring for someone who'll make you go.'

'Your face is red – you make your temperature go up.'

'Get out!'

'You mean it? You really mean it?'

'How many times must I repeat it?'

'Very well.' And as Delmuth began to attack another nail, he added casually: 'If you wanted pills why did you never ask me?'

'You!'

'Yes. Your friend!'

'You're mad!'

'So are you. I attend your request since some weeks.'

'And if I had made it?'

'I would have given you what you ask. But instead you prefer to get yourself thrown out of the sanatorium.'

'How would you have pills?'

'That is a secret.'

'Get out, Delmuth!'

'No, no. I get them from my landlady. She was a nurse. She give me pills when I not sleep.'

'Well?'

'I not always use them.' Delmuth smiled insinuatingly.

'What are you suggesting?'

'That I might help you.'

'I don't believe you.'

'I would give you one or two pills each week. Perhaps more.'

'I know you too well! Get out!'

Delmuth opened his wallet and took out a small blue capsule, which he tossed on to Paul's bed.

'Swallow it or save it – as you wish. Is just a first instalment.' He threw a second capsule after the first. 'To show good intentions,' he added.

Paul took the two capsules and was about to put them with his other pills when he became aware that Delmuth's eyelids had almost disappeared in the fixity of his gaze. He replaced the capsules on the duvet.

'Don't leave them there, you fool! Someone come in and we are both in troubles.'

Paul took the capsules and dropped them into an envelope, which he tucked under his pillow.

'That's no good. Put them with the others.'

'What do you mean, the others?'

'The other pills you've kept.'

'There aren't any others.'

'Like Bruneau, I say you lie.'

The door opened and the *femme de chambre* came into the room; seeing Delmuth, she ran across to him. Delmuth threw his arms about her and raised her from the ground, at the same time winking at Paul over her shoulder. He carried her to the armchair, sat down and pulled her on to his knees.

'Since three days we make ourselves the happiest of living peoples,' he explained. He translated the phrase into French. The *femme de chambre* nodded energetic confirmation. Delmuth bounced her up and down. 'Oooooo! Eeeeee!' she cried, waving to Paul.

'Is nice, no?' Bounce. Bounce. 'She wash twice daily in first quality eau-de-Cologne!'

'*Qu'est ce que tu dis, chéri?*'

'*Des bêtises!*' he said, pointing to Paul. He raised her skirt and slapped her thigh. 'Ooooo!' She folded with laughter. He slapped her again. She gave a smothered scream.

'She have not much hair but her scalp is good!'

'*Tu dis?*'

'*Encore des bêtises!*'

'*Petit farceur, va!*'

Delmuth suddenly parted his knees and she landed on the floor. '*Oooooo! Ça fait mal! Saligaud!*' She rubbed her haunches. There was a sound in the passage and Delmuth helped her quickly to her feet. The door opened and in came Dr. Bruneau.

'Ah!' he said to Delmuth. 'You told him?' Signalling to the *femme de chambre* to leave, he said:

'No, no. I think I forget.' Delmuth smiled blandly.

'Forgot!' Dr. Bruneau frowned, then turned urgently to Paul.

'*Monsieur*, Dr. Dubois has just arrived back in Brisset an hour ago; he is downstairs studying your X-rays and will be up immediately. Now ring for *Sœur* Rose and tell her to straighten your bed and to be on hand if Dr. Dubois sends for her.'

CHAPTER FIVE

•

Half an hour after Dr. Dubois had left the room there was a knock and Dr. Bruneau's head appeared round the door.

'May I come in?' he said. Paul put down his half-written letter to Michèle. Dr. Bruneau entered and shut the door.

'Well, *Monsieur*, you are satisfied?'

'Yes.'

'And you are changing to a smaller room?'

'Yes.'

'I didn't know that you had any financial difficulties, I thought that you drew on the purse of Croesus. Do you mind if I sit down?' He pulled up a chair. 'Dr. Dubois is very pleased with your condition.'

'He told me so.'

'It is his opinion that you have nothing to worry about. Well, it is a good thing. He says you won't have to stay here very long.'

'No more than a month or two.'

Dr. Bruneau winced.

'That is no time at all.' Then he added hastily: 'Still, Dr. Dubois is the *Médecin Chef* – he should know.' He looked at his fingernails. There was a long pause.

'He told me to come and see you, he thought that you needed to be reassured. I told him you were the last person alive to need reassuring, but he still insisted. So here I am.'

'It was very good of you to come.'

'A pleasure, I assure you.' There was another pause. Then: 'Did you tell him about our little misunderstanding?'

'No.'

'Quite right – you showed good judgement. Even the best regulated families sometimes...' Dr. Bruneau smiled painfully. 'Actually I had intended to rescind my decision, and would have done so but for the intervention of your friend.'

'You mean Delmuth?'

'Yes, Delmuth.' Dr. Bruneau crossed one leg over the other. 'He called me specifically to intercede for you. Nevertheless, his natural candour made him admit that if you did stay you would undoubtedly behave badly – you know what I mean. As your friend he felt compelled to do all he could to persuade me to let you stay; out of loyalty to me, however, his medical adviser, he could only agree that it was imperative that you should go. You must see what a very delicate situation it was for him.'

'Yes.'

'He appears very attached to you.'

'And to you.'

'Certainly. However, I was just explaining to Delmuth that in the absence of Dr. Dubois your presence was too much responsibility for me, when we heard that he had just returned! Delmuth was visibly affected and insisted on bringing you the news himself. It must have been a weight off your mind.'

'Yes.'

'Or don't you mind much either way?' The impassive tone of the inquiry was distorted by a warning tremolo.

'Of course I do.'

'Then why did you provoke the whole affair?' cried Dr. Bruneau, getting angrily to his feet. Then with an effort he reverted to his former, neutral tones. 'Well, never mind, the incident is closed, the why and the wherefore no longer matter.' He swallowed loudly. 'Your glass is set fair. Dr. Dubois has no doubts.' Again the painful smile. 'If you have the opportunity some time, you might mention to Dr. Dubois how I used to call on you to discuss art and philosophy.'

'Certainly.'

'I would be quite grateful.'

'I will remember to do so.'

'As a matter of fact, and strictly between ourselves, Dr. Dubois seems to have the notion that you're a very sensitive sort of plant!' Dr. Bruneau's painful smile developed into no less painful laughter, in which Paul also joined. Dr. Bruneau raised a conspiratorial finger to his lips.

'Don't let that get any farther – Dr. Dubois is not blessed with our sense of humour. Myself, I've always paid you the compliment of treating you the way I was treated when I was ill – doctor to doctor, man to man! No trimmings, no ceremony, no blah-blah-blah! But I'm afraid that's not Dr. Dubois' way. Still, he was your choice and it's too late to do much about it. Is everything now clear, *Monsieur*?'

'Yes, thank you.'

'And you feel suitably reassured?' Dr. Bruneau winked. Paul nodded.

'Well, *à bientôt, Monsieur*.' Dr. Bruneau left the room.

Paul resumed his letter to Michèle. He felt as if he had woken from a nightmare which had begun on the eve of Michèle's departure and which had ended with Dr. Dubois' return from Paris, and that by the act of waking everything relevant to the nightmare was invalidated. In a concise but detailed assessment of his condition Dr. Dubois had assured him that his pneumothorax was still effective and would continue to be so; that his sputum analysis was negative; that both the bacterial content and the volume of the pleural secretion were diminishing with each aspiration. In a word his body was responding admirably to treatment and, Dr. Dubois had added, the outcome of the treatment was not in doubt. Dr. Dubois's combination of kindness, conviction and authority had made despair appear as irrational as previously it had appeared inevitable.

Satisfied at last that he had set Paul's mind at rest, Dr. Dubois had inquired about the state of his finances, and, on learning that they were low, had suggested that he might care to move to a smaller room which would cost him substantially less. It was arranged that the move should take place without delay.

He was still writing when the door opened precipitately and Delmuth, bent double and clasping his belly as if a bullet had just penetrated his navel, staggered into the room. He unfolded, gave a vivid brassy laugh, waved ecstatically and folded up again. The door had swung back open after the ineffective push which he had given it; he gave it a kick then dropped into the armchair where he shook from side to side like one of the mechanical, laughing figures placed at the entrance to funfairs. Whatever effort he made to control his laughter the memory of what was provoking it would prevail, and the first words of each fresh attempt at explanation would merge into a new sequence of hilarious groans and gasps. The exuberance of his movements brought him to the edge of his chair and suddenly he found himself on the floor; he kicked his legs in the air and wagged his seat.

'Ach! God! Ho-ho-ho!' he cried. 'Is a fool! Oh! Ho-ho-ho!' He got up, his chest articulating as though in a spasm, and tottered out of the room.

When he returned he was more composed but he looked as though he were in a malarial fever.

'Bruneau!' he ejaculated. He dried his face with a soiled handkerchief which he then tied round his brow. 'Oh! Is a fool!' He laughed again, but had neither the breath nor energy to continue, and fell gasping into the armchair. Then he cried: 'Felicitations! You are a cured mans! Not *foutu!*'

'You've found that out quickly!'

'Oh yes, is why I laugh!'

'Who told you? Bruneau?'

'Wait! I tell you.' Laboriously, wheezing, panting and laughing, Delmuth recounted how he had gone into the corridor of the *Service Médical* and had overheard Dr. Dubois' raised voice behind the door of his bureau. He had pressed his ear to the panel of the door; Dr. Dubois was castigating Dr. Bruneau for his negative approach to Paul's case, whilst Dr. Bruneau was whining and protesting that Paul's outlook and mentality had made any other approach impossible. Finally Dr. Dubois had ordered Dr. Bruneau to go straight to Paul's room to reassure him in respect of his condition.

'I stand at once from the door. Bruneau come out he look like whipped worm!' The evocative power of the recollection was too much for him and it prompted a new spasm which terminated in a lusty belch: his hands sprang to his belly and he murmured:

'I give myself spontaneous pneumo if I laugh more!' Then he described how from the little which he had managed to overhear he had realised that Dr. Dubois was unaware that Dr. Bruneau intended to expel Paul from the sanatorium. As soon, therefore, as he had satisfied himself that Dr. Bruneau was well out of the way, he had knocked at Dr. Dubois' door and had requested that he might be permitted a few words in strictest confidence.

'Dubois very suspicious so at first I take care to tell him only of my concern for you, but at the same time and as if not by intention, I tell him all that Bruneau say and do and he get ever more angry and when at last I say him that Bruneau first make you want to kill yourself, and will then throw you out of the sanatorium, he nearly go mad! Oh! Ho-ho-ho!' Delmuth again broke off his narrative.

'You told him that!'

Delmuth nodded, tears streaming. He untied his handkerchief and dabbed his eyes. 'Was not all,' he gasped. 'I say him, still in confidence, that this morning I go to Bruneau to pray him that you may stay but that Bruneau say me you must go at once.'

'Whereas in fact you only wanted to make sure that Bruneau really did throw me out!'

'I know!' cried Delmuth, his state bordering on seizure. 'Is what make it all so funny!'

'But I thought Bruneau was your friend.'

'Was, but is not.'

'Why?'

'Is now enemy. Is one almighty fools. Why he declare me you are *foutu* if you are not *foutu?*'

'Well, what did Dubois say when you told him that?'

'One has no confidences in such a mans! Was mad angry – is rare, is normally cold fish. He say me: "I speak with Dr. Bruneau!" Then I say him is well known that Bruneau will oppose himself for *Médicin Chef* – in proposition to him. "Is enough, *Monsieur*! I will hear no more of that!" he say. Snubs to me! Well, no matter, he not forget, is not wasted. Then I leave Dubois and I see Bruneau in hat and coat – he think to slip out till Dubois is less angry, and I arrest him, saying: "Dubois is demanding for you everywhere!" He look very sick. "Declare you haven't seen me," he entreat. At the same moment Dubois come round the corner and shout: "Bruneau, come at once to my office!" I follow but am laughing too much to be safe to listen, so I come instead to see you!'

Paul reflected a moment.

'But I thought you said that you'd told Dubois everything in confidence,' he objected.

'I did! Ho-ho-ho!'

'Then why did he want to talk to Bruneau?'

'Is the good question. Dubois say me: "Why you tell me all this if I may say nothing?"'

'Well?'

Delmuth's face turned a deep purple and he shook gently backwards and forwards, his extended mouth looking like that section of a melon from which a slice has been freshly cut.

'Wait!' he said, panting. Then in a rush with the first available breath: 'Is the tail of the joke! I say Dubois may tell Bruneau all provided he say he learn it not from me but from you!' And once more fearing for the consequences to his respiratory system, he got up and passed unsteadily from the room.

Paul's new room, the last in the passage, had once served as the dressing-room to the adjoining suite: it was small; there was a wash-stand and bowl instead of a hand-basin with running water; there was no balcony; it faced north. Nevertheless the price was so moderate that there could be no questioning the advisability of the move. And it was not unsympathetic; with its medium-sized window, its plain furniture and its bed right in the corner it looked more like a student's lodging than a room in a sanatorium. Paul arranged with Mme. Anniette for his books and radio to be brought down from the châlet.

On the day that the patients were due to arrive from Holland, Emile and M. Halfont thoughtfully drawing-pinned a double row of miniature French and Dutch flags over the main entrance. Beneath this symbolic arch of allied solidarity, a few hours later, stumbled some fifty weary invalids; their improvised Arctic headwear, the blankets wrapped about their overcoats, and their snow-encased boots made them resemble a concourse of film extras seeking auditions for the parts of the last survivors of the retreat from Moscow. Under the direction of a uniformed Dutch official they formed up into three ragged ranks; the roll was called; they were marched off in batches to their rooms, which, formerly occupied by the students, were confined to the two lower floors, and in which they were quartered in pairs.

In the evening, under the pretext of posting a letter to Michèle, Paul went down to the foyer; it had been taken over by the newcomers, who, standing or squatting in little groups, were talking and smoking and playing at cards, marbles and dominoes. There were a few with dressing-gowns; the majority were wearing overcoats or windcheaters over their pyjamas. Dr. Bruneau, wearing a suit which looked as if he had purchased it several years earlier from a boys' outfitters, was moving from one group to another, introducing himself, shaking hands, coughing because of the smoke, laughing mirthlessly and talking German.

Two days later the *Universel* closed its doors and its patients and personnel were absorbed, as though by transfusion, into the leuchæmic blood-stream of *Les Alpes.* Porters, taxi-drivers and clients bustled down the main arteries of the reviving giant like red corpuscles newly introduced; trunks and cases, fed in great quantities into its digestive system, were distributed, separated from their contents and eliminated. The operation lasted several hours and resulted in the resuscitation of the second invalid and in the extirpation of the first.

Frequently in the last long and destructive periods of isolation had made Paul look desperately forward to the projected visit of someone who, in more normal circumstances, he would have never wished to have seen at all; the actual arrival of his visitor, in consequence, never resulted in anything beyond the intensification of his real loneliness. Now, and in the same way, Paul found that not only did the presence of the patients from the *Universel* provide far less relief than he had hoped and anticipated, it increased many times the poignancy of his separation from Michèle.

Paul found that of his former acquaintances, none remained; the novelty of encountering other patients in the passages survived no more than the first few mornings; by the end of the week life at *Les Alpes* had become indistinguishable from what it ever had been. Once again he found himself a taciturn and unwilling participant in the communal weighings and consultations; once again the self-confident exchanges, banter and witticisms of his fellow invalids acted on his stomach like an emetic. Which, he wondered, as he looked about him, were the new Mayevskis, Glou-Glous and Marelles? He hoped that he would never find out.

Traditionally, patients called upon their next-door neighbours. The occupant of the room next to Paul was one of the few patients who had been brought into *Les Alpes* on a stretcher. He was a man in whom tuberculosis had run riot – lungs, spine, kidneys, intestines and skin. An open fistula required regular treatment which it received at the same time each day from Dr. Bruneau assisted by *Sœur* Miriam and *Sœur* Denise (the new floor sister. *Sœur* Rose had reverted to her original, exclusive rôle of night nurse). The initiation of the treatment would provoke groans which, within a few seconds, would develop into screams; it was the single evidence of an independent existence that Paul ever heard from the adjoining room. One day Paul decided to call upon his neighbour, but he realised as soon as he had opened the door that his visit was neither desirable nor desired. Nothing indicated that the room was in occupation; the specially constructed iron bed, with its flat, surgical mattress, looked as if it contained no more than a head. Receiving neither a reply to his greeting nor an acknowledgment of his presence, Paul turned and stole quietly out.

The sound of typing, each morning, from a room a few doors down from his own, encouraged him in the belief that it contained a writer. Halfway through an interminable and introspective evening he determined to put his suppositions to the test. The occupant of the room gave him an immediate and indignant assurance that he was not *de ces gens là*, he was the director of a thriving mail order business and every day his secretary called to type his correspondence. Back in his bed, it seem to Paul that with every room in the sanatorium occupied, there was not one which contained a potential friend.

His treatment went on much as before; it was prescribed by Dr. Dubois but still administered by Dr. Bruneau. The presence of so much calcified tissue made the daily injection of streptomycin progressively more difficult to effect; Dr. Bruneau inserted the needle at such a variety of angles that often Paul believed the point must emerge through his chest. To avoid the tension of awaiting indefinitely his daily summons to the *Service Médical*, he took to calling there of his own accord as soon as he had finished eating breakfast. If Dr. Bruneau were available, he would give Paul his injection before commencing his morning work.

One morning when Paul was awaiting Dr. Bruneau's arrival, *Sœur* Miriam came into the *salle d'attente* and told him to return to his room. Paul inquired whether Dr. Bruneau would be sending for him before lunch; *Sœur* Miriam replied that he would not. Paul went away regretfully; on days such as these he might be summoned for his injection at any time up to ten o'clock at night.

Emile brought in a parcel of books which Paul had been eagerly awaiting for several days; an indefinable sense of uneasiness made him decide not to open it until after he had received his injection. (The exciting ritual of ordering and awaiting books was only completely realised when their arrival coincided with a good state of mind. In consequence he would only send for books when his condition was satisfactory; where it had deteriorated between order and receipt – as was often the case – he would delay opening the parcel for days or weeks.)

Delmuth called towards the end of the morning. He was in high spirits, for his wife had decided to return to Belgium and he was now able to look forward to an unrestricted relationship with the *femme de chambre*.

'Is love,' he declared fervently. 'For me is the tragedy that I not meet with her twenty years before. We are made for one another, together we make each eternally happy!' He sighed. 'In life is ever so, is ever too late!' Then more cheerfully: 'Is a wonderful thing, love – without it we are nothings, we do not exist, is not possible. For me life is the story of my love. Always, wherever I go, I attract a beautiful young girls. Why, I do not know. Is so!' He smiled in proud bewilderment. 'One day I write my memorials – it make passionate reading!'

Whilst lunch was being served, Dr. Bruneau came into the room.

'*Bonjour, Monsieur*,' he said formally, picking up Paul's temperature chart. When he had examined it, he tossed it back on to the bed. '*Monsieur*,' he said in the laboured tones which indicated that he was selecting his words with great care. '*Monsieur*, we have just learned that your bacilli are far wickeder than we had anticipated.' He cleared his throat. 'They are extremely wicked,' he added pleonastically.

The chasm opened at Paul's feet.

'I refer to your pleural fluid. How shall I put it?' In his endeavour to synthesise accuracy with tact, Dr. Bruneau rose to the tip of his toes and supported himself by the pressure of his finger-tips against the bedrail. 'Your bacilli are no longer intimidated by the action of the streptomycin. It is as if' – he searched for the homely simile – 'your daily injection had no other end than that of maintaining the level of their private swimming pool!'

'You mean?'

'What do you think I mean?'

'That I'm streptomycin-resistant.'

'Bravo!' Dr. Bruneau smiled and his heels sank to the ground – the benevolent quiz-master who has successfully coaxed the obtuse competitor to the prize-winning answer. Then, his voice lightened by a combination of wonder and enthusiasm: 'You have developed a greater resistance to streptomycin than any case within the experience of the laboratory! It's quite remarkable. Still, you're not a scientist, it means little to you.' He paused and coughed. 'It's a pity, of course, but there was no way of finding out earlier – one can't grow cultures overnight. Anyhow it reveals conclusively that your apparent progress is no more than the consequence of regular aspirations – if the exudation were allowed to re-form in any quantity your condition would revert in no time. Well, never mind – you are in good company. When a patient develops resistance to streptomycin I congratulate him and say: "That's one illusion less!" We're down to earth, we're on firm foundations. You've now got no other problems left except that of how to get well.'

'*Monsieur* – ' said Paul, but Dr. Bruneau interrupted him with: 'What are they going to do with me?' That was it, wasn't it?' he went on. 'The inevitable question. I know you now, *Monsieur*, there's very little about you I don't know. Well, I expect you've already realised that we can't go on puncturing you indefinitely. Still, don't worry about it, let us do the worrying, not you. In the end it's always the doctors who have the sleepless nights. But to get you thinking on the right lines, I'll give you a hint. Don't expect your salvation to be measured out in spoonfuls from a bottle labelled 'Miracle Drug – twice daily before meals,' it won't be that, it won't be that at all. Think rather in terms of good, old-fashioned treatment, the sort of treatment that British generals are generally reputed to rate more highly than whole arsenals of secret weapons – cold, hard steel. And, seriously now, it's not such bad psychology. Drench me with streptomycin and I put up my umbrella. Show me a knife and you won't see my heels for dust!'

He appeared ready to continue indefinitely in this strain, pursuing his fantasy like a puppy its tail, turning, twisting, somersaulting, illuminating his false analogies with fresh false analogies, rendering each successive image more fanciful and inappropriate than the last, smiling, sneering, smirking and scowling, but the set of Paul's features recalled to him the fact that with this patient it was essential to be extremely circumspect.

'Now don't start looking depressed, and don't, for God's sake, go telling Dr. Dubois that I've been depressing you just because I've been telling you the truth,' he said severely. And as Paul said nothing, he added: 'I would like your assurance that you will not tell Dr. Dubois that I have been depressing you.'

Paul shook his head. Dr. Bruneau stared at Paul's face uncertainly and a little anxiously.

'Through trying to set my patients' minds at rest I get led into saying too much, and then – trouble! Well, I've learnt my lesson. Now I behave more like other doctors – remotely, impersonally. I...'

Dr. Dubois came into the room and Dr. Bruneau, stopped in the middle of a period, turned scarlet, bowed and gave a false smile of welcome.

'I was just giving our patient a little necessary uplift,' he said. He nodded affectionately to Paul for corroboration.

Dr. Dubois picked up Paul's temperature chart and examined it. Dr. Bruneau attempted to draw Dr. Dubois's attention to the declining curve of the temperature graph.

'You see how his condition has improved despite his resistance to streptomycin.'

Dr. Dubois closed the chart so sharply that Dr. Bruneau had barely time to withdraw his finger.

'One is never wholly resistant to streptomycin. The injections have not been wasted,' he explained to Paul. Dr. Bruneau listened, smiled, nodded agreement. 'Nevertheless, to terminate your cure we will substitute a liquid form of P.A.S. for streptomycin and in a very short time you will see what satisfactory results it will produce.' And, turning to Dr. Bruneau, Dr. Dubois added: 'Carry on as at present – daily interpleural injections and weekly aspirations. A month from now I expect to see a very substantial change for the better.'

CHAPTER SIX

•

The Dutch patients were a shabby-looking crew and as time went on they grew shabbier. Excluded, like the students before them, from the mournful *salon des privés*, they consolidated their occupation of the foyer by never leaving it; the private patients, on their way to and from the main entrance, contrived to walk through the foyer as though they were crossing a desert.

Dr. Dubois and his young assistant Dr. Berry (an orphan and former patient of Dr. Dubois who had become devoted both to the man and his methods) attended to all the private patients. Not being able to add to his commitments (which extended far beyond *Les Alpes*), Dr. Dubois had delegated the care of the Dutch patients exclusively to Dr. Bruneau. The two doctors, therefore, occupied separate consulting-rooms and of all the patients in the sanatorium only Paul plied between them both.

Dr. Bruneau began first to look upon himself as joint *Médecin Chef* with Dr. Dubois, and then as *Médecin Chef* in his own right. It seemed to him that Dr. Dubois and his flock of patients were no more than refugees in transit and that they would not be staying beyond the time required to find suitable accommodation elsewhere. Speaking to Paul he would use such phrases as: 'When things will be back to normal…', 'When we will be on our own again…', 'When I shall be able to fill the rest of the sanatorium with my Dutchmen….' To give greater authority to his fantasy he tended to identify himself more and with his new patients, emulating their manners, the intonation of their voices, their deportment and their dress. Wearing corduroy trousers, sandals, a checked shirt open at the neck and sometimes a dressing-gown, a combination of invalid, pavement artist and out-of-work cowboy, he would spend much of the day and most of the evening in the foyer, where he would watch or join in the current games of poker or marbles or, appending himself modestly to the extremities of a small group (which would instantly swell about his axis), philosophise, exhort, grimace, groan, smoke, cough, King Rat of the Casualty Ward, Fagin's Recruiting Officer at work among the In-Patients, *coq en pâté*, Bruneau visibly, audibly, patently and blatantly in his element.

Before the end of three weeks there was trouble; trouble of the usual sort in respect of food and trouble of a different sort arising from Dr. Bruneau's will to power. The private patients and the Dutchmen received the same *cuisine*. When private patients complained, M. Halfont told them: 'You are paying less money than at the *Universel*, you cannot expect the same standard of foods. Besides, what we give you is basically more healthy and cures quickest.' When the Dutchmen complained he would reply: 'You get the same standard of *cuisine* as was served in the *Universel* and a private patient has just told me it is even better. If the private patients are satisfied, how have you the right to complain?' When, inevitably, each group became aware that the other was complaining, he would say to the private patients (with reference to the Dutchmen): 'The food is above them, it is too *recherché* by far, you can tell by looking at them the sort of food they are used to…' or: 'Please remember your social status and don't set these mendicants a bad example by letting them see that you're dissatisfied.' And to the Dutchmen (referring to the private patients): 'When you hear that they are complaining, remember always that they are for the most part moneyed idlers with effeminate tastes and vitiated palates. Don't be corrupted! If they like to rot their intestines with the pernicious muck served up in three-star restaurants, then that's their look-out, but for us who are here to get well and to get back to our jobs as soon as possible, it is another matter.' In a word, it was trouble of so routine a nature that, strictly speaking, and in its context, it was barely to be classified as trouble at all.

The situation brought about by Dr. Bruneau's will to power was somewhat different. Having decided to his own satisfaction that *Les Alpes* was now a *Sana Populaire* rather than a private sanatorium, he had applied himself to the compilation of a list of regulations which read as if they had been designed to maintain order in a penal institution. With remarkable ingenuity he had ruled out and proscribed every major and minor consolation of sanatorium life. In future, no wireless; no reading during the *cures*; no smoking; no drinking; no purchases of supplementary food; no lights on after nine o'clock at night; no talking in the corridors; no visits from friends, relatives or other patients without signed permission. Patients would show a proper respect both to sisters and to doctors. When addressed by sisters they would reply:

'*Oui, ma Sœur...*', '*Non, ma Sœur...*', as the case might be, and when addressed by doctors they would stand or, if in bed, lie at attention. Under the heading: READING MATTER: 'Reading can play a therapeutic rôle in the recovery of the patient, and patients should endeavour to use their enforced leisure profitably. The reading of textbooks and books potentially of use in the patient's civil occupation is wholeheartedly recommended, whilst, for diversion, novels of adventurous, humorous or romantic interest are advised. Books of a pessimistic nature, or which reflect a gloomy or morbid view of life, will not, in the best interests of the patient, be tolerated.' Under the heading: COMPORTMENT – SEXUAL. 'Sexual activities are strongly discounselled during illness and convalescence. Patients should at all times bear in mind that a single orgasm (male or female) is equivalent, in energy expended, to a five-mile walk over rough country.' The encyclical terminated with the explanation that each of the regulations had been conceived 'in the best interests of all patients', a phrase as many times repeated in the course of the argument as the compiler sensed that a doubt could have existed to the contrary. Had not Dr. Bruneau possessed a typewriter and a rudimentary duplicator it was improbable that this tender child of his fantasy would ever have been delivered into the gross world of fact.

Dr. Bruneau duplicated his regulations on a day when Dr. Dubois was presiding over a conference in Paris. In the afternoon, both as a token of his authority and as an opportunity for circulating his regulations (still viscid from their contact with the gelatinous matrix), he decided to make a formal round of all the rooms in the sanatorium. News of his projected visit preceded him; some of Dr. Dubois's patients locked their doors, whilst others vacated their rooms until he had safely left the floor. Where he gained access to patients, he was openly rebuffed and his regulations rejected. Baffled, all but broken, Dr. Bruneau retreated tragically to the consolation of his own kingdom. The next morning duplicated sheets of paper littered the floor of every corridor and drifted about the stairways and landings like autumn leaves.

Paul retained his copy of the regulations in order to show them to Delmuth. 'No, no,' said the latter, tossing them back unread. Paul insisted. Delmuth glanced casually at the opening lines; a slow smile spread outwards from his lips and he read on with fascination. 'Ho-

ho-ho!' he exploded suddenly – he had reached the section headed COMPORTMENT – SEXUAL. He made several attempts to read the passage but each time he was incapacitated by laughter. 'Ho!' he bellowed at last, his face pink and shaking. 'A five-mile walk over rough country! How he know? Ho-ho-ho! Is not much of a walker, Bruneau! I make two such five-mile walks each day over rough country and when the weather is good – three!' He laughed helplessly, hugged his belly, his breathing coming in little snorts. 'Five miles!' he gasped, dropping into the chair. 'Why five? Ho-ho-ho! What a fools! Five! Ha-ha! I make my five-mile walk always in half an hour! Is not a bad pace, I think! Ho-ho! Ten miles an hour! Indisputably I am the champion walker of Brisset!' Utter prostration. Delmuth's arms and legs hung limply over the sides of the chair, only his body working, like that of a gigantic spider giving birth. 'Ah!' he said, recovering. 'Is right, is quite right. When the country is rough is very hard work!' And between gasps he developed the image, indicating with suggestive motions the uneven surface of rough country with its mounds, dips, declivities, contours and bosky recesses, and declaring how much, nevertheless, he preferred it to flat country. Returning once more to the regulations, he noted with delight that in future he would be required to obtain permission to call on Paul.

'Ho-ho-ho! Dr. Idiot!' he cried, getting to his feet and making a deep bow and flourish in the direction of the imaginary Bruneau, 'I humbly beg your gracious authorisation to visit my friend the manic-depressive upstairs in the maid's bedroom. Ho-ho-ho!' His auto-intoxicated laughter brought *Sœur* Denise (the new floor sister) into the room, but to her outraged protestation he directed the formulæ adumbrated in the regulations, crying, '*Oui, ma sœur...* Ho-ho-ho! *Non, ma sœur...* Ha-ha-ha!' and begging her, whenever his breath was sufficient, to accompany him the next time she felt the inclination to take a five-mile walk across-country.

Trips to the lavatory, to the foyer, to the *Service Médical*: each trip by way of a window-lined corridor, a window-lined landing and culminating in a window-lined room: each window in each corridor, landing and room a single exhibit in the sanatorium's biannual exhibition of academic winter landscapes. Daylight trips, twilight trips, moonlight trips. Sanatorium windows at night; blue and gold illuminators of the fake fairyland of tinsel and icing sugar; double-paned, blazing portholes in the flanks of the stranded, ice-bound liner; refrigerated peepholes for the convenience of the meteorologically curious occupants of a building that was tropical within and arctic without. Winter watched from the stalls of the well-insulated theatre; third act of *Bohème* with real snow to compensate for the absence of music and lovers; story-book winter; rich man's winter; winter without a single rush of cold air, without the need to button up one's collar, without the need to increase the weight of one's clothing by the single addition of a scarf or a pair of woollen gloves.

The 'maid's bedroom' (as Delmuth aptly described it) now bounded Paul like a cockleshell and excluded even the concept of infinite space. As he lay staring at the walls he felt that his eyes were props and that no more than the constancy of his gaze prevented the whole structure from crumbling about him. Had it been possible he would have moved again, but as M. Halfont explained somewhat patronisingly:

'*Monsieur*, what you pay is the cost of the meals and the medical service – the room you get for nudding!' And even paying 'nudding' for the room, Paul calculated that, with the cost of his return journey to England, his means would not extend beyond the second or third month of the new year.

By December he realised that Dr. Dubois's original estimate of how long he would have to remain in the sanatorium had indicated little more than the latter's misgivings in respect of his patient's mental condition. This realisation – formulated gradually and in proportion to his capacity to bear it – brought with it no particular sense of disillusion. He acknowledged in retrospect (as at one level of his mind he had acknowledged at the time) that he had demanded to be misled, that he had allowed Dr. Dubois no alternative but to mislead him. In consequence Dr. Dubois's reassurances had been made involuntarily or, if not involuntarily, had been administered in the spirit with which, for the immediate comfort of their patients, doctors prescribe those medicaments of which the sole function is to reduce a high fever without in any way modifying its course or, subsequently, its outcome.

Nevertheless the substitution of P.A.S. for streptomycin was producing beneficial results and now Dr. Dubois informed Paul that unquestionably he would be completely well by the spring. And since he knew that Paul could not afford to stay at *Les Alpes* beyond March, he added that it would be necessary for Paul to finish his convalescence in a state sanatorium in England, and he offered to undertake the necessary arrangements with the appropriate authorities. Paul thanked Dr. Dubois for his interest but made no effort to avail himself of it – this was only one problem and it took no particular precedence over any others.

Other problems. Sick, alone, unemployable, on the verge of penury – good, decent, time-honoured, extroverted problems, unrelated to neurosis or introspection; Paul hardly considered them. If he died there would be no problems, if he lived there was one problem and it dwarfed all others. And since he thought no less in terms of living than of dying, this problem exercised him, obsessed him and constituted his major preoccupation. The problem, simple, ineluctable of how, at the first opportunity, he might rejoin Michèle.

The sane, the sensible, the common-sense decision would be to resolve to return to England with the hope that one day, someday, he would be able to rejoin her – such a decision was utterly untenable, his longing for her was too urgent and too intense, it dominated his consciousness and influenced his every thought whilst his body ached with an appetite which hers alone could satisfy.

And interminably thinking of her, he would cede to new levels of despair with the realisation that coextensively with his thoughts so her life was separately evolving, that there were those in whose lives she was an element not of memory but of actuality, that there were shopkeepers, bus conductors and passers-by who could come into casual, incidental contact with her, whilst he, who would have considered his life infinitely rich if it had occasionally permitted him to glimpse her from across a street, was confined to the contemplation of three of four claustrophobic walls. And seeing no solution and no possibility of solution, he would inevitably and invariably revert to the one constant in his life, the opinion that he had no valid alternative but to put an end to it.

Delmuth kept his promise. Two or three times a week he brought with him one of the capsules which he obtained from his landlady. Handing Paul a capsule, he would declare: 'When I know you have at last enough then for me each visit become an adventure. Or I chance to find you as you are now, or I chance to find the beauty of the sleeping wood, ho-ho-ho!'

Paul accepted the capsules noncommittally; he felt that any display of eagerness might lead to an immediate suspension of the supply.

At first he suspected one of Delmuth's practical jokes; what would be more in character than that the latter should empty each capsule and refill it with sherbet, ho-ho-ho! But so far as he could tell, his suspicions were false; in respect of taste, texture and colour, the contents of Delmuth's capsules were indistinguishable from those which *Sœur* Rose had originally given him. In this way, gradually, effortlessly, Paul found himself becoming the possessor of a lethal dose of pheno-barbitone.

There were no reservations to be made and Paul made none. He acknowledged at last and with finality that he had no possibility of resolving the one problem which committed him to life, and this being so, then the alternative was inescapable. And accepting explicitly what for some time he had accepted implicitly, his only reaction to the prospect was a diffuse and desperate gratitude that he had the means to accomplish his intentions without recourse to violence. This fact, and the fact that he had very nearly the requisite number of capsules, brought about so marked an improvement in his morale that it provoked favourable comment both from patients and from members of the staff.

The approach of Christmas became dismally apparent through the seasonal, pre-Christmas deterioration in the food (coupled inevitably with outraged protestation from the inexperienced), and through the reappearance (from Emile's grotto), of all the decorated, dusty horrors, the paper and tinsel gnomes, dwarfs and splendid little men which, like pygmy hostages, brutally seized and summarily executed, would hang suspended in rows along the ceilings of the corridors.

On the afternoon of the twenty-third of December, after a particularly painful *ponction* (during the performance of which Dr. Bruneau had been both careless and sarcastic), Paul, returning to his room, opined that he had sufficient capsules for his requirements and that the time had come to avail himself of them. He opened the door. Opposite the window, looking out of it, silhouetted against the hard north light, was a figure so familiar and yet, to his certain knowledge, so surely not there, that, believing himself to be hallucinating, he cried out and staggered back against the doorpost. The figure turned. Two-and-a-half yards, at most three, separated him from Michèle.

He held her so tightly that she seemed to have disappeared, and seeing no more than the tops of his arms and beyond them the familiar range of mountains he again believed himself to be the victim of an illusion and suddenly pushed her back, secured her at arm's length, his doubts so explicit that Michèle laughed and said:

'*Oui, chéri, tu ne te trompes pas, c'est bien moi!*'

And still he looked at her and could not believe that she was really there.

Smelling ether, and inferring from it the treatment which he had just received, she removed his dressing-gown and urged him back to bed. Paul made no resistance, sought only to adjust himself to the astonishing fact of her presence. The door opened. Dr. Bruneau came into the room, stepped back a pace as he recognised Michèle, retrieved his pace like a knitter a dropped stitch, greeted her cordially and enquired whether she had relapsed.

This possible explanation not having occurred to Paul, he looked at her in sudden alarm. Michèle shook her head and laughed – she was only in Brisset on a visit. Dr. Bruneau waved his hands in the air and retorted that everyone was in Brisset on a visit – was her visit medical or social? Michèle explained that her parents had agreed to her spending Christmas in the mountains. She would be returning to Belgium at the beginning of January.

'But it's December! You shouldn't have come before March or April,' cried Dr. Bruneau. And he explained enthusiastically that returning to Belgium in ten days' time she would be unconditioned to the prevailing epidemics and would probably succumb to them. Which room had M. Halfont put her in? Dr. Bruneau took out his notebook and pencil. Michèle replied that she was staying in a pension.

'In a pension!' repeated Dr. Bruneau, his mind orientating itself sluggishly to the concept. 'Well,' he conceded, 'if you have not relapsed, then it is quite legitimate. Still, take care that you don't waste your time and your parents' money. Be your own severest critic and warder. Impose on yourself from the beginning a strict sanatorium *régime*. Spend the whole of the first three days in bed. The second three days you might well get up for one meal, and after that we will see. And, of course, observe scrupulously the times of the cures, no reading, writing or talking...'

As the door closed behind Dr. Bruneau, Michèle threw her arms about Paul, and Paul, mentally defying Dr. Bruneau to return, pulled her beside him. How had she managed to persuade her parents to let her return to Brisset? When had it been decided? Why, why above all, had he had no word as to her intentions? Paul's questions succeeded each other so rapidly that they truncated the intervening answers.

For three months, Michèle explained, ever since, in fact, the day of her return to Belgium, she had endeavoured to obtain her parents' sanction to her passing Christmas in the mountains. But the outcome of her campaign had remained too much in doubt ever to have justified the raising of Paul's hopes. And she added that in fact only three days had elapsed since her parents had finally given their consent, and that although she could then have informed him of the news by telegram, she had been unable to resist the temptation of arriving suddenly and without warning. It had taken three months to obtain her parents' consent? Oh, yes! Paul forced Michèle's head back on to the pillow; her lips parted and her eyes closed; thought temporarily annihilated, Paul crushed her mouth beneath his own.

She left when it was dark (she had yet to unpack and install herself in her new room), but she returned later in the evening. Paul, unable to eat his supper, awaited her with an excitement which canalised his strength and left him so weak with anticipation that every footstep in the corridor first stopped his heart then doubled its rate. When she opened the door the curtains blew out through the window and her skirt billowed above her knees. Paul stretched out his arms and she ran to him; the frozen surface of her cheeks thawed rapidly against his own.

'It's cold. Let me close the window.'

'No.'

Michèle struggled, but Paul would not let her go. Suddenly she ceded. Paul drew aside the bedclothes and folded them over her, raising the sheets as high as her neck.

'I love you,' he said, and he repeated the phrase many times, devoutly, religiously. An arm rose in confirmation from between the sheets and curled about his neck. Paul turned on his side, his arm encircling her waist.

'It is strange…' he began, but the drift of his thoughts was too amorphous for concise expression. Strange that out of the worst experience of his life all that had been most precious in his life had developed (and that to have forgone the first would have been to have forgone the second). Strange that only when he had finally renounced hope, that hope (the infinitely extravagant and improbable hope that one day, suddenly, without warning, Michèle should walk into his room), had been realised. Strange that twenty-four hours earlier in this same desperate bed and staring at the same torn curtains and at the same dust patterns on the ceiling, he had believed (as firmly as he had ever believed anything) that he would never see her again.

The supper trays were collected. The night sister made her rounds. Paul and Michèle went on talking still, to their astonishment, the church clock struck ten (the hour at which all visitors had to leave the sanatorium, and the doors were locked).

Michèle got hurriedly to her feet. She said:

'There is something I had to tell you. It will have to wait till tomorrow.'

'Something to tell me! What?'

'I'll tell you tomorrow.'

Sudden panic. 'Tell me now. You must tell me now.'

'I can't.' Michèle leant over to kiss Paul on the forehead, but he caught her arms. They looked at each other. Paul thought:

'She has met someone else. She has come here to break it to me gently. She is going to tell me that when she leaves Brisset, she will never be able to see me again.' He released her arms, felt he had no longer the strength to hold them.

'Oh, it's not that,' she said.

'Not what?' he stared dejectedly down at the bed.

'Not what you are thinking,' she said, laughing and she threw her arms about him. Paul held her tightly.

'There isn't someone else?'

'Of course there isn't.'

'Then what is it you have to tell me?'

'It's nothing bad. I'll tell you tomorrow.'

'Tell me now.'

'I can't. There's not time.'

'Then it is awful.'

'It isn't awful.'

'Please tell me.'

'Tomorrow. I must go. I'll have to ring for *Sœur* Rose to let me out.'

Michèle embraced Paul quickly and left the room.

Paul remained several minutes without moving, then extinguished the light. 'What is it she has to tell me?' he wondered. He found that when his head was in a certain position on the pillow and when he breathed very carefully he could just detect the faint, fresh odour which he associated with Michèle's body; when he breathed more deeply, it was gone.

At midnight he was still awake. He got up, remade his bed, washed carefully all over, discreetly averting his gaze from the slit-eyed, crumple-faced creature in the mirror. Back in bed he endeavoured to empty his mind of the day's events, but it was like trying to wring dry a sponge whilst it was still immersed in water. At times he drifted into sleep, but at the very point or pivot he would swing back with the question: 'Is it really true that she is in Brisset?' or 'Would I really have killed myself if she had not come?' Dialogues with Michèle. Dialogues with Delmuth. Dr. Vernet, Dr. Bruneau, M. Halfont, Emile, gesticulating and shouting, closed in about his bed.

At last, in a heavy sweat, he turned on his bedside lamp and, believing himself to be in a high fever, took his temperature; it was several divisions below normal. Three o'clock in the morning. Sacrifices would have to be made if the next day were not to be intolerable.

'Trial run,' he said to himself as he staggered out of bed and extracted from his hidden cache of capsules a single, shining cylinder.

CHAPTER SEVEN

•

Paul woke with the entry of the balding *femme de chambre.* Too drugged to move, he watched her mutely from his pillow. She set down the breakfast tray on the bedside table. 'My friend makes me wear garters instead of suspenders. Men are queer, aren't they?' she said, flipping up her skirts and giving a little laugh. For the security of his stomach, Paul synchronised a blink. 'He says he wants me to wear transparent underwear, but there I put my foot down. "I'll be dressed or undressed but not a bit of both," I tell him. Still he knows what he likes, and that's something. And they say your friend has come back, so that will be nice for you, too.'

Paul pulled himself up painfully; he resolved to take no more sedatives in the early hours of the morning. 'My friend says he's got a bone to pick with you, he says you're playing him up,' went on the *femme de chambre* as Paul poured out some rusty-looking coffee. And she added: 'You bore him stiff and he still comes to see you. Well, there's no denying that he's got a really good heart.'

Delmuth, wearing a coat with a fur collar and a balaclava helmet, arrived while Paul was shaving.

'Davenants, I speak with you. Pay me your attentions, please,' he shouted, slapping snow from his shoulders to the floor.

Paul compressed that side of his nose and shaved just beneath it.

'You hear me or you are deaf and dumb?'

'I could hear you even if I were deaf and dumb.'

'Then listen to me.'

'For God's sake, lower your voice.'

'It is lowered!' shouted Delmuth. The chest of drawers rattled beneath the blow of his clenched fist. Paul turned, his face covered with lather. 'Delmuth,' he said, 'shut up!' Delmuth snorted, his lips twitched, but before he could speak, Paul continued: 'Don't go on. You're wasting your breath. I'm not interested in whatever it is you have to say.' He turned back to the mirror and continued shaving.

'Listen, Davenants, don't be so bloody rude. I come here before breakfasts to speak with you, and you…'

'Shut up!'

'I won't.'

Paul re-lathered his face.

'You are listening to me?'

'No more than I can help.'

'Christ, you make me mad!' Delmuth raised his fist, hesitated, snatched at Paul's shaving brush from the wash stand and in so doing knocked over a water carafe which crashed to the floor.

'Now you can bloody well clear that up!' Paul kicked some of the broken glass from the base of the wash-stand.

'Was your fault!'

'Clear it up!'

Delmuth pulled off his balaclava helmet, his hair pursuing it and falling into a coxcomb. As a concession to his complicity in the breaking of the carafe he kicked a few of the splinters into the corner.

'Now will you listen me?'

Paul rinsed his face with cold water.

'I come to take back from you my pills,' said Delmuth.

'What!'

'Ho-ho! You hear now! Give me back my pills!'

'Your pills!'

'My pills.'

'You've got a hope.' Paul dried his razor on a towel. And he added: 'Anyway, why do you want them? Are you thinking of taking them yourself?'

'Me! Are you mad?'

'Then why do you want them?'

'Because they are mine and because you will never take them.'

'What do you mean I will never take them?'

'Then you will take them?'

'Not necessarily.'

'Well then give me them back.' Out came Delmuth's hand. Paul tossed into it a screwed-up, squeezed-out tube of toothpaste. Delmuth swore and threw it onto the bed. 'Give me them back,' he repeated.

'But why do you want them back?'

'Why nothings. They are mine.'

'That's just too bad.'

Delmuth very deliberately removed his coat and sat down in a chair. 'If you must know,' he said, 'I want them for someone else.'

'For someone else! Who?'

'A friends.'

'So, you've got a waiting list.'

'A what?'

'So, you've got other candidates.'

'Other candy dates?'

'Delmuth, for Christ's sake! I mean is there someone else who wants the pills?'

'Not yet.'

'What do you mean "not yet"?'

'I mean not yet. But I soon find someone.' Delmuth smiled significantly.

'I see.' Paul laughed.

'So you give me them back.'

'Oh, go hang yourself.'

'You won't give me them?'

'No.'

Delmuth got up. 'Since six weeks I collect pills and you give me your word to take them and now each day I wait for you to take them and you do not. And now is back Michèle and you never take them.'

'But I haven't said I won't ever take them.'

'I not wait forever.'

'No one is asking you to.'

Delmuth looked at Paul very thoughtfully. 'I let you keep them on one condition.'

'What condition?'

'That you promise to take them tonight.'

'And I'll give you them back on one condition.'

'What?'

'That *you* promise to take them tonight!'

'Now look,' said Delmuth, making a great effort to control his voice and to speak reasonably. 'You declare you will kill yourself and for you I collect pills. Now you say me you will not kill yourself and I not say you reproaches but I ask you for the pills back. You say me no. Who, please, is right?'

'You – indubitably.'

'Well?'

'But I won't give you them back.'

'You won't.'

'No.'

'But is wrong. Is not honest.' Delmuth raised his eyes as though to a higher tribunal.

'I haven't your scruples.'

'Give me please back my pills.'

Paul replaced his shaving equipment in the drawer of the wash-stand.

'All right. Then I take them.' Delmuth looked about him. With a sudden air of resolution he pulled open the door of the wardrobe and stared defiantly at the shelves. 'Where are they?' he demanded.

'Where you won't find them.'

The telephone rang in the passage.

'That will be for me,' said Paul. He put on his dressing gown.

'For you! Why for you?' demanded Delmuth as he rummaged under a pile of shirts.

'For my injection. And I'd appreciate it if you'd refrain from turning my wardrobe upside down.'

'They still make you daily your injections?' Delmuth felt through the linings of Paul's jackets. 'It make you much pain?'

'I tell you, you won't find anything.'

'Bruneau hit sometimes your ribs?'

'Do stop crumpling my linen.'

'Why you not make your injection yourself? Is easy.' Delmuth interrupted his search to raise the fingers of one hand curved in imitation of the side of the thorax whilst he poked the forefinger of his other hand between them. *Sœur* Denise came into the room. '*Monsieur Davenant, Service Médical.*'

'Davenant, give me what I search for or I speak with Bruneau.'

'Good idea.'

'You don't believe I mean it.'

'Frankly, no.'

'*Venez vite!*' insisted *Sœur* Denise.

'Delmuth followed Paul out into the passage. 'Wait,' he cried, catching at Paul's arm. Paul pulled himself free and hurried through the mass of trailing, coloured-paper stalactites. 'I come back later,' Delmuth shouted after him.

Owing to the absence of Dr. Vernet's restraining influence, Christmas this year had infiltrated the *Service Médical*. Instrument cases had been festooned with streamers; crossed syringes had been affixed to the wall with holly at the intersection of their needles; the operating table had been converted into a *lit à baldaquin* by the addition of a striped canopy supported on four gaily decorated metal struts.

'Will Monsieur Davenant have to be pricked on Christmas Day?' asked *Sœur* Miriam as Paul lay stretched on his side under the canopy.

'On Christmas Day? Of course!'

'Oh, là-là! What a bore!' cried *Sœur* Miriam with dismay.

'Pricked – with a rubber needle!'

Sœur Miriam unravelled her knitted forehead and opened the flood-gates of her laughter. 'Pricked with a rubber needle! What next!' she asked. And she added: 'You hear that, Monsieur Davenant' Tomorrow Dr. Bruneau will be pricking you with a rubber needle!'

'And puncturing you with a rubber trocar and cannula!'

'A rubber trocar and cannula! Oh!' *Sœur* Miriam, her mouth like a blown-in front door, steadied herself against the foot of the operating table.

'And substituting old cognac for P.A.S.!' Dr. Bruneau could never discern the point beyond which a joke resisted further development.

'Substituting old cognac for P.A.S.!' echoed *Sœur* Miriam with a respectful attempt at new hilarity.

'No, no, *Monsieur*,' said Dr. Bruneau, laying a reassuring hand on Paul's shoulder, 'have no fears, we will not be pricking you tomorrow. Christmas Day is a truce. Nothing happens. The whole of creation is free to give itself up to unqualified wonder and adoration.' He picked up a plastic syringe and tested the plunger. 'Everyone knows the story of how in the first war, on Christmas Day, the Divine Spirit moved the opposing forces to lay down their arms in a common gesture of simple comradeship and self-dedication. As with war, so with disease. God concedes an interregnum in every illness so that thanksgiving may be universal.' He searched in a shallow metal tray for a suitable needle. 'In fact, *Monsieur*, I am abusing no confidence when I tell you that at a recent medical conference it was demonstrated to the final satisfaction of the highest medical authorities that between the two midnights of the twenty-fourth and the twenty-fifth of December every degenerative and deteriorative physical process is arrested, and this being so, any medical attention during that period would not merely be superfluous, it would be blasphemous.'

'Is that really so? I never knew that,' said *Sœur* Miriam.

Dr. Bruneau winked at Paul. 'This thaumaturgic dispensation is never, fortunately, projected into Boxing Day,' he went on, swabbing both his forefinger and his target with iodine. 'That is to say that God, in his mercy, not wishing doctors, nurses, chemists, opticians and the manufacturers of surgical instruments, medical appliances and artificial limbs to be deprived of their right to a relatively honest livelihood, re-establishes the status quo.'

The needle descended. One centimetre above the surface of the skin it stopped, then rose again as Dr. Bruneau endeavoured to re-satisfy himself as to the suitability of the inter-costal space which he had selected. Paul lay rigid. The needle descended a second time. Above the skin. Touching. Penetrating. He had no name and no history. He had no characteristics, thoughts, hopes or independent existence. He and the needle were isolated in a spiritual vacuum and the future was its course through the archipelago of calcified tissue between epidermis and chest-wall interior.

It arrived clearly and without incident. Dr. Bruneau pressed home the plunger then attempted to remove the needle and syringe in a simple sweep; they parted at the connection, the needle remaining embedded in Paul's side. Dr. Bruneau seized the protruding end of the needle between the tips of his fingers and pulled it free. It was followed by a thin spurt of blood which the latter avoided by an adroit flick of his elbow. '*Voilà*!' he said, affixing a small adhesive dressing. 'With a swollen pleura like yours I can never decide between trying to pull the needle out or taking a hammer and knocking it right back in!'

During the course of the morning patients whom Paul knew only by sight, but whom Michèle had known formerly at the *Universel*, called on him in search of confirmation of the rumour that she had returned. And when at last Michèle arrived, she was not alone, having encountered one former acquaintance in the foyer, a second in the lift and a third in the passage on the way to Paul's room. More arrived and it was in vain that Paul protested the smallness of his room and the fact that if his neighbour were disturbed by the noise, he would undoubtedly complain to the duty sister.

What had she been doing? they demanded. Whom had she seen? Had she spent the whole time in Belgium? Would she be staying in Brisset for the remainder of the winter? Had she had news of this one and of that one? Had she heard that de Marelle had relapsed and that it was to her that his mother had attributed the responsibility? Michèle, her ski-trousered legs over the side of the chair, answered such questions as appealed to her. The interrogation ended with the arrival of the lunch trolleys.

As soon as they were alone Paul embraced Michèle and straightway begged her to set his mind at rest in respect of what she had refused to tell him the previous evening. The request took Michèle by surprise. She replied that they had many things to talk about which were of far greater importance. Besides it was lunchtime and she must not be late on the first day at her pension. Paul seized her wrist and demanded that she should tell him.

'You're not to be worried or angry if I do tell you,' she said.

'No,' said Paul, his earlier apprehensions returning.

'It's just… It's just…'

'Just what?'

Michèle took a deep breath. 'Just that my mother knows everything.'

'Your mother knows everything!'

'Everything!'

'You mean she knows that we are lovers?'

'Yes.'

'What did she say?' cried Paul, sitting up in agitation.

'That I was never to see you again,' said Michèle laughing. She leant over and kissed Paul. 'No, don't look like that. Of course she didn't say that I was never to see you again.' And because Paul's expression still remained strained she added: 'If she had said I was never to see you again, how would I be sitting here now? I'll tell you just what she did say this afternoon. But it wasn't bad. I promise you it wasn't bad.' And with a little laugh she eluded the sweep of Paul's arms, waved to him from the door, impetuously ran forward and kissed him again, then left.

And at tea time she sat at the head of Paul's bed and told him exactly what had happened. She said that it had been quite apparent from the day of her return that her mother had divined the situation, or rather had divined the existence of a situation. Whilst she had refrained from posing any direct questions, it had been impossible for her not to draw certain conclusions from the regular arrival of Paul's letters; from Michèle's reiterated demands to be allowed to spend Christmas in Brisset; from the fact that Michèle avoided her former friends and refused to make new ones.

When finally Paul had relapsed and Michèle had received no reply to her letters, she had no longer been able to dissemble her anxiety and unhappiness and at last her mother had taken her aside and had said:

'*Mon petit, je ne veux rien savoir sur ce que ne me regarde pas, mais ton malheur me fait peur pour ta pauvre petite santé.*'

Michèle, relieved to abandon an attitude which she considered unworthy (it was the first time she had concealed anything from her mother), relieved, above all, to have someone in whom to confide, had related the whole story of her relationship with Paul, and at the end her mother had commented:

'*Je le savais déjà tout.*'

Paul listened intently and anxiously to Michèle's narration, interrupting it only to demand more precise details after which he would say hurriedly: 'Go on. Go on.' And when Michèle had finished he interrogated her in respect of her mother's subsequent reactions and Michèle said that in the main her mother had shown sympathy and understanding.

'In the main!' repeated Paul in dismay.

'In the main!' insisted Michèle. And she added vehemently: 'Which is far more than you have any right to expect. You're an enormous spider who seizes inoffensive little flies and draws them right into the centre of your web.'

'Right into the very centre of my web,' agreed Paul, seizing Michèle by the waist and pulling her to him. Michèle's arms and legs threshed the air. Paul opened his mouth very wide and bit her on the top of her shoulder. She became instantly alert. A step in the corridor. The fly reanimated with the speed of sound, shot from the bed to the armchair.

* * *

As Paul lay down to sleep, it seemed to him that Michèle's mother's attitude was far more propitious than he had ever dared hope. Perhaps, he thought drowsily, perhaps all would not necessarily end badly. Perhaps sustained pessimism was no less a deceiver than sustained optimism. Perhaps...

It was an unusual train of thought for Paul and it exercised his subconscious mind during the night and woke with him on Christmas morning. Why, he wondered, did he always dissipate all his psychic energy in anxiety and division? Why did he not employ it in resolving to be well, in doing and thinking only that which would conduce to his being well, in believing firmly and inevitably that before long he must be well? It was in this curiously amenable and regenerate state of mind that, two hours later, Dr. Dubois found him.

He shook Paul firmly by the hand, wished him the compliments of the season and said: 'My Christmas present to you is a clean pleura!' And as documentation he handed Paul a slip of paper from the laboratory on which was marked the most recent analysis of pleural fluid: B.K. – . Paul smiled involuntarily. Encouraged, Dr. Dubois continued: 'And my New Year's present to you will be its consolidation.' He went on to explain that in order to ensure this consolidation it would be necessary to continue with the daily inter-pleural injections of P.A.S. for several weeks. Thereafter it would be possible to resume the maintenance of his pneumothorax. He ended by declaring: 'For you, *Monsieur* Davenant, the New Year will be a very good New Year indeed.'

Timely Christmas present! To Michèle both its nature and the day of its delivery came as the vindication of all her hopes and prayers. Paul felt like a gambler who has placed all he possessed on a single number and has seen it come up. Plans; projects; suddenly everything seemed possible.

It being Christmas Day, there were no *cures* and no medical rounds. In the late afternoon Mme. Anniette called to deliver her good wishes. Her delight, when she heard the news, rekindled Paul's and Michèle's delight, so that by the time she left they were both again as excited as they had been in the morning.

For the first time for several months it seemed that all auguries were set fair.

* * *

On Boxing Day morning, Michèle arrived late, and when she did arrive she was in tears, looked humiliated and hunted, refused to explain to Paul what had happened, would not turn in his direction, went straight across the room and stared out of the window. Paul made a movement to get out of bed, but she stopped him with a quick shake of her head. She turned at last, her face very white, her lower lip swollen where she had been biting it. Paul took her hand. Then as Paul took her hand and she dropped to his side and lowered her face against his chest, she said that she should never have returned; that she had had no illusions as to the nature of her reception, that only her love had rendered her so insensitive and foolhardy as to come back to a place where, through no fault of her own, she was subject to insults and abuse. Paul listened incredulously. Who had dared to insult and abuse her? Michèle shook her head and her teeth bit her lower lip. She said that it was no use, that there was nothing to be done.

'You will see whether there is nothing to be done!' cried Paul. A sudden suspicion occurred to him. 'It's Delmuth. Delmuth has been getting at you!'

'No.'

'Then who? Who?'

When she whispered: '*Monsieur* Halfont and Emile,' Paul cried: 'My God!' and threw aside the bedclothes. She restrained him from getting up. 'Don't,' she said. 'My father owes them money.' And as she said this she turned away her head as though she feared that what she had yet to say must provoke in Paul an equally antagonistic reaction. 'He'll pay them back as soon as he can,' she went on desperately. 'People owe him money. He isn't dishonest. He isn't trying to get something without paying.'

And Michèle, her gaze lowered, recounted how, unknown to herself, unknown even to her mother, her father had been unable to pay her sanatorium bills. They had accumulated. Somehow he had managed to obtain credit but when the time had come for settlement he had been unable to discharge more than a fraction of his overall liability. Legal proceedings had only been averted by his undertaking to pay the balance in a series of monthly instalments. But latterly a further deterioration in his financial situation had led to his being unable to remit the amount which was currently due, with the consequence that once again there were threats of legal proceedings.

Then Michèle went on to describe how, coming into the foyer just after the end of the *cure de silence*, she had encountered M. Halfont and that in front of the Dutch patients and at the top of his voice he had declared her father to be both a thief and a liar. Seeing that his intention was to humiliate her publicly, she had tried to get away, but crying: '*Ah, non, Mademoiselle!*' he had blocked her exit. He wished her to know, he had continued, that it had been on his own responsibility that her father had been granted credit, and it had all but resulted in his losing his job. Michèle had protested that she had had no idea of the true state of affairs and M. Halfont had replied that it had been her duty to find out. And, addressing his remarks to those about him rather than to Michèle, he had gone on to say that her father's circumstances being as they were, it was perfectly clear that she should have been sent to a state sanatorium. And how, if she claimed that she were sincere, had she had the effrontery to return to the mountains? Did she not realise that the money she was spending in a *pension*, or which she had already spent on a return ticket, was money which did not belong to her, that it was money which – not to put too fine a point on it – was stolen?

Michèle had attempted to explain, to apologise, but M. Halfont had turned on his heel; his place had immediately been taken by Emile. In a voice no lower and no more accommodating than his master's, he had declared that he, too, had a large bill outstanding and that he was not disposed to wait for settlement until such time as her father had concluded his instalments to the *Société*. In a word, if the bill were not paid within twenty-four hours he would put the matter into the hands of the police.

'The police!' repeated Paul, too distracted by each development in the narrative to consider that which had preceded it. What was to be done? Would Emile proffer a charge? What would be its outcome? His mind registered a variety of possibilities, then was overwhelmed by the full consciousness of all the injuries to which Michèle had been subjected. His fists clenched and unclenched. His face became scarlet. That they had dared… That they had dared… 'By God!' he cried suddenly, jumping from his bed, 'by God, I swear they'll never speak to you like that again.'

His anger bore him half-way down the corridor with Michèle hanging on to his arm. 'Let me go! Let me go!' he repeated, trying to shake himself free. Some patients came out of their rooms and stared curiously at them both. Paul dragged forward a few more paces, then stopped, his wind broken, his heart palpitating, the fluid lapping against the inside of his chest. 'Having your first quarrel!' called out one of the patients. There was some laughter. Paul looked up furiously. 'Come back,' begged Michèle, taking his hand. There was more laughter as Paul turned and followed her back into his room.

He collapsed into his armchair, exhausted by the demonstration and by its overt futility. Thus Michèle was insulted with impunity – there was no redress and nothing to be done. As he stared desperately at the opposite wall, Michèle attempted to comfort him as though it were he who had suffered the injury. This realisation provoked an instantaneous resurgence of his anger. 'It's not finished,' he said thickly, 'they will not get away with this.' The revenge of the poor and impotent – dreams and curses. 'They will not get away with this,' he repeated.

Of course they would get away with this. If he complained, then his complaints would be disregarded. If he threatened then his threats would be laughed at. If he said: '*Messieurs, je vous dis merde!*' they would reply: '*Monsieur, nous vous disons double merde et foutes-nous le camp!*' Was there no other way? Then suddenly he demanded: 'How much do you owe Emile?' Michèle hesitated, then handed Paul a piece of paper covered with Emile's calculations.

'Twenty-five thousand francs,' murmured Paul, examining the total. Then he cried: 'But fifteen thousand francs have been paid.'

Michèle nodded. She turned away.

He noticed the date. 'It's been paid today!'

'Yes.'

'But – '

'I paid it! I paid it before I came up.'

'You paid it!'

'I didn't know how to tell you. It's all the money for my stay.' Michèle controlled her voice with an effort. As the expression on Paul's face changed from incredulity to dismay, she added: 'It doesn't matter. I've got my return ticket. And I can pay most of my expenses up to tonight.' She got up from the bed where she had been sitting.

'What do you mean?' cried Paul in alarm.

'I must catch the evening train back to Belgium.'

'Michèle!'

Michèle went suddenly over to the door as if she were going to leave that very minute. Paul jumped up and seized her.

For the second time within the hour Paul applied himself to stemming her tears. The money, he assured her, was of no account – he had more than sufficient to pay for the remainder of her stay. As for the treatment to which she had been subjected, that was a different matter. He swore that whatever happened he would force apologies from M. Halfont and Emile, that never again would they dare to insult her. But stay she must. If she attempted to leave, then he would follow her.

He made her sit down again on the bed and he dropped to his knees beside her. She protested against his being on his knees; he changed the balance of his weight from his knees to the balls of his feet. Michèle lowered her head, and, as he pressed his face to hers, her tears trickled down his cheeks. 'I love you,' he said, repeating the phrase fervently and as often as she tried to get up, whilst each time he consolidated the grip he had taken about her arms. And when he said, 'I love you,' the 'love' he felt extended to every facet of the 'you', its object. Loving her, he loved her for being poor, for her inexpensive clothes, for her father who could not meet his liabilities, for the insults and abuse which he had suffered. He loved her for her courage, for her lack of pretensions, for the tears which in the past he had made her shed. He loved her because in the base metal of his life she was the single vein of ore, all which, in retrospect, represented its sole value, all which, on the point of death, could constitute his grief on relinquishing it.

Paul did not let Michèle leave until she had promised to give up all idea of returning to Belgium. And when she had gone, his fury took him a dozen times about his room and then down to M. Halfont's office. M. Halfont's reaction was virtuous, indignant and conciliatory. He had nothing whatsoever against Michèle, she was *une fille charmante*, he was delighted that she was back and whenever he saw her he experienced a mixture of pride and admiration – 'pride, *Monsieur*, because it was us who have re-establisshed her, admiration because without her courage, re-establishment could never have taken place.' If he had spoken severely to Michèle, then he had made it clear that his severity was directed not against her but against her father. But, he continued, facts spoke for themselves and it could not be denied that her father had behaved unscrupulously. In all good faith M. Halfont had arranged that credit should be granted, had not even bothered to take up the references which he had been offered. And here was the result. (The result symbolised by the out-spreading of empty palms. The God of the Old Testament, *Monsieur*, has been replaced by that of the New. We no longer punish on the daughters the sinnings of the fathers.) He had only behaved as a good servant of the *Société*. If, as a consequence of his complaint, Michèle wrote to her father insisting on the immediate payment of what was due, then his action would have been vindicated. As for Emile – well, he could not answer for him. But he was satisfied that he would never have exceeded the limits imposed both by common courtesy and by his position as a concierge.

Emile's attitude was one of wistful reproach (fifteen of the twenty-five thousand francs now in his pocket-book and the balance in the offing). 'Like everyone,' he said, 'I was seduced by the charm of her smile. Those were my very words to her; I said: "Like everyone I was seduced by the charm of your smile."' He paused to seduce Paul with the charm of his own smile – a man all too human, betrayed into folly by his native compassion, unworldliness and susceptibility to beauty in distress. 'And of course,' he continued, 'I would never have resorted to the police – it was all only my little way of bringing to her notice that the matter was serious. Besides, I know that you are both *très liés*; you don't really think that I would have taken any action without first discussing it with you…' The smile, a compound of nostalgia, tenderness and understanding, overflowed like boiling syrup.

Paul, wishing to hear (and to see) no more, tossed a ten-thousand franc note on to the counter and turned away. Emile called him back: 'The new supply of Players is in. Would you like a packet?' 'No,' said Paul. 'Then would you like a packet and a mirror?' Emile's look grew insinuating; he winked and guffawed. 'Come here. I show you,' he said. The mirror adroitly applied to the front of the packet – the primary female sexual characteristics revealed. It was a gesture of reconciliation and of masculine solidarity.

As soon as the *cure de silence* was over, Paul listened for Michèle's footsteps in the corridor. By the end of the afternoon she had still not arrived. Feeling suddenly uneasy, Paul hurried down to the telephone booth; her *pension* was not on the telephone. He returned to his room. The duty sister knocked at the door and delivered an envelope in Michèle's handwriting.

She could not, Michèle had written, accept any of the little which remained of Paul's money. Nor could she face the prospect of further humiliation. Accordingly she had reserved a seat on the night train to Brussels. She –

Paul read no more. He rang through to Emile on the house telephone. The seven-thirty train from Brisset connected with the night train for Brussels. Paul looked at his watch. It was nearly six.

Shirts, vests, pullovers – which first and in what order? Numbed, nervous fingers pressed metal buttons into reluctant buttonholes. Before the mirror the surrealist resurrection of some sort of soldier, pyjama trouser-ends protruding below those of his battle-dress. A few minutes later he was unsteadily negotiating the snow-covered streets.

The building – low, squat, humble. He looked about him uncertainly, then instinct took him up a single flight of uncarpeted stairs to a room at the end of the passage. He opened the door. She was lying, fully-dressed, on her unmade bed, and her suitcases, packed but open, were strewn about the floor. She jumped up, white-faced, but he silenced her cry with his lips and pulled her back on to the bed. Several minutes later he went over to the window and drew the shutters, then returned in semi-darkness to the bed. 'The door,' she murmured almost inaudibly. He re-crossed the room and silently turned the key.

CHAPTER EIGHT

•

In the way that with T.B., nothing is ever final, so the next analysis of Paul's pleural fluid was positive. This provoked an agonised reaction until Dr. Dubois smilingly dismissed the result as lacking in significance. Inevitably, he declared, there still existed a few minor pockets of infection; he did not doubt but that the next analysis would prove to be negative. A new analysis was made and Dr. Dubois' opinion was vindicated.

The New Year brought with it the return of many wanderers – de la Marelle, Glou-Glou, Mayevski amongst them – whose practice it was, generally speaking, to leave the mountains in the spring and to scuttle back immediately after Christmas.

The rumour that de la Marelle had relapsed had certainly not lacked foundation. His coughing reverberated up and down the corridors, his face was moist, his gaze watery and his former plump cheeks now looked like concave testimonies to an inner state of vacuum. He took pains to avoid Michèle, whilst he behaved towards Paul with elaborate and ironic courtesy.

Delmuth resumed his visits to Paul. His pretext on each occasion was the reiteration of his demand for the immediate return of his pills. His histrionics, however, although lively, lacked conviction, thereby giving the impression that their aim and intuition was little more than the incidental exercise thereby provided. Moreover, the prospect of paternity (for he had impregnated his *femme de chambre*) was proving a mellowing influence; he would preen himself at the bottom of Paul's bed as though it were the latter who was pregnant and by his enterprise too. For fifteen years, he claimed, Mme. Delmuth's austere machinery had ground without end product: 'But now, by such a little act, so I am perpetuate!' And whatever would become of the child, he would declare, it would be the capacity to receive and transmit his own characteristics. He purchased a popular introduction to the study of genetics; he established contact with an astrologer whose headquarters were in Lyon. He convinced himself that in a hundred years, two hundred years, probably indefinitely (and despite whatever inauspicious mutations might occur), his appearance, the manner of his speech and the fashion of his thought would each be separately identifiable in his descendants; in addition (in rare though blessed combinations), there would be amongst them those who, conjoining all three attributes, would – evolution's vindication! – resemble him completely.

There were difficulties with Dr. Bruneau. The latter, perhaps (to give him the benefit of any doubt), from the best of motives, sought to impose on Paul that section of his moribund regulations which related to visits to patients' bedrooms. 'You know very well that in England such a state of affairs would never be tolerated,' he would say, to which Paul would reply that just for that very reason he had chosen to take his cure in France. Disarmed by such candour, Dr. Bruneau would modify his approach. With a suitably concupiscent leer he would exclaim: 'I, too, am the devil of a chap with the women – *I* don't have to tell *you* that!' But the point was (the argument developing) that the present was not the time and the sanatorium was not the place. 'Wait, *Monsieur*, you have your life before you, you will be able to do all that later!' And it was a bad example for the Dutchmen, for new arrivals, for all those law-abiding patients who accepted the regulations as early Christians had accepted the gospels. 'Try and look at it from my angle,' Dr. Bruneau would urge geometrically; 'try and put yourself in my shoes,' a composite manipulation which Paul would contemplate with more politeness than enthusiasm.

Patients, without exception, had taken to confining their visits to Paul to the day, accepting (as did members of the staff), that both he and Michèle – in the short time remaining to them – wished to spend their evenings alone. Nevertheless, although in the evenings there were no intrusions there was also little tranquillity – Paul's bedroom was too claustrophobically set in its context, there was too much menace in its unsecured doors. And though in theory everything promised well, and though Paul and Michèle sought to convince each other (probably too elaborately and painstakingly) that at last all was resolved and their future secure, their less guarded reactions revealed the pressure of constant anxiety and tension.

The situation restricted their relationship to two levels, one physical, the other emotional, both conditions regularly interacting and the frustration of the first contributing in no small degree to the strain of the second. They had evolved, unconsciously, a curious, erotic routine which was adapted to their circumstances; it had become so formalised through usage that one evening, finding Paul out of bed, Michèle made him sit in his armchair whilst, for his edification (and until both were weak with laughter), she took his place on the bed and mimed his customary rôle.

The general sense of strain was suddenly further intensified by the condition of Paul's neighbour. For a fortnight a '*Pas de Visites*' notice (barely necessary since no one ever called on him) had been affixed to his door. Now he was dying. His treatment was normally restricted to the evening cure. Michèle was lying beside Paul when the latter heard the rattle of the medical trolley as it was propelled up the corridor. Uneasily, knowing what it portended, he gripped Michèle more tightly. The door of his neighbour's room opened and closed and the terrible whimpering began. 'What is that?' gasped Michèle, her body rigid. 'Nothing – ' said Paul. And he added significantly: 'Yet.' Michèle's head fell back as Paul pressed his lips to her half-open mouth. There was a sudden cry from next door. Michèle twisted free from Paul's embrace. 'What are they doing?' 'Draining something, I don't know what.' 'You've heard it before?' 'Every night for weeks. I used to have to go out of the room, but now...' The whimpering changed to groans. 'I can't stand it.' Michèle tried to get up, but Paul prevented her. 'It's no help to him if you can't stand it.' He encircled her waist with his arm. 'How long does it go on for?' 'Five, ten minutes. I've never timed it.' Michèle raised herself on her elbow, her face very tense. 'He'll scream before it's over,' warned Paul, dislodging the point of her elbow and bringing her thorax to the level of the mattress. 'I love you,' he said. 'I love you,' she replied. And she added: 'I can't bear it if he screams.' 'He will. He always does.' Paul forced her head onto the pillow and crushed her mouth beneath his own.

At the first scream Michèle leapt up, her hands over her ears. 'I can't stand it, I tell you! I can't stand it!' Paul tried to seize her arm but she retreated to the middle of the floor. 'Come back!' he said. 'I can't! I can't!' 'Michèle!' More screams, like the amplified tearing of vocal tissue. 'Oh!' Michèle's hands went again to her ears. She looked about distractedly. 'Why is it like this? Why does God ever let it be like this?' she cried, clasping her hands together and separating them almost instantly as though at the same moment she had both considered and rejected the idea of prayer. Paul did not reply. He thought: 'He lets it be like this because He has made it like this.' The groans reverted to a hollow whimpering. '*Ça va! Ça va! C'est terminé!*' came Dr. Bruneau's irritable tones from the other side of the communicating door. The blunt sounds of instruments being replaced on a glass surface. '*C'est tout?*' (*Sœur* Miriam's enquiry.) '*Oui. C'est tout.*' *Sœur* Miriam started to guide the medical trolley out into the passage. '*Bon dimanche, Monsieur!*' she cried over her shoulder to the moribund as she passed through the door.

Bon dimanche indeed, though Paul's neighbour's experience of it was to be restricted since a little before dawn he slipped quietly but definitely out of range of even the longest of Dr. Bruneau's hypodermics. Emile was woken cursing from his sleep; via his accommodating shoulder one more body was set *en route* for its reward. The next day the doors and windows and cracks in the walls were sealed and disinfectant cones were lighted. Twenty-four hours after that it had a new occupant – de la Marelle!

'De la Marelle!' cried Paul incredulously when he heard the news. 'De la Marelle!' cried Michèle, echoing Paul's incredulity. What was the explanation of de la Marelle's manoeuvre? To harass his enemies? To irritate them with the knowledge of his constant proximity? To try and arouse Michèle's compassion by daily auditions of his reproachful and highly individual cough? 'Not at all!' said Delmuth. 'He move because is known to everyones that two peoples never die one straight after the other in the same room!'

Whatever de la Marelle's motives, there were other and more primary considerations. The relative indifference which Paul had managed initially to cultivate in respect of the future was crumbling. Soon Michèle would be returning to Belgium. In six or seven weeks he would have no money. What then? When Michèle would reiterate his earlier, more optimistic arguments he would become both despondent and savage and frequently he would behave towards her with a brutality and callousness which neither his condition nor his temperament excused. And what was the value of his subsequent remorse when the offense was so soon to be repeated? Loving him and having neither the capacity nor the wish to dissimulate her love, Michèle was completely at the mercy of his moods, and he, despite acute insight into both her helplessness and the odiousness of his own conduct, did little to counteract the one to moderate the other.

His mental processes were at times even more lamentable than (he hoped) Michèle ever suspected. Outraged and humiliated by his incapacity to deal with his situation or himself, he would become calculatingly destructive and in moments of apparent objectivity and detachment, questioning everything, he would even question his love.

One evening there was to be a projection of a film in the *salle à manger*. During the course of the day anyone who had come near Paul had suffered the edge of his ill-humour. Michèle, as had been arranged, arrived after supper and Paul got up and dressed; throughout the day he had treated her impersonally, distantly, much as though she had been a member of the staff who had called on him in the process of her duties. Some casual, harmless comment set him off. He turned on her, his lips already framing the sort of wounding phrase which came to them so spontaneously, but Michèle – ignoring what he was saying – threw her arms about him and pulled him down on top of her on to the bed. He resisted angrily, held on to his anger like a hat in a high wind; then suddenly the demons jumped into the pigs and the pigs ran over the edge of the cliff. He held her desperately, his love flowing back like electricity along a circuit newly completed. And he thought: 'One day I will go too far. One day I will surely lose her.'

Nor could it be denied that Michèle's spirits, normally so buoyant, were failing under the weight and regularity of the assault. And she had much else to contend with. The news she received from home was invariably disquieting. (M. Halfont was again subjecting her to haughty or malicious stares and one day he accosted her in the entrance hall with the cry: 'Instead of visiting M. Davenant you ought to be writing to your father telling him to pay his debts!') In addition, whenever she came into contact with the sisters (those bastions of repression), they behaved towards her with coldness and hostility. From Mme. de la Marelle she received an unbalanced and abusive letter in which the latter declared that news of Michèle's present conduct (and that of her parents) accorded both with her background and upbringing; she (Mme. de la Marelle) could only once more congratulate herself upon her son's providential escape. For a while she stopped coming.

* * *

Then visits resumed. There was to be an admission – one evening in the dark. An admission! Concerning what? Paul suddenly taut with curiosity. Concerning the prospect of their marriage and her parents' reaction to it, something which up to the present she had suppressed. Suppressed! Suppressed! Michèle had hesitated, then, with a rush: 'They said that they would only give their consent on the condition that…'

No mother could have demanded less – the miracle (or the folly) was that Mme. Duchesne had ever allowed her daughter to return to Brisset. The conditions were: (1) Paul, at the first opportunity, should pass some weeks at the Duchesne home. (2) He should agree both to be examined by a Belgian specialist and to accept the latter's recommendations in respect of his fitness for marriage. (3) He should be in a position to support Michèle.

'Is that all?' Paul demanded bitterly when Michèle had finished. 'There is really nothing more? You mean that when I can fulfil these three conditions I will really be free to marry you?' He sat up and turned on the bedside lamp. Glimpsing his reflection in the mirror, he studied it briefly. Brutality without strength. Weakness without compunction. 'The fact is, and you might care to explain this to your parents, that by the time I will be in a position to fulfil their conditions, we won't be needing their consent.' And he added thoughtfully: 'Nor probably will they be any longer there to give it.'

Brooding, hostile silence, then once more the recapitulation of his favourite themes. Their situation was hopeless, it had always been hopeless and always would be hopeless. They might as well reconcile themselves to the fact that this was the last time they would see each other, since there was no hope, etc., etc. ('Avoid looking into the eyes of the dog which you are vivisecting', was the advice of a doctor in a novel by Van der Meersch which Paul was currently reading. Turning away from Michèle, he realised he should have applied the advice earlier.)

'What specialist in his senses would ever pass a wreck like me as fit to get married?' he demanded. 'Or perhaps we'd advertise for one in his dotage and preferably blind, dumb and moronic as well. And then the little clause about my being in a position to keep you! What did you tell your parents? That with all my talents and connections such considerations were mere formalities. How often have I to tell you that my only expectations and prospects are the charity of the state?' Paul lowered his voice – he had no desire to make a present of all that he was saying to de la Marelle. 'It's obvious that we understand each other so little that it's impossible at times not to wonder whether there is any real basis to our relationship.'

Michèle stared down at the duvet.

'Oh, don't look pathetic,' continued Paul irritably. 'It really couldn't be otherwise. Utterly abnormal circumstances in which we both needed each other's help brought us together – that indubitably. But when the circumstances are no longer there, what then? Do you imagine that in the ordinary way of life we'd have ever thought that we had anything in common?'

Michèle did not reply, gave no indication that she had heard the question.

'Well?' insisted Paul. And again: 'Well? Well?'

Michèle said nothing. Then in a whisper: 'You don't mean it all? You mean all that you say?'

'Why should I say it if I didn't mean it?'

'Any more, that is, that you'd have told me your conditions if you hadn't meant them.'

The conditions were those of the parents, they were not hers, explained Michèle, and she spoke tonelessly, as though to herself. She had no conditions, had never sought to impose any, nor ever would. If she had dared to hope that some of her parents' conditions might have been satisfied then it had been for their sake and not for hers. But she had demanded nothing. As soon as he would have been able to leave the sanatorium she would have joined him. And had he still been ill she would have cared for him. And if he had been without money then she would have worked to have kept them both. When she had said this, she got up and left the room.

Paul woke the next morning with an exact recollection of all that he had said to Michèle. He thought: 'During the remainder of my life there is no ill-fortune which could befall me which I would not deserve.' Why did he say things which were hurtful and untrue and in which – even at the time – he did not believe? He had no longer the right to ask

Michèle's forgiveness. He could only say to her: 'At this moment I am lucid. My love for you is the air I breathe and the means by which I see, hear, think and live. Without you, life would not merely be unthinkable, it would be extinct. This is my faith and creed; all else is merely the product of my sickness.'

Whilst Paul was still eating his breakfast, Delmuth came into the room. He was fully dressed and wearing a raincoat but he had not shaved. Paul, who was feeling in no mood for his visit, asked what he wanted. Delmuth replied that either Paul would return his pills and capsules immediately or – irrespective of the consequences – everything would be revealed to Dr. Bruneau. 'I mean it! I mean it!' Delmuth's face was inexpressibly vindictive, his fist making noisy contact with anything within reach. 'Now tell me where you hide them.'

'Why not ask your astrologer at Lyon?'

'Christ, Davenant!'

'Or just get some more out of your landlady.'

'She won't give me any more.'

'Well, I can't help you.'

'I'm not asking you to help me. I'm asking you to give me back what is mine.'

'It comes to much the same thing.'

'I warn you, Davenants, I am not playing.'

'Nor am I.' Paul suddenly felt the most intense animosity towards Delmuth. 'And now that neither of us is playing, let me tell you this. Ten days ago your woman told me that I bored you stiff and that you only visited me out of the goodness of your heart.'

'What!'

'You didn't hear me?'

'Yes. Yes. I hear.'

'Well?'

'I… She… That is… She is a bloody bitch to say you so.' Delmuth was visibly shaken by the directness of the revelation.

'Not at all. But she would have been more right if she'd said that we bore each other stiff.'

'Yes. Yes.'

Paul was silent a moment. Then he said, 'Well, I'm glad you agree.' And he added: 'It's just because our association is so boring that we've modified it into a sort of game which by reiteration has become as boring as anything else.'

'A game! What do you mean, a game?'

'I mean all the day-to-day nonsense by which we contrive to pass the time. You try to get me thrown out of the sanatorium or you encourage me to kill myself, and I encourage you in your madness because I find it fractionally more tolerable than your sanity.'

Delmuth opened his mouth but he said nothing.

'And then there's the whole pathetic ritual of the pills and the way each of us pretends to believe that he is playing the other like a fish,' Paul went on. 'First I have to get the pills from you and to do this I have to pretend that I don't want them: you then have the double pleasure of intriguing to get the pills from your landlady and of encouraging me in a course of action which you have to pretend to believe I don't want to take. Then – '

'But I say you already she not give me any more pills.'

'Shut up! Then the next stage of the game is that having given me the pills you have to try to get them back. And after that – should you be successful – I would have to get them back from you. Well, it's all good, clean fun and just as tedious, and for the moment, in fact for the short time that Michèle will still be here, I'm throwing in my hand, I've got something better to do. After that, if it still interests you, we can start all over again.'

Delmuth's face had turned the colour of horsemeat bled for veal. 'You believe that?' he asked. He sat down weakly in the armchair and stared unseeingly ahead. 'Is so he regards my friendship,' he muttered.

'For God's sake, don't call it friendship.'

The wail which Delmuth emitted startled Paul – he had never heard a sound like it. Then Delmuth's face crumpled like that of a whipped clown's, his eyes turned red and pluvious and his lips curled back into his mouth.

'What on earth's the matter?'

Delmuth opened his mouth and bellowed with misery. He shook his head violently and tears poured out of his eyes. Then with the flat of his hand he slapped himself with tremendous force across the face, screamed under the impact of the blow, was breathlessly silent an instant, then intensified threefold the volume of his howls.

Paul ran into the corridor, nearly colliding with Dr. Bruneau. 'Are you making that noise?' demanded the latter, ignoring the implications of the fact that the noise was still going on. 'It's Delmuth. He's gone out of his mind,' cried Paul.

Dr. Bruneau ran into the room with Paul close behind him. One of Delmuth's eyes had closed; he was striking his forehead with his knuckles and muttering inaudibly in Flemish. As soon as he caught sight of Paul he shrank back in his chair, trembled, covered his ears with his hands and screamed vigorously. Dr. Bruneau ordered Paul from the room. *Sœur* Denise arrived and Dr. Bruneau sent her running back to her stores for morphia and a syringe. Paul tried to penetrate the throng of spectators at the door when they were suddenly scattered as the *femme de chambre* burst through them into the room. She took one look at Delmuth, raised her voice to a pitch above his own and, seeing Paul edging guiltily out of the room, threw herself upon him, striking and scratching. A dozen hands dragged her away. *Sœur* Denise returned. Delmuth gave a loud howl as Dr. Bruneau rolled back his sleeve and another as the needle penetrated his skin. The *femme de chambre* attempted a second charge, but was repulsed by a flurry of arms. Delmuth became quieter though he continued to moan; Dr. Bruneau led him out of the room with the aid of another patient. The *femme de chambre* followed sobbing.

It was not yet ten o'clock. The patients about the door dispersed to their rooms for the morning *cure*. Mayevski, who had been down in the *Service Médical* when Delmuth had been brought in, hurried to Paul's room and demanded a full account of what had happened. Paul, who was in a high state of nervous excitement, spoke incoherently and wildly. Dr. Bruneau burst into the room and, as Mayevski tactfully left, cried: 'What did you do to him? What did you do to him?'

Paul attempted to summarise the events whilst suppressing what, in fact, had provoked the crisis. Dr. Bruneau dismissed Paul's attempted explanation and declared that he must have assaulted Delmuth. 'His face is covered with lacerations and contusions!' Paul replied that when Dr. Bruneau had entered the room he could not have failed to notice that Delmuth had been engaged in striking himself. 'But why, *Monsieur*, why?' At this point a nurse hurried up from the *Service Médical* to request Dr. Bruneau's co-operation since Delmuth was once again in a state of acute and demonstrative lamentation. With a poisonous look and the assurance that he would return, Dr. Bruneau left the room.

Paul's fingers twisted about each other under the coverlet, the nails biting into the cuticles. What had he said to Delmuth? What had precipitated the intensity of his reaction? Was it all the onset of a breakdown, of mental collapse and if so would he, Paul, be considered responsible? (He envisaged the return of Mme. Delmuth, her grief, her accusations…) Would Delmuth, in his present condition, reveal the matter of their argument? Perhaps he had done so already. Hastily Paul got up and examined the surface of the floorboard under which he now kept the pills – there was nothing to suggest that it had recently been prised-up and re-secured. (And yet, like all the other hiding places which he had chosen, it now seemed the most likely, the most obvious, the one to which Dr. Bruneau would unerringly turn, the moment that the search commenced.)

Paul got back into bed. When would Michèle come? He looked at his watch. Not for another hour. Perhaps she might come early… A footstep in the corridor set his heart beating more quickly. It was the *femme de chambre*. Shaking her fist at him, she cried: '*T'es content, maintenant, avec ce que t'as fait? Espèce de petit salaud! On doît t'enfermer à clef!*' She slammed the door. 'My God!' said Paul. 'She's not going to get away with that!' He pressed the bell but she did not come. 'I must leave here,' he told himself. Well, so he would be leaving here, that much, at least, was certain. More footsteps.

It was the local electrician; he had come to adjust Paul's radio. In a single manipulation he turned the set about and removed the back; soaring squeals and oscillations superimposed upon a background of military marches poured out of the speaker like water from a tap. De la Marelle came in through the communicating door followed by two grinning *semblables*. 'Charming programme! Exquisite taste!'

He cried with a curtsy which (owing to the incautious precipitancy of the gesture) terminated in extravagant coughs. '*Oui, c'est bien bizarre*!' commented the electrician. He tapped the end of the screwdriver with a light hammer and compounded the disparate noises into the unequivocal roar of a vacuum cleaner. 'What really happened to Delmuth?' demanded one of the grinning *semblables* as de la Marelle fished in his mouth with a grubby handkerchief. There was a knock at the door and in came in the sanatorium barber. 'No,' he said in reply to Paul's request. 'No, this afternoon I've got my refill and then I'm going off. If I don't do you now it won't be until the end of the month.'

The electrician helped move the bed forward then pressed himself against the window so that the barber could pass. 'Not loud enough,' said the latter, flicking the volume control and throttling up the vacuum cleaner into a racing car. 'It can go louder than that,' said the electrician, giving the volume control a further twist. 'Well, what happened?' shouted de la Marelle, still coughing. The barber playfully sank down behind the bars of the bed, grasped them in simulated frenzy, then – to draw attention to his joke – thrust his hands between them and gripped Paul's throat.

There are moments when sanity has to be held on to like the plunging leash of a mastiff in heat. Paul shut his eyes, his ears, his mouth, his mind. 'Head forward and a little to the side.' Clip. Clip. Clip. 'A little to the left.' Clip. Clip. Clip. The superfluous locks falling in horrid flakes. 'You must have done something to Delmuth. A man doesn't get into a state like that for no reason,' insisted the second *semblable.* Paul looked up so sharply as the door opened that the barber jumped protestingly in the air. 'Could have gone through your napper like a – well, never mind. And then where would I have been?' he cried as *Sœur* Denise brought in the lunch.

'She can't be coming,' thought Paul. 'I've never seen garbage so really nicely served,' said the barber as de la Marelle raised the lid of the *réchaud.* The electrician again tapped the screwdriver with his hammer and the roaring reverted to angry oscillation. 'Still, they say you can cure on anything – pâtés, greasy soup, it doesn't matter what,' went on the barber. 'They say that if you eat you're just feeding the disease and that the time to start stuffing is when the disease has been starved to death. It's logical, you know…' The electrician turned off the radio with elaborate care. 'Something definitely wrong,' he announced authoritatively.

'Perhaps,' thought Paul, 'perhaps she has had an early lunch and will come in before the *cure de silence.*' De la Marelle tramped out with the *semblables.* The barber and the electrician packed up their respective kits and left together. Paul lay staring at his tray, then pushed it aside. Alone, the memory of his behaviour the previous evening rose up before him like a genie released from a bottle.

Two o'clock and all pretence abandoned. She was not coming. It was not surprising. What were the implications of her absence? He moved uneasily in his bed. Would she come after the *cure de silence*? Was she still in Brisset? At this thought Paul's mood changed from remorse to panic.

Sœur Denise came to draw the curtains and open the windows for the *cure*. 'M. Delmuth is a little quieter. In fact at the moment he is sleeping,' she said. Then: 'But what was it that you did to him?' Then: 'But no one would ever get into such a state for no reason at all.'

If she had left Brisset… He could not reason beyond that, beyond the void. He turned on to his side and closed his eyes. His association with her terminated and the end of all communication. Never to know where she was nor what had become of her. All that had passed between them a receding memory, the single richness in a future otherwise as grey and empty as the past. Was it only in her absence that he would know the intensity and completeness of his love? Oh! only let her not have left Brisset!

He made his way through the snow-covered streets an hour later, only to discover that she hadn't. He collapsed on her bed, and coughed his way back into her life.

CHAPTER NINE

•

Uproar without parallel or precedent. He did not care. Let them do as they liked. Let them say what they liked. 'I've got nothing to tell you and it doesn't matter,' said Paul in reply to Dr. Bruneau's hysterical interrogations. 'If I've got a new pleurisy, then I've got a new pleurisy. If the cavities in my lung have reopened, then they have reopened. If you're going to sling me out, then you're going to sling me out. But I've got absolutely nothing to tell you.'

He wondered now why he had ever worried about his condition or about the opinions of the members of staff. The door of his bedroom opened and shut; people came in and out; threats were made; his temperature was taken, checked and re-checked; his pulse was counted and expatiated upon; and the whole time he lay quietly in his bed, indifferent to whatever was happening.

He thought intensely of Michèle's room, which he had now visited twice, and from which he had now returned as a medical emergency. It did not matter. She had still been there in her room. The knowledge appeared to him to be of inestimable value, of infinite importance. And something had now changed in their lives for ever. Something was settled. Something was resolved and redeemed. What? He did not know and was in no condition to reflect upon it. But this he did know; the wellspring of his pathological behaviour towards Michèle was dry at last. He raised a hand to his sticky forehead. 'No,' he said in reply to *Sœur* Denise, 'I tell you I feel quite all right.' Perhaps, he thought, perhaps the imprudent spontaneity of his action, in visiting her in the snow, would vindicate to Michèle his love; if so, then he was ready to accept the consequences.

It was now the turn of Dr. Dubois. Unlike the others he wasted no time in reproaches. '*Toussez...De nouveau... De nouveau... De nouveau... Dites "trente-trois..."*' The plaque of his stethoscope changed from ice to branding iron as it roamed Paul's chest and back. 'You don't feel ill? No pains? No giddiness? No nausea?' Paul shook his head. Dr. Dubois ordered the wheelchair to be brought.

The X-ray cabinet, then the operating table, the iodine, the needle, the phial of P.A.S., no, not P.A.S., an unfamiliar preparation infinitely blue. 'A chemical dye,' said Dr. Bruneau, drawing the substance up into the syringe. 'I shall inject it into your pleura. If your lung has perforated, then between now and tomorrow you will spit blue. Tell *Sœur* Denise to keep your *crachoir* for my inspection.'

Paul returned to bed, took his *crachoir* and forced himself to spit, watching intently the matter he was ejecting. So far as he knew, a perforation was a *billet simple*, a one-way journey. He drew more sputum from his lungs. No sign of the dye, but probably it had not had time to filter through the infiltrated tissues. De la Marelle, exasperated by the incidental noise, hurled a heavy object at the communicating door.

Another hour measured out in enforced expectoration, its product instantly and anxiously scrutinised. *Sœur* Denise arrived with supper. '*Mademoiselle* Duchesne came but was refused permission to see you. Dr. Bruneau is going to ask Dr. Dubois to forbid you any further visits,' she said. 'Where is she? Is she still here?' cried Paul. 'No. She left half an hour ago.' 'Who refused her permission to see me?' 'It's your own fault, going out like that,' said *Sœur* Denise. 'I said, who refused her permission to see me?' 'Dr. Bruneau, of course.' 'Dr. Bruneau! Dr. Bruneau!' Paul searched wildly for words. He had had enough of Dr. Bruneau. This, at least, he would convey to him in the plainest possible terms. 'Tell Dr. Bruneau…' he said. Tell him what? Whatever it was, he had best tell him himself. 'Tell him to come and see me.' And as *Sœur* Denise went to the door, he added: 'Tell him to come now. I must see him at once.' Dr. Bruneau did not come. Either the message did not reach him or he ignored it.

The next morning he awoke sick, feverish, suicidal and homicidal. Then he remembered: his thermometer dropped from between his fingers and smashed on the floor. He seized a piece of white writing paper and spat on it. In the artificial light it was impossible to verify the colour of the sputum. He hurried over to the window. So far as he could see, there was no trace of the dye. He felt a sudden and anachronistic sense of relief. Then he put on his dressing-gown and went to urinate. He gasped, staggered, controlled himself just in time. The water which he was passing was bright blue.

Demoralised beyond all capacity for reflection, he hurried from the lavatory to the *Service Médical*. 'My whole inside is rotting,' he cried.

Dr. Bruneau listened unmoved to Paul's petrified recitation. 'So that's all,' he said. And he explained sourly that discoloration of the urine was incidental to the normal action of the dye. As Paul was leaving the *Service Médical*, *Sœur* Miriam shook with laughter: '*Monsieur*, you were given the dye to spit blue, not to piss blue,' she said.

'How do you feel?' demanded Dr. Dubois glacially, tonelessly, at the end of a further intensive examination.

'Hot,' said Paul cautiously.

'And there has been no trace of the dye in your sputum?'

'No. None.'

'That is something to be thankful for.' He stared at Paul without speaking. 'You know you're full of fluid?'

Paul shook his head.

'Well, you are.' There was another long silence. 'Do you think I'm pleased about it?'

'No.'

'Or pleased with you?'

'No.'

'Dr. Bruneau has been demanding that severe disciplinary action should be taken against you. He doesn't need to demand it – T.B. patients who break the rules devise their own punishments. I presume that an extra three months in bed wouldn't be very welcome to you.'

'An extra three months!'

'Perhaps more. Perhaps less.' Dr. Dubois sat down in an armchair. 'I'm not saying this for the sake of recrimination – what you do with your life is your own affair. The only question now is whether you still want our help and if so what we can do about it. How are your finances?'

'Bad,' said Paul. He thought: 'I shall wait till Michèle leaves, then I shall take the pills.' 'It doesn't matter,' he went on. 'Whatever my condition I'd have had to have gone back to England early next month.'

'I know that. But how do you think you'll get back?'

'I'll get back somehow.'

'You don't suppose you'll be able to travel like an ordinary passenger?'

'No.'

'Well?'

'It will be possible to make some sort of arrangement with the I.S.O.'

'*Monsieur*,' said Dr. Dubois, getting to his feet, 'I had had every hope of bringing you some unexpectedly good news. Now I can't tell you anything. For all I know, the whole situation will have changed.'

'Good news! What do – '

'And I can't answer any questions.' The tone of Dr. Dubois's voice forbade further inquiry. 'And by the way, another thing. Dr. Bruneau has made a complaint to me about your behaviour towards *Monsieur* Delmuth. I don't know what you've done and I'm not particularly interested. And I must admit that I'd have thought *Monsieur* Delmuth more than capable of looking after himself. Anyhow in the future it would be appreciated if you would try to refrain from reducing visiting patients to a state of nervous hysteria... How much longer will *Mademoiselle* Duchesne be remaining in Brisset?'

'Not long. Only a few more days.'

'You are very attached to her?'

'She is everything to me.'

'*Bon*,' Dr. Dubois suddenly smiled. '*Bon*...'

What, in fact, would constitute *good* news? *Good* news would be that he and Michèle were not to be parted; that his health was restored; that he was capable of earning a living sufficient to keep them both. News. That is to say, that there plainly could not be. There remained the fantasies. '*Monsieur*, on behalf of an anonymous donor I have been asked to present you with a thousand pounds.' '*Monsieur*, you have been selected to be the first to benefit from a new serum which arrests pleural secretions overnight.' '*Monsieur*, I have managed to persuade the parents of Mlle. Duchesne to sanction your immediate marriage.' In a word, there could be no *good* news. And he had no valid alternative but to kill himself.

Michèle's distress was so great that Paul was forced to adopt every subterfuge and expedient in his efforts to console her. Nothing would convince her that she had not been responsible for all that had happened. She had lacked patience and understanding. She should have never left Paul so abruptly on the evening of their dispute. And then she should have sent him straight back to *Les Alpes*, the moment he had arrived at her *pension*. Paul denied all this with all the vigour that his fever permitted, he claimed that the setback was no more than temporary; that Dr. Dubois had insisted that his prognosis was in no way altered. At this stage, he repeatedly reflected, it made no difference what he said.

'But what does Dr. Dubois say? When does he say you will be better?' she would demand pitifully.

At times her grief was so extravagant that Paul felt that she must have divined his intentions. Once, disconcerted by the intentness of his gaze, she had followed its direction to the place where the pills were concealed. She had given a cry, had gone straight to where he had been staring, had searched helplessly about her, intuitively aware that she had all but penetrated a vital secret. Then, having found nothing, not having known even what she had been looking for she had burst into bitter, inconsolable weeping.

What was to be done? They played sad simulacra of their games. They drew up a strange and elaborate document, an amalgam of sections and sub-sections, promising themselves each to the other both in this world and the next. They opposed the passage of time with every stratagem they could devise. And the end was always the same. Another day gone.

He reflected that, even if he had not precipitated his relapse by leaving his bed, he would surely have relapsed some other way. He would kill himself – yes, that was sure. But Michèle. He suddenly felt that were there even the slightest possibility that one day he might recover and be able to marry her, then there was nothing in the interim which he would not be willing to endure. And yet the time had come when he must acknowledge that there was surely no such possibility.

He tried to read but could not; his mind could register words but not their sequent expression. Glou-Glou drifted disconsolately into the room and asked Paul to check his pulse; he claimed that the nervous strain of timing it himself was sensibly increasing its rate. Then *Sœur* Denise brought in the temperature chart for the coming month. Paul looked at it morosely. At least he would not be requiring that. Then came Dr. Dubois. 'I've had a reply from the I.S.O,' he commented. 'The I.S.O.!' repeated Paul, mystified. 'Oh, of course! You don't know anything about it,' said Dr. Dubois.

Dr. Dubois then sat down and revealed the nature of the good news at which he had hinted a few days earlier. He had learned, he said, that the I.S.O., on winding up that department of its activities which had financed the treatment of students at *Les Alpes*, had discovered a small balance of money still to its credit. Without consulting Paul, he had written to the authorities of the association to inquire whether there was any possibility of restoring the latter's grant. Approval had been received on the day that Paul had left the sanatorium without permission. Dr. Dubois had had no alternative but to submit an amended report concerning his patient's condition. Nevertheless, the I.S.O. was still willing to undertake the cost of three months' treatment. 'And with reasonable luck,' concluded Dr. Dubois, 'there is no reason why, by then, you should not be sufficiently well to return to England.'

Paul's reaction was the confused and exhilarated surge of his thoughts. Then realising that he must make some sort of comment he produced a stumbling phrase of astonishment and gratitude.

'I trust you do not mind me having taken the liberty of accepting the offer on your behalf?' said Dr. Dubois.

'I shall never know how to thank you for all you have done.'

'You appreciate that I could not tell you about it before. There was no way of anticipating their reply.'

'Of course not.' A sudden fear. 'This doesn't mean that you will stop looking after me?'

'Not if you wish me to continue.'

'Thank you. Thank you more than I can ever say.'

'I have done nothing. No more than write a couple of letters.' Dr. Dubois dismissed his contribution with a shrug of his shoulders. And he added drily: 'Now please come downstairs. I would like to screen you.'

When Michèle arrived, she was unable to account for Paul's demeanour. 'What has happened?' she cried, running to his bed. 'Nothing,' he said, kissing her lips, eyes, nose and forehead. 'Nothing,' he repeated, laughing.

'What is it? Why are you so cheerful?'

'I'm always cheerful.'

'Tell me what has happened.'

'I can't.'

'Then there is something!'

'Perhaps.'

'Well, what is it?'

'Something I have been told.'

'What have you been told?'

'It's a secret. I'm forbidden to say. But I'll tell you,' added Paul hastily as Michèle raised a threatening hand. The hand remained poised in mid-air. 'The only trouble is, I can't remember,' said Paul.

'The slap landed lightly across the side of Paul's cheek. Paul grasped Michèle's shoulders and pulled her across his knee. Michèle seized the *carafe* from the *table de nuit*, emptied some water into her hand and tossed it backwards over her shoulder on to Paul. A sharp and rapid succession of slaps. Michèle regained a vertical position. Her hand made loud contact with Paul's cheek. From de la Marelle's room a loud roar: '*Foutez-nous la paix!*' Paul and Michèle embraced each other breathlessly.

'*Vous avez terminé? Les gens peuvent dormit?*' cried de la Marelle.

Paul started to recount what Dr. Dubois had told him. Michèle listened intently, her chin in her hands, her elbows on her knees. Paul caressed the calf of her leg. Then as he was speaking, his mood changed. In two days Michèle would be gone. What was the gratuitous provision of three months' treatment when set against the void of her absence?

'Nothing.' Paul was silent a moment, then said: 'It somehow sounded very different when Dubois told me about it. I suppose I saw it as a sort of sign. It suddenly seemed as if, after all, there was a pattern, a purpose. You see the type of rationalist I really am!'

The news sustained Paul and Michèle through the next two days. Then, in the context of Michèle's imminent departure, Paul's spirits sank. 'Don't think I'm not grateful to Dubois,' he said to Michèle. 'After you, I'm more grateful to him than anyone alive. But what does it all amount to? I've got three more months in this ghastly place and without you. And if I've got to be without you, then it doesn't matter to me where I am or what happens to me.'

'Well, it matters to me.'

He stared despondently at the cover of his duvet. 'I can't go on. Injections. Aspirations. Sedimentation rates. When you're here, it doesn't matter. But when you're not… Dubois says I should be better in three months. But they say "three months" here as other doctors say "three days". They've been saying "three months" to me ever since I arrived. The last words I'll hear when I leave Brisset will be: "We'd have cured you if only you could have stayed another three months." There's only one sure thing – I never am well, but I always will be in another three months. Well, I suppose it's about time that I faced it. And I suppose that it's about time that I, that we – ' he hesitated. Michèle's whole frame appeared to contract like that of an animal which anticipates a blow. Then he said: 'All it amounts to is that I am desperate, utterly, finally, ultimately desperate.'

As he repeated his harsh, mechanical complaints, he reflected: 'I tear at her with my love. I tear at her with my despair. And the refrain is always the same. The intensity with which *I* feel. The intensity with which *I* think. The intensity with which *I* suffer.'

Too emotionally exhausted to weigh either his thoughts or his words, he stopped speaking. And as, his eyes closed, he held Michèle in his arms, he wondered how, for the second time, he would survive the ordeal of her parting.

Partings resemble the slow opening of a main artery; like major operations, they are survived involuntarily.

Michèle had arranged for her landlady to call twenty minutes before the train was due to leave. This last evening they ate together, Michèle having purchased some provisions to supplement Paul's supper tray; from a communal glass they took alternate sips of a wine (the wrong type, year and colour), which Paul had specially ordered for the occasion. They spoke little and ate less. When the tray had been collected they took out their dominoes and set them up on the bed. Then Michèle began to cry. And as she cried she apologised for crying and as she apologised she cried the more.

Nevertheless their plans, in theory, had never been more specific. They had agreed that in no circumstances would they remain apart for longer than three months. During this period Michèle would take a combined French and English secretarial course whilst Paul would concentrate every level of his willpower and energy on getting better. At the end of three months they would travel to London. First they would find a room. Then they would look for work. If Paul were not yet fit to work then he would at least qualify for sickness and unemployment benefits. And yet despite the conclusive nature of these resolutions, Michèle cried and went on crying.

This was the waiting-room torment in which every instinct doubles upon itself demanding both the prolongation and the termination of the ordeal. Michèle, her face white and very tense, lay in a sort of hollow in the duvet. Paul kissed her until the muscles of his lips grew weak. The night was absolutely silent; on such nights, though one buried one's head under the bedclothes, though one stuffed the tips of one's fingers in one's ears, one still heard the distinct and despairing wail of the *crémaillère* as the train started its descent.

Michèle had no watch and Paul's was broken. The strain of the situation militated against even the most elementary assessment of the passage of time. Perhaps at this very moment Michèle's landlady was inquiring from Emile the location of Paul's room. 'What's the time?' Paul suddenly shouted to de la Marelle through the inter-communicating door. Three-quarters of an hour still to go.

Paul's neighbour then switched on his wireless and, as was his custom, started on a painstaking and systematic search for a programme to his liking; this involved slowly turning the indicator across the dial and then, still more slowly, turning it back again. Then he accorded slightly more prolonged auditions to half a dozen favoured stations. Then he switched his wireless off. Paul lay with his head resting on Michèle's thigh. His heart quickened as footsteps advanced towards the door, then set off back down the passage. He said: 'You say she's coming twenty minutes before the train leaves?' And he added quickly: 'Why do I ask when I know perfectly well? Let's play another game of dominoes.' By the end of the game, anxiety in respect of the time had once more become so obsessive that he again called out to de la Marelle: 'What time is it?' 'Time you bought yourself a bloody watch,' came the strangulated reply.

'You'll write to me as soon as you get back,' said Paul.

'Of course.'

'No, write to me while you are still on the train. Write to me on this paper.' He took a writing paper pad out of the drawer of the *table de nuit* and detached half a dozen sheets.

'This is the last time,' murmured Paul. 'We'll never have to leave each other again. We know that. It's not supposition. In three months no force on earth will keep us apart.'

The tentative nature of the footsteps excluded any possibility of misinterpretation. Michèle gripped Paul's wrist, her nails digging into his skin. A double knock at the door. Paul grasped Michèle in his arms. Then Michèle broke away and without turning went straight to the door. Paul jumped out of bed. The door opened. The landlady folded Michèle in her arms and Michèle lowered her forehead on to her shoulder. Then the landlady, a supporting arm about her waist, led her down the passage. Paul turned away from the door. The ineluctable traitor thought: 'I shall never see her again.' 'That is what you told yourself last time,' he muttered savagely. Then rather than lie waiting for the sound of the *crémaillère* he went off and bolted himself in a lavatory in the far corner of the sanatorium. Then Delmuth arrived.

Paul, wondering where Michèle's train had now got to, asked Delmuth the time. Delmuth unstrapped his watch and tossed it impatiently onto Paul's bed.

'Ten days ago my wife telephone me that she is interrogated by the police. I know then all is over. And tonight I receive this telegram.' Delmuth pulled a telegram from his pocket and read: '*Soignez-vous bien!*'

'*Soignez-vous bien?*'

'Is a code. It mean my wife is arrested. And next day they come for me. Perhaps they come up the passage. But whichever, is all over. This night I kill myself. But first I ask of you a request. On your response depends all.'

Paul looked at Delmuth incredulously.

'I say do you accept?'

'Accept what?'

'I think they see in from the building opposite. You mind if we turn out the light?'

'Yes. I do mind.'

'I feel safer so.' Delmuth leant over and clicked off Paul's bedside lamp. Paul clicked it on again. Delmuth pulled the plug out of the socket.

'Put that light on.'

'Listen me. There is no other living personage I can ask. Will you help me? I explain all. I – '

Paul was about to get out of bed to replace the plug when he again heard the trembling whine of the *crémaillère* in the distance. He fell back against the bolster, felt as though an adhesive dressing were being drawn back across an open abdominal wound and that it was dragging his stomach with it. The sound of the train retreated down the valley and his every impulse was to race after it in headlong pursuit. 'God!' he muttered.

'You are not listening me!' cried Delmuth in a brave facsimile of his most characteristic roar. 'Not leestening mee!' came back in angry imitation from the other side of the communicating door. Delmuth gave another roar and banged the communicating door violently with his fist.

'I see you're determined to conceal your presence,' said Paul.

'Marelle make me so mad, the fools!'

'Well, you can put the light on now.'

'Listen me, Davenants. For God's sake listen me. I ask for your help. My wife is taken. Now they come for me. Perhaps they are outside. Perhaps they come up the passage. There is no safety.'

'What are you talking about?'

'This not time to explain. Will you help me?'

'What do you want me to do?'

'I want you to accept to adopt my child.'

'What!'

'Yes. Yes.'

'You mean – '

'My mistress is two months pregnant. This you know.'

'But – '

'Do not discuss it, just say me yes. You get better. You marry Michèle and you care for my child.'

'You're mad.'

'No, no. This night I die. I kill myself. Of that there is no question. I just tell you – ten days ago my wife telephone me she is interrogated by the police. I know then is quite over. Is when I ask you for the pills.'

'You've asked me for the pills ever since you gave them to me.'

'I know. Was always, as you said, for sport. But then was suddenly sport no longer. Was why your refusing made me so upset. Now does not matter, I have other means.' Delmuth took out a cigarette but his hand was trembling too much for him to be able to light it. With a curse he tossed the matches to Paul.

'You'd better go back to bed now,' said Paul, striking a match.

'I explain you,' said Delmuth. In his eagerness to light the cigarette he stubbed out the flame. Paul lit a second match.

'Try and keep still,' said Paul, bringing the flame carefully to the extremity of the cigarette.

'Listen,' said Delmuth, puffing erratically. 'I tell you once that life is not easy in the Occupation. Or you work or you starve. I worked. Is all. Since the war me and my wife is tracked like dogs. We move all the times. We take ever new names. But always danger. Always the fears we meet someones who is recognising us.'

'Are you serious?'

'Yes, I tell you.'

'Well, what was your work?'

'I tell you, is for what I do in the Occupation.'

'What did you do?'

'I translated.'

'You translated?'

'Yes.' Delmuth was silent a moment. 'Document and evidences,' he added uneasily.

'For whom?'

'The Germans. In this way I help many of my compatriots. But will they help me now? Not so, I think. Is ever so.'

'And why should your wife be arrested?'

'She care for the women prisoners. Is true at times she go a bit far. But only with the criminals and the dregs of the ghetto. Otherwise she is very good for them. Ever you hear for the crimes of the Gestapo? You should see what is done to collaborators after the liberation. Now will you promise to take my child?'

'You're making all this up. This is your usual nonsense.'

'Making it up! Look at me!' Delmuth pushed the plug back into the socket. Paul saw that his whole body was shaking and that his face was running with sweat. 'Now you say me you take my child.'

'Of course I can't take your child.'

'You can. You must.'

'What about its mother?'

'The bitch pretend she put it in an institute.'

'Wouldn't that have happened anyhow?'

'Are you mad?' cried Delmuth. 'All my life I am wanting a child and you say me I would let it be put in an institute! Never so! Already I am telling my wife of it in order that we may elevate it as our child.' The sound of the telephone ringing in the passage brought him to his feet. 'Is for me,' he gasped. 'They send the sister to see if I am here.' He looked wildly about the room, then tiptoed over to the door and leant his ear against a panel. 'Dear God!' he muttered. 'Dear God!'

There were no developments. Delmuth tottered away from the door, his hand to his heart.

'If I am caught, what do you think become of me? Sometimes when I am translating for a compatriot he swear that if he survive he do for me. Be sure some survive. He see my photo in the papers. He come forward and give lying evidences. He claim even perhaps I am torturing him.'

'Did you?'

'*Me! You ask me!* If I am a German I have now a government pension and a position in the new West German Army. But since I am not a German I am a criminals. No. For me is no trial. For my wife is many years of prison, but for me – ' He broke off. 'Do you tell me you take my child?'

'No.'

'Say you will.'

'What's the use of my lying to you?'

'I have money. It is not money which lacks.' Delmuth pulled a great envelope from beneath his jacket. 'I put it here for you in the top drawer.'

'Take it back,' cried Paul in alarm.

'No. No. You will keep the promise you make me. In one hour from now I am dead.'

'I – '

'I am going now. In the envelope there is also some money tied with an elastic band. That money you will spend on having said masses for the repose of my soul.'

'Delmuth!'

Delmuth tiptoed back to the door. He turned the doorknob.

'You've forgotten your watch,' cried Paul.

'Keep it. It belong once to a very wealthy Jews. Is now yours.' Delmuth went out into the passage and silently closed the door.

* * *

'A visitor to see you,' said *Sœur* Denise, two days later. A heavily-built figure, dressed entirely in black, entered the room.

'*Madame* Delmuth!' cried Paul in astonishment.

Mme. Delmuth offered Paul a black-gloved hand.

'*Monsieur*, I am in a great hurry, my train leaves in under an hour. As you doubtless know, my husband was interred this morning.'

'Yes.'

'Did he at any time mention to you the whereabouts of a large sum of money which he used to keep in an envelope?'

'It's in the bottom of the wardrobe.'

'Ah! Good.' Mme. Delmuth went over to the wardrobe and removed the envelope. 'A thousand thanks,' she murmured.

'He wanted the money to be spent on his child.'

'His child! We have no child.'

'No… But…'

Mme. Delmuth hesitated, looked at her watch, then sat down in the chair which Delmuth had occupied forty-eight hours earlier. 'When did you last see my husband?'

'Just immediately before he threw himself – '

'Precisely.' Mme Delmuth's jaw clicked shut. She added: 'May I ask what passed between you?'

'He told me everything.'

'About what?'

'About your arrest and how he was expecting to be arrested at any moment.'

'Really! Have you repeated this to anyone?'

'No.'

'That's a blessing.' Mme. Delmuth gave a sigh of relief. She sat down in the chair which her husband had been occupying forty-eight hours earlier. 'What else did he tell you?'

'He told me how you telephoned him when you were first questioned by the police and how you sent him the telegram when you were arrested.'

'I see. You sound as if he had managed to convince you.'

'You mean you weren't arrested?'

'*Monsieur*, if I had been arrested, how would I be here now?' Mme. Delmuth's tone became petulant. 'Let us get this quite clear. A fortnight ago I telephoned my husband and, now that you mention it, I do remember that he asked me whether I had been questioned by the police. But that was his stock question whenever I telephoned. A few days ago I sent him a telegram saying I hoped that he was looking after himself. There was no mention of anyone having been arrested.'

'He showed me the telegram. He told me it was in code.'

'In code!' exclaimed Mme. Delmuth derisively. 'Really, *Monsieur* Davenant!' With an impatient flick she dislodged a piece of beige and amber fluff from the lapel of her costume.

'Are you trying to tell me he made the whole thing up?'

'Would that surprise you, from your own experience of him?'

'But... But... Well, I mean, he killed himself because of it.'

'He could make himself believe anything. This time he went too far.'

'But his work for the Gestapo...'

'He never worked for the Gestapo.'

'He didn't!'

'No. Though not from want of trying. But they wouldn't take him. They got fed up with his calling round ten times a day denouncing everyone he had ever known.'

'Good God! And you... You didn't work in a concentration camp?'

'I worked in a girls' remand home, though he liked to believe it was a concentration camp. After the liberation he used to send anonymous letters denouncing me to the public prosecutor.'

'He did!'

'He also managed to convince himself that he'd been a major war criminal and that he had to go "underground". This meant continually moving about under a series of false names and every other sort of nonsense he could devise. And on top of that he was ill. I tell you, *Monsieur*, that but for a legacy from his mother I don't know what would have become of us.'

'But this watch,' said Paul, unstrapping the watch Delmuth had given him. 'He said he had taken it from a rich Jew.'

'*I* was the rich Jew. It was my wedding present to him fifteen years ago,' said Mme. Delmuth with a harsh laugh. She took the watch and dropped it into her bag.

Paul looked at Mme. Delmuth incredulously. 'Did you never see a doctor about him?' he asked at last.

'Yes. But there was nothing to be done. He was not certifiable and he wouldn't undergo treatment on his own account.'

'I see.'

'Much of the time he had complete insight into what he was doing, but this wasn't always the case. And, by the way, what did you mean when you said he wanted the money to be spent on his child?'

'Well, you see...' Paul stopped in confusion.

'Go on. I'm quite used to this sort of thing.'

'He said that... I don't know how to put it. The *femme de chambre*...'

'The *femme de chambre!* Another, I suppose, of his sordid would-be liaisons!'

'Would-be liaisons! She's two months pregnant!'

Mme. Delmuth smiled icily. '*Monsieur*, I will be very blunt. Whatever may have passed between my husband and the *femme de chambre*, she is not, I can assure you, two months pregnant.'

'But – '

'But nothing. You see, my husband was, and always has been...' She hesitated, then said firmly: 'totally impotent.' She got to her feet. 'I must go now, *Monsieur* Davenant, for I have still to arrange with the undertaker about a headstone. There's nothing you would like me to send you when I return to Brussels? Books or magazines?'

'No, thank you.'

'Then there's nothing more.' Mme. Delmuth went over to the door.

'Your husband said – Oh, it doesn't matter.'

'What did he say?'

'He said he wanted some of the money in the envelope to be spent on masses for the repose of his soul.'

'I would have arranged for that in any case. You don't pray?'

'No.'

'Then it's no use my asking you to remember him in your prayers.' Mme. Delmuth showed the first sign of emotion since she had entered the room. She turned hurriedly to the door. '*Bonne continuation, Monsieur* Davenant,' she said as she left.

CHAPTER TEN

•

The three months passed, but Dr. Dubois did not conduct Paul for the whole of the journey. One day Paul saw him with his three assistants leaving the *salle d'interventions* at the close of a long but successful thoroscopy; his white jacket unbuttoned, his naked and sweating chest exposed, he looked like a jovial baker at the end of a hard day's work. The next day he was found dead inside his garage. He had had a fatal heart attack whilst turning the winding handle of his car.

Dr Bruneau wasted no time on sentiment. 'So long as each of Dr. Dubois's former patients elects to choose me as his doctor, then Dr. Hervet can have no alternative but to offer me the appointment of *Médecin Chef*,' he informed Paul. He initiated his campaign with an electoral tour of all the rooms in the sanatorium. '*Cher Monsieur... Chère Mademoiselle...* Your case... The honour to propose to you my services... Approved methods... No hesitation... In my hands...'

At the same time, and with Dr. Dubois' body still unburied, a concerted pincer movement started on *Les Alpes*. Head doctors of minor sanatoria, assistant doctors in leading sanatoria, with one accord laid down their instruments, put on their best suits, and called on Dr. Hervet. 'Signatures,' declared Dr. Bruneau. 'If every patient signs a request that I should be made *Médecin Chef*, then Dr. Hervet cannot help but...' There was a brief and formal truce as, hat in hand, the entire medical faculty of Brisset swarmed to the edge of Dr. Dubois's grave; as the earth was being levelled above the coffin, canvassing recommenced. Then a directive arrived from Dr. Hervet's headquarters to the effect that, pending appointment of a *Médecin Chef*, patients would be at liberty to make whatever arrangements they pleased with the doctor of their choice. The corridors of *Les Alpes* filled with sinister intruders. Dr. Bruneau, roaming his stronghold with the distracted mien of a menaced queen bee, shot poisonous glances at each similarly apparelled rival.

'How lucky for you in the circumstances that the I.S.O. have taken over your bills,' declared M. Halfont, coming unexpectedly upon Paul in a passage.

'What do you mean?'

'I mean that – is it possible that you really don't know?'

'Is it possible that I don't know what?'

'That the reason your room was so cheap was because Dr. Dubois paid half your bill.'

Half-a-dozen patients were less lucky; having been entirely supported by Dr. Dubois, they now had no alternative but to vacate their rooms. It would have been the same at any other period of Dr. Dubois' career: his richer patients, all unknowingly, had subsidised his poorer patients whilst he had sought no greater return from his services than the day-by-day means by which they might be sustained. His house did not belong to him. He possessed neither stocks nor shares. He left a widow, the love and gratitude of a multitude of patients and nothing else.

Paul's sense of personal loss was many-sided; one of its most relevant aspects was the fact that he now needed Dr. Dubois more than at any other time. For the first of the three months his condition had tended to improve; during the second it had held steady; now it was again deteriorating. And this deterioration was so progressive that it became each day more evident that he must abandon all thought of rejoining Michèle in the spring. 'But what is it that is going wrong now?' he would demand after Dr. Bruneau had screened him or whilst the doctor was studying his temperature chart; more often, however, he would say nothing, indifferent in his dejection to the pursuit of enlightenment.

His fever mounted. Once more he became incapable of reading. Lying all day without visitors, he took his temperature continually, his mind alternating endlessly between sexual fantasies and the wish that he were dead, between the love which he felt for Michèle and the certainty that it must now come to nothing.

Dr. Bruneau called on him late one evening. Clearly his electioneering activities had not proved therapeutic. The arcs below his eyes had retreated beneath them whilst their colour had changed from black to speckled red; the furrows of his face were deeper and their surfaces suspect. A rash was taking progressive possession of his right cheek and in an attempt at camouflage Dr. Bruneau had taken to coating it with liquid make-up several shades darker than his complexion.

'*Monsieur*,' he said, taking up his habitual position at the foot of the bed and bending over it, 'we have at last received news of primary importance in respect of your condition.' He coughed with ritualistic precision, a thesis in the art of clearing a blocked throat. 'The night air. It gets on the chest,' he commented. 'Be prepared for a shock, *cher Monsieur*. But after all, will it be such a shock? You're no longer a child, you know that something is obviously amiss. Despite a long course of P.A.S. injects, you are once more relapsing. But even two months ago you were not making the progress you should have been. Well, just before he died, Dr. Dubois arranged for new cultures to be grown and tested for P.A.S. resistance. It is now my duty to inform you, *Monsieur*, that the result of that test arrived here today…' Dr. Bruneau fixed Paul with his eye and turned his body sideways like a dueller seeking to present the smallest possible target. 'Need I tell you what it is?'

'I'm resistant to P.A.S.'

'Yes.'

'I see.'

'I'm glad you see.'

There was a silence during which Dr. Bruneau's fingertips wandered unconsciously to his rash and started to pick at it. 'Well, *Monsieur*?' he said suddenly. And as Paul did not reply, he demanded: 'What is the matter with you? Where are your questions? Why aren't you asking me what is to happen next?'

'Well, what is to happen next?'

'That, as you may imagine, is scarcely for me to say.'

'You mean I've got to go back to England at the end of the month?'

'Precisely.'

There was another silence.

Then Dr. Bruneau said: 'But if it will help set your mind at rest, I will tell you that any action undertaken by whatever doctor you may have in future will depend upon his vision and his courage. If the decision were to rest with me, I would attempt something vigorous, heroic.' He sawed the air with his fists. 'First, I'd subject you to a minute and meticulous bronchoscopy. Then, if the results were propitious, I'd strip down the ribs on the left side of your chest. Then I'd collapse the side of your chest wall on to your lung. Then I'd fix in a good drain. Then I'd – ' Dr. Bruneau started to cough. 'Then I'd…' Dr. Bruneau bent double. 'Then I'd…' Dr. Bruneau wheezed and snorted, twisting his neck and thorax in opposite directions. 'Then I'd wait and see,' he declared indistinctly as he staggered to the door. 'Good night, *Monsieur*. We'll have another chat about it tomorrow.'

As he reached the door, he seized hold of a volume of Tanguy reproductions which was lying on a table. '*Monsieur*,' he demanded, 'is this still obtainable?'

'Take it,' said Paul.

'I can borrow it?'

'You can keep it.'

'Why keep it? Don't you want it any more?'

'No.'

'Why not?'

'Because I've read it.'

'Yes. But the pictures...'

'I've looked at them very often.'

'This is not a sign of discouragement?'

'No.'

'Well, thank you, *Monsieur* Davenant. Thank you very much.'

He prised up the floorboard which split in the process; he swore quietly and listened for any change in the low snoring from de la Marelle's room. Then he removed the matchbox and the two paper-twists, replaced the board and covered it with a rug. According to his calculations either group ought to be sufficient to his purpose; in combination there should be final security. There was not above three inches of water left in his carafe; he got up and filled it at the wash-stand. Paul emptied the contents of the matchbox on to the counterpane: twenty-one pills and eighteen capsules. As far as he knew, either group was sufficient; in combination there should be final security. His water-carafe was nearly empty; he got up and filled it at the wash-stand.

As he climbed back into bed his foot became entangled in the flex of the bedside lamp, and the movement he made to save it from falling jerked the pills and capsules to the floor. 'You clumsy moron,' he muttered as he dropped to his knees and searched for the scattered capsules. Three eluded him; to avoid further loss of time, he returned to bed. He cleaned each capsule carefully with his handkerchief. Then he poured some water into his mug.

The pills would be easier to swallow than the capsules; they should be left till last. 'Well, what are you waiting for now?' he asked himself. He picked up one of the small, semi-transparent tubes and held it for a moment between the tips of his thumb and finger; then he swallowed it. Then in swift succession he swallowed half a dozen more. He paused in order to regain his breath. 'I could stop now,' he thought. The time had passed for being 'none the worse'. He swallowed three more of the capsules. This must be about the border. Now for the safe-conduct across. He swallowed two more capsules and then the remaining three.

Death should now be within him, unobtrusive but sure; like a seed in a flower pot, like a newly fertilised ovum in the womb, it would burst its envelope, consume and expand. He looked with distaste at the pills. Had he not already swallowed far more than was necessary? Were not the capsules already dissolving inside him, discharging their content on to the lining of his tissues? If it were intended that he should die, then he would surely die. And it were not… 'Intended by whom or by what?' he asked himself savagely. So even when committed there would still be backward glances. With a self-punishing deliberation he refilled his mug, poured a heap of pills into the palm of his left hand and set himself to swallowing them, indiscriminately and without counting.

The third mug of water and nearly a dozen pills still to be swallowed. His neck felt like the conduit of a stopped-up sink; for the moment he could drink no more. He lay back on his pillow and glanced at his watch. Half-past eleven. How long would it take till – He sat up, his heart beating wildly. He seized the remaining pills and, concealing them below the bedclothes, turned out the light. The door opened and in shuffled *Sœur* Rose.

'You awake?'

He lay very still.

'I said, you awake?' On went the light.

'What's the matter?' Paul endeavoured to sound as if he had just woken.

'Dr. Bruneau said I was to come and see if everything was all right. Is everything all right?'

'Of course everything is all right.'

'He said he wasn't going to have you getting up to your tricks because of the result of the test.'

'You mean you've woken me just to tell me that.'

'Ah! Your light was on.'

'It was not on.'

'Ah! Ah!' *Sœur* Rose raised her eyeshade and stared about the room.

'And what's the matter now?' Paul sat up angrily.

'Nothing. Don't get waxy.'

'*Sœur* Rose, will you please leave my room and let me get to sleep.'

'All right. All right.'

'Well, get along then.'

'I'm off. I'm going.'

'Then for God's sake, go.'

'All right.' *Sœur* Rose turned off the light and shuffled out of the room. Paul listened dazedly to the sound of the retreating footsteps. If she had arrived a little earlier and had found him on his hands and knees amidst the scattered capsules… If she had arrived a little later and had found him too drugged to respond to her presence… Several minutes passed before he felt sufficiently secure to turn on the light, and even then he took the precaution of covering the bulb with a handkerchief. Then he removed the remaining twist of pills from under the bedclothes and started to swallow. The last three would not go down; each adhered separately to his tongue and started to dissolve. Angrily he spat them out, one after the other, then rinsed his mouth to get rid of the flavour. Then he extinguished the light.

This was the way it ended – the same fœtal position in which it had all begun, he thought, as he pulled the bedclothes over his head, raised his knees and contracted his body into the smallest possible space. He remained without thinking and without moving for several minutes. Then he had a vision of the grave which awaited him, its dark interior and the earth piled at its side. Suffocating, he brought his head out from between the sheets into the cold, dry air. 'Steady…' he told himself. 'Steady…'

He lay down again. A mechanism had been set in motion which was now working of its own accord; he had no more to do than to wait quietly. No hopes. No fears. No specific train of thought. Soon he would be extinguished and extinct. He turned on his side and resumed his earlier position.

He began to feel drowsy and he found himself wondering how much longer he had to live and at what stage of the process he would die. Would it be on falling asleep or substantially later? Did one in fact fall asleep? Perhaps he would not fall asleep, perhaps death would creep slowly up and down his conscious body, atrophying one sense, organ and faculty after the other. Perhaps – that was enough. He resisted the development of his thoughts and turned over on his back.

The large family album was at his elbow. He flicked over a few pages, lingered here, passed more rapidly there. Childhood. Private school. Public school. He paused a moment. Once at the close of the holidays he had tried to hang himself: the ill-contrived noose fashioned from dog leads, the beam which he had known to be too low. What a mess he had made of it! He smiled as he turned the page. The Army. Turn over very quickly. The university. This section could bear a little scrutiny. Friends. A few. Michèle. No – she did not belong in the family album. The whole incident had been hopelessly out of character with his life. 'Out of character in every respect,' he reflected, 'save in its end.' The family album could now be taken up, dusted, secured and ceremoniously kicked down the back stairs. He raised the volume above his head, gathered his force and, in the act of sending it hurtling, crashing down, lost his balance and plunged after it.

First the spray, then Hokusai's giant wave broke over the bow, knocked him backwards, dragged him with it, drenched, drowned, water running from his hair, eyes and ears, his pyjama jacket adhering to his chest. He tried to snatch a breath. Too slow. The next wave cracked his head against the bottom of the boat. He must get up, get away before the next one. He turned, his mouth and nose discharging water. The black sky rose like a curtain. He saw Dr. Bruneau and some nurses. Then Dr. Bruneau released Paul's eyelid, which fell back into position.

'Get him out. Quickly. No, wait a moment.'

The bee was hovering above his forearm. He tried to elude it.

'Hold him still.'

The sting. It was going straight through his arm. He cried out.

'Now let's get him up.'

Another wave was coming. He tried to turn his back. Now... Now... Down it crashed. His eyes opened momentarily on a confusion of light and water. The wave had passed, a new wave was re-forming. He must get away. His arms, legs, and torso were shackled to the base of the boat. As he struggled, his face twisted sideways under one blow and back again under the next. The preliminary spray, then the body of the wave. Swamped. The boat shuddered, tipped and started to sink.

'Open your eyes. You hear me! I said open them. Davenant, wake up. Look out, he's falling asleep again.'

Sinking... Sinking...

'Get him up. Quick now. That's right.'

Everything turning, twisting, scattering; in a flurry of flailing arms he soared up past the barnacle-covered hulks and the startled, iridescent creatures, grounded, stood vertical, took in through half-open eyes the ceiling, wall and floor, then started to sink again.

'You can walk, Davenant. Start walking.'

As he fell, the weight of his body brought them all down with him.

'Get him up. Quickly. Quickly.'

His chest was solidly supported above his paper legs. Hands seized his ankles and thrust him forward. He was brought down the corridor into a side passage, his legs articulating convulsively or dragging behind like string. They brought him several times up and down the passage, then dropped him into a chair where he was pummelled, pinched, rubbed, given fresh injections and drenched again with buckets of water. A tube was inserted down his throat and removed some minutes later in a mass of blood and foam. Then he was jerked up and propelled once more backwards and forwards along the passage. The ceiling merged with walls and walls with the floor. The sea wind rose to a crescendo then was silenced as his ears dropped below the level of the water. Several minutes of intensive activity and half a dozen more buckets of water separated the relapse into unconsciousness and Dr. Bruneau's acknowledgement of the fact. He released Paul's arm and lowered the latter's body to the ground. 'Take him down to the *Service Médical* and if he regains consciousness have me informed immediately,' he said.

The twenty hours during which Paul remained unconscious were momentous in the life of Dr. Bruneau. In the morning he was warmly commended by Dr. Hervet for having dealt so resourcefully with Paul's attempted suicide. At lunchtime Dr. Hervet telephoned to say that after long reflection he had decided to ratify Dr. Bruneau's application for the appointment of *Médecin Chef.* During the whole of the afternoon Dr. Bruneau installed his possessions in Dr. Dubois's bureau and rearranged the furniture. In the early evening, just as he was robing himself before the mirror preparatory to initiating his inaugural round as *Médecin Chef* to each patient: ('*Monsieur*, I have the honour to inform you that Dr. Hervet has graciously seen fit to bestow upon me the directorship of this sanatorium. In this capacity it will be my most earnest endeavour to serve you to the limit of my humble abilities.'), he had a hæmoptysis of magisterial proportions. He was rushed to bed. A preliminary auscultation revealed that an old cavity in the lung had reopened. He would be immobilised for many months. Dr. Hervet expressed his sympathy and withdrew the appointment.

The appointment was now conferred upon Dr. Roussel, the superintendent of two large clinics in the village and Dr. Bruneau's most formidable rival. He was a brisk, sympathetic man, courteous and optimistic; when he smiled, his face looked slightly foolish. He settled into his new quarters with a minimum of delay and got to work immediately. After a rapid review of the outstanding case histories of his new patients he decided that Paul's problems were the most pressing and he determined that they should be resolved as soon as possible.

He instigated a detailed enquiry into the motives underlying Paul's attempted suicide, examined him thoroughly, studied his documents, reflected, went into conference with his two assistants, and submitted a lengthy report of his findings to the I.S.O. Then he summoned Paul to his bureau.

And, as he informed Paul at the initial consultation, they would not be unduly difficult to resolve. The reason for the failure of local treatment up to the present was the condition of the surface of his pleura. As Paul would undoubtedly have been told many times, he declared, his problem was pleural not pulmonary. If this problem could be solved there would be an end to introspection, melancholy, attempts at suicide, everything would fall into its correct proportions. And luckily the problem could be solved. The trouble was that the microbes had penetrated the surface of the pleura; it was this which had accounted for the failure of local treatment up to the present. What was now necessary was the removal of the damaged layers of the pleura and this could be accomplished by a weekly *lavage* of creosote. The treatment would be completed within a period of six to eight weeks. And how was it to be paid for? Dr. Roussel smiled. The I.S.O. had agreed to an extension of a further three months.

CHAPTER ELEVEN

•

The only significant change in Paul's life was that he no longer possessed a lethal dose of pheno-barbitone underneath a floorboard. He felt no surprise that his attempt at killing himself had failed; no surprise that the I.S.O. had extended the period of his treatment by a further three months; no surprise that he had a new doctor who promised that he would be cured by the beginning of the summer. He thought: 'How could I ever believed that I would get away with it so easily? Obviously, like everything else, to be successful it must be done the hard way.' Next time (and how could there not be a next time?), the chosen method would have to be more vigorous.

Meanwhile, Dr. Roussel lost no opportunity of reassuring him in respect of the outcome of the cure. Whilst he was preparing a solution of creosote and Paul was lying on the operating table with a cannula protruding from between his ribs, he would cry: 'How good it smells! What a lot of good it is going to do you!' And as he was injecting the creosote down the cannula: 'Make your plans. Don't get caught in three months' time without anything arranged. Are you going back to Oxford? Would you like me to write to the Head of your College? If I could tell you the number of cases of just this sort that I've cleared up with creosote...'

What in fact was creosote? In the past Paul had vaguely associated it with the washing-down of the walls and platforms in underground stations. He looked up the term in his *Oxford Pocket Dictionary* and found: 'Pseudo-Gk = meat-saver'. Was there perhaps the possibility that it might save his meat? If so its action was indirect, for he continued feverish whilst with each aspiration the fluid became thicker. 'That just shows that it's doing its work,' Dr. Roussel would exclaim enthusiastically. 'It's digging deep into the pleura and detaching all the infected part.'

Did Dr. Roussel really mean what he said? Paul might have doubted it had he not twice received independent confirmation. A patient had overheard Dr. Roussel comparing Paul's case with another which had certain characteristics in common. Dr. Roussel had concluded by saying:

'Respecting *Monsieur* Davenant I have no doubts; his condition will clear up completely. The case of *Monsieur* X, however, is basically very different and I am much more hesitant in making a favourable prognosis.' The second occasion was a consultation between Paul and Dr. Roussel in the middle of which the latter had been called away. Paul had just the time to read in his personal file a copy of the most recent report submitted by Dr. Roussel to the I.S.O.; it tallied in every detail with the views which Dr. Roussel had expressed to him.

As the weeks passed Paul's temperature increased. 'Nothing to worry about,' Dr. Roussel declared, smiling. 'Naturally with the expulsion of so much toxic matter your temperature will rise. But it's worth it. How are you getting on with your plans? I hear you are going to get married. Well, well, we will get you fit for that, never fear.' On the day that the fluid changed definitively to pus, Dr. Roussel, for the first time, looked slightly discouraged. 'Ah, *Monsieur*, if only I could get inside your pleura with a tommy-gun! I would go pop-pop-pop-pop-pop!' He went through the motion of firing a machine-gun over a wide area. Then his expression relaxed. 'No, I'm only joking. Creosote is really better than bullets.'

The inter-costal spaces were now so swollen and so filled with calcified tissue that in order to aspirate, Dr. Roussel would frequently be forced to make an incision with a lancet. 'Get the "you-know-what",' he would say regretfully to *Sœur* Miriam, at the same time smiling at Paul, after he had made several abortive attempts to pass the cannula between his ribs. On one occasion, in order to try to avoid using a lancet, he supported all his weight on the cannula. Suddenly, with a crackling sound, and accompanied by a scream from *Sœur* Miriam, it tore through the calcified tissue and penetrated nine inches into Paul's chest.

One day, after an aspiration, Dr. Roussel said to Paul: 'I had a letter from the I.S.O. this morning. They said they wouldn't be able to grant you any fresh extensions. Well, happily that needn't worry us. I have absolutely no doubt that everything will have cleared up well within the time limit.'

Paul was only able to fall asleep by concentrating on acts of violence culminating in murder or suicide. His invariable victim was Dr. Vernet.

He would take possession of him by a variety of ruses and then dispose of him in a variety of ways. Then he would direct the evocative powers of his imagination against himself. The vividness with which he would both envisage and, at one remove, experience the action would bring its own relief and he would at last fall asleep.

This was a bedtime sedative; by day he was more objective. He could not doubt but that soon Dr. Roussel would have to confess that the creosote treatment had failed; it was essential that in that eventuality he should have decided what he intended to do. Or rather not what he intended to do but how he intended to do it. Since he could have no further recourse to barbiturates, the obvious, the economical solution would be for him to throw himself from the window. But that particular solution was good for no more than the promotion of sleep – he knew that in practice he would be incapable of attempting it. He thought longingly of his service revolver and of the five years during which it had remained in his possession.

Paul's resolve in no way lessened his dependence upon his love for Michèle. He had concealed from her his attempt at suicide, but little else; when he wrote to her (his only opportunity for communicating with someone to whom the changes in his condition had any significance), he found himself all but incapable of dissembling his true feelings. On a day of great depression and after a particularly bad aspiration he wrote to her that his case was hopeless and that although his love for her had never been greater, he had no longer the right to continue to engage her affections and that they should end their correspondence.

The manner in which the letter had reached Michèle could not have been less fortunate. Her father had collected the post during breakfast and in answer to her enquiries had at first denied that there had been a letter from Paul. Then he had conceded that he might have been mistaken, that he had noticed a letter with a French stamp but that he had not noted to whom it had been addressed. Michèle had begged him to give her the letter at once; her father, intent on teasing her, had laboriously searched each of his pockets. Then, by a ponderous sleight of hand he had produced the letter from the back of his collar, had held it out of her reach, had juggled with it, had placed it on top of the picture rail and had finally allowed her to snatch it from between his fingers.

Whilst her family had laughed at her eagerness, as she had started to read, her expression had changed to despair; without a word she had handed the letter to her mother and had run from the room.

She had replied to Paul immediately; had she not done so, Paul – appalled by what he had done – would have had to have written to implore her to disregard his earlier injunctions. At it was, the degree of consolation which he experienced was grotesquely unrelated to the context of the situation.

For what did it serve at this stage to love Michèle and to know that his love was reciprocated? And yet he could not dispossess himself of her image, could not but think of her incessantly. One night, a little before the dawn, he had a slow, strange, formal dream, Monteverdian in its progress. He dreamt that he had been separated from Michèle for several years and that the news had just reached him that she was about to marry someone else; he had hurried at once to her former room in *Les Alpes* where he had found her dressing for a ball which she was to attend with her fiancé the same evening. They had exchanged no greeting: Michèle had appeared barely conscious of his presence and had continued with her preparations. Nevertheless, he had sat beside her (hardly daring to raise his eyes from above the level of the floor), disregarded but conscious of a deep and undivided unhappiness as the wounds of the years during which he had been separated from her were healed by this moment of proximity. She had left for the ball; he had slept and risen early the next morning. Whilst he had dressed he had reflected that in order that he might be able to see her again, he had to do no more than let it be known that he intended to stay another night. With this realisation he had immediately re-experienced the intense and unearthly happiness of the previous evening. He had woken only gradually from the dream and with much overlapping of the two states; whilst the strange sensation of happiness had remained with him like the afterglow of a sunset. And even after it had faded, its memory persisted, alluring, golden and ambiguous.

Two weeks later, whilst Paul was eating his supper, M. Halfont came into the room. 'Davenant,' he said, looking approvingly at the tray, 'it gives me great pleasure to see that you have at last become a reasonable man and that you eat what we give you.' (Defeated by the *cuisine,* and no longer able to afford to supplement it, Paul had at last reverted to a semi-carnivorous diet.) Slabs of meat, the flesh of fish in which the veins were visible he still could not eat; made-up dishes, dishes the content of which bore little resemblance to the raw materials from which it had been derived, he managed to eat somehow.

Then, sitting down, he continued: 'Well, Davenant, everything, as you see, comes to an end. I am very glad for your sake that you are leaving.'

'That I am leaving?'

'Yes. We shall miss you. No, I mean that sincerely. In some sense, you are our *enfant gâté*. When Dr. Roussel told me this morning that you would be leaving next week, I could hardly believe my ears…'

Paul looked up sharply. 'He told you I would be leaving next week?'

'Yes. There isn't much time and it of course falls to me to make all the arrangements with the I.S.O. Still, don't worry about that, that's my worry. And now tell me. What are your plans? What are your projects?'

The next morning brought formal confirmation. Whilst examining Paul, Dr. Roussel said: 'Well, *Monsieur*, I think that the treatment has served its purpose; it is time for it to be stopped. Obviously you are not completely well, but you are certainly fit enough to return to England, and my advice is that you should do so without delay. Now don't look like that, this is good news I am giving you.'

And with an enthusiastic smile he repeated: 'This is good news. Stop looking as if I have just delivered a death sentence. Now what is the matter with you?'

Paul said nothing.

'Well, cheer up, then. Haven't you had enough of sanatoria? Don't you feel that it's about time that you had a change? Or does it depress you to learn that you are better? After all, it's not as if I were chasing you out of one sanatorium into another. When you get back to your own country, your sanatorium days will be over.'

'My sanatorium days will be over!'

'Precisely. Oh, don't misunderstand me. I'm not saying that you'll be fit enough to compete in next year's Channel Swim – neither next year's nor the year after's. But a quiet, reasonable life – that will certainly be well within your scope. And all the time you will be getting progressively better.'

'But my fever... the aspirations...'

'Your temperature will undoubtedly tend to settle now that we are stopping the treatment. And such aspirations as you will need can always be carried out by your local T.B. doctor. Besides, why must you always look on the black side? There's absolutely no reason why the secretion should go on indefinitely. Now I hope with your approval to get you away from here some time next week, though at the moment I can't tell you when. Anyway, in the meantime we'll meet again and go really thoroughly into any questions you might have to ask me.'

Paul learnt that in two days' time a famous Swiss specialist was to address a conference at Brisset. Through Dr. Roussel he made application for a consultation. In preparations, routine X-ray plates were taken.

Professor Klauss was an enormous man, bald, bearded and frock-coated. He bowed deeply and gravely as Paul entered Dr. Roussel's bureau; Paul, slightly self-consciously, bowed in reply. Dr. Roussel and his two assistants were in attendance. Said Dr. Roussel: '*Monsieur* Davenant is one of those rare birds – an Englishman who speaks French.' '*Monsieur*,' said Professor Klauss as he took Paul's hand, 'I will not say that I am enchanted to make your acquaintance; it is too often only in circumstances as unpropitious as these that members of my profession are brought into contact with their illustrious contemporaries. Now be so good as to strip down to your chest.'

'Very fast!' declared Professor Klauss, as he timed Paul's pulse by the sweeping second hand of a great, gold Omega. Then he added playfully: 'But I choose to believe that that is because *Monsieur* is moved to be seeing me!' Dr. Roussel and his assistants laughed respectfully.

Paul was then screened, after which he was told to go and sit down in the waiting-room; he was re-summoned to Dr. Roussel's bureau a few minutes later. Three wooden chairs had been drawn up behind Dr. Roussel's desk; in front of the desk, facing a glass screen, were two armchairs; on the screen was displayed Paul's most recent X-ray. Professor Klauss took Paul by the arm and brought him to an armchair; Dr. Roussel and his assistants sat down on the wooden seats behind the desk.

'Now, *Monsieur*,' said Professor Klauss, 'I will ask for your closest attention. Some two-and-a-half-years ago you had the induction of a pneumothorax; it was succeeded by an inevitable series of accidents which have persisted more or less uninterruptedly up to the present day.'

'Inevitable,' repeated Paul. 'You mean it never had a chance of succeeding.'

'Perhaps one chance in ten or twenty. But don't misunderstand me, *Monsieur*. You were a dying man and your doctor had to try something. And at that time there was nothing else.'

Professor Klauss picked up a wooden pointer and pressed a switch which illuminated the glass screen. 'Now this, *Monsieur*, is your latest X-ray: so far as the condition of the pulmonary tissue is concerned, it is a great improvement on the X-ray which was taken when you first arrived here. Unhappily that is not the whole of the story. For over two years, as you are no doubt only too well aware, your pleura has secreted great quantities of fluid; the consequence of this is that your lung is now rigid, whilst your pleura is as hard and as thick – ' Professor Klauss looked about him – 'as the edge of that window-ledge!' He pointed dramatically across the room. 'But all this you know. What you have invited me here to tell you is what you do not know. Your question, if I interpret it rightly, is: "What am I to do?" Am I right, *Monsieur*?'

Paul nodded.

Professor Klauss tossed his pointer on to the occasional table and sat down in the adjoining armchair. 'Now let me make it quite clear from the start that I am not an oracle. There are certain questions to which there are no answers; there are others to which, by their very nature, the answer will appear unsatisfactory and inconclusive. You ask me what you should do. Suppose I replied: "You have put up with this state of affairs for two and a half years. You might as well put up with it indefinitely." Would you consider that a satisfactory reply?' Professor Klauss paused for some sort of comment. Paul turned away and stared at the tips of his bedroom slippers.

'No, *Monsieur*,' continued Professor Klauss, 'you are probably too polite to say so, but you would not consider that a satisfactory reply. And for that matter, nor would I. Very well, then, let us attempt to be more positive. Let us consider one or two possible forms of treatment. We could, for instance, give you a drain. A rubber tube could be fitted just here between your ribs.' He sprang up from his chair and indicated with his pointer the exact place of entry on the X-ray plate. 'It would not be a painful process and it could be carried out with the use of local anæsthetics. At least one of the advantages will be immediately apparent to you – no more needles! And there are others which are more significant. For example – ' A sudden idea occurred to Professor Klauss. 'I am not speaking too quickly, *Monsieur*?'

'No, *Monsieur*.'

'You will stop me if there is anything you don't understand?'

'*Monsieur* Davenant understands everything. He is one of those rare birds, an Englishman who – ' Dr. Roussel remembered that he had just employed the phrase a moment before. 'I mean he is quite at home with French medical terminology,' he added with some confusion.

'Very well, then. But before we spend too much time developing the advantages of a drain, let us consider some of the disadvantages. In the first place a drain would do nothing to help clean up your condition. In the second place – and this is a graver objection – it would be the means whereby new germ strains could be introduced into your chest. I think, therefore, and without going any further, that you will accept my word when I assure you that the advantages are in no way commensurate with the disadvantages and that in consequence we have no alternative but to reject the idea *in toto*.' Professor Klauss resumed his seat.

'You are now probably thinking to yourself: 'Klauss is very good at telling me what he does not recommend. But what, in fact, does he recommend?' Well, let us consider the next possibility. Our problem is essentially one of how to stop a secretion. What would happen if, to put it in its most elementary terms, we resolved to close the aperture in which the secretion has its origin? No aperture, no secretion! And we could attempt to close the aperture – ' Professor Klauss got to his feet and indicated a section of the illuminated X-ray with his pointer – 'by stripping down these ribs and collapsing the side of your chest on to your lung. What would you think of such an idea, *Monsieur*?'

Paul made no reply.

'I said what would you think of such an idea?'

'It depends… I don't know…' Paul looked about him. What was he meant to say? 'How many ribs would have to be removed?' he murmured.

Professor Klauss led the chorus of laughter. 'You train them well in France!' he cried delightedly to Dr. Roussel. 'How many ribs, indeed? My goodness, what a question!' He blew his nose loudly. 'You mean,' he continued, turning to Paul, 'that if I said six ribs you would accept, but that if I said nine you would refuse! It's too rich!' He started to laugh again. 'Oh, but let's not concern ourselves too much with exact calculations, for I am once more leading you up the garden path! In theory the procedure has much to recommend it, but, in practice, despite whatever ingenuity the surgeon might employ, a small pocket of fluid would almost certainly remain and we would be where we were before.

'Now, *Monsieur*,' he continued, sitting down, 'we have considered and rejected a variety of possibilities and – ' he glanced at his watch – 'our time is running out. Therefore, let us swiftly recapitulate. Since it has not yet yielded to prolonged treatment, we can no longer cherish any illusions about the condition of your pleura. And your lung, despite a certain degree of radiologically substantiated amelioration could – though I don't say it will – perforate from one day to the next.

'A year ago I would have been very diffident about advising you. This is not the case today. The employment of antibiotics has enabled our surgeons to make great advances in operational techniques, and it is for this reason that I tell you, categorically, that you must have your lung and pleura out. But before we consider the details, there is a more immediate problem...'

Professor Klauss glanced round at Dr. Roussel, who nodded his head. 'The performance of an operation of this nature,' he continued, 'presupposes the possession of one sound lung. Now your latest X-ray – forgive my bluntness – reveals your formerly sound lung to have relapsed.' Professor Klauss paused. Paul's lips moved, but he did not speak. 'You will appreciate that before anything radical can be attempted, the condition of what will be your remaining lung must be stabilised. Since you are resistant to the relevant antibiotics it will be a question of bed-rest – probably a year to eighteen months. Or, since there is some urgency in the matter, it might even be advisable to consider inducing a second pneumothorax...'

'And now, *Monsieur*, I would be failing in my duty if, before terminating, I failed to warn you not to delay in coming to a decision. You are, to employ a popular metaphor, on the edge of a precipice. Owing to the suspension of all local treatment there is nothing now to check the spread of the disease. As I have said, your lung could perforate. This being the case you will appreciate that the risks incidental to the operation are, to all practical purposes, irrelevant. Now, are there any questions which you wish to ask me?'

Paul hesitated, then gave an almost imperceptible shake of his head.

'Professor Klauss wants to know whether you have any questions to ask him,' prompted Dr. Roussel.

'*Monseiur* has just indicated by a shake of his head that he has no questions to ask me,' said Professor Klauss. Then to Paul: I hope that your disinclination to interrogate me is in no way a sign of discouragement.'

Paul shook his head a second time. He got to his feet.

Soon after he returned to his room, there was a knock at the door and in came Emile, carrying a letter in his hand. Paul suddenly felt faint as he recognised a Belgian stamp. Then he saw that the writing on the envelope was not Michèle's.

He opened it and read:

Cher M. Davenant,

It is a very unhappy mother who at last finds herself forced to take up her pen, and she counts upon your honour as a gentleman that the contents of her letter should remain forever a secret. Each new letter you write makes my little girl more desperate and yesterday her father (who loves her dearly) lost his temper with her, for he is no longer willing that she should waste all her youth in waiting for you. I have always supported you up to now, *cher* M. Davenant, but at last I have to admit that my husband is quite right. What happiness will you ever be in a position to offer her? The years are passing and with them all Michèle's beautiful youth. God knows what will become of her if this state of affairs goes on indefinitely.

And so, as you will by now have guessed, I am writing to ask you a great sacrifice. Give up Michèle. Neither write to her nor answer the letters she will undoubtedly send you, *whatever* they contain. It is a mother who begs this of you. If you love her, as I believe you do, you will see where your duty lies. There is no more to say. Life, alas, is not a novel in which things somehow contrive to come all right in the end. I expect no reply to this letter and I trust to your sense of honour that it will ever remain a secret between us both.

The letter was signed 'Mme. Duchesne'.

There being no scope for further procrastination, nothing mattered. And yet he could well have done without the letter. 'It alters nothing,' he told himself. Why did he feel such an intensification of grief? 'Nothing is altered,' he repeated, half-aloud. He covered his eyes with his hand. 'Stretch me no more on this rough world.' The phrase came irresistibly to his mind. Where had he read it? He stared at the titles of the books on his bedside table and picked up Haydon's *Journal,* turning to the last entry which the artist had made just before killing himself:

'22nd God forgive me. Amen.
Finis
of
B. R. Haydon

'Stretch me no more on this rough world' – Lear.'

Something was grotesquely wrong. He opened his Shakespeare.

'... O, let him pass! He hates him
That would upon the rack of this rough world
Stretch him out longer.'

'The rack,' he murmured. 'Haydon forgot the rack.' And, his mind still exercised by the strangeness of the omission, he stared across at the half-open window.

Published in Great Britain by:

Ashgrove Publishing

an imprint of:

Hollydata Publishers Ltd
27 John Street
London WC1N 2BX

Originally published in 1958
by William Heinemann Ltd

ISBN 978 185398 160 9

Reprint 2023

Book design by Brad Thompson
Printed and bound in England